So Far, So Good

'A fascinating self-portrait of one of the world's greatest horsemen. This new book gives a unique insight into the pressures of being a top eventer' *Horse and Rider*

'A much more gripping read than the average horsey biography' *Eventing*

'A three-day eventer is always defined as a Jack of all trades, master of one. The Jack part is dressage, showjumping, endurance and steeplechase; the master part is cross-country, the testing to the limit of horse and rider over the most fiendish and terrifying obstacles that man can devise. The definition works for every three-day eventer that ever took on the ultimate challenge of horsemanship. But not for Todd. Impossibly, he is master of them all' *The Times*

'[An] enjoyable biography' *Independent* (Sports Book of the Week)

'Having been possessed by the legal thrillers of John Grisham lately, I have to admit that it was with a little reluctance that I broke off to read Mark Todd's autobiography for the purpose of review. In fact, it was the latter, *So Far, So Good*, that proved to be the truly gripping read ... His candour in revealing what motivates him has you hooked' *Horse and Hound*

Mark Todd was born and raised in Cambridge, New Zealand. He began his three-day eventing career as an amateur whilst pursuing an apprenticeship in general farming. After the 1978 World Championships in Lexington, Kentucky, he moved to England in order to concentrate on his riding and has since become a leading figure on the international three-day event circuit. He now lives in Gloucestershire with his wife and two children.

So Far, So Good

Mark Todd

ORION

An Orion Paperback
First published in Great Britain by
Weidenfeld & Nicolson in 1998
This paperback edition published in 1999 by
Orion Books Ltd,
Orion House, 5 Upper St Martin's Lane,
London WC2H 9EA

Copyright © Mark Todd 1998, 1999

The right of Mark Todd to be identified as the author of
this work has been asserted by him in accordance with the
Copyright, Designs and Patents Act 1988.

All rights reserved. No part of this publication may be
reproduced, stored in a retrieval system, or transmitted, in
any form or by any means, electronic, mechanical,
photocopying, recording or otherwise, without the prior
permission of the copyright owner.

A CIP catalogue record for this book
is available from the British Library.

ISBN: 0 75282 633 6

Filmset by Selwood Systems, Midsomer Norton

Printed and bound in Great Britain by
The Guernsey Press Co Ltd, Guernsey, C.I.

ACKNOWLEDGEMENTS

When Susan Lamb first approached me about doing this book, probably at one of the horse trials at which her horses were competing, I was very reluctant to say the least. I'm sure there have been many times during the months it has taken to get the book completed when she must have wished she had never mentioned the idea. I'm also sure the book would not have been finished without Susan's invaluable expert help, mostly gentle prompting and tremendous encouragement, and that of Caroline Oakley, whose job it has been to oversee the project.

Also a huge thank you to Minty Clinch, who made numerous trips from London down to our home in Evenlode and had the unenviable task of prompting and listening to my inane ramblings on the life of an event rider and turning them into coherent text.

My late grandparents were the initial catalyst for my love of horses and country life, and my parents, Norman and Lenore Todd, although lacking in equestrian knowledge, were always tremendously supportive and encouraging throughout my early years. For the past eleven years my wife, Carolyn, has taken over this role and has been a constant source of love and inspiration through good and bad times.

Judy and the late Bill Hall also deserve a special mention, for without their help and belief in me, my international career might never have started.

Finally I owe a huge debt of gratitude to the many people who have tirelessly worked for me over the years, and to the owners who have provided wonderful horses for me to ride – all have contributed to my success in this my chosen career.

CONTENTS

CHAPTER ONE

RURAL RIDES

'ONE DAY I'M GOING TO RIDE FOR NEW ZEALAND IN THE Olympics.' I can't remember what age I was when I told Mum that. 'Yes, of course, dear,' she replied, picking another shirt off the pile of ironing. Naturally I had no idea of what it would involve, but I did know I loved horses and as I was always very determined, I dedicated my childhood to making sure I spent as much time with them as possible.

As a small child, every Christmas I wrote to Santa asking for a pony. As a result, I always got books on horses, models of horses, pictures of horses and eventually even a saddle. The first thing I'd do on Christmas morning was get out of bed and run to the backyard to see if there was a pony there – but there never was. In fact, my introduction to the real thing wasn't that promising. The first one I ever saw was The Mare, the horse my grandfather used around his farms. She was a right bitch, a real snakey old thing who used to chase my sister Kerryn and I out of the field.

Neither of my parents liked horses, although when they were young horses were still widely used for transport. Mum used to ride to school, but she was very nervous and I never saw her on a horse. Dad came from a town called Taumarunui in the back country, so he had no choice either, but he always preferred machinery. I only saw him ride once. When I was about fifteen, I was given a retired racehorse, Coup de Grâce, by a family friend, Ray Coles. For some reason, Dad decided to ride him back from Ray's property, with me on another horse. We got along all right until we passed an irrigation system spraying jets of water into the air. The sight of them sent Coup de Grâce berserk. Dad very quickly dismounted and led him the rest of the way home, much to my amusement.

When my parents, Norman and Lenore, married, they settled in Cambridge in the Waikato region on the North Island, to be near Mum's parents, Ted and Linda Nickle. Cambridge is a very pretty, small farming town on the Waikato River, the focus of a traditional dairy area, but with a strong Thoroughbred-breeding industry. It has a population of about 3,000 so it's not big, but it's definitely a town. The Nickle farms, five or six miles outside Cambridge, have been in Mum's family for five generations, ever since her ancestors arrived from Ireland by way of Australia.

On Dad's side, the original settlers were Scottish, David McAlister Todd and his wife, Mary Emma. I've seen the family tree but I can't remember much about the details, except that there was a bit of French blood on Dad's side as well. None of them were convicts or anything like that, just farming folk looking for a new life. The early settlers brought livestock with them, cattle for dairy farming, horses to work the land and Thoroughbred stallions to improve the stock. I'd say they chose well because New Zealand is a wonderful place to bring up children. It may be a bit of a backwater in the sense that it's so far removed from the main centres of world politics, but I knew no different so I didn't care. It's not until you get out and travel that it strikes you that you're living in a very new country.

I'd say that I had a normal happy childhood. I was nearly a leap year baby, but I held out until 11.10 a.m. on 1 March 1956. My sister Kerryn is four years older than me and my brother Martyn four years younger. My parents weren't wealthy at that time, but we were comfortable, we never went without. Dad worked very hard, setting off early in the morning and returning late in the evening, so we kids rarely saw him during the week. He was a mechanic by trade and he gradually built up a big business with several garages. He was a bit of an entrepreneur. He also had a logging company and he was the first person in town to have a computer company, Computer Services. He didn't know how to use a computer himself, but he appreciated what they could do and knew how to make money out of them. Initially he had them set up to do his own bookkeeping, then he sold the same service to other businesses in town. That would have been in the seventies. One way and another, he built up quite an empire.

He was always strict about discipline and he used to keep a leather strap to enforce it. One of my first memories is of running outside and hiding the strap in the hedge when I was due for a hiding. He never found it but I still got the hiding. We've always clashed a bit. It's probably because we're alike in a lot of ways, determined, strong-willed and not prepared to give in easily. We have very different interests and we've always had tremendous rows but I respect him. He's got a strong temper, though no worse than mine, and he can be quite tough. He came from the old school and his family never had enough, so he worked for everything he had.

Mum is much more mellow and we always got on very well, perhaps because we're both Pisces. When I had a problem, I always took it to her, partly because she was much more available than Dad. My first memories are of her but they aren't precise. I wouldn't say she spoiled me and I wouldn't say I was rebellious. Well, I could be quite stroppy, but otherwise utterly charming! Pretty much like my own son, James, I expect.

I was always very close to my grandparents, Pop and Mumma, perhaps because I was the oldest grandson. They'd had three daughters and Pop in particular always looked on me more as a son than a grandson. Ever since I can remember I've loved going out to their farm. No doubt they spoiled me shamelessly! Pop had a dairy farm and a sheep farm and, as I instinctively loved animals, I'd spend as many weekends as possible there. My parents would come and pick me up to go to Sunday school which I hated. When I knew they were coming, I'd head out across the farm which didn't amuse them at all, especially as by the time they found me it would be too late to go. They were nominally Church of England, but they sent me to Sunday school more out of convention than religious conviction.

I have Pop to thank for taking me riding when I was quite small, six or seven. His next-door neighbour, Kenny Browne, offered to lend me a wonderful old pony called Shamrock. Pop would take me with him on The Mare to pick up the pony. Then we'd turn round and have a race back up the hill on the wide grass verge. Shamrock was a grey, about twenty-three years old, but she still jumped. She was probably only 12.2hh so it was lucky I didn't grow too early. My parents, anxious about my safety, took up a friend's offer to let me wear a policeman's hat. There's a photo of me sitting on Shamrock wearing it, but the irony is that I'm barefoot which is extremely dangerous. My parents really knew very little about horses and I knew even less; not that I cared as long as I was on the pony.

The main thrill I got out of riding at that age was speed, but Mumma decided that I needed technique as well so she gave me my first formal instruction. She had learned the basics as a necessity because in those days you had to ride and drive a gig, and she passed them on to me. She'd stand by the gate to the paddock in front of their house and I'd walk Shamrock away from her and trot back, with her shouting, 'Up, down, up, down, up, down'. The pony wasn't bad-tempered, nevertheless, coming back towards Mumma meant she had to stop when she reached the gate. As I improved, I'd trot away from her and canter back.

After a few weeks, Mumma had taught me all she knew and I progressed fairly quickly to building small jumps from tin cans and bits of wood. Shamrock was a cunning old thing. You had to watch out if you were going downhill or she'd put her head down and make off or go under low branches and swipe you off. It was a bit of a contest, which she won as often as not, but I never hurt myself in the early days. I remember Mumma saying, 'You aren't a good rider until you've fallen off three times.' When the third fall came, I was thrilled because it meant that I was a good rider at last.

In the end, it was Pop who relented over buying a pony. Although he never did anything competitionwise, he loved the races and the horse sales. He'd lived with horses all his life, broken them for the plough and all sorts of things, so he was very knowledgeable. Well, he was supposed to be. Anyway, he went to the sales and bought an unbroken three-year-old called Hunter to be my first pony. A very wise choice! He probably paid about NZ$20 for him. Mum often took me out to see my grandparents after school but on this occasion she was excited.

'Pop's got a surprise for you, Mark,' she said, and sure enough, there it was, a bay pony tied to a tree in the orchard.

Any pony was perfect as far as I was concerned but Hunter didn't stay with us for more than two months. Of course, I begged to get on him at once, but Pop said no and I never did get to ride him, which was a huge disappointment. The plan was for Pop to break him in a bit by mustering sheep around the farm, but his flapping raincoat startled the pony while Pop was getting back on after opening a gate. Hunter promptly bucked him off, breaking Pop's ribs and booking himself an early return to the auction ring in the process.

As Pop was in his mid-sixties, you would have thought he'd have gone for something quieter the next time, but he could never resist a bargain, or what he thought was a bargain. The second pony was called Rusty, obviously a chestnut and also very young, and I didn't have him long either. He was poor and wormy when he arrived so he seemed quite docile but once he had some good grass in him he got a bit full of himself. This time I was the first victim. I jumped on him bareback to ride him down to the paddock to turn him out. When he broke into a canter, I put my hand on his wither to balance myself and he bucked me off straight into the garage. I landed on my head in the gravel with my feet up against the wall. After that Pop decided he'd better ride him to get the sting out of him. Again it was his flapping raincoat that led to his downfall. When Rusty bucked him off and broke more of his ribs, he was sold immediately but we heard later that he'd developed into quite a good showjumping pony.

By now Pop was getting the message. At the age of ten, I was ready to go to Pony Club and the third pony, Nugget, was sensible enough to take me there. I had an old saddle my parents had given me for Christmas even before I had Hunter. Mum thought it should be cleaned up, so she shined it with brown shoe polish until it gleamed. The problem was that it was like sitting on glass and the polish came off on my breeches. By the time I got to Pony Club, we'd sorted that out and I had a proper riding hat, but most of my kit was borrowed. I remember Poppa Todd gave me a new body brush one Christmas and that was a great excitement. I just loved anything to do with horses.

I rode to the Cambridge Pony Club from the farm, four or five miles each way I suppose. I'd learned to ride in a very natural way, galloping round Pop's farm and going over to Kenny Browne's. He was well known on the New Zealand horse circuit as a leading jump trainer and amateur rider. He also did a bit of showjumping and represented

New Zealand at polo. He had lots of jumpable logs and ditches on his land and as he was a family friend, he let me use them whenever I liked. My cousin Jonelle, who is a couple of years older than me, was quite keen on riding and we used to take turns galloping Nugget round a twenty-acre field on Pop's land. I'd get on and canter down the fence line, then belt back up it as fast as I could. Then we'd swap. We used to do it all afternoon. I don't know how poor Nugget survived, it's incredible what ponies will take.

The first time I went to Pony Club, I thought I was quite good at riding, so I was mortified when they put me in the bottom group after the assessment. When I recovered from that setback, Pony Club became the highlight of my life. It took place every other Sunday and as my parents weren't interested in driving me to shows, I waited impatiently for the next meeting to come round. I don't think anyone saw me as a great talent and as I wasn't competing, there was nothing to set me apart from the others. I failed my Pony Club B certificate, the second highest of four tests of equine skill, on two occasions. The first was for incorrect bandaging and the second for my riding! I couldn't be bothered to do it again after that but Pony Club was excellent training, lots of fun and no pressure. I enjoyed the company of the other kids as well, but I expect I'd have had the same career whatever instruction I'd had at that stage.

My next pony, a part Arab called Little Man, cost my parents NZ$70. I never had a well-schooled pony so there was always some kind of problem. I can't think why they bought him, but he did jump. Time and time again, I've seen parents unwittingly buying ponies that are just dreadful but we were lucky because Little Man was a good pony. Pop hated him because he couldn't get near him, probably because he'd been beaten up by a man at some stage. On one occasion, Pop went into the corral to try to catch him and Little Man jumped straight out over the rails. On another, when I tied him to a five-barred gate, he pulled back and galloped off with it trailing behind him. He was quite spooky, which meant I had my first real accidents during the years I had him.

My sister and brother never showed much interest in riding but we kept Nugget so that Martyn could go to Pony Club as well. He never had much of a chance because I had the saddle, while he had to make do with a sheepskin strapped on with a surcingle. He gave up when our pet duck came out quacking and the pony took off. When we got Little Man, my parents rented a field near our house so I could look after him myself. We shared the cost with a girl from an English family, Anne Wrigglesworth, who was mad keen on horses. We used to go riding together after school, mostly on the wide grass verges beside the roads. We'd gallop for miles and jump road closed signs, ditches and wire fences. Even Pony Club competitions have wire fences in New Zealand so it seemed sensible to practise!

Little Man won me my first ribbons for jumping at the local shows. There was a popular competition called Round the Ring – one circuit of the arena over three sloping white gates and a double brush in regular classes, or two circuits plus a turn up the centre and over a wire fence if it was a championship. Each combination went round individually, with the prize going to the one who went fastest and stood off furthest at the fences. I'd say I was quite good at that. When you're a kid, any rosette is wonderful. The prize money was no big deal in those days, a token two dollars or so, but the amount didn't matter.

It was Pony Club that first introduced me to eventing. The sport originally evolved as a multiple test for cavalry horses in response to boasting in the mess halls over who had the bravest and fastest charger in the regiment. Initially restricted to army officers, eventing made its first appearance as an Olympic sport in the 1912 Games in Stockholm. The Military Event, as it was then known, took place over four days, starting with a 50 km endurance ride, followed by a 5 km cross-country course. On the second day, there was a 3.5 km steeplechase, on the third, a showjumping test and on the fourth, a ten-minute dressage test that included some jumping. In a clean sweep for the home side, Lieutenant Axel Norlander won the individual gold on Lady Artist, with the Swedish Army taking the team event.

In the 1928 Games in Amsterdam, eventing was opened up to male civilians, but women weren't allowed to compete until the Tokyo Olympics in 1964. By that time, the current three-day format was well established, with dressage on the first day, speed and endurance on the second and showjumping on the third. By the late sixties, the sport was growing fast in Europe and North America, but it hadn't really taken off in New Zealand. However, there was a groundswell of enthusiasm for it at a grass-roots level, and nowhere more so than in the Pony Club, an organisation dedicated to improving standards in all branches of horsemanship.

I was thrilled when Little Man and I were selected to train with the Cambridge Pony Club; some of our early efforts were fairly dramatic. I remember going to a cross-country practice with the Pony Club and one particular fence, haybales with a plastic cover, spooked Little Man. After he stopped dead the first time, I was determined to get over it so I whacked him two strides out. He stood off, landed on top of it and rolled on me. He scrambled up and galloped off but I was out cold for quite a while. I woke up in the car on the way to the hospital with my anxious parents. The end result was that I'd broken my jaw, bruised my lungs and cracked my ribs. I was in hospital for about a week, which was fairly major, but it didn't take too long to get back in the saddle. I have to admit that I was a bit nervous for a while afterwards.

As Little Man and I became more experienced, we began to do a lot better. For the National Pony Club Championships, each area, rather than each Pony Club, was allowed to send a team. This meant that I had to be selected for the Waikato Area Team in the face of very strong competition from the members of local Pony Clubs. As Little Man and I were placed in every one-day event in my last season in the Under-17s, I felt I was in with a good chance when it came to the Waikato Area Trials. Unfortunately we came fourth so I was reserve for the Pony Club Championships team, which meant I stayed at home. Little Man had always been in the first three but when it counted he missed out. I was hugely disappointed. Mind you, we would have had quite a problem getting there if we had been selected because the blooming pony would not go in a trailer or a lorry with a roof on it. The solution was to hire an open cattle lorry so we'd arrive at events with just one pony in this huge vehicle. When I got my driving licence at fifteen, the legal age in New Zealand, I bought an open single trailer, borrowed my dad's car and we were away.

This may sound as if I did nothing else but ride but that was not the case. I was reasonably quick at school so I managed to get by with a minimum of work, despite my mother's best efforts to make me put education first. When I got back from school, she'd say, 'Homework first, Mark, then you can go out riding.' 'Yes, Mum,' I'd reply. Then I'd spend half an hour in my room reading a horse book until it was time to meet my friends. However, she did have some control because she made good grades a condition of not going to boarding school, always the ultimate threat for any serious misdemeanour. In moments of extreme frustration, I'd shout, 'Well, send me then. See if I care,' but she never did and I stayed at home throughout my school career.

I went to Cambridge Primary, Cambridge Intermediate and Cambridge High School and passed my school certificate at fifteen. Anyone who stayed at school after that took the university entrance exam, regardless of whether or not they wanted to go to college. There were two possibilities, continuous assessment on classwork throughout the year or, if you failed that, written exams in six subjects. The first year I failed the assessment so was forced to sit the written exams in maths, English, accountancy, geography, biology and chemistry. I had no great aptitude for maths, but I was quite good at English and okay at things like geography and biology. Even so, I didn't do well enough to pass so I had a second year of continuous assessment, this time successfully. I was a prefect in the intermediate school so I suppose I was quite responsible, although I remember being severely reprimanded for smoking behind the gymnasium. My father used to smoke and I'd tried it out with a friend on summer holidays at the beach. We'd buy a pack and cough our way through it.

I'd also drink the occasional can or so of beer for a laugh. My parents only drank socially but I got legless at one of my sister's birthday parties. As the designated barman, I was supposed to serve the alcohol to my relatives, so I mixed all these drinks and took a sip from each to test them out. After a couple of hours, I was absolutely plastered and saying outrageous things. I told my auntie, 'You're looking a bit tired. If you want to, you can lie down behind the sofa and no one will notice.' It wasn't long before I was violently ill. As I came from a rural community and a straitlaced family, this was a rare opportunity for experimentation, but it wasn't a great success.

We were fairly close rather than very close as a family, but we did go on holiday together regularly. In winter, we sometimes went skiing at Mount Ruapehu, which is near where my father's family came from. The sport was in its infancy on the North Island and we probably only went twice, maybe three times, but it's amazing how that early learning meant that I could always do it. When I next tried it in the Alps in my twenties, it was much easier to pick it up. I suppose riding helped because both require good balance.

My grandparents had a house on the beach where my mother and her sisters went when they were kids. We spent wonderful summer holidays there, mostly surfing, swimming and having barbecues. I was never that keen on the fishing, although I'm not against bloodsports. I quite enjoy hunting, but I've never really been a fishing and shooting type of person.

My parents believed in the Protestant work ethic so we were all encouraged to get holiday jobs whenever we were at home. Dad was very competitive in business, he really thrived on it, and Kerryn, Martyn and I all take after him to some degree. We were brought up with the idea that if you wanted to get anything in life, you had to work for it. Not that we were ever forced but we knew we had to get on with it. Because of the big age gaps, we rarely did things together outside family activities. We had television and we went to the cinema occasionally but there wasn't much else to do outside sport.

Mum and Dad encouraged us to do all sorts of sports, at least as much as school work. Martyn and I played tennis, rugby, soccer and hockey, but my speciality was athletics. I was athletics champion at school on a couple of occasions, excelling at high jump and hurdles. I could jump over my own height at one time but I don't think I was very tall then. Up till I was about sixteen I was one of the shortest in the class and then suddenly I shot up. I only competed at school and I've often wished that I'd concentrated on athletics a bit more, if only to see how well I could have done at a higher level. Even now, I sometimes regret not knowing how far I could have gone.

Kerryn and Martyn were also good at sports, which is surprising because neither Mum or Dad played anything, not even tennis or bowls. Kerryn was good at netball and a pretty tough competitor. Martyn and I both reached a reasonable standard at tennis and squash. Later he got into go-kart racing. It must have been a nightmare for my parents having to take us to all these different things. When we won, we weren't allowed to bask in glory. I was reasonably shy, certainly too shy to push myself forward, and I preferred to let my actions speak for themselves. After the success I've had, I've come to appreciate praise but on the rare occasions it came in those days, I was almost embarrassed by it.

I started dating in a minor way on school outings in my mid-teens, but my parents were pretty strict about it. Dad would say, 'You're far too young for that sort of thing, Mark.' Neither of my parents talked to me about sex. The school put on a sex education talk which Dad drove me to, but he never referred to the subject matter. Anyway I knew all about it by that time. Initially, I'd tell my parents that I was going to the movies with some of my mates and we'd arrange to meet girls there. It should have been an advantage being allowed to drive at fifteen but I wasn't allowed to use Dad's car to race around the streets. Anyway I was pretty shy with girls in those days so it wasn't as useful as it sounds.

After I passed the university exam, I was allowed to leave school in November 1973. What a moment of liberation! I never considered actually going to university because I planned to be a farmer. Of course, I could have studied agriculture but I preferred to learn on the job. From an early age, I knew how to lamb a ewe, calve a cow, fix fencing and water systems. New Zealand farmers are pretty practical. On the farm, you get a very good education in life and death. My grandfather was from another era, he milked his house cow, killed sheep for the table, knocked on the head lambs and calves that weren't right. I've always thought that was a straightforward way of looking at life.

Before I left school, I was torn between racing and joining the farming cadets. If I'd wanted to make other choices I probably could have but riding was the number one priority and an eventing career wasn't an option in those days. Until I shot up in my mid-teens, I dreamed of being a jockey. It was optimistic really because my father is over six feet tall but anyone can dream. When I was fifteen, I was asked by the trainer, Doug Fisher, to ride work with his racehorses before school but my parents wouldn't allow it. I met Doug through the Pony Club so they must have rated me a bit for him to offer me the job. Immediately after I left school, I filled in time by working for a racehorse trainer called John Boyte. He specialised in breaking young Thoroughbreds and he always put me up first. I also used to ride his racehorses on the track which was invaluable because I learned about pace, balance, and riding short.

When I was forced to accept that I was too tall to be a flat jockey, I joined the farming cadet scheme run by the Federated Farmers. Its aim was to help young people to get into farming through a combination of work experience and college courses. The farmers who subscribed to it took on the cadets as working pupils and allowed them a set amount of time off to go to college and on field trips. After three years, you took a written exam for a Diploma in Agriculture.

The rules of the scheme meant that I had to change farms at regular intervals. I only worked for people who let me bring a horse and I was very lucky with my employers – but, then, I planned well. I interviewed them and they had to fit my bill! The first to pass the test were Barry and Vicky Rae, a young couple I joined in February 1974, just before my eighteenth birthday. When I'd grown too tall for Little Man, I'd sold him for NZ\$1,500 and used the proceeds to buy a big brown horse called Killarney. Like my grandfather, I loved horse trading, buying cheap, selling on and buying another bargain. I could only manage one at a time in those days, but I turned a profit on them.

On a New Zealand dairy farm, you get up at 4.30 a.m. to milk the cows, then work through till 6 p.m. I'd ride after that. I think I had one weekend off a month to go to events. There wasn't much social life at Barry and Vicky's and I was never really interested in going to the pub. It was a bit lonely so I moved to the Harveys, another family with a small involvement in horses, in November 1974. I already knew them because I'd had a holiday job there when I was still at school. Barry and Betty have four children. Bronwyn, who'd been at school with me, the twins, Bruce and Judith, who are a bit younger, and Suzanne. I spent eighteen months with them and we're still good friends today.

They allowed me a bit more time off to go to shows and I discovered that Killarney was reasonably useful as an all-rounder. He show-jumped in the summer and evented in the winter, with a bit of hunting thrown in, so he was a real jack of all trades. One of my good friends at that time was John Nicholson, Andrew's older brother, and he and I went around the shows and events together. Killarney jumped in some of the bigger classes in New Zealand without being wildly successful, but he did reach grade A, the top showjumping classification. I had help with my dressage from Ted Harrison, who'd taught us in the Pony Club. He was English, a stickler for detail, and he insisted that we sit in the correct way. He was the first major influence on my flatwork.

As I always found instruction interesting, I never had an attitude problem about doing what I was told. I also learned a lot from watching the riders I admired. It didn't matter what they were doing, racing, polo, or whatever it was. If I thought they were good, I tried to analyse why and copy them. I copied Pop initially as he rode one-handed round the farm, more like a cowboy than anything else. I learned to sit on a bucking horse, arguably better than he could, given his record with my first ponies! We'd break young horses together and I'd always get up on them first. When I break in a horse now, I do it in the same way Pop did, with a few refinements of my own.

As I was still mad about racing, I was easily persuaded to go into partnership with Barry Harvey on a cheap steeplechaser. Barry and I went to a sale and bought Mr Papagopalus. He'd run a few times, maybe won a couple of races, but we got him for NZ$200. Unwanted racehorses are never worth much, but a price tag as low as that should have told us something. In the end, it was the jockey who'd ridden him who gave us the bad news: he wasn't too complimentary, to put it mildly! However, nothing could discourage Mr Papagopalus's new owners, so we took him home and trained him for a chase at Rotorua races. It was a lighthearted enterprise from the start, a small investment in a bit of fun. Barry and I didn't really care if he won or not because we enjoyed being owners, saddling the horse up and leading him round the parade ring, doing all the bits and pieces at the track.

On the great day, Bruce Harvey, who is even taller than me, was in the saddle. When the tape went up, he set off in front but at the second fence Mr Papagopalus was startled by a flock of seagulls. Shying sideways, he crashed through the running rail and Bruce came off. On the first two circuits of the track, the field had to race round an extra loop adjoining the main course. That was fine with Mr Papagopalus. He took the shortest route, stopped at the junction until the others rejoined him and galloped through the whole field. At the end, he led them past the winning post, ears pricked as if he'd won. The crowd was in hysterics, transfixed by the antics of this wretched horse rather than the race itself. That was the last time Bruce rode Mr Papagopalus, but the horse did run into a place with another jockey while he was still in our ownership. Barry and I had another venture into racing with a mare called Hasty Decision, but that also drew a blank. Nowadays Bruce and his wife, Maureen, are among the best preparers of yearlings for the Thoroughbred sales, so he learned something from the fiasco.

All I learned was that I was fatally bitten by the racing bug and it wasn't long before I was the owner of a third racehorse, a five-year-old black gelding by Crown Lease called Crown King. I answered an advertisement for him in a racing paper and when I went to see him, I realised I'd helped to break him in at John Boyte's three years earlier. He was as unmanageable as ever, difficult to steer and a dedicated bucker, but I still liked him so I bought him for NZ$500. Initially I thought of him as a showjumping prospect but Crown Lease's progeny were beginning to make their mark as steeplechasers and when I checked his pedigree, I realised he was a half-brother to three winners. I took him down to the local training track to try him over some practice fences and discovered that he was a quick, clean jumper. I also discovered that I couldn't hold him, so the next time I went I put him in a pelham bit with a curb chain to exert more control, which amused the other trainers.

Crown King's first race was at an informal country meeting at Taupo. He ran in the ladies' flat race with Carol Marshall on his back and came sixth so I entered him for an amateur chase at an official meeting at Rotorua. He went well in that race, his first over fences, and finished fourth, so I was delighted. Lyall Keyte, a friend who lived down the road from the Harveys, took over the ride for the next amateur race at Te Rapa and came second but their next outing ended in disaster when a horse jumped across Crown King and brought him down. Lyall and Crown King took a very heavy fall. Both were okay, but as it was the end of the 1977 jumping season, the horse went out for a spell. By this stage, I thought that he had a great future but, as an impoverished farming cadet who was hoping to go to the USA in 1978, I couldn't afford to keep him in training the following season. Although he'd showed promise, no one wanted to risk serious money on buying him so I leased him to a Thoroughbred agent called Doug McKenzie. He raced him in partnership with trainer Fred McCawley and Crown King won five races the next year, including three major steeplechases. That's racing for you.

In 1976, I had my last chance to be selected for the Under-21 Waikato Area Team for the National Pony Club Championships. By way of preparation, Bruce and I used to career madly round the farm jumping the fence lines as they came up. On one occasion, he galloped off in front and took off over a hedge, not realising that there was a single-strand electric fence on the other side. He must have landed in an awkward position because although he was trying to yell at me not to follow him, the words wouldn't come. I realised what had happened in time to go round and pick him up, slightly bruised in a certain part of the anatomy. Later the same day, Killarney and I followed him into a wire fence supported by rotten posts. Bruce's mare hit it so hard that it swung back towards me but Killarney and I were already committed. He cut his legs on the wire so badly that he was out for the rest of the season.

Killarney wasn't especially brave across country but he was going well and I was very disappointed not to have the chance to qualify. However, I got lucky when Lyall Keyte offered me a replacement ride on Top Hunter. He was a big, rangy chestnut who'd hunted ever since he retired from the track as a four-year-old. He'd tried out as a steeplechaser but at that time he was too immature and gawky to make the grade. When I took him over in the summer of 1976, he'd never done a day's dressage in his life but he was a naturally free mover and did surprisingly well. He was brilliant across country but once again I was selected as reserve so I never got to ride for the Waikato team in the New Zealand Pony Club Championships.

I liked Top Hunter so much that I tried to persuade Lyall to let me buy him.

'I can hunt him all day with one hand on the reins and the other on my hip flask so why should I want to sell him to you?' he asked.

Fair enough, but he gave in eventually! I sold Killarney quite well as a showjumper and Top Hunter was not expensive at NZ$1,200. I had also bought my first car, a Humber 80 station wagon which really struggled to pull my horse float, but at least I had control over my schedule.

After eighteen months with the Harveys, I had to move again under the rules of the cadet scheme. My next employers were David and Ann Goodin, large-scale dairy farmers with 400 cows and one of the first rotary milking parlours in New Zealand. They also did quite a bit of showjumping. David sometimes let me take his horses to the shows while he worked the farm, which suited me just fine. Social life? Forget it. I either worked the farm or worked the horses and that was it.

David had some land in the hills near his farm where he grazed his cattle in winter and turned out young horses to mature in summer. Part of my job was to keep an eye on the stock and I can clearly remember the first time I saw a particular little almost-black colt grazing the hill pasture. He was one of half a dozen horses bought cheaply in a job lot from the breeders, Daphne and Peter Williams, by David Murdoch, who ran New Zealand's only three-day event at Isola. I remember looking at the four-year-old and thinking, 'That's a smart little horse. Pity he'll never be big enough for me.' I could hardly have been more wrong. That was the first time I saw Charisma.

CHAPTER TWO

WIDER HORIZONS

W HEN I FIRST SAT ON TOP HUNTER AT LYALL KEYTE'S farm in 1976, I had no premonition that he would take me to the World Championships in America but I did know that he was something special. He was a lovely mover, a big horse, about 17hh, a liver chestnut Thoroughbred who'd raced. He was easy to train and a very scopey jumper. I think if I had him now, with my greater experience, he'd have been brilliant. With all the steeplechasing and hunting he'd done, he was a very competent jumper and he quickly cottoned on to the dressage. I worked on him and got quite good results. There were huge gaps in the competitive calendar in New Zealand so we had to go in for anything and everything to get an outing. While I was with the Goodins, I concentrated on showjumping and Top Hunter reached grade A, but he was never going to make it to the top, even by New Zealand standards. The bigger jumping shows quite often had a dressage competition as well and we were usually placed so it was a nice little earner. When you're on a tight budget, even NZ$20–25 helps. In those days, there were only three or four one-day events and just the one three-day event, so I concentrated on those from February to June.

In 1977, Top Hunter won the Waikato Horse Trials, the opening one-day event of the season, on his dressage score of 17. He also won his second event, the national one-day championships, which meant that he upgraded to intermediate before competing in the open class in his first three-day event at the National Equestrian Centre at Taupo in June. By today's standards, conditions on the eventing circuit were pretty spartan. We slept in the horse truck, scraping the muck out of the back, putting down an old carpet and setting up camp beds, a table and a cooker. Not that we did much catering, just nipped off to the pub for a few beers. As with horse events all over the world, it was pretty sociable, with drinks served in the back of the trucks, but even then I took it seriously enough not to go too wild the evening before a cross-country. There were very seldom any proper yards or stables so we made little pens for the horses out of electric fence standards and battery electric units, using the truck as a windbreak. Sometimes a horse would get the wire round its leg and go berserk and there'd be absolute pandemonium, with as many as thirty horses galloping down the main road, but usually the system worked well enough.

Taupo was a decent, small-to-middling sized, advanced course, well built and quite difficult. At least, it seemed so then. I wasn't cocky but I did feel confident. Why not when the horse was such a good jumper and I had nothing to lose? Everyone just went out there and gave it their all and, in typical New Zealand fashion, we didn't worry too much about the dressage; nor, in my case, about the showjumping because Top Hunter was accustomed to much bigger courses. When it came to the cross-country, we went flat out. There weren't many alternatives so all it took was big bold jumping. The strategy worked pretty well and we finished third behind Carol Harrison on Topic. Carol was married to Ted Harrison, the instructor who helped me a lot in the early days. The others who finished strongly were Joanne Bridgeman and Bandolier, Nicoli Fife and Never Dwell and Mary Hamilton, who had two horses, Vladivostock and a grey called Arranshar.

It was Lockie Richards who suggested that we five should form a squad with a view to entering the World Championships at Lexington, Kentucky, in 1978. He was a New Zealander but he had been away training in America and Britain, competing himself and teaching dressage. He'd also helped the New Zealand twins, Paul and Tony Harris, when they'd made a fairly successful circuit of American events a year or so earlier. By this time, Lockie was the Chief Instructor at the Wills Equestrian Centre at Taupo so he was well placed to look for fresh talent and, in the absence of any international exposure of our own, we were eager to hear what he had to say. At the end of the event, he got the five of us together and said, 'You should make up a team to go to America for the World Championships.' If anyone said that now, my reply would be, 'You're mad. I've only done one three-day event,' but what I said at the time was, 'Well, that sounds like a good idea.'

We'd all read about eventing on the other side of the world, Badminton and such like, but we'd always believed that there was them and there was us. Lockie was in a position to compare standards and horses so, although we were amazed that he felt we could compete at that level, we were prepared to give it a go. Lockie was keen for New Zealand to make a breakthrough in eventing and he had the contacts we needed. Of course, he didn't think we could win, only that we would get some experience that would stand us in good stead later. When he put the idea to the New Zealand Horse Society, they agreed to name us as a squad for Lexington and we duly assembled at Taupo for a training course with Lockie in November. There was also a veterinary examination which none of our horses passed. The vet was accustomed to working with two-year-old Thoroughbreds for the racetrack so there was no way our mature horses were going to meet his standards. He came up with the most amazing reasons for failing them – flat feet, knees that didn't flex sufficiently – pathetic reasons basically, but they gave the Horse Society the excuse they needed to say, 'If you want to go, it's off your own bat, but we won't pay for you.' They probably didn't have much money but by refusing to confirm our status as an official team, they made it very difficult for us.

The Championships were nine months away at that point so at least we knew what the score was while we had enough time to do something about it. There had been quite a lot of publicity within the sport about the fact that we were going to Lexington, so we decided to raise the money ourselves. My parents could probably have financed me, but some of the others were less fortunate in that respect and there was a strong sense that we were all in it together. As Mum and Dad had brought Kerryn, Martyn and me up to be independent, I didn't want them to give me money, but I did accept a loan of NZ$7,000, which I later repaid. I believe that the effort of earning money on my own account is an important element in my success. In my opinion, the problem with some of the younger riders in both Britain and New Zealand is that they now expect everything to be handed to them on a plate.

You didn't earn much working on farms in those days so I left the Goodins and moved in with my parents. I'd got my Diploma in Agriculture by then so it was a good time to take a break from farming. I didn't see the trip to America as the start of a glittering career in eventing, only as an adventure. I was a twenty-year-old kid, I wanted to see the world and, in my circumstances, this was the most obvious way to start. I got a job at the local dairy factory doing shifts packing milk powder, fairly monotonous work but the other guys were good fun and I knew it wasn't going to last forever. It was a big factory preparing dairy products for export, butter and so on, and the milk powder department operated around the clock. For reasons of hygiene, we wore white gumboots, white suits and hats. You put a bag under a huge silo full of powder, pressed a button and filled it up, then sewed up the top of the bag. Then you did it again and again until the shift was over. The only let up was the odd occasion when you hit the wrong button and the milk powder spilled everywhere. My fellow workers helped me in every way they could. Best of all, they swapped shifts with me so I could compete at shows. To get the whole weekend off, I'd have to do a double shift but no one ever told the bosses. Occasionally, when they'd seen me on both shifts, they'd look a bit surprised and say, 'What, are you still here?' but they never realised what was going on; or if they did, they turned a blind eye.

After the day shift ended, I'd often spend the night at a local stud keeping an eye on the mares that were due to foal. Top Hunter fitted in as best he could; it never came to riding in the dark. I also earned a bit extra by breaking in horses so, all in all, it added up to the kind of workload you can only manage when you're young and sleep isn't so important. I don't remember feeling exhausted because there was purpose to it, but I can't imagine doing it nowadays.

All through this period, I joined the other members of the squad in an intensive fund-raising campaign. We begged prizes from local companies – a weekend for two in some holiday place, a bottle of whisky, a grocery hamper, that sort of thing – and set up raffles.

Unfortunately my father had nothing worth raffling, other than a tractor which we certainly wouldn't have got off him, or a few nuts and bolts, so he wasn't on our list. We wanted to announce that the raffles were 'In Aid of the World Championships Eventing Team', but the Horse Society wouldn't let us use the title because they said we weren't an official team. I think they were embarrassed in case we didn't do well. Our deal with them was that we paid our own way until we qualified for the World Championships, at which point they would enter us as the official team. We had to raise NZ$20,000–25,000 each to pay for the transport and our living expenses in America. It doesn't sound a lot now but starting with nothing, it took some getting. We sold our cars and whatever else we had. When you're young, you're not thinking about setting up home so possessions aren't important. Once we were in America, the New Zealand Horse Society gave me NZ$3,000 because I had the best results in the run-up to the Championships, but the others had to make do entirely on their own.

By February 1978, we'd scraped together enough to go to America. Carol was the only one who was married so she followed on in May. The only time I'd been out of New Zealand was on holiday to Norfolk Island so travelling on the plane with the horses was a huge adventure. We were based at Skycastle Farm at Chester Springs, about half an hour's drive from Philadelphia. It belonged to Elizabeth Streeter, a friend of Lockie's who supported eventing in a small way. She was a wonderfully kind woman who liked young people and she had the space available, so she let us have it for a minimal rent. The property consisted of a barn divided up into five or six stables in the middle of a field. We lived in a tiny duplex down the road, with a small kitchen, living room, two bedrooms and a bathroom. I was used to communal sleeping in the backs of trucks on the show circuit, so it wasn't a huge deal living with four women, but it was an eye-opener. Nicoli and Mary shared one room and Joanne and I the other. When Carol arrived, she moved in with us.

We had rosters for everything and cooked in strict rotation. Chicken and mince were the cheapest things so that was what we lived on. I hadn't done much cooking but I was ready to give it a try, with a little help from Mum's parting gift, a book of easy-to-cook meals. There were the inevitable disagreements here and there, usually over trivial things, like whose turn it was to clean up, and we learned an awful lot about each other and ourselves. It was probably fortunate that I wasn't romantically attached to any of them but over the months we did develop strong bonds. Mary and Nicoli were good friends, so Joanne, Carol and I were pretty much thrown together.

A team of colonials was something of a novelty in the area so we made a lot of friends and received a lot of dinner invitations in the six months we spent at Chester Springs. Before I crossed the Pacific, the only Americans I'd seen were the worst sort of tourists, so I was pleasantly surprised to find that many of the people we met were fantastic. Sue Stevens, another good friend of Lockie's who lived across the road from Elizabeth, was at the top of my list from the start. She was a lovely, kind person and she's been stable manager for the last three Olympics so I always keep in touch.

We explored Philadelphia and New York, short trips in all conscience but even so they suggested a vastness that was far beyond anything we'd ever seen before. The rollerama disco, roller skating to disco music, was very big at the time so we had quite a few fun evenings trying that out.

Elizabeth herself was totally eccentric. Her mother was one of the wealthiest people in Boston, as we discovered when we went to stay with her for a competition. The house was palatial, with servants. If you left your clothes in a heap, they were gone by the time you got back to your room. Twelve hours later, they'd be returned, immaculately washed and pressed. I'd never seen anything like it. Maybe Elizabeth rebelled against the grandeur because she lived in a totally ramshackle style. She had an equally eccentric farm manager, a herd of belted Galloway cattle and her own pack of Basset Hounds, always thickly covered in ticks. Not that that was her fault because the ticks flourished in the long grass and invaded everything. We had to inspect the horses' manes and tails everyday and burn them off; and not only the horses. We'd go through each other's hair to get them out. They used to crawl up your legs and get into all sorts of inconvenient places.

Although Elizabeth was fabulous, she was most un-American about cleanliness. We went over to dinner at her place and the kitchen was in a less than hygienic state, which made us a bit nervous about what we were eating. She kept a turtle in the bath and a lamb that lived indoors and sometimes chewed through the telephone wires. When Kerryn and her husband, Martin, came down to visit us from their home in Canada, I took them over there for drinks. Elizabeth was serving iced tea on the verandah, using mint covered in bird muck and ice cubes that had been licked by her dogs. I'll never forget Kerryn's face! I think she poured her tea discreetly into the bushes.

Our training facilities were pretty basic. We used the jumps that belonged to the local Pony Club, but we had no arena. Lockie had arranged a mini-van for us to get around in and Mary's father bought us a horse truck. It wasn't that old but we were unlucky because the engine blew up in sweltering heat on the Massachusetts Turnpike near the end of the nine-hour drive to a competition at Ledyard Farm. We rang the event and Ralph Hills, one of the members of the American team, sent his parents with another truck to pick us up from the side of the highway so that we could take part in the event.

The Ledyard cross-country was designed by Neil Ayer, who later devised the course for the Los Angeles Olympics, and it was the most demanding I'd ever seen, especially as the ground was extremely hard compared to what we were used to at home. After I walked the course, I kept my fingers crossed as I said, 'It's a good course for a bold galloping horse,' and luckily Top Hunter proved me right by finishing sixth at the end of the cross-country. This was our first taste of competing in the extreme heat we could expect at Lexington but it was Nicoli, rather than the horses, who suffered most. After going clear on Never Dwell, she collapsed and had to be treated with the oxygen provided for the exhausted horses.

Top Hunter was an experienced and reliable showjumper, but the twisty course caught him out on this occasion and he dropped two rails to finish in seventeenth place. Nicoli also had two fences down which put her down to twenty-third, while Joanne, who had fallen at a complicated cross-country combination called the Eyelash, went clear to end up twenty-ninth. Arranshar had already been eliminated and Carol thought that the ground was too hard for Topic so our fortunes were mixed at best and we were still a long way from home.

At that age, life's luxuries aren't important so we were perfectly happy operating on a shoestring but it did mean that we didn't have much of a cushion for emergencies. As we couldn't afford to hire a replacement truck, we had no choice but to hitch rides back to Chester Springs for our horses and ourselves with our new American friends.

I was encouraged by my Ledyard result because the leading Americans, Bruce Davidson, Jim Wofford, Mike Plumb and the reigning Olympic champion, Tad Coffin, were all in the field so I was holding my own at the highest level. Riding against people I'd heard about for years made me realise that they were only human after all. Maybe they were better and more experienced than I was but I wasn't a mile behind them so I should be capable of catching them up.

Two weeks after Ledyard, the final selection trial for the American team took place at Bruce Davidson's place at Chesterland Farm. Boy Caro, the representative of the New Zealand Horse Society, had flown in to assess our progress at the two-day competition. As there were no official qualifications for the World Championships in those days, the decision on whether or not our team should be entered rested with him. He was very correct, almost English, in a tweed jacket, cap and tie. Back in New Zealand, he'd come up to me at a competition and said, 'Look, son, if you ever want to get on in life you want to dress more like me.' As a teenager accustomed to wearing jeans, that was the last thing I wanted. There was another incident back in New Zealand when we were stabled on a racecourse for an event, but were forbidden to use the track for training gallops. Ted Harrison, Carol's husband, got up at 5 a.m. and took his horse for a gallop down it, leaving hoof prints which the staff complained about to Boy Caro. Somehow Boy Caro blamed me for it and gave me a right ticking off, which made me very indignant as I hadn't even had the fun of doing it. As a result, I didn't like him very much at that time, but I grew to respect him later and I've had an excellent relationship with him ever since. After our trip to America, he and his family did everything they could to promote horse trials in New Zealand, so I've got a lot to be grateful to them for.

The day before Chesterland, the garage in Boston rang to say that our truck was ready so I flew up to collect it. After driving it back to Chester Springs through the night, I only managed a couple of hours sleep before we loaded the horses for the journey to the event. Though I don't like to admit it, too little sleep always makes me a bit tetchy which partly explains what happened next. Lockie was working us in for the dressage, watched by Boy Caro and his wife. I felt Lockie was interfering too much too early on in my warm-up routine so I said, 'Would you leave me for a few minutes so I can work the horse?' He said, 'No, you gotta do this.' Well, I let rip, called him all the names under the sun. The Caros got an awful shock, Lockie got an awful shock, and I stormed off on the horse and did my own thing anyway.

With so much at stake, it was important to get a good start, but Top Hunter picked up the tension caused by the row and we did our worst dressage since arriving in America. However, we made up for it by galloping round the relatively straightforward cross-country course in one of the fastest times of the day, while most of our rivals went slowly in order to save their horses for the big one at Lexington in four weeks' time. Meanwhile Joanne got so lost on the roads and tracks that she never checked in for the cross country and Carol decided to withdraw Topic after the showjumping because of the hard ground. Overall, it wasn't a great dress rehearsal but Boy Caro decided we'd done well enough for the New Zealand Horse Society to finalise arrangements for our Championship entry. Much to our relief, our great gamble had paid off.

The row at Chesterland was the only major fall out. Otherwise we all got on very well with each other and with Lockie. He was a brilliant trainer and incredibly generous, giving his time and expertise for nothing, and we developed a great camaraderie during the five months we were together. Lockie raised a lot of laughs by banning me from having sex before an event because he said it turned my legs to jelly in the dressage. As far as I know, the girls didn't have boyfriends in America, but he said sex would be fine for them because it would make them more relaxed.

As the only man in the group, I got away with quite a lot. I had several girlfriends in my ten-month stay, all of them briefly serious. There were a couple who got a bit intense so they had to go. No doubt they made the first approaches because I was a shy sort of character, but I was eager to widen my experience. I hadn't had a serious girlfriend back in New Zealand and I certainly wasn't up for anything long term in America, but I enjoyed my new freedom. Any relationship that lasted for two or three weeks was doing pretty well, either in New Zealand or America. Not surprisingly, the girls on the team were fairly dismayed by my behaviour!

Lockie had been in America long enough to pick up the fitness habit, yoga and five-mile runs every day, and that gave me a chance to pay him back for the sex ban. He may have been a bit ahead of his time, but none of us reacted very well when he suggested we should join him on a run. Carol and I were the only smokers so we'd jog 200 yards up the road, hide behind a tree and sit down for a cigarette. Nicoli and Mary were more diligent and Joanne made a token effort. As I was quite fit, and pretty young compared to Lockie, I decided to challenge him. We didn't exactly race, but I got home first. That night, I was so stiff I could hardly walk up the stairs, so that was the end of my fitness regime. Still, I did beat him so I felt I'd proved my point.

At Chester Springs, we looked after our horses ourselves. None of us had ever had a groom and we weren't easily persuaded that we'd need them for the Championships. Lockie was very friendly with Sally O'Connor, an Englishwoman who was married to an American. She rode with Lockie and evented a bit and she suggested that her sons, David, who won Badminton in 1997, and Brian should groom for the team at Lexington. Jan Mossman, a New Zealand girl who was working for the racehorse trainer Dwayne Murty at his Long Island stables, offered to groom for me. Initially it was very odd to have someone else take over the horses but Lockie said, 'Come on, you've just got to let them get on with it.' Once we got used to it, we got quite keen on the idea, but I think I forged a much closer partnership with Top Hunter by doing everything for him.

For most of the time, I doubled as the team farrier. I wasn't trained but I'd always shod my own horses for reasons of economy. When I was working for John Boyte in his racing stable, I learned on one of his old horses. I don't suppose the horse ever walked again, but I'd improved over the years! We'd all had several sets of shoes made up to take to America, so it was just a question of trimming the feet and nailing them on. When it came to the Championships, we got a proper farrier but up till then I saved the team money. I didn't get any other extra duties for being the only man. After all, they were big strong girls accustomed to doing lots of work. We had a rota for looking after the horses so that we all got some time off. We'd also work each other's horses and swap advice, but Lockie was always there to keep us on the right track overall.

Lexington was incredibly well organised, especially the Kentucky Horse Park, which had benefited from a million dollar facelift in preparation for the Championships. The riders were put up in hotels, which meant that we had the rare luxury of our own rooms. There were very grand parties, the likes of which we'd never seen before. I didn't have any smart clothes, but this was the time of *Saturday Night Fever* and I certainly thought my flared trousers, platform shoes and shiny shirts with big collars were the height of fashion. I've always loved dancing and if there is good music played at a party you can guarantee I'll be up there. Like all sportsmen, I have a natural sense of rhythm and balance. I certainly wasn't a John Travolta clone, but some of the more traditional Kentuckians may have wondered what I was doing.

As Lexington is on the fringes of the Deep South, the hospitality was incredible, no expense spared, huge ice sculptures, fabulous food. It would have been hard not to be impressed. Being a New Zealander, I took a laid-back view of it all, but it was certainly very different from anything I'd seen at home. The organisers did it to impress and up to a point it worked, not just for me, but for everyone. You soon learn what's genuine and what's not, but our hosts went out of their way to do things for us and make us feel welcome. I made some lifelong friends, among them Bruce Davidson, Sally O'Connor, her son David, and Karen Lende, who later became his wife.

Lexington was my first opportunity to meet British riders who would also become lifelong friends. Lucinda Prior-Palmer (now Green), one of my childhood heroines, was over for the Championships, along with Jane Starkey, Chris Collins, Lizzie Boone (now Purbrick), Jane Holderness-Roddam and Richard Meade. Although the team stuck pretty much to themselves, I chatted a bit to the Brits because our horses were stabled near theirs. One of the things I remember was how they had team meetings in their tack room every day. We thought that was incredibly efficient so we used to eavesdrop to find out what we were missing out on. That's how we knew about their elaborate plans for putting runners out on the course to feed back up-to-date information on how each fence was jumping. Not that the strategy was of much use to us because we didn't have the manpower to mount such an operation.

At Lexington in July, the first thing that struck us was how incredibly hot it was, far hotter than Ledyard, which had been bad enough. Today, everyone would demand a shortened course if they were competing in such temperatures, but no one knew anything about heat stress in horses in those days. The organisers had recognised the problem to some degree and tried to offset it by providing ice and oxygen. We New Zealanders had got our team there fit and raring to go, or so we thought, so we were pretty pleased with ourselves in that respect. Mary's grey, Arranshar, had gone wrong with an abcess in his foot – pricked during shoeing, I daresay – but the giant Vladivostock had been flown over as a replacement, so all five of us made it to the starting line. Carol was the most experienced rider so she went first on Topic, followed by Nicoli on Never Dwell and Joanne on Bandolier, with me as anchorman. As Mary had had to switch horses, she rode as an individual.

The New Zealand Horse Society added to our team spirit by sending over black-and-white saddle cloths and warm-up jackets for us and our grooms, but we had to find our own tail coats and top hats for the dressage. Chris Collins, who was on the British team with Smokey, kindly lent me his. He was the only rider of roughly the same height, but he was a lot broader, so the coat hung off me like a sack. Top Hunter was going very well, placing in most of the events, but Lockie thought we had a better chance as a team than as individuals so that was our biggest goal as the great day approached.

By this time, we knew that the American fences were more complicated and better presented than the ones back home, but they hadn't seemed much more formidable until we first walked the course at Lexington. Then our eyes were opened and we thought, 'My God, this is big, but we're here, we've got to do it.' There wasn't any feeling of, 'we can't do it', probably because ignorance is bliss. The World Championship was my second ever three-day event and my horse was the least experienced, but my months in America had proved that I was competitive so I was quietly confident. It is incredible to think, now, that I expected a horse who had done no more than ten one-day events and one three-day event in his entire life to be competitive in a World Championships – the optimism and ignorance of youth.

Even so, I would hardly have been human if I hadn't been a little nervous when the moment came to trot into the dressage arena. With his long relaxed stride, Top Hunter was a natural on the flat and he'd profited from his training with Lockie to the point at which he was beginning to go very well. I was scheduled early on the second dressage day, so I'd ridden him as near to the stands on the first day as I could to get him used to the electrifying atmosphere. When the time came, he gave 110 per cent, doing everything as well as he could and even maybe a little bit better. The result was a fantastic test by our standards so I was the best Kiwi, not that far off the lead in tenth place. Carol usually got the best dressage marks among us, but Topic had freaked out on the first day and ended up last. The others were in the middle, with Joanne scoring higher than Nicoli and Mary, but as it turned out the dressage played almost no part in the final line-up.

On cross-country day, we weren't any more worried about the heat than anyone else. The pattern was that the humidity built up through the morning, often developing into thunderstorms in mid-afternoon. As the last team member to start, I was due to ride when the conditions were at their worst, but as news of the carnage came in, followed closely by a stream of exhausted horses and riders, I sensed that I could improve my position considerably if I could put in a good performance. When a reporter asked me about the course, I'd replied, 'Oh, any good New Zealand Pony Club horse could get around!' so I already had a bit to prove as I was counted down through the starting gate in the sweltering heat of the early afternoon.

Phases A and C, the two sets of roads and tracks, were longer and faster in those days. The optimum time for phase B, the steeplechase, was five and a half minutes and the track included a bullfinch, a double brush, a water jump and a post and rails, in addition to the customary chase fences. Top Hunter really stood off at a post and rails with a big water ditch behind it and landed on the uphill slope on his nose. Even so, I was half a minute inside the time, the second fastest round of the day after Lizzie Purbrick on Felday Farmer, who was even madder than I was.

Top Hunter pulled up a bit unlevel at the end of the steeplechase, but I walked him at the start of phase C and by the time he reached the ten-minute box for the inspection before phase D, the cross-country proper, he felt fine again. Lockie was in a high state of excitement as he updated me on the misfortunes of our rivals. The British team had been eliminated, the Americans had just one rider round clear at that point and the Canadian leaders had all gone very slowly. Meanwhile, Carol had clocked the third fastest round of the day, even after missing her line at the Sinkhole and having a run out. Never Dwell had been withdrawn before the cross-country because he was lame but Joanne had completed, despite falling at the third fence, the Park Pavilion, and again at the Open Water.

'I think we'll be in the medals if you go clear,' Lockie told me and I set off with the determination to give it my all. We cruised round the early fences, Top Hunter jumping with his usual honesty, but when we reached the Old Fort Lexington combination, he didn't want to know. He jumped in over the first element, a small cabin, but absolutely refused to consider the big bank and ditch that came up four strides later. I presented him three times, but it was hopeless and we were eliminated, walking glumly back to the stables with all our hopes shattered.

I was devastated because the only time Top Hunter had refused with me before was at his first-ever cross-country, ironically at another, though very small, bank. Obviously there was something seriously wrong, but it was only when I took the bandages off and saw his swollen tendons that I realised why he'd stopped. In my ignorance, I'd gone too fast and the bandages had slipped or he'd injured himself when he pecked on the steeplechase. Since then, I've always used boots rather than bandages on the cross-country.

I've never seen anything like the carnage in the stables later that night, with horses lying everywhere with drips in them, just like a battlefield. Again, it was ignorance that did the damage but at least the lessons of Lexington were well learned. Nowadays, speed and endurance competitions in such extreme conditions would be reduced to protect the horses from over-exertion on that scale, or cancelled altogether.

When all the scores were up, there was some consolation in the fact that we were not alone in our disappointment. The Canadians had been rewarded for their caution with first place in the team competition, with the Germans and the Americans filling the minor places after losing one rider each. In the individual, Bruce Davidson, the reigning world champion, went clear on Might Tango, but the seven-year-old grey was so exhausted that he had to be supported from both sides at the end of the cross-country course. They worked on him through the night to get him ready for the showjumping and he passed the vet's inspection and won, giving Bruce an unprecedented second successive victory, but the horse never appeared in top-class competition again. Carol and Topic went clear in the showjumping and finished in sixth place, a fantastic effort and a very creditable start for New Zealand in world-class competition.

I was annoyed with myself because I thought I'd done a little too much preparation, pushing Top Hunter past his peak. As you always do after a failure, I kept thinking, 'if only, if only, if only ...', but when I was able to look at it more rationally, I realised that I'd been tenth after the dressage so if I'd gone clear as we always had, I could have finished near the top of the order, so I didn't feel totally defeated. I'd proved myself to a certain extent in the run-up to Lexington and, if anything, the disappointment at the Championship made me even more determined to succeed at the highest level. Although I had no immediate plans for extending my travels, I decided that wherever I went next, it wouldn't be back to the farm. As the dust of Lexington settled, I set about building the next stage in my career.

CHAPTER THREE

... AND WIDER STILL

We'd always known that we would never be able to afford to take our horses back to New Zealand; they were all in America on a one-way ticket. Of course, I was sad to sell Top Hunter. He'd done so much for me, he'd taken me overseas, given me a taste of international eventing and he was a lovely, kind horse as well. After the cross-country at Lexington, his forelegs were like bananas, but oddly enough he was never lame. Jan Mossman did an amazing job on him. She was used to working with legs from her time with Dwayne Murty's racehorses and she treated Top Hunter round the clock for three days. When the bandages first came off after the cross-country and I saw his legs, I was in despair about the prospect of him doing anything in the near future, let alone selling him, but within a week you'd never have known there'd been a problem.

After his sixth place, Carol had no trouble selling Topic to a woman in California who gave him a very nice home. Carol kept in touch with her for a long time afterwards so she knew her horse was well and happy, which is a bit of a luxury in our business. Typically, Joanne was in a dither over what to do. Bandolier was a stunning horse and several people wanted to buy him, among them Lucinda Prior-Palmer and Lady Hugh Russell, whose daughter was eventing at the time. I rang Joanne from my room in the hotel after the competition and put on this really posh English accent.

'Hello,' I said, 'I'm Lord so and so and I want to buy your horse for my daughter.' Then I offered her this astronomical sum of money and she fell for it, hook, line and sinker, so I arranged to meet her to discuss the details and rang off. All our rooms were adjoining so there she was, running out of her room into mine screaming, 'Guess what, guess what.' The others were in the room with me when I rang her and we managed to keep straight faces for about thirty seconds before we burst out laughing. She nearly killed us.

Eventually Overseas Containers Limited (OCL) bought Bandolier for Lucinda so he went to England where he was rechristened Mairangi Bay. In fact, he never suited Lucinda so David Green, who later became her husband, rode him for a while. Their most memorable moment became a famous footnote in Badminton's history. It occurred at a big combination near the end of the Badminton cross-country. Mairangi Bay jumped in and somehow David and he parted company, leaving David with both legs on one side of the saddle facing backwards while Mairangi Bay went on jumping. David hopped off on the other side of the fence and there was no harm done.

Bandolier and Topic went to their new owners straight from the Kentucky Horse Park but Top Hunter had to return to Chester Springs. Karen Lende (now O'Connor) came and tried him, as did Jurg Zindel, a Swiss dealer who eventually bought him for the Italians. Carol had flown straight back to New Zealand, but Nicoli and I went on a trip in the mini-van down to Florida to see Disney World. After Top Hunter was sold, Joanne and I drove across America from the East Coast to the West Coast, just for the hell of it. The owners of the car wanted it delivered and we were only too glad to help them out! We only had about three days to complete the trip but it was such a smart car that we just switched on the cruise control, put our feet up on the dash and watched the countryside go by. We even slept in it one night. I remember enjoying the journey much more than I'd expected but the sheer distance was imposing. I'd never imagined driving flat out for seventy-two hours almost non-stop to get from one side of a country to another. We must have been lucky because we didn't get any speeding tickets.

After Jurg bought Top Hunter, he asked me if I'd like to look after him when he travelled to Britain in October, three months after the World Championships. I was still in a happy-go-lucky mood, keen to follow wherever destiny took me, provided it added to the sum of my riding experience, so I joined Top Hunter at Jurg's yard between Newbury and the M4. Joanne was looking after Bandolier while he settled at Lucinda's yard near Andover so I had a friend in the neighbourhood. I'd always wanted to go to England, but the timing wasn't great because I arrived at a time of year when there was no eventing and it was freezing cold. When Jurg sold Top Hunter to the Italians, it was a sad parting of the ways; you definitely develop a special affection for a horse from the farm down the road that takes you to your first World Championship. I said goodbye in a bit of a daze and was sad to learn later that he'd damaged a tendon again and retired from eventing.

After a few weeks in England, Jurg offered me a job the following year riding young horses for him, so after Top Hunter had gone I returned to New Zealand with the specific aim of buying a horse to take back to Britain for the 1979 season. Jurg paid me US$25,000 (NZ$50,000) for Top Hunter so I could afford a decent advanced horse, provided I could find one. Lockie had returned to New Zealand after Lexington and he told me about Jocasta, a horse owned by Diane Guy that had proved his reliability across country by completing two three-day events. I went down to the South Island to see him, but I can't imagine why I bought him because he was lame when I tried him and I never particularly liked him. I suppose I was used to following Lockie's recommendations but, with hindsight, I don't think he had a particularly good eye for a horse. Jocasta was a fizzy little character, not the sort I'd been used to, part Hackney, part Thoroughbred, but on his record he was reasonably priced at NZ$10,000.

I returned to England in the New Year and Jocasta followed. When he arrived at Jurg's, he had a couple of dodgy looking tendons so we gave up on the idea of Badminton, which was probably a blessing. Although the tendons never looked totally right, they didn't affect him at all so I followed my game plan by competing at a lower level. He was quite highly strung, very difficult to ride on the flat and I never really came to terms with him, but we got a few places and I ended up qualifying for Burghley. I must have been terribly brave in those days!

Burghley 1979 was my first British three-day event. The venue is very impressive with that magical house and parkland. At Lexington the fences were themed but at Burghley it was all big timber, much more natural. Neither course remotely resembled the ones in New Zealand, which were more like hunter trials than anything else. Jocasta's legs still looked dodgy and the vet said I shouldn't take him, but I ignored that. Everything was much more carefree then! Jocasta had a rigid back and a bone-jarring trot so we didn't do too well in the dressage but we got round the cross-country with two stops. The first was at the Waterloo Rails, a formidable fence built on undulating ground with a big drop which Jocasta always hated. I had to ride hard to get him over the second time and he protested at the pressure by stopping again at the next fence, but went clear after that.

Burghley that year was memorable because, apart from being my first one, I met the Irish riders, David Foster and Brendan Corscadden, kindred spirits in the vital matters of drinking and partying, who have become lifelong friends. We lived in the caravan park and gathered with some of the other riders – Andrew Hoy, Sarah Bouet and Tim Thomson Jones among others – in whichever caravan had the best bar, maybe even mine. One night, we were making so much noise that Reggie Purbrick put on his Colonel voice and bellowed at us to shut up. I remember thinking, 'Who is that pompous prat?' little realising that he, too, would soon be one of my closest friends. Another evening, Brendan and I got stuck into Tom Hudson's whisky until the wee small hours. Tom was a colourful personality, a showjumping and horse trials commentator, and a very generous host. When it was time to go back to our billets, Brendan announced that he'd lost one of his contact lenses so the three of us peered around in the grass in the dark, too far gone to have a hope of finding it, but determined not to quit until we'd given it our best shot.

I looked after Jocasta myself and got on well with many of the grooms so I was never short of drinking companions; not that that was my aim, but the partying was one of the best things about eventing in those days.

Although I didn't see Jocasta as the ideal Olympic partner, the prospect of realising my childhood dream by riding in the 1980 Games in Moscow became increasingly viable as the 1979 season progressed. Although there was no prospect of New Zealand fielding a team, the

Horse Society was keen to build on Lexington by paying my expenses from England to Moscow to compete as an individual. My performance at Burghley was not going to impress the selectors so I took Jocasta to the Boekelo three-day event six weeks later. It was an unorthodox gamble, but it paid off because he went very well and finished seventh, my best result to date, so I was wildly excited and encouraged.

Nowadays Boekelo is almost a local event, but in those days going to Holland was a marathon trek. I travelled with Clissy Strachan, one of the first British riders to come up and make friends with me. We just hit it off from the word go and we've always been great mates. She had hair down to her waist and when she got you on the dance-floor her flying hair would whip you round the face. By the time I got to Boekelo, I realised that eventing people partied in much the same way all over the world, not so much because of the pressure but out of sheer *joie de vivre*. I've always loved a good party – still do – and at twenty-three I had the stamina to ride effectively on very little sleep so why would I resist Boekelo's fabulous hospitality? The Poles and the Russians got tanked up on vodka till they dropped and I got blind drunk on genever, so much so that I've never been able to drink it since.

As I was the first New Zealand eventer to come to live in Britain, I was accepted as much for my novelty value as anything else. I was able to get around because I'd bought what I thought was quite a smart car, a second-hand Datsun 180B. That was fine until I wrote it off on the way to Heathrow to pick up a girlfriend who was flying in from Italy. I was low on petrol and I knew there was a garage just up the motorway, but what I didn't know was that an accident had blocked all three lanes. I wasn't paying much attention and drove straight into the back of the pile-up. The car was a write-off and as it wasn't fully insured, I had to replace it with a low-profile Austin 1100.

I went to dinner at Lucinda's from time to time and I was also invited to Wylye by Lord and Lady Hugh Russell. I knew the Russells because their cross-country course at Wylye was about the only place you could go for schooling in those days, and then only if you had lessons with Lady Hugh. She had a reputation for fierceness but I wasn't overawed by her which is probably why I was asked to dinner. It was all new territory for me. I'd never met a Lord before and it seemed pretty formal, especially to someone who didn't even own a suit, just some dreadful jacket and tie. I didn't bother much with clothes in those days. In fact, I still don't.

Meanwhile the young horses I was bringing on at Jurg's were going quite well and selling quite well but we had no written agreement regarding the commissions on the sales that I thought we'd agreed verbally, so it eventually led to a disagreement.

I had no other income so a parting of the ways was inevitable. It was a meeting with Baroness Barth Von Wehrenalp at the Ascot Sales that actually triggered the move in the autumn of 1979. She'd seen me at events so she introduced herself and invited me over to Harwood Lodge, on the other side of Newbury, for dinner. Penny was an over-the-top English eccentric. Her husband, Uve, was German and they were both pretty wild characters, fond of throwing grand parties in their huge house. As commissions are an accepted part of horse dealing, they were indignant at Jurg's failure to pay me, so they offered me a new home with them. In a characteristic spirit of adventure, they came over to Jurg's yard in their ancient horsebox and removed Jocasta and the rest of my possessions. I'd never done anything like that before so it was pretty nerve-racking, especially as Jurg and I had half shares in the horse. Inevitably the writs soon started landing on the Von Wehrenalps' doormat, but we managed to settle out of court and I kept Jocasta. Since then Jurg and I have got on very well together and done several deals over horses.

Uve and Penny had a few horses that they had bred themselves and I looked after them in lieu of my keep. They were in their heyday when I lived with them and we had a lot of laughs. They'd bought Harwood Lodge when it was derelict after being gutted by fire and completely done it up. Penny was very arty and innovative and she enjoyed hosting the great and the good, though the only famous person I remember meeting there is the ladies' underwear designer Janet Reger. The parties were fairly riotous, no drugs but lots of booze. Penny loved champagne and she was a great one for opening another bottle. I discovered later that the money came from Uve's mother, who owned a large publishing company in Germany. I stayed with them through 1980. A couple of years after I left, they went their separate ways.

When I went home for Christmas in 1979, I planned to spend the remains of my Top Hunter money on a horse that would give me a more realistic chance of doing well at Badminton and in the 1980 Olympics. I rang Boy Caro to ask if he knew of any suitable contenders and he got back to me a week later with the suggestion that I should consider Southern Comfort, or Monty, as he was always known. I remembered him from 1977, mostly because his owner, Shirley Woods, had ridden him round a cross-country course on her dressage saddle after forgetting to bring her jumping saddle. Various members of the Woods family had hunted him, he'd competed in the Pony Club Championships, he was a grade B showjumper and he'd completed two advanced events in 1979 when ridden by Sue Thompson, a friend of Shirley's.

Encouraged by these credentials, I went to try him and got on well with him from the start. He was a big bay horse, 16.2hh and nearly full Thoroughbred. He was a very smart mover, but his dressage was at best all right, definitely not good at that stage. He jumped in an odd style, with his head too high, but he was very careful and he did quite well when I rode him in grade B classes in New Zealand. Initially, I was worried he might be too cautious across country, especially as I'd been advised by friends not to buy him because he'd been known to stop. He also had a heart murmur, the kind that can be heard at rest but disappears with exertion, but the vet seemed to think he would be capable of doing three-day events and I liked him enough to take the chance.

I travelled back to England on the horse plane with David Green and Andrew Nicholson. David had a little grey horse called Swift Deal, which he was going to take to Lucinda's. He'd met her in Australia and he boasted on the journey that he was going to marry her. Andrew and I laughed and said, 'Are you sure?' It was an awful flight, with seven stops over two days, but Andrew and David were excellent company. The plane was a regular Noah's Ark, with cows, live eels and 100 rams which we dropped off in Buenos Aires. There weren't any frills, no airline meals or anything like that, but there were facilities for heating up your own food and we could stroll around and talk to the pilot in the cockpit, so there were advantages over commercial flights.

Monty and I arrived at Harwood Lodge in March 1980, just six weeks before Badminton, but we got going so quickly that I decided to enter him. Nowadays, I'd find the thought of bringing a horse over and doing that pretty daunting, but then I just cracked on and did it. Frank Weldon was in his heyday and the courses were big, particularly so in 1980 because of the upcoming Olympics, but I'd walked round Badminton the year before and thought, 'Yes, I can do this.' I'd experienced nothing since to make me change my mind. I prepared by taking a few dressage lessons with Bridget Maxwell, who was teaching Lucinda at the time. Lucinda herself was very driven and focused, but she did help me in her own way. She was always very friendly and very charming but in a slightly distracted kind of way. One minute she'd be talking to you and the next she'd be off talking to someone else. She wasn't a big party girl and I was a bit in awe of her. I'd read books about her triumphs with Be Fair when I was still living in New Zealand.

I took Monty for some cross-country lessons with Lady Hugh and I was confident he was very fit. He went well in the advanced classes at Frensham, Rushall and Brigstock, where he finished eighth, but we certainly weren't among the favourites for Badminton. That year the money was on Mark Phillips with Columbus, Richard Meade with Kilcashel, Mike Tucker with General Bugle and, of course, Lucinda with Killaire. Andrew Nicholson agreed to groom for me at Badminton as a gesture of goodwill. My test was scheduled early on Thursday morning. We both overslept and ended up plaiting Monty at great speed, one starting at the head and the other at the withers. I had my own top hat by then but I was still borrowing Chris Collins's tail coat, with the New Zealand silver fern pinned on top of the Union Jack. I was really pleased with Monty's test but we ended up about fortieth, which wasn't very promising.

Andrew and I were staying in the caravan park and Penny moved in for support. She always believed in omens so she was optimistic about my chances because she'd worked out that 1980 was the Year of the Monkey in the Chinese calendar, just as the year of my birth had been. The night before the cross-country, a group of us started on the whisky and most of us got absolutely ratted. Maybe Penny was right about the favourable omens because I was the only rider from that little session who completed the cross-country without mishap!

I'd walked the course three times and it was pretty impressive but there wasn't any one fence that especially worried me. Sally O'Connor was over from America and she walked round with me on one of my circuits. I also got some inside information from some of the more experienced riders, including Clissy who had the same approach as me, although she rode very differently. Lucinda was very technical, always jogging up to the fence on the exact line she planned to ride it. I felt, 'God, should I be doing this? What am I missing out on?' but Clissy and I just decided to go for it. There weren't many long routes in those days, so there wasn't all that much choice anyway.

I must have gone fairly early on because I didn't know when I started that nobody had got round clear. The hangover was under control after coffee, orange juice, Disprin and far too many cigarettes, and I completed the roads and tracks and the steeplechase without penalty. While I was out on the roads and tracks, I heard over the public address system that Mark Phillips had retired Columbus at the second Luckington Lane crossing. I didn't think, 'Oh my God, if he didn't get round I may find it difficult,' but rather that losing one of the favourites gave me a better chance. Other than that, I had no news about the state of the competition as I met up with Sally in the ten-minute box before the start of phase D. The truth was that the course was causing absolute mayhem and Sally was torn about whether to tell me or not. In the end, she decided to say that everything was fine and I just went out there and rode the course. I don't think it would have bothered me if she'd warned me because I was confident about where I was going to jump every fence. By this time, I'd come to terms with eventing in Britain and my preparation was very thorough. I had a clear picture in my mind's eye of where Monty was going to jump and how he was going to jump. I'd always tried to make myself visualise my round in advance and I set off with everything to gain and nothing to lose. As I didn't own a stop-watch, I decided to go as fast as possible and see what happened. It was very different from Kentucky; in fact the weather was ideal, sunny but not hot, with dry going so there was less danger of slipping than if it had been muddy.

We went round anti-clockwise that year, starting off across the front of the house, with the Pardubice brush and ditch coming up at the third fence. I took almost all the direct routes, but not at the Vicarage V because I thought it was a horribly daunting fence. I remember being most impressed later by the way Lucinda jumped it, just cantering up and popping over, as if it wasn't there. The Footbridge came next and it was huge. I missed my jerk coming in, got in a bit deep and Monty landed just on the lip of the ditch on the other side, pitching down on his nose and skidding along on the ground. Luckily his body stayed fairly straight and I managed to stay on board until he picked himself up and off he went. The Footbridge turned out to be the most influential fence, with both Sue Benson and Lorna Clark falling as they attacked the direct route. Lorna broke her leg and Sue ended up in the nettles at the side of the fence.

Monty gave me a fabulous ride round the rest of the course, with no problems at the Lake, the Normandy Bank, the Ski Jump and the Quarry. There were only six clear rounds all day and only three of those, including mine, were within the time. Helen Butler on Merganser was in the lead on 57.0, Lucinda on Killaire was second on 61.4 and Monty and I were third on our dressage score of 64.6. With a five-point penalty for each knock down in the showjumping, Helen had one fence in hand over me, and Lucinda could not afford to have a fault.

Back in the stables, the big drop fences and the dry ground had taken their toll on the horses, including Monty, who was a bit foot-sore. Andrew put cooling poultices on his legs and Peter Scott Dunn, the British team vet, gave him 20ccs of bute, a perfectly legal remedy for any kind of soreness in those days. After lunch and a celebratory bottle of champagne, Andrew and I went back to the stables to prepare a hot bran mash, a routine chore that turned out to be more dangerous than riding round the cross-country course. The problem came when I tried to light the antiquated gas boiler. I'd never seen one like it but I assumed it lit from the bottom, so I leaned underneath with a lighted match and the flames exploded in my face. There was a terrible smell of burning hair and I lost my eyebrows and my eyelashes, but luckily my eyes were okay.

I only had one pair of white breeches so I washed them and got the people in the village store to dry them. Then I put them under the mattress to press them while I slept. I had an early night on the Saturday, partly because I was exhausted and partly because I was worried about the vet's inspection. As it turned out, I needn't have been because Monty passed with flying colours. I was in a state of euphoria, having gone into my first Badminton with the idea that I'd be doing really well if I finished in the top ten. Now I was third after the cross-country, far higher up the order than I'd ever hoped, and poised to do even better. The showjumping was in reverse order of merit so I concentrated on the clear round I needed to be sure of retaining my position before turning my attention to the two in front of me. We all knew Helen's horse, Merganser, was an unreliable showjumper so Lucinda was favourite to win a record fifth Badminton.

Monty went in and jumped a lovely round, no rattling poles, no risky moments. When I got to know Lucinda better, she told me she'd thought my horse was a bit of a dodgy showjumper, but when she saw me whack up a big fence in the practice arena, she realised she might have been wrong. I still didn't rate my chances of coming first; Lucinda didn't make many mistakes when she was in a position to win. However, Killaire spooked at his first sighting of the water jump and when he came to jump it, he landed in the middle. You don't wish ill on your rivals, but of course you're very happy when they end up below you! Poor Helen had four poles down and that was that. I'd won! When the poles fell, the television commentator, Dorian Williams, said in his plummy voice, 'And Lucinda has won her fifth Badminton. No, no, of course it isn't Lucinda, it's that Mark Todd from New Zealand.' I was in a complete daze but my friends went berserk, with Penny and Uve in tears and the others cheering themselves hoarse.

I've often watched the television pictures of the Queen chatting away as she presented me with the Whitbread Trophy but I can't remember what she said, only that she was very easy to talk to. I'd seen female winners curtseying to her but I wasn't sure what I should do so I scraped together some sort of bow. I won a saddle and lots of money, about £3,000, which went a long way in 1980. I was in shock when I did the lap of honour but the reality of it all struck me when I spoke to my parents from the press tent. I woke them up at four o'clock in the morning their time. I got Mum first and said, 'Guess what?' She said, 'What?' and I said, 'We won.' At first she thought I was joking but once I'd persuaded her it was true she was very excited. That was the most emotional moment, the first time it actually sank in that I'd really won. I was in tears. Mum and Dad were as shocked as I was, as shocked as everyone was, but an underdog that beats the favourites always gets a lot of support so I had a very warm reception wherever I went. Penny, Uve and I drove the old lorry to our local pub in Wootton Hill, ordered drinks all round and put the Whitbread Trophy – a fabulous silver horse – on the bar. Regardless of its value and the fact that it had to go back, we left it there for a week.

Afterwards I was overwhelmed by the letters I got from people in Britain, most of whom I didn't know. I had a very nice letter from Sue Benson, née Hatherly, one of the most competitive event riders at that time. Best of all, there was a poem of congratulations from Ginny Holgate, as she was then. I don't remember exactly when I first met her, but it must have been sometime the year before. I was very attracted to her but she always had a fairly aloof aura and I was too shy to make the first approach. I didn't see her often because she lived down in Devon, but Clissy came from there so I'd been able to make some discreet enquiries through her! The poem was the catalyst and Ginny and I got together soon after Badminton. She was my first serious girlfriend and our relationship blew hot and cold over the next four years.

CHAPTER FOUR

A Horse in a Million

Horses being horses, it was inevitable that the Badminton magic wouldn't last long. The disappointments started with the boycott of the Moscow Olympics as a protest against the Russian invasion of Afghanistan. New Zealand was quick to join the boycott but I didn't feel so bad because the other leading eventing nations, Britain, America and France, also pulled out, so it would have been a hollow victory. I was invited to represent New Zealand at the alternative Olympics at Fontainebleau in northern France, but Monty was lame so I had to take Jocasta. Although he'd gone well at Punchestown in May six weeks after Badminton, he certainly wouldn't have been my first choice because his dressage wasn't as good as Monty's and he was a less reliable jumper.

That was my first Punchestown but I can't remember much about it because it was, and is, an exceptionally sociable event. The roads weren't good so, as with Boekelo, getting there was quite a marathon. The horses were stabled at the racecourse and we slept on site in caravans. Nowadays we arrive in time for the vet's inspection but in the early eighties the thinking was that you needed two or three days to settle in. It was all much more amateur and I didn't have a big string of horses waiting at home, so time was not so important. Jocasta wasn't a natural dressage horse – being a quarter Hackney didn't help his action – but he did his best test to date at Punchestown. The cross-country was quite a decent track but he was braver at that stage than he would be later on, and he went clear within the time. We pulled up to second place behind David Foster at the end of the second day and retained it with a clear showjumping round.

After Punchestown, I took the horses down to Simon and Bobbie Neville, who had the yard that had belonged to Flavia Phillips, Mark's aunt, at Great Somerford near Chippenham in Wiltshire. The geography was favourable, too, because Ginny had moved from Devon to a yard in Acton Turville near Badminton; Great Somerford was a great deal closer to her than Wootton Hill. My nature is to go with the flow and when the opportunity to move to Great Somerford came up, it seemed worth taking. I left on good terms and, in fact, it was Penny who introduced me to Bobbie after meeting her at a health farm. They got on well because they were both equally eccentric. I seem to have an affinity with eccentric women and my amazingly long-lasting novelty value as the only New Zealand rider based in Britain was still opening a lot of doors.

Bobbie had five daughters, Amanda, Cazzie, Hetty and the twins, Arabella and Victoria. While I was there, Hetty died from a head injury after falling from her horse onto the road. She was just a kid, fifteen or sixteen, and really nice. She was out hacking, her horse shied and her hat came off as she fell. I wasn't there when it happened, but I went to see her in hospital and she died shortly afterwards. It was horrible, a pointless accident, and we were all deeply shocked and saddened.

Fontainebleau was scheduled for the last weekend in August and I travelled to France with Irish rider Eric Horgan, who is now the director of Punchestown, in Tub Ivans's lorry. Ivans used to show stallions and he also invented some portable stables known as Tubby Boxes. It seemed that every signpost on the way pointed to Paris, which gave us some problems. We couldn't ask the way because none of us spoke French. I was the lone Kiwi, but as I'd come with Eric and I shared a sense of humour and a devil-may-care attitude with other Irish riders, they adopted me for the duration. Helen Cantillion, who is now the Irish chef d'équipe, was also riding. The cross-country course at Fontainebleau was difficult and I walked it four times, maybe even five. It was in and out of the woods, which made it hard to remember which fence came after which bend. Every time you walked it, there were a couple of points where you couldn't think what came next. Control was essential, which may have been a factor in the story that the colourful Irish rider, Van de Vater told about his own performance. Realising it would be difficult to hold his hard-pulling horse in such tight conditions, he claimed he threw the bit into the bushes on Phase C of the roads and tracks, telling the organisers that it had broken and he would therefore have to withdraw from the cross-country.

I managed to keep Jocasta's fiery temperament under control in the dressage and I was pleased with his score. After Badminton, I was recognised wherever I went. It's amazing how much your dressage marks improve when you have a success like that, whether or not your test gets any better, so that may have had something to do with it. I wasn't up with the leaders but I wasn't that badly placed as I went into the cross-country. The going was sandy and quite good and Jocasta was very fit, so I was reasonably optimistic. Early on, there was a long, artificial hill with a big log on the top. Because Jocasta was a bit cautious, I came up the hill fairly strongly and instead of just popping over it as I expected, the horse took off. I thought we were never going to touch down again, or that if we did we'd be in a heap, but amazingly he picked up all right and went on. We had a stop at the water, which was partly my fault, and continued to the third last fence, which was like the earlier one, only much, much smaller. The log was probably only eighteen inches high but Jocasta absolutely refused to jump it, so obviously he remembered that he'd frightened himself. In fact there was a long way round and why I didn't take it, I can't imagine. All I can say is that I was still quite green. So Jocasta stopped three times and we were eliminated. It's always easy to be wise after the event and to think what you might have done differently, but whichever way I looked at it the fact remained that this was my second international championship and I hadn't finished either one.

Back in Great Somerford, things didn't get much better. We still hadn't got to the bottom of Monty's lameness, and it kept him out of the autumn events. We eventually discovered it was caused by a piece of gravel lodged inside his hoof. I was living off the last of the money I got for Top Hunter, and found I had to rely a lot on people's kindness. I rented a one-bedroomed flat over a garage, down the road from the Nevilles, on a lovely property owned by Jane and John Irwin. They were keen hunting people but not really involved in eventing. My place was tiny, beautifully furnished and very cosy. I didn't have an expensive social life. Andrew Hoy, the first Australian rider of his generation to compete successfully in British events, winning Burghley in 1979, was working for Mark Phillips so I ran with the Gatcombe crowd – the grooms rather than the royals. After I started teaching the Neville girls, word of mouth soon brought me more pupils, a useful supplement to my income. At about this time, I met Mimi and Tom May at a drinks party and Mimi started bringing her horse over for lessons. She also helped me out by lending me her Range Rover and trailer to take my horses to events.

My parents came to stay for Badminton in 1981. They slept in my bedroom and I was on the sofa, which would have been fine except that we had freak snowstorms and the power was cut so there was no heating. One night I went to a ball with Ginny and it snowed and snowed and snowed. She lived fifteen minutes away from me under normal conditions, but on this occasion I was tempted to stay over. Then I thought Mum and Dad might be worried so I set off in the Yellow Peril, the clapped-out Ford Capri I'd bought to replace the Austin 1100. I was having a hell of a job driving through the snow when suddenly there was a tree blocking the road. I thought, 'God, I'm going to be stuck here all night.' I couldn't move the tree so I broke off some of the branches, then ran the car at it and somehow managed to get through. The Yellow Peril stopped more often than it went, but on this occasion it excelled itself and got me home to my anxious, freezing parents.

I did get to Badminton with Jocasta but only after the most awful lead up. He'd never recovered his nerve after Fontainebleau and he'd fallen in every event he'd been to since, either not taking off or half taking off. If I'd known then what I know now, I'd never have attempted Badminton. As it was, I was the defending champion and my parents had come over so I felt I had to have a go. The cross-country course went clockwise so we went through Huntsman's Close to the big Elephant Trap, at which Jocasta duly fell. We got up and went on but he stopped again at the next fence, the Quarry, and I thought enough was enough. My parents had been to Lexington to watch me and that hadn't worked out, and now to Badminton which hadn't worked out either, so they were beginning to think they were a bit of jinx.

My finances started to run seriously low at this stage and I reluctantly decided I'd have to sell Monty. He was sound again but he wasn't fit in time to compete at Badminton. Torrance Fleischmann bought him for £45,000 – I'd paid £5,000 for him – which was fair enough because he was only eleven and he'd won Badminton. I was much happier to see the back of Jocasta when I sold him to Eddy Stibbe for £3,000, hunter money, but he was going like a drain most of the time. Fortunately, we had a post and rails that he actually enjoyed jumping so whenever anyone came to try him, I galloped him at them and he'd pop over them eagerly. Eddy thought that was pretty good. In America, Monty was leading horse of the year with Torrance and she took him on to the World Championships in 1982. She made some cock-up on the roads and tracks or the steeplechase and got a horrendous number of time faults, but otherwise she would have been well placed. She polished up his dressage and he was pretty smart. Not surprisingly, Jocasta was never heard of again.

With both of them gone, I was without a ride until Mimi came to the rescue with Felix Too, the horse she brought over for her lessons. She offered him to me to compete on at novice level in 1981. He was pretty much a Thoroughbred, chestnut with a big white face, and fairly hot tempered. He moved well and he was a good jumper, very bold and brave, but he tended to rear up a lot. At the beginning of our partnership, we both had a bit of a temper on us, but after a while he knuckled down and started going well. Mimi had hunted him and he went through to advanced in his first year of eventing. I rode him for the love of it because I'd have lost my amateur status if I'd been paid to ride and that would have meant that I'd be barred from the Olympics. You could receive prize money but any other kind of payment had to be justified as expenses.

The World Championships were coming up the following year in Luhmühlen, but Felix Too was inexperienced and I had no hope of getting there until a Northamptonshire farmer, David Lloyd-Thomas, rang me up out of the blue and offered to lease me an advanced horse called Milton Tyson. The horse had a problem with his spine which had to be constantly corrected by a chiropractor, but I decided to give him a try and he went well enough for me to take him to Burghley. After coming seventh in the dressage with a competitive score of 48.15, I wanted to impress the New Zealand selectors so I took all the short cuts, a policy that ended in a refusal at the Duck Blind hedge bounce and an awkward landing at the Trout Hatchery. That put the horse's spine out of alignment and although the chiropractor got it right for the showjumping, it was too risky to rely on him for Luhmühlen, especially as I knew he wasn't top class. All in all, it seemed like as good a time as any to pack up and go home.

I didn't agonise about the decision because it just seemed inevitable. I wasn't really homesick but the thought of settling down to farming has always been in the back of my mind. Of course, I was disappointed not to have a world-class horse but I'd always seen my time abroad as a period of development, even a period of self-indulgence, before I took up my real career as a dairy farmer. After Burghley in 1981, I had a big farewell party in the Seagry village hall, just down the road from Great Somerford. I invited all my eventing friends and all the local people who'd helped me, about fifty in all. We decked out the hall with candles on the tables, and I mixed up a punch. There was no food, just bacon and eggs later on, so everyone got very, very merry. We had a disco and everyone danced till dawn. The locals said they couldn't remember a livelier night.

Whenever I went home to Cambridge, it was as if I'd never been away. By now, I was a hero in riding circles, but the general public didn't have a clue what the Badminton Horse Trials were, let alone any idea of their significance. Pop had said I could take over as a share milker on 1 June 1982, when the new farming year began and I had enough money in my pocket to buy his cows, 120 cross-bred Jersey Friesians, for NZ$350 a head, not top of the market but not cheap either. I didn't want him to give them to me, partly because it would have sparked a family row and partly because I wanted to make my own way in life, just as I did when I raised the money to go to Lexington rather than taking it from my parents. John Murdoch had been on the farm for the past twenty years as a share milker, but he was ready to retire so the timing was good. Under that particular share-milking deal, Pop owned the farm and the herd and Murdoch did the daily grind and sold the milk for a percentage of the proceeds.

When I became a share milker, I owned the herd, Pop owned the farm and we had a fifty:fifty split on the milk cheque. In that way, both of us had a financial stake in a partnership that provided me with a job and Pop with a proper income from his land. I don't think he ever quite believed I was going to stay, but he gave me every chance to build a profitable career as a farmer on my own merits rather than his generosity. He probably knew me as well as anyone, but he was always tactful with me and we got on very, very well.

As our deal didn't come into operation until the following June, I had time on my hands and Ginny came over to spend some of it with me. In one of the most relaxed periods in our romance, we drove around the country seeing the sights and looking at horses. I suppose she was checking out New Zealand with a view to living there but we both knew the timing was wrong. She'd been the European junior champion in 1976 and her star was very much in the ascendant in the early eighties. Her two best horses, Priceless and Night Cap, were in the early stages of their careers, so there was no real likelihood of her packing it all in and settling down in Cambridge.

I felt a twinge of envy as she left to prepare her horses for the spring season but I consoled myself by moving into the house that my great-grandfather had built nearly a century earlier, a lovely, somewhat ramshackle, tree-shaded property surrounded by forty hectares of grazing land. Pop said I could keep one or two horses on the farm, but it soon crept up to eight or nine. I had a sixteen-year-old lad, Scott Wickens, to help with the cows and Rosemary Barlett to help with the horses. I was given a half share in a 17hh part Cleveland bay, part Thoroughbred called Beaumont, a talented horse but I couldn't hold one side of him. In the three-day event at Taupo in early June, he was so strong on the steeplechase that I had to pull up to get a fresh grip on the reins and he was still eight seconds inside the time. We finished in second place in the advanced section and I was also second in the intermediate section on Shogun, a horse I was riding for Joanne Bridgeman. In New Zealand, there was a burden of expectation as a result of my Badminton victory, but Beaumont did well enough for the Horse Society to approve an entry for the World Championships in September if I'd wanted to go.

As he was relatively inexperienced, not to mention totally exhausting to ride, and as I'd just taken over the farm, I decided not to take up their offer. In those very early days, I was enjoying the farming. We had a very old-fashioned cowshed, a walk through in which you had to bend down and put the cups on each cow as she reached her allotted space. In a modern shed, you stand in a pit and attach them from below. I did the milking night and morning, except when I was away at a show. Even when I was, I'd hurry back to help Scott if I possibly could. I also did quite a lot of horse trading, buying what I hoped would be bargains at auction and bringing them on to the point at which they could be sold at a profit. Depending on the problems of each individual horse, it could take weeks or months, but the Japanese were trying to establish themselves on the international scene at the time and I made more money out of the horses than the cows in 1982. I was also doing a bit of teaching, so although I had to work very hard, it was a good time financially. I don't think I could do it now.

Of course, I was still young and single so I also partied a lot. Friends would come round and we'd stay up till three or four in the morning, which left me an hour or so to sleep before I started work at 5.30 a.m. The tanker came to collect the milk at 7.30 so it had to be ready by then. Sometimes the party continued in the milking parlour and sometimes I fell asleep on the job, but I think I only once had to ask the driver to come back later. It was a fun time, but in the back of my mind there was the knowledge that I hadn't yet fulfilled my Olympic destiny. Although I knew that I couldn't be a farmer and a full-time international event rider, I did believe that I could make successful excursions into the big time. All it needed was the right horse.

When the showjumping season started in January 1983 I went on the road with Beaumont and Snowstorm, a grade A horse owned by Pop's neighbours, Kenny and Ann Browne. Snowstorm had previously been ridden by their son Roger, who'd been killed playing polo in Australia. As we were long-time family acquaintants, they asked me to take over the ride. I was delighted to get back on the circuit and catch up with all the old gang. There weren't many shows and most of them lasted several days, so you'd see the same people at all of them. When we arrived, we'd park our trucks next to our mates' trucks, well away from the mothers and kids, so we could turn up the music, break out the booze and party late into the night without disturbing anyone.

Snowstorm had a habit of stopping if he didn't meet a fence on exactly the right stride, but gradually we came to an arrangement. He was second in the big derby at Isola and won five out of five starts at the next show at Taranaki. Kenny and I thought he might have a chance in the World Cup showjumping competition, so I took him down to Wellington for the qualifier. The courses were huge but we came second in the morning so my hopes were high. By the afternoon, the rain was so heavy that I could hardly see the fences and the wind so strong that the officials had to hold on to the uprights to prevent them falling over. Half-way round, Snowstorm crashed through a huge parallel and staked himself through the fetlock joint so that was that for the season. Meanwhile, Beaumont had nearly died of a blocked intestine so he, too, was off the road for months.

That left me clean out of experienced horses so Mimi May's phone call was particularly welcome. After I left England, she'd given the ride on Felix Too to Angela Tucker. She'd done well with him at Bramham so he was entered for Badminton, but a month before the event Angela had a bad fall. Mimi had said before that if Felix ever qualified for Badminton, she'd like me to ride him, so with Angela sidelined, she suggested she fly me over. I played hard to get for about two minutes, then rang straight back to accept. April is a quiet month on a New Zealand farm and I had a return ticket, so there was no reason to believe that the trip would be anything more than a brief interlude in my farming career.

When I arrived, Felix was lame with an abcess in his foot. His shoe was on and off as they poulticed it, but he was sound when it counted. Angela is a superb dressage rider and she'd done a great job on his flatwork so we did a pretty good test, ending up in the top third. The course was big and Felix was still inexperienced at that level, so I didn't push him across country and he gave me a lovely ride, clear with 17.5 time faults. With hindsight, he made so little of it that I wished I'd asked for a bit more. On the other hand, it may be as well that I didn't because his leg swelled up overnight and we had to work hard to get him through the vet's inspection the next morning. He jumped a clear round, but again with time faults, which meant that he retained the ninth place he held after the cross-country.

Immediately after Badminton, he too was bought by Torrance Fleischmann, but she was never able to ride him. He was not a horse you could dictate to. When she tried to say, 'You will do it my way,' he'd never agree. He was a young horse, nine or ten, and she paid a lot for him, as I know because Mimi paid me a very generous commission, but I don't think Torrance ever competed on him. However, the story has a happy ending, as I learned when I was in Atlanta for the 1996 Olympics. A girl came up to me and said, 'Do you remember a horse called Felix Too? I'm still competing on him.' He must have been well into his twenties so he really was a tough cookie. Hopefully, he still is.

While I was in England, I got a call from Virginia Caro, Boy's daughter and the publicity officer for the New Zealand Horse Society, asking if I'd like to ride a horse called Charisma. The eventing season was just getting underway and, with Beaumont sick, I had no experienced horses so I was prepared to grasp at straws. According to his breeders, Daphne and Peter Williams, Charisma, or Stroppy as they called him, was born a champion. His dam, Planet, was out of a Thoroughbred mare, Starbourne, by a stallion called Kiritea, who was one-sixteenth Percheron. Planet, who was only 15hh, had been hunted by Daphne, then jumped by her two daughters, reaching grade A. When she moved on to Sheryl Douglas, she became the first mare in New Zealand to jump her own height. When injury put an end to her career, she returned to stud on the Williams's 3,000 acre farm in Wairarapa on the North Island. She was sent to the Thoroughbred stallion, Tira Mink, and Charisma was born on 30 October 1972.

The Williamses told me that the colt foal loved the girls so much that he had to be separated from the fillies at an early age. Even as a baby, he cultivated the laid-back attitude that served us so well later, sleeping in his pen until Daphne arrived with his bucket, then getting up to eat and lying straight down again.

'He was quite unreal when he was weaned,' Daphne recalled. 'He never put a foot wrong. When we taught him to tie up, he tied. You could see him thinking, "It's rather a bore, but I suppose if I have to stand here for an hour or so, I'll have to." He was the dearest boy.'

Even before he was weaned, the foal was spotted and bought by David Murdoch, then planning to set up the Isola Equestrian Centre after an extended learning trip to Britain and Europe. When he went on a horse-buying mission to the Williams's, Charisma was standing 300 yards away in the paddock. David told me that he knew he wanted to buy him the moment he saw him.

'It was his outlook that impressed me so much, his bold look, bright eye and air of intelligence. He seemed to be saying, "Hey, watch me, I'm special." He was always a real show-off!'

David collected him as a yearling and, during the journey home, installed him overnight in a field surrounded by a four-foot wire fence. The next morning he'd jumped out in search of greener pastures, which was very much the shape of things to come. He spent much of the next two years running wild on David Goodin's farm at Te Kauwhata, where I'd first seen him in 1976. David had him gelded as a four-year-old and broke him in slowly. At that stage, he was very obliging, quick to learn, calm and confident, with a terrific jump. In 1977, David sold him for NZ$3,500 to Sharon Dearden, a young working pupil at the equestrian centre. In those days, he was still Stroppy or 'the little black gelding', but when he revealed his true personality, Sharon knew he should be called Charisma. Later that year she took him to her parents' property fifty miles outside Christchurch and started training him. No one said it had to be easy and it wasn't, partly because he'd covered four mares before he was gelded so he was a bit 'colty'. In the early months, they argued over everything. Even when he won a maiden hack class at a local show, he had an ace up his sleeve: as Sharon was presented with the rosette, he dumped her and did his victory lap on his own. Within six months she was jumping grade B tracks.

In 1981, she would have won the Pony Club Championship if Charisma hadn't shied and missed the flags at the finish of the showjumping, relegating her to second place; but, all in all, she did a good job, qualifying him as a grade B showjumper and an intermediate eventer. In 1982, Sharon and Charisma were listed as possibles for the New Zealand event team for the Los Angeles Olympics, but she needed to do a year's work experience for her teaching career so she decided to sell the horse she referred to as her 'best friend'. She'd already turned down large sums of money for him because she wanted him to have a family home, so the lucky buyer was Mrs Fran Clark from Taupo, a mother who was interested in dressage and showing. Things didn't quite work out as planned so she lent him to Jennifer Stobart, who'd taken over from Lockie Richards as the Chief Instructor at the National Equestrian Centre. She liked him so much that she'd worked him up to Prix St Georges level dressage 'just for fun' by the time Virginia got in touch with me.

I'd heard of his successes so I told Virginia I'd try him as soon as I was back in New Zealand. By the time I drove over to the Equestrian Centre at Taupo, where Fran kept him, it was early May 1983 and well into the autumn. Charisma always grew a long winter coat and he'd been doing dressage with Jennifer all year so there he was, a shaggy, fat, overgrown pony standing in the paddock. I looked at him and I thought, 'What on earth can I do with this horse?' It didn't click with me that I'd seen him at the Goodins' all those years earlier, but with the eventing season about to begin and the three-day event only six weeks away, I was desperate enough to try anything. As soon as I started riding him round, I knew I wasn't wasting my time. He was a beautiful mover with a very big stride on him so he didn't feel like a little horse. He was quite highly trained, though not as I would do it. He used to float along with his head in the air, doing all the right things but not in the outline I'd have liked.

He came up to my place and we got cracking on him at once. My neighbour, Kenny Browne, had a 1.6 km racetrack with an 2 km spur leading to a private airstrip at the top of the farm, a long, uphill pull that was perfect for getting horses fit. Charisma was a real athlete and very fast, but did he like to eat! That was his Percheron blood coming out and it earned him his nickname, Podge. With the help of Greg Keyte, a friend who is now an international polo player, we divided up the old barn into stables so that we could control his diet. He was always bedded down on strips of newspaper because it was the only thing he wouldn't eat and I had him out on Kenny's gallops every other day in order to get him fit in time for the three-day event. He won his first two one-day events, then the National One-day Championship and the National Three-day Event at Taupo, leading in the dressage and going clear in the cross-country and showjumping.

As a start to a partnership, it couldn't have been better and the victory had an added piquancy because Ginny was there to share it with me. We'd got back together when I was in England for Badminton, but basically the situation hadn't changed. Our relationship was never stormy, just on and off because of the logistics and because neither of us was prepared to make the sacrifices that were needed for us to settle down. The truth of the matter is that we were both used to getting our own way and our behaviour was totally in character. Ginny had been in Britain's gold-medal-winning team in Luhmühlen the previous autumn, placing seventh as an individual, so she was even less inclined to leave England than she had been previously. However, she did come out for Taupo. Joan Gilchrist, the press officer for the trials, had asked me to choose a top international rider to compete so I suggested Ginny who was lent Casino, a horse who did a decent test, but occasionally stopped across country. She only had two weeks to get used to him; enough to win the dressage phase in the intermediate section, but not enough to prevent a stop at a combination near the end of the course. After the event, she returned to England but with Podge improving with every outing, I thought it wouldn't be long before I saw her again on her home turf.

When Podge and I first got together, he jumped a bit cautiously on the cross-country so I put him in a rubber bit to try to make him take hold. As his confidence grew and grew, he developed into a brilliant cross-country horse, very bold and scopey, very fast and nippy, a perfect combination really. On the flat, he was elegant, but inclined to go above the bit and, as he was a tough little bugger who knew how to fight, we had some pretty decent rows over that. I'd feel he wasn't going correctly, he'd decide he didn't want to toe the line, and we'd be at it for an hour or more until we left the arena steaming, his eyes red, my eyes red, and neither of us sure who'd won. It didn't always happen, just on the days when he couldn't be bothered. It was his ability to fight combined with his mental toughness and bottomless energy that made him so exceptional. He was and is lovely to have around, a really sweet horse who loves people and gets on well with other horses.

By leading from start to finish, he impressed everybody at Taupo and the New Zealand Horse Society immediately approached Fran to ask if he'd be available to go to the Los Angeles Olympics. She said yes, but that he was not for sale. In December, they arranged an official trial at Taupo for the Olympic hopefuls, excluding Andrew Nicholson with Kahlua and Mary Hamilton with Whist, who were already in England. By this time, it was recognised that there should be some kind of qualification for the Olympic Games so the chairman of the FEI, Vicomte Jurien de la Graviere, came out to New Zealand to give certificates of capability to all those who jumped well on the cross-country course. I took Carlsberg, a horse with the same sire as Charisma out of a half sister of his dam, as my second string. He was small and dark brown like Charisma, and quite good, though not as good. Podge won easily and Carlsberg, or Bert as we called him, came fifth so we were all selected, along with Andrew Bennie and Jade. In the process, Podge won the Vicomte's heart. '*Petit cheval – très, très bon equilibre. Peut progresser en dressage. Cavalier superbe,*' he wrote in his notebook on 18 December 1983, comments to which he later added a footnote: 'I am glad and proud to have met that marvellous horse before he came to Europe.'

As my excitement over Charisma grew, I knew that I would never be a full-time dairy farmer, but I still believed I could combine it with international eventing at the highest level. However, Pop had other ideas. He pointed out that you can't farm if you're half-way round the world and that, as he was getting older, he didn't want the responsibility of not having me there full time. Ultimately, he forced me to make a decision, which was hard in one way because I was giving up my heritage, but not in another because I knew what my answer had to be. I sold the cows for NZ$500 a head, which was a nice profit, and I had another stroke of good fortune when Judy Hall, one of my pupils, said that her husband, Bill, might sponsor me. I was very nervous when I went to meet him at the headquarters of his company, Woolrest International, in Hamilton but he was amazing. I told him I wanted to represent New Zealand in Los Angeles and he said, 'Okay, we'll help you. What do you need?' He gave me NZ$35,000 with no legal contract, just on his word as a gentleman, so we shook hands and that was that.

Fran Clark didn't want to sell Charisma, but after lengthy negotiations, she agreed to lease him to Woolrest until after the Olympics for ten cents and to allow him to be entered for other events in their name provided they paid all the expenses. Bill also bought Carlsberg for NZ$5,000 and we rechristened him Night Life, a name more in tune with Woolrest's main business, which was the manufacture and export of pure wool sleeping pads.

When I joined Mum and Dad for Christmas, my aunt predicted that 1984 would be the pinnacle of my career. She claimed she had reliable sources for this information, but refused to reveal them. Like most event riders, I'm very superstitious and I remembered that the Baroness had been right about the Chinese Year of the Monkey before Badminton in 1980. As I planned my next journey to the other side of the world, I made myself believe that my aunt was right. She needed to be because this time I'd really burned my boats, so there could be no turning back.

CHAPTER FIVE

ON TOP OF THE WORLD

W HEN I ARRIVED IN ENGLAND TO START MY OLYMPIC campaign in February 1984, I had the funds to have a yard of my own for the first time. I'd arranged to rent a place before I left New Zealand, but when I arrived I found that it was miserable. I caught a bad cold because the flat was so damp and when I spent my twenty-eighth birthday on my own, I thought, 'I don't like this at all.' Shortly afterwards, I moved to Priory Manor in Kingston St Michael near Chippenham, the home of Charlie and Sarah Cottenham. They'd both given up eventing so I rented their yard and a cottage on their estate. The horses came over shortly afterwards with Helen Gilbert, an English groom I'd met while she was working for Toby and Gail Sturgess in Great Somerford. When Helen broke up with her fiancé in the middle of 1983, she came to New Zealand and later agreed to return to England to work for me. I was on a pretty tight budget in those days, but the expenses still mounted up. Once the eventing season started, I allowed £15 a week for stabling, £15 for bedding, £50 for feed and hay, £10 for shoeing, £30 for vet's fees, £50 for travelling, £35 for entry fees, £30 for accommodation, £35 for food and £25 for miscellaneous expenses.

Podge caught a bug on the plane that stayed with him for the rest of his career. He had an infection in his sinuses that caused a slight discharge from his nose. A few years later we took him to Bristol Veterinary College and they discovered that all his sinuses had disintegrated, but at least he never lost his appetite. When we turned him out in the paddock after a forty-eight-hour flight, he glanced at the frosty Wiltshire countryside, rolled and started to pick at the frozen grass. Poor old Bert caught a fever in transit and arrived with a high temperature and a runny nose so he was off work for a while. Once again, I was dependent on one horse and for the first few events, it appeared that it wouldn't be enough.

When I took Podge to Aldon, he had a run out on the cross-country, which was a bit of a shock after being unbeaten back home. He was a bit cheeky and caught me off guard while I was being blasé, showing off my new horse. Worse was to follow at Rushall, where we had a fall. The ground was very heavy, which he never liked, and I strangled him coming into a bounce so it was probably my fault. He hit the rail and I came off. I was beginning to think that Badminton wasn't such a good idea so I went to Brigstock the following week with the thought that if we didn't go clear, I wouldn't go. Fortunately we did so my resolve wasn't put to the test, but I can tell you there was a huge sigh of relief.

Badminton was a bit of a rise in class for Podge. He'd done an inter-mediate three-day event with Sharon Dearden and the open class at Taupo, the equivalent of a decent two-star event, with me, but there were still questions to be answered at the highest level. In New Zealand, lots of people had said, 'Why are you taking him to England? He's just a Pony Club horse. You'll never make the Olympics,' so I had a lot to prove. In England, people were more encouraging, especially Colonel Frank Weldon, the director of Badminton, who previewed the championship in *Horse and Hound*. 'It would not surprise me to see Mark Todd win the Whitbread Trophy again,' he wrote, 'for Charisma, unbeaten in his five outings at home last season, is infi-nitely more experienced than Southern Comfort was when he came to Badminton four years ago.'

Fran Clark came over for the event and also my sponsors, Bill and Judy Hall, which could have added to the pressure. I told them that Podge was going well but that he'd never seen a course as big as this and the Halls said, 'We really don't expect anything spectacular so don't worry about us. We'll just stay out of your way and let you get on with it.' If only all sponsors were like that! At Christmas, my parents had promised to come to Badminton as a prelude to a second honeymoon. Initially they'd been doubtful, following the disasters at

Lexington and Fontainebleau, in case they brought me bad luck, but they'd allowed themselves to be persuaded.

I was delighted with the way Podge settled immediately in the practice arenas. I'd been having dressage lessons from Bill Noble and he came to help me warm up on Friday afternoon. Luckily it wasn't one of Podge's peacock days and he relaxed immediately. I had my own tail coat this time, one I'd had made in New Zealand by a tailor who hadn't a clue what a riding tail coat was supposed to look like. He copied it from a photo and it fits so well that I'm still wearing it today.

I was fifth last to go, following Ginny and Night Cap, so I knew what the standard was. Podge was pleased by the crowds, which he knew were there just for him, but he remained supple and obedient and we did our best test yet. This was especially gratifying because the same judges had already been appointed for the Olympics. When all the scores were up, Lucinda was first with Beagle Bay on 51.2 and I was sixth on 57.4, well in touch for the rest of the competition.

The next day, my closest shave came even before I got to the start of phase A. As I was due to start near the end of day, I had plenty of time on my hands. I decided to go to my caravan, do my times for the different phases and put my feet up to relax for five minutes. I have never done it before or since, but that day I fell asleep. For some reason I woke with a start, looked at my watch and realised I had about seven minutes to get to the start of phase A. In my panic I completely forgot about my carefully worked out times and raced to the start to find a very anxious looking Helen. With literally seconds to spare I jumped on, yelled at Mimi to fetch my times and meet me at the steeplechase and set off. During phase A I had time to collect my thoughts and mentally work out the times, so when a breathless Mimi came flying up to me at the steeplechase start, I calmly said, 'Oh it's all right, I don't need them now!' She nearly expired on the spot.

On the steeplechase, Podge didn't understand that he should brush through the tops of the fences so he ballooned over them, making it difficult for me to judge a stride accurately. It was an alarming ride and I thought he might have taken too much out of himself so I leapt off and ran beside him for the first kilometre of the second roads and tracks so he could get his wind back. The cross-country itself was anti-clockwise, as it had been for Southern Comfort in 1980, not quite so big but testing for a relatively inexperienced horse. I'd walked it four times so I was confident of taking the right line, always provided Podge was up for it. He thought his way round the first part of the course, jumping well but carefully. Then we got to Horsen's Bridge, two fences before the water, and he took a bit of a look. I gave him a crack with the stick and he changed gear completely, flying round the rest of it to finish within the time. That meant we ended the day on our dressage score and in second place behind Lucinda, who was also clear within the time.

Podge was never out of sorts after the cross-country and he came out and jumped a clear round the next day, a bonus because he was apt to hit poles with his front feet. As Lucinda was more than five points ahead of me, she would win even if she knocked one fence down and I really couldn't hope for her to knock down two. In the event, she jumped clear so she was first and we were second. My father was the most excited man at Badminton that afternoon, opening bottles of champagne and saying, 'It's third time lucky, the third time we've come to see Mark and this time he's come up trumps!' Maybe it wasn't such a thrill for me as winning with Southern Comfort, but for the first time I really believed I was going to get to the Olympics. All that remained was to make sure that we would be in the best possible shape.

With three months to go before Los Angeles, Podge took a well-earned rest in the field while I planned the campaign with the New Zealand Horse Society, a long-distance negotiation that wasn't always easy. As this was the first time they'd sent an event team, no one was quite sure what was required. Initially they planned to economise with two grooms for the four horses, which was ludicrous. It was partly ignorance and partly meanness but there's no point going to an Olympic Games scrimping and saving to the extent that you can't do the job properly. Eventually I got that one sorted out but they still wanted Katherine Dalrymple to double up as groom and dressage coach. I was appointed captain because I was the only rider with international form, so I got a bit of what I wanted and that included Bill Noble as my dressage trainer. I said I'd pay his fare myself, but two weeks before we left the Horse Society came round to my way of thinking and sent the money for his ticket. None of the others had dressage trainers, so he helped us all. We had a chef d'équipe to organise the details and a trainer to train us, so being captain was an honour rather than a big responsibility. We were all friends on the team and roughly the same age so it wasn't as if I was an older statesman bestowing the benefits of years of experience on younger riders.

When Podge came back into work, he was more than living up to his nickname, so I put him on a strict diet of oats and a little hay, with no sweet mix or calorie-laden carbohydrates. He had to have sufficient food to provide enough energy for his work but the weight had to go, and fast. Helen worked him round the roads for hours to get him fit and harden his legs. I only had two horses in those days, so I was able to do a lot myself as well, certainly much more than I do now. I took him over to Bill once a week for a dressage lesson. He and his partner, Trish Gardner, lived in Great Somerford down the road from Mimi. Initially, I had lessons with Trish but she didn't really have the time, so Bill took over.

I took Podge to two warm-up one-day events, at Tweseldown, where he was fourth, and Castle Ashby, the final advanced competition for the British team, where he was third. In both cases, several of my rivals for Los Angeles finished behind me so morale was high as the day of departure, 18 July, approached. Podge was normally very sound but we had a few days of total panic just before we left when he developed a swelling on a tendon in one of his back legs. When we ran him up, he looked slightly lame so I called our team vet, Wally Niederer, who'd come from New Zealand to accompany the horses on the flight. He thought it was just a bump and he was right, but it was an anxious period while we waited to see if it would go down.

Podge, accompanied by Helen, flew out to Los Angeles with the British and Irish horses on a charter plane; Andrew Nicholson, Mary Hamilton and I flew on Air New Zealand out of Gatwick. Our fourth rider, Andrew Bennie, had travelled to Los Angeles from New Zealand two weeks earlier with the Australian team, a good strategy as he'd managed to secure a block of stables on a slight slope that would catch any air that was going. After thirty-six hours in quarantine, all the horses moved into the permanent stables at Santa Anita race-course, a complex of big airy boxes, each with its own fan. We'd been very worried about the heat after Lexington, especially with the levels of pollution in southern California, but the climate is less humid than it is in Kentucky so we were hoping for the best.

The practice facilities were superb. There were sand arenas for dressage and jumping and the grass racetrack, with its 800 m uphill spur, for fast work. Everything we needed was laid on, but if we could think of any shortfall we had merely to whistle and Davida, our effervescent liaison officer, came running to our rescue. She'd turn up every day with her wide Californian smile and ask, 'You wanna go fishing? You wanna go shopping?' Her job was to supply our every need and she did it to perfection!

We stayed in the Olympic Village at the University of California in Los Angeles (UCLA). We'd never seen anything like it. There were huge food halls open twenty-four hours a day, a big gourmet selection to cater for all the different nationalities and all free, but I couldn't benefit to the full because I, too, was on a diet. Because Podge was so small, I made an effort to get my weight down as close as possible to 75 kgs, the minimum for the speed and endurance phase. I looked like a scarecrow but I was successful; Podge's two Olympics were the only times I needed my saddle to make the minimum weight. In hot weather, it's no great hardship to diet. I ate a lot of fruit and yoghurt which I don't normally eat, and the weight just fell off, helped by sweating it out in the sauna. We didn't drink much alcohol because you couldn't buy it in the village, although the New Zealand team did have its own supply of beer. Andrew Nicholson and I were Olympic virgins and we went crazy when we first arrived, racing around the athletics track, playing tennis, leaping over the high hurdles. I hadn't done much fitness training up till then and it wasn't a brilliant time to start. The next day we could hardly walk so we went to the massage facility, expecting to find some nice sympathetic females but the masseurs turned out to be big burly blokes. We were in the New Zealand section of the compound, sharing with the boxing and wrestling teams. The other athletes weren't accustomed to being around smokers, so my habit of light-ing up in the common areas in our flat resulted in a complaint and a reprimand from the New Zealand team management.

The main inconvenience was that Santa Anita racecourse was an hour away from the accommodation and we were entirely dependent on the Olympic bus service. We'd get up at 5 a.m. so we could ride before it got too hot and the first words we'd hear were, 'Athletes, have a nice day!' followed by 'All athletes on the bus.' Since then, we've done the Olympics in greater luxury, with our own cars and rented accommodation near the stables, but I have to say that those Games were the most enjoyable. I don't know if it was because it was the first attempt for all of us, but it was a tremendous experience and a huge amount of fun. Living in the village and meeting all the other athletes, seeing living legends I'd read about in the papers, was a great thrill. Sadly, we missed the opening ceremony because the three-day event took place early on and we had to be out at Santa Anita for the vet's inspection.

As the rider with the best form, I was the automatic choice as the anchorman for the team, which meant that I went last. After much soul-searching, the team, in collaboration with Peter Herrick, our chef d'équipe, decided to start with Andrew Nicholson on Kahlua. Andrew Bennie on Jade, the least experienced combination, went second, which left the third spot for Mary Hamilton on Whist.

From the moment he arrived in California, Podge felt very well and very fit. In those days, you were allowed to use running reins in practice, which was fortunate because I doubt I could have held him on the racetrack without them.

Each team was allowed half an hour in the main dressage arena to get the horses used to it before the competition started. As it turned out, the practice was valuable because the stadium was absolutely packed. The racecourse grandstand formed one side of it and they'd enclosed the rest with temporary stands to make quite a daunting arena. I think there had been some mix up with the tickets and the spectators thought they were going to see something else because three-day event dressage doesn't usually attract such a large crowd.

As the moment of truth approached, Podge warmed up very, very well, so I went straight into the stadium and did an extended trot down one side of the arena to get him going forward. He had a spectacular extended trot and the American crowds, who didn't understand that dressage required intense concentration, erupted into spontaneous applause. It was a shame because Podge took off in fright and although I got him back under control, he was a little on edge throughout his test. Although I knew he could have done better, he performed pretty well, ending up fourth behind Switzerland's Hansueli Schmutz on Oran and the American pair, Bruce Davidson on JJ Babu and Karen Stives on Ben Arthur, one of the less-fancied American pairings. The American judge put me first with 173, but the Swiss and French judges gave me 147 and 142 respectively so there were big differences of opinion. When I rode over to Bill Noble after I came out, I expected him to say, 'Well done.' No such luck. He just looked at me and said, 'He can improve on that by ten marks.' Both Mary Hamilton and Andrew Bennie finished in the middle of the field, but Andrew Nicholson and the very inexperienced Kahlua were fourth last, which didn't bode very well for the team competition.

We'd also had to find time to walk the cross-country course, a further hour's bus-ride away at Del Mar, San Diego, on the Fairbanks Ranch, once the home of Douglas Fairbanks and Mary Pickford. The developers had incorporated the fences into a new golf course on a 140 acre site, 20 per cent of which was taken up with lakes. They'd restricted the terrain still further by building all these condominiums round it. Although these limitations meant that the course was tight and twisty, the designer, Neil Ayer, had done a wonderful job with the track. It wasn't huge, not as big as Badminton, but it was definitely a decent size, with lots of variations, not hilly but undulating. The first problems came at the fourth and fifth, the Mark of Zorro and the Crescent Oxer, which were genuinely big. Neil incorporated California's history and fauna into his design so there was a Rattlesnake fence at the thirteenth and a fully fledged Western town at the fourteenth, with a saloon – you either jumped through the picture window or over the hitching rail outside – a jail, a blacksmith's shop and a cemetery with famous names on the tombstones. The only thing we hadn't seen before was the water complex early in the second half. You jumped in over a big upright rail, then ran through the lake, jumped up two waterfalls into the top pond and out over another rail. The spray from jumping the first waterfall obscured your vision for the second and we didn't know how the horses would cope with that.

Overall, I thought such a twisty course would suit Podge because he was so nippy.

When we moved the horses down to the coast on the evening of the day the dressage finished, my mood was upbeat. It's nice to have a good dressage because you're up there instead of playing catch as catch can. The horses were in temporary stables and the riders were put up in a neighbouring hotel. As the next day was a rest day, we had a few drinks in the bar, the first watering hole we'd seen since we'd arrived in America. The idea of having the speed and endurance on the coast was to take advantage of the sea breeze, but it wasn't much in evidence the next day when we walked the course for one last time. On this occasion, I made sure I had an early night and my virtue was rewarded when I woke up to find that the skies had clouded over and the promised breeze had arrived. After the baking heat we'd had on the dressage days, the temperature dropped to 32°C, not exactly cool but containable, so everybody's worst fears were never realised.

As Kahlua isn't a Thoroughbred, it was fortunate he went early in the coolest part of the day. There hadn't been enough horses round the course for me to have any specific advice for Andrew so I just told him, 'Go round carefully for a clear. If he's got any energy left in him at the three-quarter mark, step on it a bit.' He followed these instructions to the letter, finishing clear with one time fault, but the other Andrew wasn't so fortunate on the eight-year-old Jade. The horse nearly fell in the middle of the Ghost Town, then ran out at the Golfer's Bench, tipping his rider off as he swerved. Andrew remounted and finished but incurred eighty penalties for a stop and a fall. That left Mary Hamilton and Whist to go for a slow clear for the benefit of the team, which they duly did, coming home safely, but with twenty-four time faults.

As our dressage marks hadn't really put us in contention as a team, I had carte blanche to go for the individual gold. The steeplechase was on hard sand which suited Podge and he absolutely flew the fences, seizing the bit in his teeth four or five strides out and launching himself over them with me hanging on for dear life. Because I knew we'd have no hope of recovery if he made a mistake at that speed, I kept trying to exert control, but without much success. My friend,

Pat Daley, who was helping at the steeplechase said, 'Christ, if he can run like that, he should be racing at Cheltenham!' All was well and we came in twenty seconds ahead of time. As at Badminton, I ran beside Podge for the first kilometre of the second roads and tracks before vaulting back into the saddle for a bit of a let up myself. When I was on my first loop on phase C, I caught up with Lucinda and Regal Realm on their second and we trotted along together for bit which encouraged both horses. Pat was waiting with Bryn Powell at the watering station half-way round to throw buckets of water over Podge and he was as bright as a button again by the time he trotted into the inspection box before the start of the cross-country.

Going late in the day is good in that it allows you to watch some of the early starters – seeing that the fences are jumpable really does give you confidence – but it's also bad because you have more hours of white-knuckle tension. At this stage, I was more focused on getting round clear than on winning a medal. I knew that the overnight leader, Hansueli Schmutz, was out of the running after a stop, but Karen Stives and Ben Arthur had finished on their dressage score, which meant they were ahead of me, and Ginny and Priceless had just 0.4 of a time fault so they weren't far behind. Bruce Davidson and Lucinda, who was now out on the course, could be expected to go clear as well. Some of the other contenders had massive amounts of time faults, so I drained my orange juice, stubbed out my cigarette and set off as if I meant business. The first three fences were inviting but I had to get Podge back for the fourth, the Mark of Zorro, so as to take an accurate line into the corner. Because of his size, I jumped the Crescent Oxer on the right-hand side where the drop wasn't quite as big as on the direct route. The first water, the Bridge and Walkway at the seventh, had caused problems, not least for Tiny Clapham who took a spectacular – and much photographed – fall from Windjammer, but I got Podge back to a slow canter so he could fit in two short strides before the jetty. Then he hopped on and bounced back into the water very neatly.

The middle section was fairly straightforward. I didn't get my line quite right at the Rattlesnake and Podge had to adjust himself for the third element. The direct picture window route at the Ghost Town was on a long stride, but he bowled happily through it and on to the

Watts Wall. There were two options at the Fairbanks, but all the New Zealanders chose the longer one because it placed less strain on the horses at this late stage on the course. Not many risked the direct route, but according to Major Derek Allhusen, who timed all the competitors through it, those who did took between twelve and fourteen seconds to complete the combination. The longer route took the others between twenty-one and twenty-five seconds, but Podge did it in nineteen, which shows how nippy he was. After negotiating the Waterfalls, I had my only real moment of anxiety at the Ski Jump and the San Dieguito Ramps. The approach to the Ski Jump was on level ground, but the fence itself had a six-foot drop, followed by two downhill strides to the first element of the Ramps. Like most of the horses, Podge peered over the drop, kicked off the edge and took a stride. Then his back feet skidded and I thought, 'Oh God, we're going to slide straight into the fence,' but somehow he picked himself up and banked it. It was a bit of a scramble but we managed somehow. Mary and I had worked out a cunning way of saving time at the curved Osuna Brand rails. Even so, I reckoned I was slightly down on the time, so I gave Podge a bit of a kick and let him go. He took off and finished full of running in the fastest time of the day. With an optimum time of thirteen minutes, it was a very long cross-country course, but he was under the time. And, as it turned out, he was in second place, because Bruce Davidson had had a fall, leaving me just two points behind Karen and Ben Arthur.

Given Podge's robust health and soundness, I had less worries than most about the trot up at Fairbanks Ranch the next morning. When it was over, the convoy of horses and riders headed back to Santa Anita to prepare for the showjumping the next day. With rest days before and after the cross-country and two days of dressage, it was actually a six-day event, which made sense, given the heat and the travelling. However, it did give me another day of anxiety about the showjumping, never Podge's most reliable phase. He'd gone clear at Badminton, but he liked to feel his way a bit and every so often he'd get it wrong. He was more reliable on a hard surface, which the sand in the stadium provided, so I didn't have to worry on that score but there was still a big question mark in my mind as the hours dragged by.

Back in England, I'd been taking him up to Ted Edgar for help in the final phase and, as Ted was training the Australian showjumping team in Los Angeles, he agreed to walk the course with me and give me a hand in the warm-up. The track was very long, with lots of gallops between jumps, which probably made it more difficult, and very bright and colourful, which was probably an advantage because it made Podge look at the fences. Ted told me to let Podge relax on the gallop between each fence before picking him up for the next one because he'd get too tired if I kept him bottled up all the way. At the warm-up, I trotted and cantered him around to get his muscles working. Normally I'd start jumping over a cross pole, but Ted put up a parallel at about three feet, with a trotting pole on the ground eight feet in front of it. I trotted in and, boom, he knocked it down. I came round again, and boom, he knocked it down again. It's a very difficult exercise and Ted kept trying to make it more difficult by edging the trotting pole closer to the fence. The steward would tell him to move it back a bit because there are set guidelines for practice fences and Ted was stretching them to the limit. At the third or fourth attempt, Podge made a huge effort to clear the fence and Ted said, 'Stop.' I wouldn't have attempted a routine like that if Ted hadn't been there to supervise it and it was certainly nerve-racking when Podge kept hitting the fence, but I appreciated the need to get him thinking so he'd jump cleanly in the ring.

As the showjumping is in reverse order of merit, I was second last to go. All this time Karen Stives was warming up Ben Arthur, a horse I knew pretty well because Mary Hamilton had been his previous owner. Karen had the best American showjumping trainers and riders there to help her and they'd obviously done some homework on the horse because he never looked like hitting anything in practice. When Ginny and Priceless went clear, she put some pressure on me, but I did have one fence in hand over her so I had a small cushion. When I went in, I was thinking more of defending my silver medal than of winning the gold. As my turn approached, Ted had me jump an upright and a parallel, both at maximum height, and Podge cleared them really well so I went into the ring on a surge of confidence. Because I'd done so much showjumping in New Zealand over bigger tracks, it didn't freak me out as much as it did some of my rivals, and

I was relaxed enough to do the best I could. Podge loved a big crowd and I enjoyed the buzz so it was an uplifting atmosphere for us both.

The second fence was a cartful of fruit with a couple of rustic poles over it. Podge gave that a good tap, but it stayed up. After that, he went round really well, just as Ted and I had planned it, until the second last fence, a treble with an upright in, a parallel and an upright out. I was worried about it because you seemed to be approaching a blur of candy-striped poles, with no clear idea of which element was which. He rattled the first part, then made an effort to clear the next two. At the last, I gave him an extra lift and there we were, Olympic silver medallists!

Karen was already in the arena but because I'd seen Ben Arthur jumping outside, I was convinced he'd go clear. I lit a cigarette and Ginny rushed up with a hug and a drink of water as I stood in the tunnel, determined not to watch Karen. There was this deathly silence in the arena, you really could have heard a pin drop. Occasionally there were a few oohs and aahs, but only because Ben Arthur was so spectacular. Finally I couldn't bear not to watch any longer. I had no idea where Karen was on the course so I came up to the entrance and saw her jump the two fences before the treble. Ben Arthur was still jumping huge and I thought, 'He's so extravagant, the treble might just catch him out.' He jumped in, took the two strides to the parallel and took out the front rail. What a wonderful moment! Olympic gold!

I put my hands over my head and walked away again, then everyone closed in on me. When Karen came out, I went over and gave her a kiss and said whatever you say, 'Bad luck, but thanks,' something like that. She was pretty pleased with silver, although she'd been so near to the gold so, of course, she was disappointed.

By this time, drug testing was routine for the horses and for all medal-winning riders. Podge was tested after the dressage and again when he won, and I was tested at the end of the event. They searched me first, and sent me into a cubicle to provide a urine sample. As far as I know, no one tested positive.

When Karen, Ginny and I rode into the arena for the medal ceremony, we had to keep behind the officials as they walked slowly towards the podium. We thought we'd never get there. I dismounted and climbed on to the podium and Jean, Grand Duc de Luxembourg, put the gold medal round my neck. After he'd presented the silver to Karen and bronze to Ginny, I pulled them up to join me on the top step and gave Ginny a spontaneous kiss that set tongues wagging and printers whirring around the world.

There were a few tears, a few gulps when they played 'God Defend New Zealand'. I don't know what it is about the anthem and the flag going up, but it always stirs up more emotion than you expect. I hadn't thought about representing my country while I was actually competing, but at the medal ceremony I was very aware of being part of the New Zealand team. As the three-day event came so early in the programme, mine was our first medal, so the team officials were there in force to encourage and praise. Helen was in floods of tears as she stood there holding Podge. At the exact moment the medal went round my neck, he nipped her on the arm as if to say, 'Hey, don't I get a look in too?' When it was over, I remounted and led the lap of honour at a sedate canter but when Podge insisted on a flat-out gallop, I let him go. No horse deserved his moment of glory more.

For Karen, Ginny and I, the press conference seemed to go on forever. I have no idea what they asked me or what I said, but they did let me ring Mum and Dad. For some naive reason, I thought they wouldn't have heard that I'd won but of course the Olympics, unlike Badminton, were on television so the party with Pop and Mumma and the neighbours was in full swing. Despite being at Badminton that year, they felt they might jinx me so they didn't come to either of Podge's Olympics. When the questions were finally over, it was time to join the party which had already started in the stables.

Peter Herrick had bought a case of champagne in anticipation of some kind of celebration and they'd finished that, then headed for the American stables to drink theirs. When that was gone, they sent out for more so everyone had had a fair amount by the time I got there. I'd made a start on the champagne in the press tent so it didn't take long to catch up. The British, the Kiwis and the Irish were the hard core of the party, but everyone joined in. As things warmed up, we commandeered a golf cart and there was a huge water fight. Joan Gilchrist, always a big supporter of New Zealand eventing and currently the editor of *Horse and Pony Magazine*, was hiding in the tack room but I dragged her out, rolled her in the sand and doused her with the hose. I also dumped her in a water trough, a bit of a precedent as it turned out because I did it again at Seoul. She was a largeish lady in her forties, but she took it all in good part. I can't remember how long the party lasted, but at one stage I put my medal in the fridge for safe-keeping.

Podge enjoyed the party too, hanging over the stable door to get his fair share of the praise, but he slept a lot the next day, which is more than I did. The celebrations continued the following evening when a whole bunch of us went to a pub-cum-nightclub in the city. We got fairly well sewn up and I finally returned to the Olympic Village at seven or eight o'clock in the morning. I'd been invited to lunch with the New Zealand ambassador and was picked up in a limousine for the drive into Los Angeles. It was all I could do to keep awake through a long formal lunch, so I don't suppose I was particularly entertaining company. On the return trip in the limousine, I passed out in the back.

By that time I was tired of all the hoohah so I called Nina Patterson, a girl I'd met when Joanne and I drove out to Los Angeles in 1978. She wasn't a girlfriend, little more than an acquaintance really, but we'd kept vaguely in touch and she offered to take me to the beach for the day to relax away from the crowds. The New Zealand journalists were desperate to interview me, but they couldn't find me so they came up with headlines like, 'Todd's done a bunk'. It was naive of me to go off at a time like that, but I didn't realise how much a gold medal meant to a small nation or how big the story would be in the newspapers and on television back home. When I returned to the Olympic Village, they had a big blackboard outside the New Zealand quarters with my name at the top of the medals table. It was a good omen because we went on to win a record eight gold medals, several of them for rowing. The joke was that all our medals were won sitting down!

The other cause for speculation was that kiss I gave Ginny on the podium. The photograph appeared in newspapers everywhere, accompanied by lavish fantasies about the love between Ginny and me. The irony was that the journalists had missed the heat of our romance, only catching up when we were near the end of the road.

Our careers were developing very much in tandem at this point, as they would continue to do through the mid-eighties, with major successes for Priceless and Night Cap as well as for Podge, so we were in constant competition. Obviously I was pleased when I beat her, but no more so than when I beat anyone else, and I'm sure the same was true for her. As I was now based in England, the logistical barriers to getting married had gone, but although we enjoyed ourselves at the Olympics, we both knew it wouldn't last.

Andrew Nicholson and I came home long before the closing ceremony which, with hindsight, was a big mistake. We should have stayed and enjoyed the razzmatazz while we could. The news that I was on the plane was leaked – could it have been by Andrew? – so it was champagne all the way. When I got back to my little cottage, I found that Mimi and Tom and the Cottenhams had hung a huge banner outside saying, 'Well done, Toddy'. In New Zealand my father was Toddy but in England all my friends call me that. Lots of local people arrived with drinks so we had another party at the cottage. The press kept going for a few days of phone calls and interviews, then it was time to get back to real life. As far as I was concerned, that meant Podge, still in Los Angeles with Helen, while Fran Clark decided his fate – and mine.

CHAPTER SIX

CONSOLIDATION

WINNING AN OLYMPIC GOLD MEDAL FOR NEW ZEALAND had been the summit of my ambition for twenty years, almost as long as I could remember, so it was inevitable that I should feel a bit flat once I was back in England. It was only mid-August, with a third of the eventing season still to come, and Night Life was standing in the stable in Kingston St Michael waiting his turn. When it came, he must have wished we'd stayed at home because I did my dressage test with only one spur and got lost on the cross-country. In the first week of September, we went to Burghley, had a fall on the cross-country and had to retire. It was a reasonably straightforward fence, a small jump onto a bank, one stride and another bank. For some reason, Bert, as we still called Night Life, half tripped up the first bank, stood on an overreach boot and went slap into the second one and off I came. So much for the Olympic champion!

On the other side of the world, my victory had put New Zealand eventing on the map; and not only eventing – Charisma was hailed as a star in his own right and one newspaper judged me to be the country's most eligible bachelor! Naturally I was eager to cash in on my new status and the opportunity came in November when I went back for my annual visit. In Cambridge, there was a ceremony in the main square and they presented me with a gold chain with a bar of gold, representing the freedom of the town. I was astonished by the size of the huge crowd who turned out for it; it was a real hero's welcome.

The Auckland area of the New Zealand Horse Society organised a special international one-day event at Pukekohe near Auckland. They invited some of the riders who had done well at the Olympics, including Karen Stives, Torrance Fleischmann and Mike Plumb from the USA, Mark Phillips, Ian Stark and Ginny from Britain, as well as an Australian team including Andrew Hoy, so the programme read like a roll of honour. Owners lent experienced eventers and the riders came out a week or so before to get used to them. We were able to ride several horses each before we made our final selections and most of them went pretty well. The only loser was Torrance, who chose one that did flash dressage, but dumped her on the cross-country.

At the same time, NZBC (New Zealand Broadcasting Company) televised their first-ever *This is Your Life* programme and I was the subject of it. As is customary, it was all shrouded in secrecy so I had no idea what was going on. We were trying out the horses and I was saying, 'Oh God, I've got to go now to get down to Wellington for this chat show.' They said, 'Oh yeah, okay,' without revealing that half of them were going to be there as well. As soon as I left, Karen, Ginny and Mark must have scarpered to catch the next plane. When I was called and the presenter said, 'Mark Todd, this is your life,' you could have knocked me down with a feather.

My parents were there and a couple of schoolfriends I hadn't seen for ages and the Baroness, who'd been flown out from England specially for the occasion. I have no idea how the programme organisers knew about her, presumably through my parents. Once I got over the shock, I enjoyed it and I was told that the show went down very well with the public. That night is also memorable because Ginny and I finally decided that we had no future together. Who knows how these decisions come about, but somehow we both knew that it was time to move on and to go our separate ways.

The autumn was overshadowed by negotiations over Podge's future that took months to resolve. He returned to Britain with the other Olympic horses and enjoyed a well-earned holiday in the Cottenhams' field, a break that he enjoyed all the more because all dietary restrictions were off. In Woolrest's original contract with Fran Clark, it was agreed that, 'the owner will let and Woolrest will hire the horse from the date of this deed, February 1984, and expiring on 30th November,

1984 or upon the horse being returned to the owner at Taupo, which-ever event shall occur first'. The fee for the hire of the horse was a nominal ten cents, but Woolrest had to insure him for NZ$82,000 and pay all his expenses while he was with them.

Initially Fran was very happy with the arrangement, but when it was made none of us thought he would win in Los Angeles. When he did, she talked to the New Zealand press, one moment saying she missed Podge and wanted him home so she could ride him herself, and the next that she wanted to sell him. What became clear was that whether she sold him or kept him, it was unlikely that I would be riding Podge in the immediate future. Fran's husband Kevin had originally bought Podge for her as a birthday present. He and I hadn't always seen eye to eye, but by the time I took Podge to England to prepare for his first Badminton in 1984, I felt relations were civil. Fran came over to watch Podge there, but I was pretty preoccupied with the competition, as well as with my parents and the Halls, so perhaps I didn't spend as much time with her as I might have done. She didn't come to Los Angeles, but rumours that the horse was for sale were already circulating at the Olympics.

Clearly he was now worth a great deal of money, though not perhaps the NZ$250,000 price tag she put on him when Woolrest wanted to buy him for me. The New Zealand Horse Society were equally keen that I should keep him, but they came up against a brick wall when they tried to broker a deal for Woolrest. Fran claimed she'd had fabulous offers from Japan and here, there and everywhere, none of which appeared to materialise.

I realised how serious she was about preventing me from riding him when calls started coming in from some of the major players in international eventing. First on the line was the American rider, Karen Lende, saying that Fran had offered Podge to her and asking what the story was. I said, 'Well, yes, he is for sale, but I'm trying to buy him myself,' so she said she'd stay out of it. Sally O'Connor was on next to tell me that Fran had selected her as her agent to sell Podge in America. Sally, too, wanted to know what the position was, so I gave her the same answer and she backed off as well.

Eventing is a tightknit circle which I was part of in a way that Fran never could be, but even so I was touched by the way my friends put my interests above their own. Come January, with the situation still unresolved, friendship was put to a yet greater test when Lizzie Purbrick, the British rider I'd first met at Lexington, came into the equation. She'd met Fran briefly at Badminton in 1984 when her husband, Reggie, asked her over for a drink one evening because he thought she seemed a bit lost. Nine months later, the Purbricks were staying on Lizzie's brother-in-law's farm in New South Wales when they received a call from Fran offering them Podge. Reggie knew nothing of the publicity surrounding the horse in New Zealand but he stalled, saying that Podge would make a wonderful birthday present for Lizzie, but that he'd have to ask her first.

By the time the Purbricks rang me in New Zealand, I was desperate to break the stalemate. Podge was still in England, doing his basic fitness work for the 1985 season with Melanie O'Brien near Swindon, and I wanted the green light to prepare him for Badminton in April. When Lizzie told me about Fran's call, I asked her if she'd consider buying the horse and selling him straight on to Woolrest. Although she was embarrassed at deceiving a woman she'd befriended, Lizzie is enough of an anarchic spirit to appreciate a good challenge. She's also a gambler, with a passion for playing the stock market, so I was lucky that Fran picked her. Lizzie leads a frenzied life, doing ten things at once, driving the car, talking on her mobile, putting on lipstick and reading the *Financial Times*. Sometimes it comes off, but not always. She has been known to crash the car!

When Lizzie got back from Australia, she met Fran at the Cavalry Club in London to discuss the deal. On a snowy midwinter day, the two women thrashed out Podge's future, with Fran quizzing Lizzie exhaustively as to her intentions and Lizzie responding with a fabrication about a new sponsor who would come up with the asking price of £50,000. The next hitch came when Fran insisted Lizzie should try Podge before buying him. It was a reasonable demand in the circumstances, but Lizzie was three months pregnant – something she certainly couldn't mention because it would make Fran suspicious – and she didn't want to risk her baby by riding a strange horse. In the event, she was lucky because a timely snowstorm blocked the M4 motorway in Wiltshire, making it impossible for her to get to Melanie's yard before Fran's plane left for New Zealand that evening. Before she took the flight, Fran signed the contract so Woolrest transferred the funds to Lizzie's account in Hungerford and two days later she wired the money back to Fran in New Zealand.

You can imagine my relief when Podge was finally mine. Until Fran and Lizzie came to terms, I was planning to live in New Zealand and event internationally as and when the opportunity came up, but once Bill told me I could keep Podge for as long as I liked, I was able to plan my return to Britain. I already had excellent proof that Bill's word was his bond and when I rang him on 19 January 1985 about sponsorship for the World Championships, scheduled for May 1986 in Gawler, Australia, he promised me a further NZ$50,000 for Charisma and Night Life.

I was all the more grateful for his renewed support because I knew he wasn't really getting his money's worth out of his sponsorship, not anyway in Britain, which was one of Woolrest's main export markets. In those days, sponsorship was in its infancy in eventing and the rules were both strict and illogical. Woolrest's money had to be channelled to me through the New Zealand Horse Society, so there was no controversy on that score. Podge and Bert were allowed to run in the company's name and we had team colours, with branded rugs for the horses and sweatshirts and T-shirts for me and my grooms. Horseboxes could be painted in the company colours, but logos were forbidden when the horses were actually competing.

A television commercial for Woolrest made in the autumn of 1984, featuring me completing a showjumping round and being greeted by a radiant New Zealand Miss World, could be shown in New Zealand, but not in Britain, where attitudes towards sponsorship were more ambivalent. We'd first run into trouble when Bill placed an advertisement in the *Daily Telegraph* in the run-up to the Olympics. It was a picture of Podge and me over a caption saying how proud Woolrest was of its association with our Olympic bid, innocent enough but sufficient to arouse outrage in the upper echelons of the British Horse Society. They took it up with the New Zealand Horse Society, who fined me a nominal NZ$5, but the downside was that the scope for promoting my sponsors in Britain was severely curtailed.

As far as I'm concerned, the Fran Clark story ended shortly after I got back to England on Valentine's Day 1985 to start my new campaign. I picked Podge and Bert up from Melanie's yard the next day. Podge is one of those horses that love people so he's friendly to everyone, rather like a Labrador dog. He wouldn't come over whinnying when I appeared after a long absence but he always knew who I was. Four days later, I gained a certain amount of perverse pleasure by ringing Fran.

'Guess what?' I said. 'I've got the horse.' The entry in my diary reads, 'Shit hit fan!' and that's the last time I spoke to her.

My new season with Podge got off to a superb start, with wins in the one-day events at Crookham, Aldon and Brigstock. At Badminton, he came second in the dressage to Finvarra with Torrance Fleischmann. That was the year of the terrible snowstorm on the speed and endurance day. I got the worst of it on phase C, but luckily it wasn't nearly as bad when I got to the cross-country proper. Because the going was deep, I didn't have such a nice ride but we still got round clear within the time. Podge had a lovely action and he liked to bounce off harder ground, but tended to get rather bogged down in muddy conditions. He was very confident by this stage, cocky even, and he was very strong at the beginning of the course so I checked him a bit, to say, 'Hey, don't get too carried away.' There was very little response to this so I decided that the time had come to exchange the rubber snaffle I'd always used for a metal one that would exert more control.

Torrance miscalculated the time on the steeplechase and got 2.4 penalties which put her behind me, though only by a fractional amount. Ginny had gone clear with Night Cap, so she was in third place going into the final day and then showjumped clear to hold her position. Torrance was not so fortunate. She went clear up to the final combination where she missed her stride coming into the first part, then crashed through the next two elements and all but came off.

Mimi May, who had sold Felix Too to Torrance after the 1983 Badminton Horse Trials, claimed that she might have had something to do with Torrance's showjumping disaster. Mimi had bred the horse out of her old hunting mare and she was very fond of him – and she was especially pleased to have bred a horse that had gone so well at Badminton. She and Tom had been on a trip to the States earlier in the year and decided they would call in to see Felix Too since they were going to be in the area. When they phoned to make arrangements in advance, they were initially told that Torrance was not at home. They had, however, already spoken to Torrance's mother-in-law, who had said she knew Torrance was in the yard because she could see her car in the driveway. Phoning again, they eventually got Torrance on the line and she said she was far too busy to show Mimi the horse. Naturally, Mimi was very upset at not being able to see Felix Too and, moreover, upset at Torrance's attitude towards her.

Jokingly, I said to Mimi that she should give Torrance the 'evil eye' – Mimi and her friend Annie duly positioned themselves at the entrance to the showjumping arena and glared at Torrance as she was about to start. Torrance went in and had her disaster and Mimi exclaimed in horror: 'God, I'm a witch!' The horror may have been tinged with some understandable glee!

Podge followed, needing to go clear to stay ahead of Night Cap. He jumped one of the very best rounds of his life, but the distance between the last two elements in the final combination was quite short and he just rolled the very last pole to let Ginny in.

I was disappointed at being second again, but Podge had a jinx about three-day events in England, coming second twice at Badminton and once at Burghley. As I was concentrating on the 1986 World Championships in Australia, I thought it would be less gruelling for him to compete in one-day events in the autumn of 1985, rather than going to Burghley. He did five, winning first time out at Heckfield, then blotting his copybook at Dauntsey, where he had a fall on the cross-country. I was staying with Mimi and Tom at Great Somerford for the event and she had a party the night before, with Clissy, Rodney Powell, Rachel Hunt and Tanya Longson among the guests. The wine must have been bad because all of us had the most terrible hangovers and every single one of us had a fall the next day. In fact, Rachel had two falls on different horses. Podge was miles in front, but I was going too fast and it was very boggy so he just tipped up on landing over the last, turning certain victory into defeat.

He redeemed himself a week later at Gatcombe, winning the British Open in exceptionally wet conditions. The heavens opened from early morning, reducing the course to liquid mud, and a lot of my rivals withdrew but I was lucky because my second ride, Susan Welman's

Michaelmas Day, acted as a pathfinder for Podge. Although Mick went early when conditions were at their worst, he coped really well and I realised that the rain had come down so fast that the ground was wet rather than heavy, which meant that Podge would gallop through it, rather than sinking in. He had already wasted his dressage advantage by knocking a fence down in the showjumping so he started exactly level with Jonquil Sainsbury on Hassan. As the cross-country was in reverse order of merit, she went ahead of me by virtue of my better dressage score and she certainly didn't hang about, but Podge beat Hassan by one second so we were the winners.

He won again at Bourton and at Castle Ashby, where he had an extraordinary dressage score of 15, the best ever given in an advanced event. It came rather out of the blind side because he was a nightmare while I was riding in, mostly because the warm-up area was near the start of the cross-country. After a frustrating forty-five minutes of high jinks, I went into the arena expecting to muddle through at best, only to have him change immediately into a totally co-operative partner. After that, it was easy – despite knocking a showjump and clocking up 7 cross-country time faults, we finished on 27, 15 points ahead of Mike Tucker on General Bugle. It was a perfect end to an almost perfect season; but for Mimi's wine supplier, we would have won every one-day event in which we competed.

In other respects, 1985 was the year in which I started to put my business on a sound financial footing. Although Woolrest ensured that I was in good shape financially, I knew I wouldn't always be able to depend on sponsorship money. The other alternatives were teaching, which I was beginning to develop through word of mouth, and buying and selling young horses, which I've always had a talent for. But first I needed a more permanent base, which meant moving from Kingston St Michael. Charlie and Sarah Cottenham had plans to convert their stables into flats and in any case, I had to have a larger place if I was to increase the size of my string. Initially I rented a yard in Mere in Wiltshire, a good place with a lovely cottage down the road for me to live in. My Swedish working pupil, Erik Duvander, lived in a mobile home at the yard and kept an eye on the horses at night. The deal only lasted for a few months because the building contractor who owned the yard ran into problems and I decided it would be best to move on quickly.

I heard about the equestrian centre in Cholderton on the edge of Salisbury Plain through Moisie Barton, the mother of one of my pupils. Previously the place had belonged to Debbie and Ronnie Clarke, with Sue Benson, their regular rider, in charge of the yard. The Clarkes sold out to Dalgety's, the agricultural suppliers, who had ambitious plans to turn the yard into an equestrian centre. They signed up Richard Meade to run it and built no-expense-spared facilities, including an outdoor school and a fabulous indoor school. When the scheme came to nothing, John and Mary Cornelius Reid bought the property, which also had around twenty acres of land. Their business was old peoples' homes and they knew nothing about horses so they were prepared to listen when Moisie suggested I might be interested in renting the yard.

Initially Mary Reid was a little reluctant because she didn't want too much activity; my main worry was whether I'd be able to pay the rent. The yard at Mere was already bigger than anything I'd had before and Cholderton, with its nineteen boxes, seemed enormous. Philip Leischman, a television presenter I'd met in New Zealand, was over with his wife and I invited them down. I didn't know them well, but my dilemma was discussed and they said go ahead, which turned out to be the right advice. That was the first element in a learning curve that has taught me that every time you move to a bigger yard with empty stables, horses arrive to fill them. Over the first two years, I supplemented my income by running unaffiliated showjumping and dressage competitions in the indoor school. They were hell to organise, but they kept my cash flow on track and the rent was never in jeopardy.

The main plank in my business scheme for 1985 was getting more horses, either by buying or borrowing. Although I'm much more choosy now, I'd get on anything in those days. In addition, I bought horses in the expectation of turning a profit rather than finding a champion. Temperament has always been my top priority, on the assumption that every horse is potentially for sale and no one likes riding a difficult horse. The horses I buy must be reasonably good movers and they must be good jumpers, but there's a bit of leeway. Some might not be such good movers, but really good jumpers, or vice versa. They must have sound limbs and no obvious confor-mational faults or injuries.

I'd lost faith in Bert after Burghley 1984, so felt I had to sell him to make room for better prospects. He went to Germany in March 1985. He fetched a reasonable price and did a decent job for his new owner. Not so long ago, I had a letter from a woman who bought him as a hack when he retired from eventing so he had a good long life as well. With Bert gone, my second string was Michaelmas Day, a big tough sort who turned out to be one of my better first horses. He was a bit of a favourite, a strong brown horse, very hard pulling and usually a very good jumper, but every so often he'd take a serious liberty at a fence. That was because he was exceptionally brave to the point of not always thinking what he was doing, but the thought of stopping never entered his head. He was a nice old boy, very good-natured but difficult in the dressage because he didn't move particularly well and he was very stiff and hard. After a long but interrupted career, he became quite famous without winning any major championships.

Back in 1981, his owner, Susan Welman, had rung me out of the blue to ask me to take a horse called Hijack to Osberton and we'd won, which was a very good start to what has been a very long association with the Welmans. Mick had done an awful lot when he was young, going advanced as a six-year-old with Susan's regular rider, Phoebe Alderson. When she gave up eventing, Susan offered me the ride and Mick had come to me in the spring of 1984. Our part-nership got off to a promising start when we won the Rotherfield three-day event in June. By the autumn of 1984, he was ready to move up a grade so I took him to Boekelo in October, where he finished third.

In October 1985, we made a second assault on Boekelo. He was in quite a good position after the dressage and I'd completed the steeplechase and roads and tracks without incident, so I was feeling pretty optimistic as I waited in the ten-minute box. To get to the first fence, you had to cross a little bridge about 50 m from the start and the officials warned me to keep to the left because the right-hand side was starting to give way. It was taped off so that seemed clear enough and we set off at Mick's normal pace, which was very, very fast. After a moment or so, we galloped onto the bridge and he went straight through, just totally disappeared. It was the most unusual feeling. One minute he was galloping along, the next I was on the ground with no horse underneath me. Somehow he didn't actually go into the ditch, but skidded across to the opposite bank, picked himself up and galloped off. The clock was running so I chased after him and eventually caught up with him. The breastplate and the reins were broken so I couldn't go on, but the officials insisted on starting me again after giving me a bit of time to regroup. While someone ran off to fetch new equipment from the stables, they repositioned the start to cut out the bridge. Then we were off again, with Mick totally unfazed by his experience. If he'd been a less confident horse, he might have been put off, especially as we had to go over a similar bridge later in the course, but he took absolutely no notice of that and went round clear within the time. The next day, we completed the showjumping and finished third, but it was a pretty hair-raising incident, and also a pretty lucky one because he could easily have broken a leg.

I think that was the most alarming thing that has happened during my career, mostly because it was so unexpected. It certainly wasn't the most painful because I've broken both ankles in unrelated incidents. The first was in New Zealand when I was training a young horse on the flat. He slipped on the grass and fell down on my leg in such a way that the stirrup iron cracked my ankle. The second time a young horse got its legs tangled up while schooling over cavaletti (low fixed jumps) and did the same thing, but to my other leg. Neither was put in plaster, but I couldn't walk for a while. It's ironic that both accidents happened while schooling because I've had some horrific falls in competitions, but no serious injuries, touch wood.

Usually the falls are over too quickly to feel fear, but the slow ones are terrifying. A year or so ago, I was coming too quickly into a big bounce at Upton and the horse took it on too strongly and got a bit close. That brought him in too deep. He tried and failed to fiddle a stride for the second element and still didn't stop. He hit the upright rail above his knees and we had one of those slow-motion falls where he stood on his head, I was thrown to the ground and I knew he had no place to land except on top of me. It was probably only a split second before he came squarely down on my lower back, but it seemed like an eternity. I was quite badly winded, but not seriously hurt so I was able to walk away. Again I was lucky because that's the kind of fall that can easily smash your pelvis.

Once I was at Cholderton, my gold medal was a magnet when it came to attracting new custom, despite the fact that owners often got a bit of stick from the British Horse Society for giving horses to me, a New Zealander, to ride. I really appreciated Michael and Susan Welman's support because I know they took a lot of flak for sending Mick to me rather than to a Brit. Then she bought a second horse, Welton Greylag, for me to ride. Sam Barr had bred him by his jumping stallion, Welton Crackerjack, in 1980 and his wife, Linda, had done a couple of novice events with him before I took him over as a five-year-old. He was a very attractive horse, a flashy mover and a good jumper. Susan has always been a fabulous owner, my second proper one after Mimi, and she's still got a horse with me today. Most people thought my Badminton win in 1980 was a bit of a fluke, but after the Olympics they said, 'Maybe this guy can ride a bit', and the phone at Cholderton started to ring. A lot of my first horses were real pullers, and some of them had terrorised their previous riders but, for better, for worse, I accepted them all and soon I'd doubled my number of competition horses from three to six.

Larking About was a very good example of the best kind of horse trade! I bought him in 1985 through the agent, Susie Pragnell, for £7,000 and sold him a year later for £35,000 after he won the three-day event at La Granja in Spain. Obviously he'd impressed his hosts because some Spaniards rang me up in England and made me a most generous offer. I don't know how he did; I never saw or heard of him again.

I also bought Joint Venture, a lovely big chestnut horse from Scotland, in partnership with Mimi. He made an excellent start to his three-day career when he won Osberton, with an impressive dressage score of 31, a clear round across country and ten showjumping penalties. I was offered £50,000 for him at that juncture, but I liked him so much I refused it. More fool me. The next year, he slipped on landing at the last fence at Aldon, his seasonal debut, and broke down so badly that he was never able to compete again. Another of my horses was Arctic Flight, a really good jumper that I chose for

Jane Irwin when she decided to take up eventing at the age of forty. She had a bad fall so she offered me the ride and a half share in the horse. I won Osberton with him the next year and we sold him on to Eddy Stibbe.

As my thirtieth birthday approached, I turned my thoughts to the tantalising prospect of the World Championships, due to be held at Gawler in South Australia the next May. No one had ever been Olympic and World Champion at the same time but Podge had the class and I believed that I had the skill and the temperament. If only we could get it right...

CHAPTER SEVEN

EVERY EXCUSE FOR A PARTY

WHEN YOU TURN THIRTY, YOU SUDDENLY THINK YOU'RE old, at least until you turn forty, when you think you're really old and thirty seems young. Fortunately my birthday falls outside the eventing season so I can always celebrate it to the full, especially important in a landmark year like 1986. A bunch of riders, including the showjumpers, Graham Fletcher and Geoff Billington, plus Clissy, Mel and me, had been invited to a showjumping competition on snow at Kössen in Austria that January. Although the competitions were not all that serious, they were great fun and we were shown such a good time by the Austrians that I knew where I wanted to be on 1 March. Our hosts were pretty keen we should come back, so I got a group together and booked us into the same hotel for a weekend's skiing over my birthday.

Clissy Strachan and Bettina Overesch, the German event rider who is now based at Gatcombe with Andrew Hoy, signed up, along with Bryn and Sue Powell, Rodney Powell and a few others. The girls got the festivities off to a good start by ordering a huge feed of scrambled eggs and bacon for everyone to be served in my room on my birthday morning, so we all ended up having breakfast in bed together. After that, we skied all day and partied all night to take my mind off my advancing years. The Austrians love parties so they joined in but there were no formal celebrations and definitely no speeches. In those circumstances, I found it easy to convince myself that thirty was just a number to be used as an excuse for a serious party before I settled down to the business of trying to win the World Championship.

Mark Todd top row, fifth from left – next to the Burgess twins in 1961– and I can still remember most of their names!

Mark Todd aged nine, and Nugget, on Pop's farm – wearing the policeman's helmet that doubled as a hard hat

With Shamrock on Pop's farm – with Kenny Browne's in the background

With Killarney at the local Pony Club jumping show - I was seventeen or so

Mum and Dad - Lenore and Norman Todd

Pop in his nineties: on the land that he farmed all his life

Mumma and Pop at a family
celebration

With Carolyn on our wedding day, Wellington
Cathedral, 1986

In New Zealand at Mum and Dad's for Christmas 1995 with our children, Lauren and James

Carolyn on Done For Fun at Luhmühlen – third place – 1991

Lauren at Heythrop Pony Club camp, 1997

James, age four, on Bagpuss in 1997 with our nanny Sarah Mann

Taupo, 1983, Charisma and Mark Todd winning the New Zealand National three-day event: our first together

In the dressage arena during the 1984 Olympic three-day event

Charisma jumping a clear round at Los Angeles

1984 OLYMPICS STARRING:
SCENE: THREE DAY EVENT
ACT: STADIUM JUMPING

A spectacular recovery at the water in Luhmühlen, August 1986

Charisma during the dressage test at the 1988 Seoul Olympics

Victory parade in Queen Street,
Auckland in 1988

Charisma with Helen Gilbert,
his groom

Charisma opening the Commonwealth Games in Auckland in 1990 - the first and only horse to do so to date

New Zealand 1st, 2nd and 3rd at Badminton, 1994, Mark Todd (left) on Horton Point, Blyth Tait (2nd left) on Delta, Vaughn Jefferis (3rd left) on Bounce; Bruce Davidson, USA, on Eagle Lion was 4th

Bill and Judy Hall at home with my parents – the Halls bought Charisma, so that I could continue to ride him after our Olympic success

I was glad to get home because I was looking forward to seeing Carolyn Berry, a stunning blonde New Zealander who was studying for her Assistant Instructor's exam (AI) with us at Cholderton. When our mutual friends, Martin Dobson and Tony Cosgrove, first introduced us at the Hawkes Bay show back in 1982, Carolyn was wearing very short shorts and I remember thinking, 'Wow – she's cute.' A couple of years later, fate took a hand when her father, Keith, published *Todd's Ride*, the book I wrote with Sally O'Connor after the Los Angeles Olympics. When I went to see him in his office in Wellington, he asked me to sign a copy for his horsey daughter, Carolyn. A week or so later, we talked and danced for ages when we met by chance at a party given by a mutual friend, but Carolyn had a boyfriend so that was that for the time being.

A year passed before our next encounter at a talk I was giving in the Civic Center in Wellington. Carolyn and Martin interrupted me in mid-flow by walking in late and knocking over a chair. It seems she'd written to me to ask about studying for her AI at Cholderton, but I hadn't replied. She figured that was because I didn't have a pen so she presented me with a box of them when we met up after the talk. The upshot of this banter was that we agreed she'd come to Cholderton in January. When I got back from the snowjumping with Clissy and Rodney in the middle of the night, she was in the extra bed in my room, the only place she could find to sleep. The three of us crashed out in a state of exhaustion, and by the time we woke up in the morning, Carolyn had moved out into the housekeeper's cottage.

It wasn't a particularly promising start, but as the winter progressed we realised that there was a certain chemistry between us. We have a lot in common apart from horses – the same taste in music, the same sense of humour and we both love dancing. Working pupils didn't usually argue with me, but Carolyn did and I enjoyed the banter. She soon passed her AI exam but she agreed to stay on at Cholderton while I went to the World Championships in Gawler. Erik Duvander was there as well, so I knew the place would be in safe hands while Helen and I were away.

Podge was back on hard rations and well into his work by the time I returned from my birthday bash. There was just time to take him to a one-day event at Aldon before he went into quarantine for Australia. He started where he left off the year before, with a victory, which put me in a positive frame of mind when I moved him to Lady Hugh Russell's yard at Wylye. All the British, Irish and German horses were gathered there as well for the preliminary month of quarantine. When it was up, they flew out to Australia and spent a further ten days in isolation on Torrens Island before they were allowed up to Gawler. I don't know what diseases the Australians were trying to target, but it was all a load of nonsense because it's impossible to make an operation like that totally watertight. Still, we followed the instructions rigidly at Wylye, walking through a trough of disinfectant every time we entered or left the stableyard, and Australia was as free of disease after our visit as it was before, so I suppose there was no harm done.

I was lucky the authorities chose Wylye because it is only twenty minutes away from Cholderton. The whole estate was in the quarantine zone, which gave us a huge area of Salisbury Plain to ride over. As I was accustomed to doing all my fast work there, I didn't have to change Podge's programme at all. Although it varies with each horse, there are certain ground rules involved in any fitness regime. You start with roadwork to harden the legs and build up muscle, then you do a lot of slow cantering to increase stamina, followed by a certain amount of fast work so that the horse can sustain a gallop without running out of steam. In the late seventies, there was a vogue for interval training, a predetermined pattern of fast and slow work designed to increase fitness without strain. Basically it's good if you only have flat land to train on, but I prefer to use hills because they're easier on the horses.

Wylye may have been compulsory, but it was great fun. All the riders knew each other pretty well and it was instructive to see how the others worked their horses. The Brits and the Germans had resident trainers, but I had Bill Noble only on an occasional basis so I had more independence. Podge was able to show off on the gallops by competing with Clissy's horse, Delphy Dazzle, who was also very fast. Because the horses weren't getting the competition they needed for Gawler, the organisers staged a mock one-day event. Podge was at his most stroppy, tearing round the cross-country course and hitting one of the fences really hard. His stifle swelled up quite badly and it hadn't gone down by the time he took the flight to Australia so that was a bit of a worry. However, it settled quickly once he arrived.

The Brits had a formal dinner with Lord and Lady Hugh every night and, unlike the German riders, I was often invited to join them. It was a proper sit-down affair, not quite black tie, but we had to wear smart clothes. We had to mark down our pre-dinner drinks in a little book so we could pay for them later. Obviously such an honour system is open to abuse: I remember one evening someone just wrote 'one gin', but meaning one bottle rather than one measure.

In the real world I was working my other horses and taking them to the spring events. Clissy and the Scots rider, Ian Stark, kept some of their horses at Cholderton, so we were able to combine forces on occasion, though not always with the best possible results. In April, we went to Dynes Hall, Chris Hunnable's place in Essex. Clissy took her own horses but Scotty and I sent ours with Helen and drove up together in his car. It tipped down with rain all day and all the lorries had to be towed out, but there was only one tractor so gridlock was inevitable. Scotty won a section so our lorries were well down the line by the time we got back from the prize-giving. I said, 'Sod this, let's go and have a drink while we're waiting,' as good a cue as any to break open the emergency supplies in the lorry. Quite a few people joined us and the line never seemed to get any shorter so we kept on drinking. With hindsight, my behaviour, especially in view of what happened next, was at best irresponsible but, in my own rather weak defence, there was less sense of public outrage about drink driving in those days.

When our lorries were finally towed out and Clissy and Helen were safely on their way, Scotty and I headed for his car.

'Oh, I'm feeling a bit pissed,' he said and I said, 'I'm fine, I'll drive.' About ten miles down the road, I said, 'I wouldn't mind another drink,' so we nipped into a pub and had a couple of stiff gin and tonics before setting off again. Scotty had won a magnum of champagne which we were getting stuck into while driving along the M25 when I saw a blue flashing light in the rear-view mirror. I told Scotty to stay in the car while I got out, trying desperately not to look sozzled. The police claimed I was doing nearly 100 m.p.h. in fog with a visibility of fifty metres so it is hardly surprising that they weren't convinced I'd just thought the windscreen was fogged up! When they breathalysed me and I registered nearly twice the legal limit, they said, 'You come with us and your friend can drive.' I said, 'You can't let him drive, he's even worse than I am,' so we went in convoy to Maidenhead Police Station, with one of them driving Scotty's car.

Back at the station, I was breathalysed again, booked and put in a cell where I lay down and promptly fell asleep. I'd already used my one phone call to tell Carolyn to come and get us, but I'd hung up without telling her where we were so it took her a while to track us down to the right police station. Meanwhile Ian was stomping round the hall and crashing into the glass doors, so they threw him out into the car park until Carolyn and Erik rescued us.

When the case came up, I got a good lawyer and pleaded guilty, but with the mitigating circumstances that, as a sportsman, I rarely drank so even a small amount would have a very extreme effect. That went down pretty well and I lost my licence for only a year.

Badminton was one of the last events before we flew to Australia. I took Michaelmas Day and Any Chance, a lovely light bay Thoroughbred who'd reached advanced with his previous rider, Frances Hunter. He was a sharp sort of horse, a little bit tricky on the flat, but a wonderful jumper. I heard he was going cheap because he was an insurance write off. Probably he should never have competed again, but as he was only eleven years old, I thought the risk was worth taking. Mimi persuaded some wealthy friends of hers that they would enjoy owning an event horse and they bought him for £2,000. It wasn't a huge outlay for them and they certainly got their money's worth at Badminton.

Indeed he might easily have won if I hadn't challenged the gods with a rash prediction before the competition started. The BBC were conducting interviews with prominent riders at the most challenging fences out on the course. When I was asked about the sunken road, two-thirds of the way round, I said, 'I think Frank Weldon [the designer] has been quite kind to us this year and the fence shouldn't cause too much trouble.' Rarely have I regretted my words more because both Any Chance and Mick were clear and in winning positions when they approached it. Mick fell at the rail coming out and

Any Chance jumped it too boldly, put a back foot in the ditch, lost all his momentum and stopped at the final element. Even with twenty penalties for the stop he finished fifth overall, and Mick, with an added sixty penalties for the fall, was eighteenth, so I was left to dream of what might have been.

Any Chance had given me a magical ride, jumping effortlessly and maintaining a rhythmic gallop throughout, but shortly after Badminton, he hit his stifle on a cross-country fence and that was the end of his eventing career. He went to Steve Gittins, who said he was one of the best team chasers he'd ever had. Although our partnership was brief, less than a year, I was sorry to see him go because he was such fun to ride.

When I joined Podge and Helen on Torrens Island, I met up with my fellow New Zealanders, Trudy Boyce, Tinks Pottinger, Merran Hain and Blyth Tait. The facilities were minimal, but the ten days we spent there gave the European horses time to relax after the long flight. The organisers had ploughed up a sand track for hacking, but the going was so deep that we couldn't use it safely. Conversely, the cantering track was so hard that we were afraid to use it in case the horses went lame. Things improved a lot when we moved into the Roseworthy Agricultural College outside Gawler, a small town to the north of Adelaide. As team captain, I'd flown out a year earlier to help Trudy, Tinks and Merran with the Gawler dress-rehearsal event, so I knew what to expect. Blyth was the newcomer to the team, but his horse, Rata, died of a heart-attack during schooling before the competition started. If he'd had a replacement in Australia, he could have ridden that, but as it was he had to wait a little longer to make his impact on the eventing world.

Podge had got a bit bored with his confinement on Torrens Island but he always had a sense of the big occasion. As Olympic champions, we were obviously among the favourites, which put a bit of pressure on me, but not on him. He was getting more consistent by this stage, especially in his dressage, and his cross-country had always been superb, but the showjumping was still a bit hit and miss. He cheered up when we went to a one-day event at Reynella, a two-hour drive from Gawler. Clearly it was risky running so close to the big one, but he always went better in a three-day event if he had a preliminary competition to take the edge off him. On a small straightforward track, the chances of him damaging himself were pretty slim. He tended to bolt round the easier courses, but he usually managed to look after himself and so it came to pass this time. With a lot of my rivals pulling out before the cross-country, he won his fifth consecutive victory, a good note on which to start the Championships.

As I only had one horse to ride instead of six, the month I spent in South Australia was something of a holiday. Although the hospitality wasn't as glamorous as Lexington, the Australian welcome was at least as warm and we were invited to lots of barbies by the big property owners round Gawler. We had plenty of time to visit country fairs and vineyards. Naturally there was lots of tasting, but purely in the interests of research because Australian wines were just starting to flood the shelves in British off licences so we needed to know what was what. On one occasion, a bunch of us – Mel, Clissy, Scotty and the broadcaster Lorna Clarke, who was on the British team – went water skiing on the upper reaches of the Murray River. We hired this little speed boat and as the most experienced skier, I went first. Then it was Scotty's turn, with me driving the boat. I don't think he'd done much before, but he got up first time and he was looking quite cocky until I told my passengers to hang on and opened up the throttle. When I went into a tight turn, he was flung outside the wake at ever-increasing speed until he came off and skipped across the water like a pebble. It was a silly thing to do, but it was very funny at the time, and luckily he didn't hurt himself.

As the anchorman, I did my dressage on the second of the two days, a very windy one as it turned out. Podge worked in brilliantly, but once we got into the arena he was irritated by the flags flapping in the wind. Also there weren't many spectators and empty stands are worse than full ones because you get an echo from every clang and bang. As we were among the favourites, there were a lot of television cameras and whirring motor drives, so Podge had more distractions than some of his less-fancied rivals. The upshot was that I was sitting on a volcano, holding on rather than letting him flow forward as I would have liked. Even so, he looked pretty good and did a nice test, coming second to Torrance Fleischmann and Finvarra, the last time he was beaten in the dressage phase of a three-day event.

The cross-country course had been completely rebuilt since my visit the year before and the result was a strange mixture of big, testing fences and silly little ones. I'd known the terrain was hilly but after all the training at Wylye Podge was extremely fit and raring to go, so I had no anxieties on that score. The biggest question for all the competitors was the water complex, Dead Man's Pass, at fence nine. There were three elements, a small rail, a log with a five-foot drop down into the water and a rail on a slight angle in the water. If you jumped the angled rail on the left it was a bounce from the log, but if you jumped on the right, it was too long for a bounce and too short for a stride. On the extreme left, there was a very long route that looked safer, but wasted a lot of time.

Tinks was the first to go for New Zealand on Volunteer, a bold long-striding horse who had no trouble taking the bounce on the left, just as we'd planned when we walked the course. There weren't many competitors at Gawler, so I only saw three other horses attempt the fence, none of them successfully, before I had to get on for my own round. My team-mates said, 'Tinks has jumped it fine, you'll be right,' but no one told me that the other competitors who jumped on the left weren't making the bounce, whereas those who jumped on the right were fiddling a short stride and mostly getting away with it. Torrance, for example, jumped on the right and although Finvarra bashed his nose on the rail and had a nosebleed, she managed to get round clear, though rather slowly because of the blood. Although we foresaw the problem, we didn't read it quite right; the fence jumped differently from what we expected. By the end, everyone was jumping on the right, but because Tinks had taken it so well on the left, I decided to do it her way, which turned out to be a big mistake.

The start of the course was downhill on slippery going, very testing on a horse as keen as Podge. I was worried about the second fence, an upright logpile, but he jumped it neatly. Scotty had had a slip up at the Jubilee Js, so I chose a route that eliminated the sharp turn between the two rails and Podge handled it impeccably. As most of the course up to the water was downhill, Podge was still very strong when we got there. I was on a holding stride, whereas I wanted a more forward stride to get the kind of jump we needed to make the bounce. Because I was checking him, Podge landed short into the water, a long way off the angled rail. He still tried to bounce it, but bellied it instead. For a split second, I thought he might keep his feet but down he went. It was a spectacular fall, but I really couldn't blame the horse. As I climbed back into the saddle, I just thought, 'Sod it, I've blown it.'

Getting going again after total immersion is never easy. Podge had water in his ears, I had water in my boots and I was slipping around the saddle like crazy. Motivation was low but I knew I had to keep going for the team because Tinks and Trudy had gone fast and clear, but Merran had had two falls with the six-year-old Chief. I gave Podge a couple of cracks with my stick to tell him to get on with it and he fairly flew the next fence, an imposing double oxer brush. After fence thirteen, there was a long uphill climb which tested fitness to the limits, resulting in stops for a couple of horses at the Brewery Drays just before the summit. I didn't go flat out but Podge was unaffected by the hill and finished full of running with twenty-two time faults. When I pulled up, I felt very fed up, even more so when I was approached by a couple of uninformed local reporters. One asked, 'Will you be able to make it up on the showjumping day?' and the other one capped it with, 'Now that you've had this fall, do you wish you hadn't come out here?' Bad timing on their part, but at least I had an outlet for some of my anger. I left them in no doubt as to what I thought of their idiot questions.

Back in the New Zealand camp, the good news was that Tinks was in the lead, with Trudy lying third. Even with my eighty-two cross-country penalties, the team was on track for a gold medal. The bad news was that Volunteer had bashed his knee and might fail the vet's inspection the next morning. I tried to join in the rather muted celebrations, but I felt bitter about the advice I'd been given and depressed that I'd deprived Podge of the chance for double glory. Once the competition starts, you tend to stay with your compatriots, but if I'd called on my friends in the British camp, I would have been better informed. Clissy had fallen in the water when Dazzle lost his footing going the longest route of all, but because she went early, she was able to watch a lot of the other competitors. Afterwards she said, 'If only you'd asked me, I'd have told you not to attempt the bounce.' The Brits were well organised, with spotters out on the course to bring back up-to-date information on how each fence was jumping, but we didn't have that kind of back-up. As it turned out, Volunteer was the only horse to jump the bounce successfully all day. I don't, of course, blame anyone but myself, but in different circumstances we might have had a different result.

The next morning, Volunteer was a little bit off, though not limping or hopping lame. It was obvious that he'd whacked his knee rather than damaged his tendons or anything more serious. He probably could have completed a round of showjumping without doing himself any harm and I've certainly seen lamer horses get through the trot up, but this vet didn't see it like that and Volunteer was out. Vets have a certain amount of discretion in such matters and it must have been a difficult decision because the guidelines say that if the cause is obvious and jumping wouldn't harm the horse, he should be allowed to take his chance. Obviously, the interpretation depends entirely on the individual vet but it was hugely disappointing for Tinks and the team. After the showjumping, the Brits took the team gold medal and Ginny the individual one, with Trudy's fantastic performance earning her the silver medal. I had two fences down and ended up in tenth place, which goes to show how much trouble there was on the cross-country.

Win, lose or draw, the New Zealand supporters always have one hell of a party and so it proved on this occasion. Things were only just getting going when we joined them in their tent so we thought we'd see how our British friends were getting on in their supporters' tent next door. We expected a tremendous victory celebration but instead there was this quite sober gathering. The Brits were easily persuaded to join us and we had one hell of a night. Scotty and Mark Phillips were up there dancing on the tables, and I'm sure I got up there at some stage. It was spur of the moment but the place was packed and everybody had a really good time. We were commiserating to a certain extent but we cheered the Brits and they cheered us so there was an excellent spirit.

On my return, I received a welcome if unexpected offer of sponsorship from the investment bankers, Merrill Lynch. The mid-eighties were boom years for such companies and Stanny Yassicovich, the managing director of Merrill Lynch Europe, approached me out of the blue. He liked riding, especially playing and watching polo, and he thought it would do the company good to be associated with an Olympic equestrian gold medallist. When it came to sponsorship, there was a certain amount of rivalry among the top riders to get the best deals. Lucinda was the pathfinder with her contract with Overseas Containers Ltd, but by 1986 she was less competitive than she had been in her prime. Ginny was at her peak in the mid-eighties, as Citibank recognised when they agreed to support her. The Merrill Lynch contract, which ran for the two years up to the Seoul Olympics, gave me around £60,000 a year to spend on the horses as I thought best, crazy money that you couldn't hope to match nowadays. The horses ran in the sponsor's name and wore rugs in the corporate colours with the Merrill Lynch logo on them and we wore their team livery when we went to events. Otherwise I didn't have to do anything much, other than turn up for the occasional function.

Merrill Lynch also took over my Woolrest horsebox, a faithful servant that made me a lot of money over the years. Bill Hall bought it originally and gave it to me when his sponsorship ended. When I sold it to Merrill Lynch, they did it up and had it painted in their colours. As they'd written it off in their books, I was able to buy it back again for very little money when the sponsorship ended. It was my first horsebox with a living area, sleeping for four or five, a cooker, a fridge, heating and of course a drinks cupboard, and I spent a lot of time in it. I love staying at events because you don't have to worry about getting on the road in the early morning after a heavy night.

Over the next few weeks, Carolyn and I became progressively closer and I took her to visit friends like Mimi and Tom May to see if they approved. I kept things light by introducing her as my chauffeur until my friend, Alfie Buller, an Irish property developer who worked in London in the week, jokingly offered her a job. I asked her to be my groom for the La Granja three-day event in Spain. We travelled in Clissy's lorry, with Mel, Mark Mingo and an Australian called Shaun and were joined there by Mel's future husband, Mick Duff. Shaun was supposed to be Clissy's boyfriend, but he was a bit of a smoothie and he was taking a bit too much of an interest in Carolyn which prompted me to step in. We took an overnight crossing, one of those six-hour jobs from Portsmouth to Caen, and spent the night chatting and laughing in the living space in the lorry. The next evening we stabled the horses outside Biarritz and drove into town in the lorry. After dinner, we went to a bowling alley and then a nightclub before retiring to our hotel room. Gossip spreads like wildfire in the eventing world and the news of our romance was filtering back to England on the grapevine even before we reached La Granja. After Larking About won the event, we all went down to Marbella to stay on a boat owned by some friends of Bryn and Sue Powell. We were joined by Rodney Powell, Rachel Hunt and another Aussie rider, Scott Keach, and we partied twenty-four hours a day for a week, one of the happiest holidays of my life.

Back at Cholderton, I took a long hard look at Podge's future and decided that retirement was not on the agenda. My disappointment at Gawler had been all the more intense because I thought it might be his last international three-day event. He was fourteen, an age when horses can deteriorate very rapidly. Although there was no sign of that with him, I knew that if anything did happen, he might not recover so quickly. I couldn't say with any confidence that I planned to take him to Seoul in two years' time, only that I would have to take it step by step. At the end of the forty-eight-hour return journey from Australia, he had a bad experience when the pilot slammed the plane onto the tarmac at Luton Airport, landing with a thud that swept horses and humans off their feet. There were a few minor injuries, grazes and bruises, but typically Podge emerged completely unscathed. He was so fit and keen that I entered him for Luhmühlen at the beginning of August, a less strenuous event than Burghley, although it took place a month earlier.

His obvious well being didn't stop people criticising me for taking him to a three-day event so soon after Gawler so it was particularly gratifying when he put in one of the best dressage tests of his life, returning a score of 29.2, with three tens, indicating movements perfectly performed. A score of under thirty is remarkable in an international three-day event and Podge must be one of the few horses to have achieved it.

We'd done the test on the first day of competition and I had a day to spare before the cross-country, so that evening we had a bit of a party to celebrate the result. Carolyn and I were staying in the La

Romantica Hotel, one of those typically German establishments with frills and cherubs and gilded mirrors. As our romance was less than two months old, it suited our mood perfectly. We hadn't really talked about the future, but that night I asked Carolyn to marry me. It seemed quite spur of the moment, but I'd been mulling it over in my head. She said yes immediately. Well, she claims she asked for five minutes to think it over, but I don't remember that.

I always thought I would get married. My parents have a very good relationship so I had a positive outlook on marriage. I believed I'd know when the time – and the person – was right. I can take a long time to make up my mind about certain things, but I can be quite spontaneous, as I was on this occasion, and I felt sure I was doing the right thing. After all, I'd turned thirty so, in theory at least, I was ready to face up to new responsibilities.

The next thing was to ring our respective parents with the glad tidings. We tried mine first. I got Mum and said, 'Guess what, I just got engaged,' and she said, 'Who to?' She'd never met Carolyn and the last girlfriend she'd heard of was Jane Swallow. Then we rang Carolyn's father at work and he was so thrilled he rang all the New Zealand papers. They splashed it across their front pages so we were headline news. First thing the next morning, I woke Brendan up to tell him that our bachelor days were over. It was a nasty shock for him, but he knew I was serious because I asked him to be my best man. Later that day, Carolyn and I announced our engagement officially at the event, which resulted in a flood of television interviews. The decibel level was so high that people were telling us to be quiet because other competitors were trying to concentrate on their tests.

Podge responded to the mood of the moment with a clear cross-country round within the time over a big but reasonably straightforward track. My only anxious moment came at the water complex, which I over-rode, perhaps to compensate for under-riding it at Gawler. This time we went in over a big log with a drop into water, then for about twenty m through the water before we jumped onto a bank and bounced back into the water over a rail, took a few strides to another bank and out over another rail. Podge jumped boldly into the water and powered up the bank and over the rail so eagerly that I was fired up his neck. He screwed in mid-air but landed safely, with me hanging off one side of him, and we somehow scrabbled over the next bank and rail without parting company. On the third day, I was in the lead with a fence in hand over my nearest rivals, Bettina and Lucinda, but I didn't need it because all three of us had one down so the placings were unchanged. I was also in a winning team for the first time, a Commonwealth one made up of Lucinda, Scotty and me. We won by over 100 points from Italy and Germany and Luhmühlen has banned composite teams ever since.

Podge got his well-earned rest after that while I concentrated on my other horses. With Mick coming ninth at Burghley and Pedro the Cruel winning the three-day event at Le Lion d'Angers in France, Merrill Lynch were getting good value for their money. We were also concentrating on wedding plans. I am quite a traditional person in a lot of ways, certainly in anything to do with family, and I always assumed I'd have a formal white wedding. I may not have been a regular at Sunday school, but the religious aspect of marriage was important to me. Fortunately, Carolyn and I both wanted a church ceremony so the talk was over detail, rather than form.

We set the date for 29 November, but as we could only get back to New Zealand two weeks ahead of time, much of the organisation fell on Carolyn's mother, Betty. My parents came to pick us up when we flew into Auckland early in the morning. They are fairly easygoing and I was confident they would like Carolyn, but she was a bit nervous, as I was at meeting her father again as his future son-in-law. Brendan arrived the next week, with Clissy, Mel, Mick, Rodney, Jane Starkey and Dot Love, a Danish friend who lives in Ireland. I'd arranged for people to lend them horses to ride in the three-day event at Pukekohe. Dot loved her horse and went really well until the showjumping when the damned thing napped and dumped her. Clissy rode a horse belonging to the New Zealand Olympic showjumper, John Cottle, but she blew her best-ever chance to win a three-day event when she had one down in the showjumping.

The wedding took place with full pomp and ceremony in Wellington Cathedral in front of 200 guests. Carolyn wore a dress she'd bought in Harrods and I was in morning dress. I was very nervous, but not as nervous as Brendan, who was afraid he'd drop the ring and forget his speech. Carolyn stuck with bridal tradition by being late so that prolonged the agony. She'd done some modelling when she was younger and I was well known so it was a high-profile occasion, with coverage on national television and crowds of well-wishers waiting to greet us as we came out of the cathedral.

Because it was such short notice, we couldn't get Carolyn's first choice of venue for the reception so we decided on the Overseas Terminal, a large converted building on the waterfront. The wedding was at three o'clock, followed by champagne, a sit-down dinner, cutting the cake and witty speeches from Carolyn's father and Brendan. Once the formal stuff was out of the way, things got going. I'd booked a Cambridge band called The Politicians, with Ian Jeffries, and Carolyn had invited a trio, made up of some friends of hers, to take turn and turn about with them. As things warmed up, they combined on some of the numbers and everyone danced until they dropped. Carolyn and I were two of the last to leave at around 1 a.m. We had our friends from overseas, plus a lot of local people we hadn't seen for a long time, and this was our big day, so there was no way we were going to slip off early. We had a fabulous night and we drank another bottle of champagne in our hotel room before we finally retired.

Pop lent us his house on the beach at Mt Maungnanui for our honeymoon and we broke with tradition by inviting our friends to extend the celebrations for another week. Everyone just dossed in with the chores, as you do in that sort of situation, and we had a wonderful time. Our wedding was a romantic catalyst for several of the group. Mel and Mick soon tied the knot and Clissy got together with Edward Bleekman in Los Angeles on her way back to Britain. She'd fallen for him at Boekelo in October, so she took the opportunity to get to know him better on neutral ground. The next year, Brendan met Sally Hercock, the daughter of a Leicestershire Master of Foxhounds, at Punchestown. At their wedding, in June 1988, he returned the compliment by asking me to be his best man so it was my turn to sweat over the ring and speech.

Carolyn and I had planned a more conventional honeymoon in the Maldives on the way back to Britain after Christmas, but I had a three-year-old filly racing at the time called Sounds Like Fun. I'd bought her as a yearling at the January Sales in 1984 and she was entered in the New Zealand Oaks, which is run at Wellington. She'd won her previous two starts and she was among the favourites so there was no way I was going to miss the big one. I owned her, but I'd leased a half share to my parents so it was an exciting family occasion, especially when she finished second. In a career that lasted until 1988, she won eleven races in all and won NZ$500,000, so she was by far the best racehorse I've owned to date. After finishing fifth in her last race, an A$1 million contest in Australia, she was retired to stud on our farm in New Zealand.

Needless to say, Carolyn and I never got to the Maldives. Many newly wedded wives would whinge about that sort of thing but not Carolyn, so I knew I'd made the right choice as we headed for Britain and our new life together.

CHAPTER EIGHT

HIGHS AND LOWS

As OUR ROMANCE HAD BENEFITED SO MUCH FROM Carolyn's temporary employment as my driver, it was appropriate that our first home should be called Chauffeur's Cottage. Moisie Barton had approached Lady St Just, the owner of Wilbury Park just down the road from Cholderton, on our behalf while we were in New Zealand and we met her as soon as we got back. Maria St Just was a White Russian, a ballet dancer and an actress, who'd been to the same drama school as Marilyn Monroe. Later she'd married Lord St Just, from the Grenfell banking family, but he'd died by the time we knew her and her daughters were living in London so she was on her own at Wilbury.

Maria was accustomed to an incredibly smart lifestyle, with lots of staff, as she called the people who worked for her. At our first meeting, she introduced us to her general help, Toogood. 'Toogood,' she said imperiously, 'this is Mr and Mrs Todd.' Carolyn said, 'Oh, just call me Carolyn,' whereupon she was whisked away by Maria. 'Dizzy, darling,' she said – she always called her Dizzy because she was blonde – 'you really cannot have the staff calling you by your first name. You are Mrs Todd.' She was a wonderfully eccentric character locked into a bygone age and she soon became a close friend.

She'd originally earmarked a different cottage for us but when she showed it to us, it wasn't quite what we were expecting. She must have taken a bit of a liking to us because when we looked disappointed she said, 'I'll show you another cottage, but I'm not sure you can have it.' That was Chauffeur's Cottage, which was gorgeous and beautifully furnished. As soon as we saw it, we said, 'Oh yes, this is perfect,' but it turned out that Taki, the Greek millionaire and journalist, used to spend time there. When he said he no longer needed it, Maria agreed to rent it to us.

When we'd been there for about two days, she went off to New York and left us with the keys to the house so we could feed and exercise her two huge dogs. It was an extraordinary act of trust because the place was full of valuable paintings, furniture and silver and she didn't know us from a bar of soap. She was away a lot of the time, visiting friends all over the world, but whenever she was in residence, she'd cook kitchen suppers for us. She suffered very badly from arthritis so we helped her out as much as we could and she was very good to us. Wilbury was a bit run down, but it had as much character as its owner and we loved living there.

Maria's circle of friends included the film-makers James Ivory and Ismail Merchant, and the house was used in *A Room With a View* and *Maurice*. Maria had a small role in *A Room With a View*, but that was several years before we arrived. She had wide-reaching artistic connections – she was an executor for Tennessee Williams's estate, for example – and she'd hold big celebrity dinner parties when the mood took her. On one occasion, she said, 'Bryan Ferry's coming to supper. You must come and meet him,' but unfortunately we were away. I'd hate to have been on the wrong side of Maria, but she was brilliantly funny and entertaining, a real 'giver of life', as one journalist put it.

Although she knew about Badminton because she was friends with the Duke of Beaufort, she always pretended that she didn't understand about eventing. She'd introduce me as, 'Mr Todd who does horse racing', and she'd ask, 'Are you off to another race, dear?' Mind you, I gave her some cause for confusion that spring because I rode in a point-to-point on I'm Bad, a horse I'd bred myself in New Zealand and brought over to England in May 1985. Despite my mixed fortunes with Mr Papagopalus and Crown King, I'd always retained my passion for racing. I bought my first brood mare at the Claudelands Sales when I was living with my parents in the run-up to Lexington in 1978, so I had a couple of horses of racing age by the time I took over Pop's dairy herd in 1981. I paid knockdown prices for the mares because they were old and I sent them to unfashionable stallions, but the excitement of breeding is that you never know what you're going to get.

I sent a mare to Cry Baby and bred a filly that jumped quite well. She didn't have the speed for racing so I sold her to John Cottle, a regular member of the New Zealand showjumping team. Then I sent the same mare to Superstud, a son of Cry Baby, and the result was I'm Bad. As his name suggests, he was a right bastard, but he was a good jumper and quite quick when he felt like it, so I thought I'd try to event him. That plan went on hold when he cracked a pastern galloping round the paddock at Mere as soon as he arrived and put himself out for a year. When he finally recovered, he ran away with Carolyn on Salisbury Plain and tried to scrape me off on the wall of the indoor school, so I sent him to Moisie Barton to sell. She took him out with her point-to-pointers and he enjoyed the competition so much that she suggested qualifying him for the local Tidworth Hunt point-to-point in the spring of 1987. As it coincided with Badminton, I had no plans to ride in it myself, but when the event was cancelled, I was keen to have a go.

I'd always loved jumping at speed, but riding with a wall of horses in front of you so that you can't even see the fence is something else again. In a way, it's more frightening because you are going quite a bit faster, but it lacks the variety you get in eventing. At that time, my experience was limited to third place on a horse called Tariana in a hurdle race at Taupo in New Zealand as a teenager, plus a couple of point-to-points when I was with the Nevilles in Great Somerford. Bobbie's friend Simon had a share in a horse he kept with Robert Dickinson, a cousin of top trainer, Michael Dickinson, and he asked me to ride him in the spring of 1981. First time out we fell at the third fence, but the second time, at the Beaufort meeting at Didmarton, the horse went really well until the last, when he fell again. We were vying for the lead, but he was hanging towards the horse on the outside, which gave me the choice of asking for a long stride or holding him on a straight line. If I'd asked for a long one, he'd have taken the other horse out so I held on, he fiddled a short one and down we went. Maybe I could have won but as the last fence was right in front of everyone, I'd probably have been disqualified.

Despite our joint inexperience, I'm Bad gave me such a good feel in the Tidworth point-to-point that I thought it would be worth putting him into training for the 1987–88 National Hunt season. Mick Duff and Alfie Buller took shares with Carolyn and me and we sent him to David Elsworth at the end of October. His first run was at Cheltenham in quite a smart novice hurdle and he got beaten by a neck, starting at 66 to 1. Sadly we were in New Zealand, but Mick and Alfie got their money on so it was a lucrative start for them.

David Elsworth found us a buyer who was prepared to pay £50,000 for this supposedly useless horse that I'd bred out of a scrubby little mare by an unfashionable stallion, a horse, in other words, that you couldn't give away. However the Cheltenham winner was quite a smart novice hurdler so we turned the offer down and sent I'm Bad to Kempton Park, where he started favourite, but got brought down at the third fence. It was quite a nasty fall and it probably put him off because he didn't run that well next time out. Undeterred, we entered him in a stayers' novice hurdle at the Cheltenham Festival in March 1988. He was a bit of a funny character and he'd lost a lot of condition so we weren't surprised when he had to be pulled up. I remember John Francome, who was commentating on TV, saying, 'This is I'm Bad, but they call him I'm Mad at home.' True enough, because he had a habit of galloping off in whatever direction took his fancy as if his brain had flipped. He was happier at the races, though there was always a possibility of trouble at the start.

Despite the Cheltenham fiasco, David Elsworth thought there were still grounds for hope, so we turned him out for a spell in the spring, then put him back into training over fences in the autumn. David Elsworth must have thought quite a lot of him because he selected a listed race at Ascot as his first steeplechase. His rivals had won several good races between them, but I'm Bad ran very well and finished third. Next time out, he came down a class or two and started hot favourite, but his luck ran out when another horse galloped into him and sliced through a tendon in his hind leg. Elsworth took him home but the wound became infected and he had to be put down. Although he had his moments of glory, he was exceptionally accident prone and, with hindsight, we wished we'd taken the money while we could.

1987 was the year the Whitbread Trophy had Podge's name on it, or so I believed. He'd come back into work as strongly as ever and he proved his well being by coming fourth at Dynes Hall in early April. As Mick had finished second, I had two strings to my bow as I loaded the lorry for the short journey to Badminton. Tinks and Trudy were based at Cholderton for their first assault on the classic and we were all packed up and ready to go when Clissy rang.

'Don't bother,' she said, 'the ground's too wet. It's all off.'

I was devastated. If I kept him in training the following year as a sixteen-year-old, it would be to defend his Olympic crown in Seoul which would rule him out of Badminton, so he'd missed his last chance. There was some consolation for him in the crowds of dejected New Zealand supporters who flocked to Cholderton to pay their respects. He always thrived on adulation, at least until he got bored with all the meeting and greeting and turned his back on his fans. However, a photo opportunity was not to be missed. Helen always enjoys the story of a couple who were treated to a view of Podge's hindquarters until they wandered off to take photos of the yard. The stable door was open and Podge, never normally one to leave even an empty manger of his own free will, was out like a flash to pose in front of them.

After a bit of fast footwork, I got him a replacement fixture at the Saumur three-day event in the Loire Valley. By this time, he was pretty much unbeatable at three-star level and he duly won the dressage, went inside the time across country and jumped clear in the showjumping. Two months later, we went to Stockholm, where he again won the dressage. Only two horses finished the steeplechase within the time and unusually Podge wasn't one of them. He hated the heavy sand and, for the only time in his career, he was a couple of seconds over. It didn't matter much because he was clear within the time round the cross-country and were still in the lead at the end of the speed and endurance. However, I wasn't counting my chickens as I warmed up the next day because the showjumping was on the same kind of sand as the steeplechase. Podge always liked to tap the rails, but he didn't allow for sinking a few inches into wet or heavy ground. Sometimes he got away with it, but this time he was hopeless, knocking down four fences and dropping to sixth place.

I was particularly cross because there was a car, a Volvo, as a prize. I have won a car in a showjumping competition, but there haven't been many opportunities in eventing. Bruce Davidson won the Volvo, and asked for it to be painted in his colours, fire engine red, and shipped to America. If only Podge had made a bit more effort!

My best new horse for the 1987 season was Big Red Willy, better known to the public as Wilton Fair. He wasn't my usual sort of horse, a big chestnut, with Irish draught blood in him. He was intermediate at the start of the season and his owner, Lucy Robinson, didn't want to take him any further so she offered me the ride. He was quite difficult on the flat initially, but a good enough jumper. We went to Le Touquet, a fabulous two-star three-day event right by the sea, and he came fourth which qualified him for Burghley. He'd gone very well, but he was quite inexperienced for an event of that calibre so it was a push to get him there. I took him to a couple of advanced events to see how he'd tackle the bigger fences and he was second to Podge at Rotherfield, so I decided to let him take his chance. If I'd known what was to happen, I might have decided differently.

As had become his custom, Podge won the dressage at Burghley. In the weeks running up to the event, he'd developed a habit of flicking his head while I was schooling him. It could have been the flies but as he'd never done it before, I was worried that the sinus trouble he'd developed on his first flight to England in 1984 was catching up with him at last. I was also worried that he would do it in the arena and ruin his test but he didn't, performing just below his best to lead the field, with Big Red Willy in fairly close contention in fourth or fifth place.

Burghley was big that year and only six horses got round clear within the time. Four of them were ridden by New Zealanders, and two of those were Podge and Will. For Podge, the event was a test to see if he'd be my first choice for the Seoul Olympics the next year. If he'd felt tired or lost enthusiasm round Burghley, I'd have retired him immediately, but he gave me one of my best rides ever, jumping the fences effortlessly and speeding round with his usual enthusiasm. Will wasn't a fast horse, but he'd gallop forever and he didn't pull so you didn't have to check him much for the fences. That helped with the time and he too gave me a fabulous ride, finishing second to Podge at the end of the cross-country day.

If they'd ended up in that order, how happy I would have been, but of course the showjumping was still to come. Podge had a fence in hand over Will so I was cautiously confident that he'd win his British major at last. Naturally he had other ideas. After Will jumped clear, Podge knocked two down so that their placings were reversed. I'm prepared to share the blame for the first error at two related fences, a spread to a wall, half-way round the course. He should have jumped the wall, but I made him put in a short stride so he clipped a brick. Okay, so I got anxious and over-checked him, but he wasn't that wrong and he could have tried harder. Even so, he would have won if he hadn't knocked an element in the combination. That was his fault, sheer carelessness, and I was really disappointed. Photos of the victory circuit show me riding Will, ears pricked with excitement, and leading Podge, ears laid back in anger; or perhaps he knew that the cheers weren't for him. Either way, we'd blown our last chance.

Podge wasn't a King William, that great horse of Mary King's who'd readily knock down five fences when he was in the lead on the final day, but I never really sorted out his showjumping. I got advice from professional showjumpers like Ted Edgar, but Podge was always hit and miss. He jumped brilliantly when he wanted to, but he never saw the point of clearing fences that came down so easily and I was always worried that he'd get more contemptuous of them as he got older.

In 1987, I started riding four promising new horses, Bahlua, Jued Lad, Pedro the Cruel and Peppermint Park. Andrew Nicholson's brother, John, had bought Bahlua through Dummy Myers, a well-known showjumper and successful racehorse trainer in New Zealand. I was down visiting John one Christmas and we went to the racing trials at Hawera in the middle of the North Island. Horses have to finish in the first three to qualify for proper races but Bahlua was very immature and there was no way he was going to do that. In fact, he finished last but he was by Valuta, the sire of the Grand National winner, Seagram, so Dummy thought he had jumping potential. As John and I were leaving the racecourse, he said to me, 'Hey, take this one, he'll do you right,' but he wasn't a particularly good-looking horse and I was rushing back to Cambridge and on to England so I said, 'Sorry, no time,' and left.

John was living down there so he took Bahlua from Dummy and

passed him on to Andrew to bring to Britain. Andrew did a couple of events with him, then put the word about that he was for sale so I took a girl to try him. I didn't know Bahlua's recent history, but he seemed familiar so I asked Andrew if he'd got him off Dummy. I can't always recognise horses but he had a distinctive head on him with a slightly Roman nose. My client didn't like him, but I did so I went back later and bought him. He had a very nice jump and seemed well priced at £6,000.

I nicknamed him Baxter because he looked how I imagined a Baxter would look, very worried and serious, although he was only six. He was a dark bay, not as dark as Podge, but a strong rich colour. It doesn't make any difference to a horse's performance but I've always liked dark bay best. Baxter was an exceptionally kind horse, always trying to do his best to please but over-anxious when he didn't get it right. He wasn't really nervous, but you had to be a little bit careful because he tried so hard and bullying really upset him. In our first three-day event at Breda at the end of May, he finished a respectable ninth.

Jued Lad was owned by Jackie Wright, a woman who used to race motor bikes. She had a bad accident and broke her neck so she chose eventing as a safe alternative. She took Jued Lad through novice to intermediate, then realised that he had more ability than she was going to get out of him. I took over the ride and a share in the ownership. He was a good jumper, an English Thoroughbred by Tower Walk, bred to be very fast but in reality rather slow.

Pedro the Cruel was on loan from Lizzie, one of her series of horses named after mad kings. He was very handsome and very fluent on the flat, but he wasn't the most generous horse over a fence. He was pretty quirky, a nightmare to break in by all accounts, and initially you had to be very careful how you got on and off or he'd take off with you. You could never wear a raincoat on him. He thought a lot, which was a pity because he didn't always come to the right conclusions.

I bought Peppermint Park from Penny and Martin Podmore, dedicated all-rounders on the equestrian circuit. He was a big handsome grey, a good mover with an okay jump. Penny had done some ridden showing, showjumping and hunter trials with him, so the basics were in place, but he'd never evented. He was Irish bred, by Teaspoon, and my first impression was that he might be a bit heavy for the job. As it turned out, the more he did, the finer he got. He wasn't exactly vicious, but he was a bit of a narky beggar and I can't say I took to him straightaway. Our partnership didn't start that well because he got very tense and over-excited when I asked him to do a dressage test, but once he came right he was a very good horse, one of the best I've had. Was I mad when I entered Pedro and Pepper, the quirky and the narky, for Le Lion d'Angers that October? Apparently not, because they finished first and third after performing impeccably in all three phases, which shows that you never can tell.

A love of riding wasn't a pre-condition for marriage but I rarely met anyone outside my field so it was pretty inevitable that my wife would be a horsewoman. Even if Carolyn hadn't wanted to compete at the outset, she would have been bored out of her mind trailing round after me so I knew that sooner or later I'd have to bow to the inevitable. Naturally my attempts to teach her resulted in the first blazing rows of our marriage. I'd say, 'Do such and such', and she'd say, 'But I am', and I'd say, 'No you're not', and she'd say, 'Well, get on and do it yourself,' or words to that effect, which I sometimes did. I've always been much more worried for her than I am for myself, especially across country, both because I want her to do well and because I don't want anything to happen to her.

I originally saw Done for Fun, her best horse to date, when he was cross-country schooling at Aldon. He was a nice sort, a dun gelding by a Thoroughbred stallion called Precipice Star, out of a part Connemara mare. I was with Scotty and we both liked him. Scotty thought he might suit his wife, Jenny, and I thought I might turn a quick profit on him, but his rider said he wasn't interested in selling. I left my phone number anyway and later he came back to me, so I got lucky.

I started riding him myself but Carolyn's current horse, Bloody Clive, had broken her collarbone and ribs in the indoor school so Carolyn needed a substitute. Before we had him, Merlin, as he was always known, bucked and bolted so much that he almost went to the knacker's yard, but he injured his knee during one of his escapades and his owners broke him when he was on three legs, which saved his life. He always thought like a pony and he had a knack of crossing his jaw and running out ten strides away from any fence he didn't like. Carolyn came to terms with that eventually, but it wasn't easy. At Longleat in 1987, her first one-day event in England, she had two falls and one run out, but she stuck with it to complete so it was a start.

The Spanish rider, Santiago de la Rocha, first came to train with us at Cholderton in February 1987. Sante was an airline pilot, about my age and with very little eventing experience, and he'd asked me to find him a horse when we first met him at La Granja the previous year. We got him the veteran Mr Todd from Erica Jewitt, an Irish friend of mine who'd bought him to hunt in his retirement. Mr Todd had done a lot of eventing with his previous rider, John Watson, and Erica said he was just what Sante needed. How right she was! We'd thought the old schoolmaster would nurse the new boy through his first low-level three-day events, but both Sante and Mr Todd had ideas far beyond that station and they ended up going to the Seoul Olympics and the European Championships.

Sante had a full-time job as a pilot with Iberia, so we'd prepare the horse and he'd roll up for odd training weeks and events. Mr Todd was the most appalling jumper at home and I used to hate schooling him, but he was as honest as they come. Sante was one of the last of the Corinthians, riding with tremendous determination, as if getting to the other side was the only thing that mattered, but he never interfered with his horses. They made their own arrangements and, one way or another, they usually worked. Sante was lucky that Mr Todd and Kinvarra, the second horse he had with us, understood his system and were willing to go wherever it took them.

Sante's three-day campaign started at Windsor in May. Neither partner had much aptitude for dressage, Mr Todd had a tendency to knock down showjumps and Sante wasn't the most accurate rider, but they went clear across country. Sante was thrilled, especially as the result qualified him to ride for Spain in the European Championships at Luhmühlen in August. So there they were, the rank amateur and the battle-scarred hunter, competing against the best in Europe after just one two-star three-day event together. As non-Europeans couldn't compete in those days, I was able to give Sante the benefit of my full attention when I went out to Germany to help him. The course was quite big and I counselled caution, especially at the water.

'Don't take the most difficult route,' I said. 'Go the slightly easier way. It's not a lot longer.' I watched on closed-circuit TV and there he was, riding straight for the middle. I said, 'My God, he's going the quick route!' Only one other person attempted it all day, but the old horse just went pop, pop, pop and they were through. At the end of the speed and endurance, they were clear and in the top ten so I didn't have the heart to say, 'I told you not to do that!' The next day, they had four showjumps down and ended up twelfth, but I've rarely seen anyone on such a high as Sante after the cross-country. Whoever says dreams don't come true?

Carolyn and I went back to New Zealand in November in time for the first anniversary of our wedding. We were always keen to start a family and, after an early miscarriage, Carolyn became pregnant again in October so we had a double cause for celebration in Cambridge that Christmas. Although we spent as much time as possible with our families, I had plenty of riding commitments to keep me busy during our winter breaks. That year, I went to a clinic given by George Morris, a top American showjumper who'd become a celebrated international trainer. The clinic was held at Clevedon, near Auckland, and organised by John Cottle, who'd jumped as an individual for New Zealand at the Los Angeles Olympics. It was there that I met up with Merran Hain, a fellow member of the event team at Gawler in 1986. She'd always done a bit of everything and she had this New Zealand-bred showjumper called Bago, by the part-Hanoverian stallion, Winnebago. The New Zealand Horse Society was thinking of sending its first-ever showjumping team to the Seoul Olympics and she asked me if I'd like to try to qualify him.

He was a strong horse with a huge jump, just a bit careless, but no fence was too big for him to take on. He had tremendous scope and what he lacked in technique, he more than made up for in courage. He was a bay horse, nicely mannered and quite straightforward to ride. Merran had done a good job training him and he'd jump rather than stop, even if it meant ploughing through the fence. When we came second in a qualifying Grand Prix at Isola, Merran offered to fly him over to England so I could do some competitions with a view to taking him to Korea. As befits an Olympic junkie, I agreed immediately. Where horses are concerned, you can never have too many strings to your bow.

CHAPTER NINE

CHAMPION OF CHAMPIONS

THERE IS ALWAYS AN EXTRA BUZZ ABOUT AN OLYMPIC year, especially when you know you're in with a chance; or, in my case, two chances, as I confirmed by taking Bahlua to Saumur in April. It was his biggest event to date and he went really well to finish second. He booked his ticket to Seoul with that result but he was young and relatively inexperienced at that level so I was always going to ride Podge if he felt right.

The plan was to start Podge's campaign at the spring one-day events and miss out Badminton. I thought two major championships in one year might be a bit much for a sixteen-year-old horse, though in his case I was probably wrong. In the belief that an old horse should be kept up to the mark, I got him three-day fit in the spring, and in that I was certainly wrong. We started at Belton, where we came second, and went on to Brockenhurst, where he gave me one of the worst rides of all time. He was in the lead after the dressage, but as soon as he saw the showjumps, he went berserk, charging round the ring and knocking two down. On the cross-country, he bolted at the fences, pulling my arms out and taking the sort of liberties that could easily have ended in disaster if he'd made a mistake. Luckily he didn't and we finished third, but he felt so fit and well that I nearly rang the Badminton office to see if I could get a late entry. I'd have been tempted to run him if I'd entered him at the right time, so it was probably fortunate I hadn't, given the barrage of criticism I was already facing for even thinking of taking such an old horse to the Olympics. Realising that I'd got him too fit too soon, I had to let him down a bit before he exploded.

At Cholderton, Olympic anticipation built with the arrival of Tinks and her two possibles, Volunteer and Graphic, in the early spring. Sante was also back in the saddle, with both Mr Todd and Kinvarra on his Olympic hit list. Bago arrived on 13 May so, with Podge and Bahlua, there were seven Seoul hopefuls in our yard. In July, Bago went to the Royal International Show at the National Exhibition Hall at Birmingham, where he jumped okay, not disgracing himself but having the odd fence down. I got some help from Jeff McVean, a British-based Australian showjumper who was married to a New Zealand girl, before I took him to Hickstead and some other big shows. He kept on jumping, but his form in Britain was never better than average.

I also increased my race riding experience in a charity fundraiser for the British Olympic Equestrian team at Kempton Park. It was an invitation race, a mile on the flat, and Scotty, Ginny, Lucinda, Robert Lemieux, Jane Holderness-Roddam, Maureen Piggott, Michael Whi-taker and Annette Lewis were in the line-up. Various trainers lent horses and as I'd had I'm Bad in training with David Elsworth, I asked him if he had anything suitable for me to ride. He said he did, and quite a good prospect too, which had the added advantage that I would carry top weight. I dieted as much as I could, but I was still worried I wouldn't be able to make it until someone offered me some diuretic pills. I hardly ate anything for the twenty-four hours before the race, then I took them just before I left for Kempton Park. When I arrived, I went straight to the sauna where I found Scotty trying to take off those last vital pounds. As it turned out, I overcooked it, ending up several pounds too light and having to carry a weight cloth.

My horse was a front runner so he jumped out smartly and was still in the lead as we turned into the straight. At that point I thought I could win the race but I got progressively more feeble as we neared the winning post. I probably should have won, but I didn't have the strength to ride it out properly and I got swamped on the line, ending up about fourth. Robert Lemieux fell off at the finish and I was so exhausted I could hardly pull the horse up. When I jumped off, I nearly keeled over. At the official prize-giving, we were all standing round during the speeches when my vision suddenly went from colour to black and white. I've never fainted, but that was the nearest I came. Luckily Malcolm Wallace, the British chef d'équipe, had done quite a lot of race riding so when he saw me leaning on Lucinda and Scotty, he realised what was happening. He led me off back to the jockeys' room and made me drink fluids and sugary tea until I revived.

The Brits had so many fundraisers that we decided to hold the Alternative Olympics without horses at Cholderton to raise money for all the other teams. Helen and the girls built cross-country and showjumping courses in the indoor school and we did dressage on hobby horses. It was a fancy dress do, led by Robert Lemieux in fishnet tights. I should think there were a couple of hundred people and it was tremendous fun. What with entry fees, drinks, auctions and raffles, we made about £2,000 and had a hilariously successful evening.

1988 was also the year of the televised challenge between the jump jockeys and the eventers. The deal was they would ride round Gatcombe and we would ride round Aintree. I rode Mr Todd so it was Todd on Todd. He was a tough old boy and a great survivor, but it was also one of the most terrifying experiences of my life because he didn't care how hard he hit the fences as long as he got over them. The only one he respected was Becher's, which he jumped beautifully and before it was modified too, but although he rose to the big one, he certainly didn't leave much brush on several of the others. That spring, he took Sante round his first Badminton as part of his Olympic preparation. Rather him than me!

Although she didn't compete that spring, Carolyn kept on riding until two days before Lauren was born. Merlin was quite steady and the doctor said it was all right so long as she didn't feel uncomfortable. She never ballooned out, so she was able to get on and off without too much difficulty. On the evening of 23 July, we went to a Michael Jackson concert at Wembley with the Purbricks and the Duffs. It was pouring with rain but Mick had got the tickets some time before and Carolyn was determined not to go into labour until it was over.

She only just made it because she had to go to the hospital early on Sunday, 24 July and Lauren was born on the Monday evening. I spent most of the time with her, but I went out occasionally for a cigarette and I must admit that hearing all these women screaming was pretty unnerving. Carolyn planned to have a natural childbirth, but as the pain dragged on and on she wanted whatever they could give her, so she had an epidural. Then Lauren appeared. I don't know what I expected but, as Carolyn said, it was just like calving a cow. Having seen lots of animals born, we were both more prepared than some people might be. We didn't know in advance whether our baby was a girl or a boy, and we didn't mind either way as long as he or she was healthy and normal. The first thing we did was count how many fingers and toes she had and there was a tremendous moment of relief when the doctor said, 'You've got a nice healthy baby girl.'

We'd been looking forward to the birth for months and it was great when she arrived. She looked incredibly fragile but, again, a farming background is helpful because you have experience of the survival instinct in very young creatures. We discussed all sorts of names and decided on Lauren Grace. It wasn't a family name for either of us but funnily enough, my mother told me later that she nearly called my sister Lauren and my sister nearly called her daughter Lauren. Carolyn wanted Lauren or Michaela, which I didn't like, so Lauren it was.

I'm certainly not one of those men who can't stand, or is nervous of, tiny babies and I did my share of nappy changing. Right from the word go, I enjoyed picking Lauren up and cuddling her. For the first few weeks Carolyn breastfed her, so I couldn't help much with that, other than getting up to bring her into the bed. Carolyn fed her every three hours and still Lauren cried all the time. Some wise person suggested she might be hungry, so we gave her a bottle and she slept for five hours. Carolyn thought she'd died, but what a relief it was to get all that uninterrupted quiet. As it was the middle of the eventing season, I was away a lot so much of the burden fell on Carolyn. A baby brings a whole new dimension of responsibility. You have this other person who is totally dependent on you so you can't nip out to the pub or go to the movies or whatever; not that it was a great sacrifice because we were too tired to go out after the wakeful nights.

By now, it was crunch time for Podge. If he came back into full work in top condition, he would defend his Olympic crown. If he didn't, he would retire. The first test came at Holker Hall, the final Olympic selection trial for the short-listed British riders, in August. Podge was so full of himself that he did his worst test ever. He then skittled four or five showjumps and tore around the cross-country like a thing demented. By this stage, he was very cocky and he thought he knew it all. He was also very keen to get on with it after his break. His performance may have silenced those who doubted his physical well being, but as Bahlua was second in an advanced section, it was inevitable that people should think he might be a better choice for me to ride at Seoul.

Needless to say, I was not one of them. I knew I'd neglected my eventers in my attempts to improve Bago's Olympic chances by taking him showjumping, but I put a fair amount of work into Podge in the week before the British Open Championship at Gatcombe. In front of large crowds of enthusiastic supporters, he responded with an impeccable performance, leading the dressage, going clear in the showjumping and skipping brilliantly round the cross-country. None of the British Olympic team ran their horses across country, but I reckoned the risk worth taking because Seoul was still five weeks away. Podge won the competition by ten marks from Robert Lemieux which shut my critics up, at least for the time being. When one of the reporters asked if he was going to Seoul, I said, 'Yes, and he'll be even better there,' because I knew I still had a bit of work to do on him. That was his last run in England, a fitting ending to that part of his career, and it did wonders for my confidence as we prepared for the journey across the world.

Sheer numbers worked in our favour when it came to the quarantine regulations and we were granted a dispensation to keep Podge, Bahlua and Bago, along with Volunteer, Graphic, Mr Todd and Kinvarra, in isolation in the bottom yard at Cholderton for the last three weeks before the flight. They travelled to South Korea with the British and Irish horses in a newly built plane, with much better facilities than the DC8 that had taken them to Los Angeles. The flight was reduced from twenty to fourteen hours when the Russians gave permission for it to fly over Moscow. The horses spent a further thirty-six hours in quarantine before they moved into the stables at Kwa'Chon race-course, half an hour's drive from the city centre.

I knew what to expect because Carolyn and I had stopped off for a recce in February on the way back from New Zealand. As is customary in Asia, the racetrack and the facilities had been built on a money-no-object basis and they were excellent. With no infrastructure to build on, the Koreans had travelled the world to see what was required, then replicated it in their own backyard. There were no fields to turn the horses out in, but otherwise everything was perfect, with brand new stables, gallops and training areas.

I travelled to Seoul two weeks before the Olympics began in early September and Carolyn arrived just before the start of the three-day event. We left Lauren at home with a friend who also had a young child and a nanny because we thought it was too risky to take her to Korea. In any case, Carolyn was exhausted due to her night duties by that time, so it would be good for her to have a break. We lived in the Olympic Village, which consisted of spartan apartments, very small and with just the most basic furnishings. I shared my apartment with Andrew Bennie, and Tinks was with Marges Knighton, who'd joined us from New Zealand. By this time, the New Zealand management had realised that they could minimise team disruption by giving the riders their own floor. We underlined their good sense when we invented a drink called Sustagin. Because of the heat and the danger of dehydration, the medical team suggested we drink Sustalyte, a lemon- or lime-flavoured electrolyte-replacing preparation. Tonic was quite hard to get hold of so we were quick to take their advice, adding it liberally to our duty-free gin. It proved very popular, both with the medical team and with the other athletes, who sampled it eagerly once they'd finished their events.

As in Los Angeles, there were all the exercise facilities you could use, though I didn't go quite so crazy this time. That may have been partly due to the kick in the groin Baxter gave me by way of greeting. I was picking out his feet and he lashed out, catching me just where it hurts most, so I had a huge bruise for several days. Again I was dieting so I couldn't take full advantage of the twenty-four-hour international buffet provided for the competitors. There was a pre-Olympic promise that no cat or dog would be served – both are delicacies in Korea – and I'm sure it was honoured, but there were a lot of complaints about the food. Actually it wasn't too bad, so long as you avoided the local dishes. Almost everything else had to be imported and they did a reasonable job of catering for large numbers of people with very varied tastes.

We used to travel out by bus from the Olympic Village each day with a motor-cycle escort equipped with sirens and flashing lights. The drivers thought that gave them precedence over everything else on the road and we'd tear straight through red lights with no regard for traffic crossing from other directions. We'd compete to get the back seats because it was so terrifying to sit near the front. As far as I was concerned, that was the most dangerous part of the Olympics.

My other accident blackspot was a visit to Itaewon in the heart of Seoul with the French riders. We'd brought photographs of European fashions, suits, ski suits, jackets, and we got the local tailors to copy them incredibly cheaply. Less sensibly, we went to eat in the shanty town at one of those little stalls where they cook the food in front of you. It was mostly won ton and cabbage, with lashings of soy sauce, which didn't suit me at all but the French seemed to like it. They also recommended the rice wine, so I got stuck into that and by the end of the meal I was feeling a bit woozy. That didn't stop me going on to a Seoul nightclub, but after half an hour I felt so bad I knew I had to get out. All I could say to the taxi driver was, 'Olympic Village'. I was completely gone and I spent most of the journey throwing up with my head sticking out of the window. He took me to the wrong gates at first, then by some miracle to the right ones. I stumbled out, practically threw some money at him, rushed in and collapsed on the bed. I've never felt so dreadful and even now the smell of that sort of cooking or rice wine finishes me. One of the French riders disappeared for two days, so I guess the refreshments had an even worse effect on him.

The Koreans were incredibly friendly and tried very hard to make everything work as smoothly as possible. For years afterwards, I received Christmas cards from the President of the Korean Equestrian Federation. They had copied the event layout in the Seoul Equestrian Park from the Los Angeles Olympics. Kwa'Chon racecourse had mountains in the background, just like Santa Anita, and the organisers had made it very attractive, with flags and flowers and bright colours. From the moment Podge arrived, everything seemed to fit into place, as if he knew this was his big moment. To do justice to it, he was feeling and going incredibly well. When you wanted to do a training gallop, you started by the main dressage and showjumping arena, then went round the track and back towards the arena to pull up. One day, he was pulling so hard that it was all I could do to stop him before he ran into a line of portable loos. He never actually got away with me, but that was one of several times he came close. He never bucked but he'd seize the bit, set his jaw and off he'd go. I'd be pulling on the reins and his head would come down onto his chest but he just kept on going faster. At home, he pulled himself up at the end of the gallops, but at Kwa'Chon he didn't know where to stop so he kept on going.

Staging a repeat Olympic bid obviously brings a measure of pressure but it was relieved a bit because so many people thought Podge was past his peak. In any case, you never go into a competition thinking, 'I've got this one sewn up', no matter how well your horse is feeling. It was hot, but that was probably to Podge's advantage because he wasn't bothered by it and some of the others were. He had his favourite surface, fairly firm sand that would never get deep or heavy, for the dressage, the steeplechase and the showjumping. On the cross-country, they'd done a lot of work on the grass and it was perfect. As a team, we thought we had a handy sort of chance, although we were definitely not the favourites. Tinks was strong and respected internationally, Marges was a bit of an unknown quantity because she hadn't competed outside New Zealand and Andrew's horse, Grayshott, was average.

The dressage arena was on the racetrack, with the permanent stands on one side and temporary ones on the other three. Unlike Los Angeles, there were hardly any spectators, just a few curious Korean farmers, some noisy children and the people involved in the competition, so it was a huge echoing bowl. The judges were Colonel Anton Bühler from Switzerland, Berndt Springorum from Germany and François Lucas from France. On the first day of dressage, there was a downpour in the afternoon which caught the early riders in each team including Marges Knighton and Mark Phillips. Afterwards Marges said, 'My legs were all over the saddle like slippery fish,' so I was lucky that it was dry on the second afternoon when my number came up. From the moment I got on Podge, I was able to ride him exactly as I wanted and he gave his best performance ever, going into the lead on 37.6. Germany's Claus Erhorn and Justyn Thyme, the horse Anne-Marie Taylor rode for the British team in Gawler, were second on 39.60, with Ginny and Master Craftsman a close third on 43.20 and Scotty and Sir Wattie in contention on 52.

Although Podge had a lower penalty score at Luhmühlen in 1986, dressage marking is always subjective and I believe that the Seoul test was even better. The *Horse and Hound* dressage correspondent, the late Pegotty Henriques, clearly agreed with me because she wrote, 'The test they showed together was as good as you need to see at this level and probably more faultless than the Grand Prix Special that the gold medallists Uphoff and Rembrandt performed.' She wasn't alone in her opinion because a lot of people said that Podge should have been further in the lead, but neither Bühler nor Lucas gave him the marks that I felt he deserved. Bühler had, in the past, trained some of the Italian team and he gave one of their riders 172 marks, just one less than Podge, whereas Springorum and Lucas gave the Italian 149 and 110 respectively; such are the vagaries of top-class dressage markings. Tinks, Marges and Andrew, who finished eighth on 52.20, all performed to the best of their expectations. As a team, we were third on 155.60, behind Germany on 137 and Britain on 146.40, so morale was high as we went into the speed and endurance phase.

The FEI had appointed Hugh Thomas, an event rider who'd represented Britain in earlier Olympics, to build the course. Again we had to relocate, this time to Wondang Ranch, an hour's drive away from the Seoul Equestrian Park. The stabling was in tents, for all the world like a set from *M*A*S*H*, but we were put up in hotels which made a welcome change from the Olympic Village. Although it wasn't a golf course, the site was as limited and undulating as Fairbanks, and Hugh had to use considerable ingenuity to build a suitable course. It is always difficult to design an Olympic test that stretches the horses from the experienced nations, while allowing the less experienced ones to get round without too much grief. It sounds very conceited but we New Zealanders were a bit disappointed when we walked it because we'd hoped it might be more challenging. The Brits wanted the jump into the water lowered, but we said, 'No, leave it as it is.' However the Ground Jury instructed Hugh to lower it by three inches and to remove the first element of the Wondang Walls, fences twenty-seven and twenty-eight near the end of the course. Under the circumstances, with the weather and everything, we were quite happy with it in the end.

As far as my own performance was concerned, my first impressions of the course were correct because I had absolutely no anxieties on cross-country day. My diet had worked and I weighed in at 11 st. 8 lbs fully clothed, which meant I had to carry my saddle to make the 11 st. 11 lbs minimum, just as I had in Los Angeles. The roads and tracks were entertaining because they went through paddy fields and backyards. You could see women going about their chores – cooking or squatting down to do the washing – inside the houses, which was a bit different from the customary views of fields and woods. The men were out and about, performing their normal farming duties, but they barely looked up when we passed. I don't know what they thought of it all. At strategic points, there were guards with guns cocked ready for trouble, presumably because we were quite near the border with North Korea and our hosts were taking no chances. As always, Podge took an intelligent interest in his surroundings but when it came to the steeplechase, he bolted off as eagerly as ever, with me having to keep a tight rein all the way round. Even so, he finished twenty seconds under the time. When I finally got him back under control, I got off and ran beside him for the first part of phase C, but he was so onward bound that there was some question as to who was leading who. Although much of the going on the roads and tracks was unyielding concrete, there was never a moment when I thought, 'Oh my God, is he all right?' He felt so good that I was able to give every phase my best shot and the further we went the more confident I felt.

In the ten-minute box, Helen and Carolyn cooled Podge down with fans and ice while I got up-to-date news of my team-mates. The course was causing more problems than we'd anticipated, perhaps because it was hilly and twisty, and good horses were finishing quite tired. Marges was round with three stops, the last at fence thirty, the Taxi Stand, where Enterprise stopped out of sheer exhaustion. Andrew had had a fall with Grayshott at fence twenty-five, the zigzag barrier, but managed to complete, and Tinks and Volunteer were the first combination to go round clear within the time. This was a tremendous boost for me, not least because it showed it could be done. It also meant that the team were still in with half a chance, so I had everything to play for as Podge stormed out of the box like a demon. I'd planned to start at a sensible pace then build up the speed if things were going well, but he had other ideas and I could only restrain him as best I could without making too much of a fight over it. To my amazement, we were already fifteen seconds under the time at my first four-minute checkpoint. I'd known we were going fast, but surely it couldn't be that fast!

After that, I let him cruise at his own pace and each time I checked, he was up on the clock. I took all the direct routes with the exception of Chosun's Choice, a combination fence, with a rail to a wide left-hand corner. Podge had run out at a left-hand corner a year or so earlier at Gatcombe and I wasn't prepared to take the risk, especially as the longer way didn't waste much time. He jumped everything immaculately and effectively reduced the Olympic track to a Pony Club course. When I asked him to gallop over the final uphill fences, he was off and he finished full of running in the fastest time of the day. Show-off that he was, he pulled up doing an extended trot, as if to say, 'Beat that if you can'. They were monitoring the heart rates at the finish and he had one of the lowest. When they monitored him again five minutes later, he showed the best recovery rate of all and he stopped blowing completely within ten minutes. So much for being too old to compete!

At the end of the speed and endurance, Ginny and Scotty were my nearest rivals, but both had had some cross-country time faults which meant that I could have two fences down showjumping and still win the gold medal. As a team, we were competing with the Brits for the silver, with Germany out of sight for the gold. The silver started to slip away from us when Enterprise was spun at the vet's inspection. Greyshott didn't help by having five fences down in the showjumping and we ended up with bronze, New Zealand's best result to date. Sir Wattie went clear for Scotty so they ended on 52.80, but surprisingly Ginny had two down with Master Craftsman, which put her behind him on 62. As a result, I had three fences in hand as I went into the arena which I felt should be enough, even for Podge.

He'd come out for the vet's inspection as cocky as ever, with no hint of strain or stiffness. Basically I was happy with the showjumping course – again modelled on Los Angeles – and the going was perfect. I knew he'd rattle the jumps if he wanted to, but I'd come to believe that the more relaxed he was, the less likely they were to fall. Working on this principle, I kept my warm-up to a minimum so he wouldn't get excited. He started carefully enough, but then he knocked the first element of the treble and the heat was on. He rattled the eighth hard and I had to resist the temptation to look back to see if it had stayed up. Fortunately it had and by the time I got to the last two fences, I knew I could have them down and still win. I felt like letting go and galloping at them out of sheer relief, but again I resisted temptation and he jumped them clear. In the end, he beat Sir Wattie by 10.20 penalties, an unusually large margin for a major three-day event. There were some very good horses still further behind, so I felt that his runaway victory confirmed both his class and his tremendous form.

Although the competition was immaculately staged, the Korean public had no knowledge of eventing and they stayed away in droves. In Los Angeles, we'd been overwhelmed by the cheering crowds, but here our audience was limited to the Kiwi faithful and the other foreign supporters. I shared the bronze medal honours with my team-mates, then stood alone on the podium to receive my individual gold, with Scotty and Ginny on the lower steps. You bet I was glad I'd beaten them, for all that they are such close friends! I didn't feel more patriotic or less than in Los Angeles, but I'm very much a New Zealander, now as then, and I was very proud that we'd come so far in such a short time.

That evening we had a party, but it was a muted affair compared to Los Angeles, partly because I wasn't too keen to go out on the town after my rice wine experience and partly because the Olympic showjumping competition started the next day. We opened up the champagne in the stables and I rode Podge out of the barn in his headcollar so he could join the celebrations and acknowledge his fans. Glutton that he is, he accepted anything on offer and that certainly included champagne. Later Joan Gilchrist got her customary ducking in the horse trough, before Carolyn and I headed into town for a night in a five-star hotel, my reward for victory from the New Zealand

Olympic Committee. The American and Australian Equestrian Federations may pay big bucks to the Olympic medallists, but Carolyn and I appreciated our night of luxury in one of the few places with western-style food.

The three-day event gold medal has only been won back to back once before, by the French-sounding Dutchman, Charles F. Pahud de Montangnes, on Marcroix in 1928 and 1932, and it certainly takes an exceptional horse to do it. I was very touched to receive a telegram from his widow saying how proud her husband would have been to see me follow in his footsteps. In Los Angeles we'd gone in as unknowns and ended up as winners, but in Seoul I'd planned our campaign and victory was all the sweeter for it. From the outset, I'd said, 'Win, lose or draw, Podge will retire after the Olympics,' and I couldn't imagine a more perfect way for him to go. From a physical point of view, he could have competed for another year or even longer, but he was beginning to get a bit fed up with the daily grind. He still loved the excitement of the big competitions, but he was bored with doing flatwork at home. I'd have hated to see him go downhill. Before the Olympics I'd booked him onto the post-Games flight to New Zealand, with Helen as his escort and Bago as his companion. I was never tempted to change my plan.

Once the party was over, I joined up with my new team-mates, Harvey Wilson, John Cottle, Maurice Beatson and Colin McIntosh, for the practice round of the showjumping. They'd come directly to Seoul from New Zealand, but we'd all known each other for years. I was relatively inexperienced in this discipline and realistically I knew I had no chance of winning a medal because Bago almost never jumped clear. He was lazy with his front end, often catching the uprights and the front rails on oxers. On the other hand, I was confident he'd jump round whatever track they built and I was looking forward to the new challenge. In the practice round on the first day, Bago knocked four fences and had one time fault for a score of 17. Maurice Beatson with Jefferson Junior and Harvey Wilson with Crosby had 4 faults each, Colin McIntosh with Gigolo had 8 and John Cottle with Ups & Downs had 12, so I was the worst in the New Zealand contingent and my prospects of getting into the team looked bleak. However, Bago improved dramatically when we schooled him the next day. He also had the advantage of being competition sharp after a summer in England, whereas the other horses had come from the off season in New Zealand, so he was preferred to Gigolo, who had a tendency to jump violently to the left. On the day of the team competition, Ups & Downs was sore so Gigolo replaced him.

In the seventies, huge Olympic tracks put a premium on sheer jumping ability but Olaf Petersen, the designer in Seoul, built courses that emphasised the importance of technical skill as well. His philosophy was that a balanced horse that responded well to the aids and an intelligent rider who was able to adjust to technical distances should have the edge on a partnership jumping on raw power. Basically that's sound thinking, but none of the New Zealanders had had the opportunity to develop the skills to do that kind of job at this level. In the team event, Maurice and Jefferson had a combined score of 48 penalties for the two rounds, Colin and Gigolo had 52 and Harvey and Crosby had 36.5. That left Bago to carry the flag, with three down in the first round and two in the second for a creditable 20.5. We finished in twelfth place out of sixteen, but as the team rounds were part of the qualifying competition for the individual event, Bago was still in with a chance of being in the hunt on the last day of the Games. That chance became reality in the individual qualifier when he had one fence down, finishing joint eighteenth on aggregate.

The final gave me the chance to ride in the main Olympic stadium in Seoul, the first time I'd been there. Again there was a sense of disappointment because the stands – much bigger ones this time – were pretty empty. All the qualifiers started the competition with a clean slate, but the fences were huge so I didn't feel there was any great cause for optimism. When I walked the course with my fellow competitors, we identified the main problem as the diagonal line at 6, 7, 8 and 9, a double to a big oxer to another double over water to a final huge oxer. Typically, Bago jumped those beautifully, only to have three of the more straightforward fences down. However, it was enough of a thrill for me plan a return assault on the Olympic showjumping in 1992, provided I could find the right horse. The next day, the eventers and the showjumpers made their mark on the closing ceremony, with me snaking round the stadium at the head of the Kiwi equestrian cobra.

We were eager to see Lauren after the long separation, so Carolyn and I flew out that same evening. Podge and Helen stayed on in Kwa'Chon for a further four weeks of quarantine with the New Zealand and Australian horses, a period of some strain because the Koreans lost interest in administration as soon as they were off the world stage. Podge stopped over in Melbourne, where he was able to gallop round a field for the first time in two months. He discovered that he could dig up the top soil to reveal a layer of chalk that was perfect for rolling in. Each day, he'd dig a little deeper and emerge a little greyer. As he was still on northern hemisphere time, he grew his winter coat so that by the time he walked down the ramp in Auckland to claim his kingdom, he resembled nothing so much as a woolly black teddy bear.

Wrightsons general stores sponsored a nationwide victory tour of the North and South Islands, covering 17,400 miles in six months. Podge appeared five days a week, with Helen in attendance, usually in a pen inside one of the stores, with the public crowding round to pat him. Often, he'd have to walk through the front door of the shop and up a flight of steps to reach the designated spot, but none of it fazed him. He also visited shows and old people's homes, winning more friends wherever he went, especially among the disabled, who appreciated his gentleness. I joined him for the New Zealand Olympic Victory Parade on the streets of Auckland that autumn. He was being led, the crowds were thronging round, something made him whip round and he knocked an old man over. Luckily the man wasn't hurt; in fact he was quite proud to be knocked over by the great Charisma, so there was no harm done.

When the tour ended, he went to Judy Hall's for a bit, then to a beautiful farm outside Tirau owned by Pam and Dick Bailey. One of his last guest appearances was at the Miss Waikato Beauty Pageant, where he walked on stage, got an erection and had to be hustled off. What a wonderful end to a wonderful career!

CHAPTER TEN

NATIONAL HEROES

ALTHOUGH WE HAD TO SPEND A FEW WEEKS IN ENGLAND to wrap up the 1988 eventing season, Carolyn and I could hardly wait to introduce Lauren to the rest of her family. My parents love children so they had a big party to celebrate their first meeting with her in November. Kerryn had three children so Lauren wasn't their first grandchild, but everyone made a big fuss of her. I never really considered raising my family in New Zealand, but that's not to say there wouldn't be advantages. I'm always torn when I see Kerryn's kids doing the sort of things I did as a boy, but the longer I stay in England, the harder it is to leave. Kerryn and her husband, Martin O'Brien, lived in Canada until they had children, then returned to Cambridge to educate them. Their eldest son, Nicholas, went to the local athletics club, just as I did, and he's already broken the New Zealand junior 100 metre hurdle record. He's eighteen so he could be in the line-up for the Sydney Olympics, fulfilling those athletic dreams I never pursued. I don't know if he's inherited the Todd competitive spirit, but he's a very nice kid with an excellent attitude, and it would be great to see another Todd in the Olympics, even one masquerading as an O'Brien. In Britain, kids become more worldly more quickly because so much more of the world is so much more accessible to them. I can never decide whether that's good or bad.

It is important to me that people associate my success with New Zealand, even though I spend so little time there. New Zealanders are mad about sport, any sport, and it doesn't really matter which one you do so long as you do it well. Three-day eventing is relatively new and it is impossible for a young rider to get the exposure required to reach the top without wider international experience, so I've always felt I had to base myself in Britain while remaining a New Zealander at heart. Blyth Tait and Andrew Nicholson share my view, whereas Vaughn Jefferis has managed to compete from home, but usually with only one top horse. From 1984 to 1990, the sport put me in the public eye in New Zealand, and not just me because Charisma was a national hero in his own right. Wherever I went, people would rush up and seize me by the hand. Most of them just wanted to say, 'We're proud of what you've done for our country, congratulations on your success.' Some said, 'Aren't you the one who rides horses?' and some wanted me to sign things, anything from toilet paper to body parts. My most startling moment came when a woman pulled her bra down at an event and asked me to sign her breasts. I obliged, of course.

Although we spend up to three months in New Zealand most years, it's always a rush to get everything done. By the time we've caught up with our friends and done the things I have to do officially, it's time to leave. In 1988, I made a television commercial for Bell Tea, who have been fantastic long term benefactors of all equestrian sports in New Zealand. It shows me, tastefully dressed in a primrose yellow sweater, galloping a dark brown horse through green fields in the early morning before going indoors for a welcome cuppa. At one point, I jump a big stone wall, a high risk business as I'm not wearing a hat. A year or so later I was doing another commercial for them and I came off in a water jump, which caused great hilarity – at least I was wearing a hard hat.

After Bago's relative success, I was hooked on showjumping, partly because there is more money in it, which is always useful for a growing family, and partly because it was a new challenge. I had no specific plans to buy a top-class prospect when I went back to New Zealand towards the end of 1988, but fate took a hand when Carolyn and I saw Mum and Dad's neighbour, Penny Stevenson, riding a young horse called Double Take in her outdoor school. He was bred on a station as a shepherd's hack, but Penny had spotted his potential when a farm worker took him to one of her showjumping clinics. She always had a good eye for a horse – and indeed for a buyer – so when she saw us, she said, 'take a look at this' and popped him over a couple of fences. Seeing that I was impressed, she offered me a ride and I realised he was something special. He was part trotter, hardly fashionable breeding, but I was influenced by the fact that Jappeloup, the French horse who won the Olympic gold medal with his amateur rider Pierre Durand, had some trotting blood. Double Take, or Squiff as he was known, felt amazing when he was jumping, with tremendous scope and yet very careful for a young horse, so Carolyn and I thought he was worth a gamble. I didn't want to go to Bill Hall because he'd already done so much for me, but when I mentioned it casually in conversation, he jumped at the chance. He paid serious money, a record price for a showjumper in New Zealand at the time. By the time the Woolrest sponsorship ended, Bill was a good friend, always ready to help on a business or a personal level. When we finally got round to christening Lauren about two years after she was born, Bill and Judy agreed to be her godparents, so that was another bond between us.

During our 1988 trip, we also bought Mayhill, the New Zealand stallion I still have standing with Clissy and Edward Bleekman in Devon, for a relatively modest NZ$3,000. He was owned by Dorothy Johnson, an eccentric woman aged seventy or so with some pretty odd ideas. She used to be my auntie's biology teacher so I'd always known about her. She bred blue healer dogs, grew camellias and advocated comfrey as a cure for any kind of illness or pain. Although she was an intelligent woman, she was totally disorganised and her property at Tirau, twenty miles from Cambridge, was a complete mess. She had a herd of horses, colts, mares and foals, that ran wild over the land, with hardly any fences to keep them apart. Half of them had huge cuts on their legs where they'd got tangled up in the barbed wire. We went to see her one day and spotted a four-year-old unbroken colt running with three others. He was a bright bay and we liked him as soon as we saw him trotting around the field, so we bought him immediately before he could come to any harm. He was by Auk, who was by Sea Bird, so he was smartly bred, but the price tag was quite high for a horse who'd never done anything. Kenny Browne was keen to try him on the racetrack, but Dorothy preferred to sell him to me. We rounded him up and got a headcollar on him without too much difficulty. After a couple of days of handling, we loaded a retired hunter into our truck and went over to pick him up. Carolyn led the hunter up the ramp and Mayhill followed without turning a hair.

We didn't have time to break him in before we left for England so we took him to Dean Phillips, an ex-steeplechase jockey who often worked for Kenny Browne. He did an excellent job and seven weeks later Mayhill was on the plane for England with Double Take. The grooms who travelled with the horses said he was immaculately behaved all the way, always relaxed enough to eat and drink, unlike some of his more experienced companions. A lot had happened to him in a very short time, but his temperament stood up to it amazingly well. As I was going to compete on him, I hadn't planned to keep him as a stallion, but we turned him out with the other horses and he behaved just like a gelding. We had no mares in the yard at the time, so I left well alone. We thought of putting him into training as a hurdler and got as far as taking him over to David Elsworth to see what he thought, but his training as an event horse was going so well that it seemed a pity to risk spoiling him on the track.

On our trips to New Zealand, after I've re-stocked my stable and completed my official duties, we usually manage to snatch a break at my parents' place on the beach, but in 1988 we celebrated the Olympic success with a proper trip. Together with Lizzie and Reggie Purbrick we hired a forty-five-foot launch to cruise in the Bay of Islands. Although Reggie had been an army officer, his military career had not included training in seamanship and I'd never driven anything other than a speedboat, so we weren't entirely confident when we went to hire the launch, not that you'd have known it.

'My dear chap,' said Reggie to the owner, 'I assure you I used to be a Baltic sea captain.' The guy believed him and allowed us to head out to sea on our own, which he could well have regretted.

Five minutes later, Lizzie said, 'You know, I don't like the sea and I don't like boats,' but Reggie and I had the bit between our teeth and there was no turning back. Our basic supplies, wine and beer and a bit of food, saw us through the first evening, but we needed to stock up again the next day. When we came to a lovely big bay, we headed in and dropped anchor a few hundred yards from the shore. There were no other boats there, but what the hell. Lizzie and Reggie and I decided to swim in, while Carolyn rowed with our clothes and money, but it seemed much further once we were in the water. The next thing we saw was the dinghy flip on the shore, with Carolyn trapped in the sand underneath it. I started swimming like fury, a spurt that lasted for about fifty yards before I ran out of steam and reverted to my trusty breaststroke. Carolyn was rescued by someone on the beach, fortunately, because it was another ten minutes before the three of us panted ashore. Our clothes, sunglasses, watches and money had gone missing but we fished around until we found most of the stuff, then walked the mile or so to the village. By the time we got back, the waves were so big that we couldn't launch the dinghy so we had to beg a tow from a speedboat to get back aboard. From then on, we avoided deserted bays, however appealing.

Things improved after that. We knew Ginny was coming out to New Zealand with Mike Huber on an ocean liner at about that time, so we ventured out to sea on the chance of meeting it. The huge ship came into view and Reggie used the boat's radio to ask if Ginny was aboard. Apparently she was, but no one was able to get hold of her before it was out of range. Back at anchor, the guy on the next door boat recognised me and offered us some wonderful scallops he had just harvested from the seabed. Carolyn cooked them up and I don't think I've ever tasted anything so delicious.

There was also the night of the possum barbecue, held on a beach under a tree, an ill-chosen venue as it turned out. We'd gone through all the hassle of loading and unloading the provisions, gathering wood, lighting the fire and getting the cooking underway when a possum appeared. As a joke, I told Lizzie and Reggie that possums had a habit of dropping out of trees and scratching people's eyes out. We must have had a bit too much to drink because they believed me and started throwing stones into the branches. That scared the possum off for about five minutes. Then he was back with his mates, an ever more daring band determined to plunder our dinner. They made such a nuisance of themselves that we had to decamp and eat on the boat.

Reggie and I thought we were right on top of the sailing by this stage, mooring at docks and dropping anchor as if we'd been doing it all our lives, but there were further lessons in store. One night a storm came up as it was getting dark, so we followed a fishing boat into a bay, moored for the night and eventually went to sleep. At about 2 a.m., I heard the fishing boat leave but I just thought, 'Okay, he's going off fishing, what a dreadful job,' and went back to sleep. Two hours later, we awoke with a start to hear the graunch, graunch, graunch of a creature in pain, the sound as it transpired of a boat stranded on rocks by an ebb tide. Reggie and I investigated and found we could step off onto the beach, which wasn't much help. We scrabbled around for the tide tables, then realised that there was nothing we could do except sit it out. Carolyn and Lizzie were shouting, 'You useless bastards,' the usual kind of thing, but in fact there was no harm done, or none that we knew about. When the tide came in, we floated off and took the boat back to its owners. Hopefully it's still afloat.

When I returned to the real world, I had to tackle my tax status, something I'd been putting off for years. As I was a New Zealand resident in Britain on a visitor's visa, no one knew where I should be taxed, so I kept a low profile and chugged along until Bill Hall said I'd better get it sorted out. He was using a high profile firm of accountants for his business at the time, so I consulted them. In the end, it took so much time and money that I've often thought it would have been better to let sleeping dogs lie. Although I only paid 60 per cent of their final bill, it still ran into five figures and there was all the back tax as well, but at the end of it we were a company, M.J. and C.F. Todd.

Basically, our business isn't complex and we were much less busy then than we are now. We've always had a secretary to handle the entries and prepare the figures for the accountant, but over the years Carolyn has taken over most of the administration. I still plan which horses are going to which events and vaguely keep an eye on the accounts, but she does everything else. Somehow the correspondence has increased and multiplied, with ever more demands on my time. Loads of people want to come for work experience or jobs, others want me to make public appearances or answer questionnaires, small things on the whole, but they add up to a lot of work.

I've never had any trouble making money, but however much you make it's never enough where horses are concerned. The bills for feed and entries and vets and travel and wages are endless, so you always have to be on the alert for ways of making a profit. Whether you're good at producing horses or not depends on what you buy and how well you bring them on and we've been pretty successful on both counts, partly because we've always had excellent staff. After Podge's tour was finished, Helen stayed in New Zealand, eventually getting married there. Debbie Cunningham, who'd been with me for a short time while I was down at Mere, joined me at Cholderton before Helen left and stayed for eight years. The responsibility wasn't so great when I was able to supervise the day-to-day running of the yard myself, but we had about fifteen horses by this stage, which meant I was riding more and staying away for competitions more. I needed somebody responsible so I could be sure that everything was done properly while I was away. Helen was very good and so was Debbie.

Towards the end of our time at Cholderton, we had a staff of six. In June 1990, Debby Slinn joined us as head groom, on the recommendation of her previous employers, Lizzie and Reggie. Brook Staples, an Australian rider currently based in England, came as a working pupil in 1992 and they later married, one stable romance that had a happy outcome. Normally we actively discourage affairs because they end in squabbles, but Debby and Brook were not to be deflected. When I'm hiring, I look for people who are self-motivated, responsible, hard-working and good fun. I also get a stream of letters and phone calls from people wanting to come as working pupils. If they want to bring a horse, they pay, otherwise they don't, but they don't stay for long if they're not good riders. So long as they do their job, I don't mind what they do in their spare time, but we do try to keep an eye on them. Mostly we've been lucky, although I did have to get rid of one English boy because he arrived for work drunk on several occasions.

I train the working pupils when I can and they ride in the school with me so I can point them in the right direction, but there's no formal teaching programme. They can see we're very busy and they respond to that, especially when the horses are doing well. In a lean period, everybody gets depressed. Sometimes you get a run of bad luck, just a series of little things, no rhyme nor reason for it, and that gets me down. If the same problem keeps repeating itself, you can do something about it, but the random problems are very frustrating. Normally the younger ones are terrified of me to start with, perhaps because they are in awe of my reputation and nervous about riding in front of me. I try to keep it that way as long as possible, but it doesn't usually take them long to suss me out! They give me a bit of cheek, but as long as they know where to draw the line we get along fine. We have them all up to dinner now and again and sometimes we take them for dinner at the pub. We have had some very funny evenings over the years.

With horses, deals that go wrong are part of the territory. Whenever I've turned down offers of large sums of money for horses – Joint Venture and I'm Bad spring to mind – I've lived to regret it. There's a saying that your first offer is your best, and nowadays I usually accept it. I always get a lot of phone calls offering me horses for sale and I'd advise people to keep trying because most of the ones I buy are through word of mouth. I went the *Horse and Hound* route for a while, but the owners always said their horses were fabulous, then you'd travel miles to look at them and find it not to be true.

Getting back on Podge at the start of each season was like relaxing in a favourite armchair so I missed him when it was time to prepare for the 1989 campaign. He was such a lovely horse to have around and such fun to work with that he left a huge gap in the yard, but we didn't have time to mope around. In any case, I knew I'd see him each year in New Zealand, so I had that to look forward to. I also knew it might be a long time before I had another horse of his standard – if, indeed, I ever did – but I wasn't short of contenders for the top three-day events. I'd celebrated my return from Seoul the year before by taking Peppermint Park and Jued Lad to their first three-star three-day event at Boekelo and they'd finished second and sixth to Scotty on Murphy Himself. A fortnight later, Pedro won Le Lion d'Angers for the second successive year, and he too made a promising debut at three-star level when he came sixth at Saumur the following April.

In March 1989, the Koreans made me an offer for Peppermint Park that even I couldn't refuse and I sold him for a decent profit. He had an excellent record and he turned out to be a great servant for them, with clear rounds in the World Championships in Stockholm in 1990 and the Barcelona Olympics two years later. I was sorry to see him go but I still had four advanced prospects in Bahlua, Jued Lad, Welton Greylag and Pedro.

Although Jued Lad hadn't been jumping very well in the early spring events, he was my only Badminton entry. He did the dressage quite well, given how green he was, but when I jumped him over the practice fence afterwards, he didn't feel quite right. As he was young and promising, but out of form, I thought it would be stupid to go across country so I withdrew him. If I'd only had my own horses to call on, I would have been left without a ride, but Rodney Powell had broken a collarbone the previous weekend and he asked me to stand in for him on The Irishman II. Rodney was a friend and The Irishman was a pretty decent sort of horse, so I found it easy to say yes. He was a real three-day type, a big honest bay, with excellent flatwork and a good jump that was slightly spoilt by a very high head carriage. Rodney took a bit of stick from the British Horse Society for offering him to me, but he wanted The Irishman qualified for the European Championships at Burghley that autumn and he also believed he could win Badminton, so he wasn't about to be persuaded to change his mind.

I went down on the Tuesday to have a cross-country school round Debbie Kent's intermediate course at Doddington Park. I hate schooling over big fences because you're always thinking about what could go wrong rather than getting your blood up to the level required to ride well across country. This was especially true on this occasion, with the Badminton vet's inspection the next afternoon. After I got the feel of The Irishman, he started jumping quite well, but then he stopped dead at a simple chicken coop. It was partly my fault because I was dribbling into it, but a refusal of that kind comes as a bit of a shock. Luckily the fence was out of Rodney's sight, so I didn't have to confess, but I thought, 'Oh God, this is a great warm-up for Badminton.' Despite the setback, the horse clearly knew his job. His size and shape, his attitude and his style of jumping reminded me of Southern Comfort so I thought, 'Yes, I believe I can deal with you.'

The Irishman was well schooled on the flat and he did an excellent dressage test on the first day, but it was on the cross-country that he really excelled and he gave me a sensational ride. He was a great galloper and very fit, so we got it together on the steeplechase and by the time we set off on phase D we'd clicked. Rodney and I are about the same height so The Irishman may have felt at home with me and I certainly didn't feel as if I was riding a strange horse. Apart from steering him and hopefully putting him in the right place at the fences, I encouraged him to go in his usual manner. I took all the direct routes, he answered all the questions and we finished just inside the time in the lead.

I'd never ridden him over a showjump and although he wasn't careless, his style was a little unusual. We did the best we could but he trailed a hind leg and had one down, an expensive mistake which relegated us to third place behind Ginny and Master Craftsman. That was the second time I'd handed her the Badminton Trophy by having a showjump down and although I was delighted to have done so well on a chance ride, I was also a bit peeved because I always hate losing, especially from a winning position.

Throughout the 1989 season, I was assessing the form of my advanced horses with a view to making the best choice for the first-ever World Equestrian Games. They were due to be held in Stockholm in 1990 and, as is customary, there was a practice three-day event on the site the year before. The setting was a municipal park and the roads and tracks wound through the streets and over the bridges that earned the city its nickname, 'Venice of the North'. The Swedish army had a base nearby, so the horses had temporary stables in the barracks. The practice event was held in July, the same time of year as the Games and, although the cross-country course was to be totally replaced for the big competition, it was a good opportunity to get a feeling for the place. Greylag did the best dressage out of my Games possibles and he was a consistent jumper, both cross-country and showjumping, so he was my first choice at that stage. He was a bit of a tricky customer, always very full of himself with a tendency to be on the hot side, but he improved with training. Bahlua, my second choice, was the better jumper, but he didn't have the same potential on the flat because he was so stiff. In these circumstances, it was logical to take Greylag to the preliminary competition and he rewarded my faith in him with a clearcut victory in Stockholm. In September, Bahlua and Jued Lad confirmed my strength in depth by finishing first and third at the Achselschwang three-day event in Germany.

Meanwhile Pedro was making his usual erratic progress through the season. When he went into the lead after the dressage at Luhmühlen in the summer, I felt it could be a banker weekend, but I was counting my chickens too soon. I remember being told with true German precision, 'Zere is a storm coming. At 3 o'clock ze storm will arrive.' My start time for the cross-country was 3 o'clock and, almost to the moment, the forecast came true. I was in the ten-minute box when the heavens opened and I could hardly see as I set off. I remember thinking I should take the long route at the combination in the woods, but when I got there I went straight and Pedro needed no further invitation to run out. It was a crazy decision because I ended up ninth, whereas I could have won with a few time faults, but that's eventing for you. In October, Pedro hit his banker weekend when he redeemed himself by winning at Boekelo, with Greylag third. That gave me a hat-trick of three-star three-day event wins, plus several top placings, in my first season without Podge. In terms of numbers of good results, 1989 was my best year ever.

Sales were good too, and not only for me. In addition to Peppermint Park, who was settling well for his new Korean owners, World Games hopefuls included Tom Thumb, a horse I'd ridden into twelfth place at Saumur in 1988 before selling him on to someone in Spain, and Wilton Fair, who was going well for David O'Connor. When some Swedish owners bought Jued Lad early in 1990, I had four of my ex-horses in the line-up, which did my reputation as a trainer no harm at all.

1989 was also the year that Carolyn got going on the three-day circuit. It had fallen to me to sort Merlin out after the Longleat fiasco in 1987, but he was still more than capable of the odd run out, as he'd proved at his first three-day event at Windsor in 1988. Carolyn was seven months pregnant, so I was riding him. As was his habit, he crossed his jaw ten strides away from a cross-country fence he took exception to and there was nothing I could do about it. Naturally Carolyn was delighted! I'd got him to advanced by the time she took over a week after Lauren's birth. She started on a high by winning a combined training competition at Wilton a few days later, then rode him in intermediate classes that autumn and did her first advanced at Dynes Hall the next spring. She was thrilled because she beat Ginny and Master Craftsman in the dressage, then completed a double clear to finish seventh. She was a nervous wreck at her first three-day event at Windsor that May, but again did brilliantly to come tenth.

She was hooked after that, taking Merlin to two more three-day events that year, Waregem in Belgium, where she again finished tenth, and Le Lion d'Angers, where we joined up with Andrew Nicholson to form a New Zealand team. We'd have won if I hadn't had a rail down in the showjumping so you can imagine how much flak I took for that! At Saumur in 1989, Carolyn moved into the big time with her first three-star three-day event, but Merlin took typical exception to the third fence, a shadowy jump into water, and stopped twice. Carolyn had given up by the third attempt, but he'd decided it was okay so he jumped and she nearly fell off.

My popularity hit a new low at Luhmühlen in early July, just before the World Games. In my capacity as groom, I was supposed to tell Carolyn when to leave the ten-minute box to go to the start of the cross-country, but I fell down on the job. When she finally did go, she circled round waiting for the starter to give the signal until I asked when she should start. He shrugged and said, 'Whenever she likes,' but by that time the clock had been running for a minute. After she finished third, clear but with an extra minute's worth of time penalties, I protested to Patrick Connolly Carew, the head of the Ground Jury. He said, 'Shall we let bygones be bygones and split the difference?' and, like a fool, I agreed. Even with the extra penalties, she could have won the next day if she'd gone clear, but all three leaders had one down so she stayed in third place. We were bitterly disappointed because it was her best chance to date of winning a three-day event, and one that had special memories for us because we'd got engaged there three years earlier.

After Luhmühlen, Merlin had a slight injury to his suspensory ligament, so he didn't come back until Saumur in 1991. Typically, he remembered the water at fence three and stopped again, then refused at some steps near the end of the course. He was always good at steps so Carolyn suspected the injury had recurred. When the vet confirmed her diagnosis, it scuppered our plans for Burghley. For a non-Thoroughbred like Merlin, the problem was not the competition itself, but getting him fit enough to do it. We felt the extra work needed to get him to four-star level would put an unfair strain on him. Our neighbours, the Clarkes, had always wanted him, so we sold him on to them to event at a less demanding level. He gave Louisa Clarke invaluable experience and gave her a thrill by winning the three-day event at Necarne and is now happily retired as Madeleine Lloyd Webber's hack. We also started looking for another horse for Carolyn, but for years we couldn't find anything she loved like Merlin.

When the eventing season draws to a close I normally can't wait to get back to New Zealand, but in 1989 I was offered my first ride under National Hunt rules. The race was the three-mile Colne Valley Amateur Novice Chase run over the Gold Cup fences at Cheltenham on 10 November, and the horse was the New Zealand-bred Robert Henry. His owner said he was a good jumper and an honest plodder and would I like to ride him. I said I'd love to, but I'd have great difficulty making the weight. She said, 'Oh, that doesn't matter.' It's amazing how people imagine that if you can ride a bit in one discipline, you can switch to another, but the reality is that the steeplechase phase of a three-day event bears no relation to riding round Cheltenham. I did air my doubts about my ability to do the job as well as she thought I could, but she was still keen to put me on, so I schooled him and he jumped fine. On the day, we acquitted ourselves reasonably well, albeit lacking a bit of professional style at times. We came home third, behind the easy winner, Shipwright, and the fast finishing Celtic Reserve, who overhauled me on the hill up to the winning post. Okay, so three of the eight runners fell, but the sense of history in riding at Cheltenham and the excitement of jumping at speed against other horses made it one of the greatest thrills of my life.

CHAPTER ELEVEN

CENTRE STAGE

THE NEW ZEALAND PUBLIC HAD NEVER SEEN ME RIDING Charisma since I first took him to England in 1984, so I was delighted to accept an invitation to the Commonwealth Games in Auckland in January 1990. The organisers planned a surprise celebrity opening with me and Peter Snell, the champion middle-distance runner, but they were keen to keep our identities a secret until the last possible moment. We'd spent Christmas in Burford with Bill and Judy Hall and we left Lauren with them when we flew out to New Zealand on 21 January 1990. From the moment we arrived, it was a hush-hush operation. Carolyn and I were smuggled through immigration at the airport, whisked down to Cambridge to stay with my parents and told to lie low.

Pam Bailey had done a great job smartening Podge up for his starring role. On the day, he was kept hidden and I arrived at the stadium in ordinary clothes so the people who saw me wouldn't think I was the mystery guest. I was sneaked off to change into riding clothes, mounted Podge and we were on. It was a truly amazing moment as we came out of near darkness into the glare of the spotlight that tracked us round the stadium. I held the Commonwealth flame aloft as I kept the exuberant Podge at a sedate walk so that he wouldn't rip up the running track. The stands were packed and they cheered us to the echo, as they did Peter when he took over the flame for his circuit. Podge was in his element because he knew that the crowds were there for him, and him alone. I didn't cry, not quite, but it was magical to ride him in front of my countrymen at a time when New Zealand was the centre of the world stage. If ever there was a time for national pride, that was it and I was really choked up. The ceremony ended on a more downbeat note when Carolyn and I were left stranded on the pavement outside the stadium. The limo failed to pick us up and we had to hitch a ride back to the hotel with the actress Susan Hampshire and her husband, who'd come out to watch the Games and support the British team.

It was a momentous occasion and I'm all the more grateful for the invitation because it meant that I saw Pop in the last days before his death. Mumma had died just after the Los Angeles Olympics. One afternoon, she said to Pop, 'I don't feel very well.' Then she lay down on the sofa and drifted off. They'd been married for sixty years so it was very hard on Pop, but he was a strong character and he went on living on his farm on his own. He was always extremely active but early in 1990, he got gangrene in his foot and had to have his leg amputated below the knee, a major operation for a man in his mid-nineties. He didn't know Carolyn and I were coming out, but we dropped in to see him in the hospital in Hamilton as soon as we got off the plane. It was 8.30 in the morning, definitely not visiting hours, and the staff weren't going to let us in but I managed to persuade them. Pop was over the moon, a very emotional moment for both of us. He'd recovered from the operation and he seemed in quite good health, but he said, 'I knew you'd come out,' almost as if he felt it might be the last time he'd see me.

After that, I went every day and wheeled him round in his chair while we reminisced about the past. On a couple of occasions, he got depressed about learning to walk again or being permanently in a wheelchair. He watched the opening ceremony on television and I saw him again the next day. That night, he went into a coma and he died in the morning, with Mum and the family round his bed. He was buried next to Mumma in the cemetery in Cambridge before Carolyn and I flew back to England on 1 February. It was wonderful that I was able to say a proper goodbye to the man who had done so much to foster my love of horses and to help me in every possible way, when I could so easily have been thousands of miles away.

When the Merrill Lynch deal came to an end after the Seoul Olympics, we were without any sponsorship for over a year, but Reggie

Purbrick came to the rescue that January by introducing me to Helmut Rietzner, whom he'd met when he was posted in Germany during his army days. Helmut owned a computer company called Alpha Components and we went to Cliveden, where he always stayed when he was in England, to sign the contract shortly after our return from New Zealand. The deal included a new lorry, a top of the range Mercedes car – we called it the Whale – and £50,000 over the next year. Less than six months later, he discovered that one of his colleagues at Alpha was embezzling money and the sense of betrayal was so great that he took his own life, a terrible tragedy – he was a fantastic man. His executors had to wind up the company so they didn't want to continue with the sponsorship, but they honoured the contract by giving us the lorry outright in lieu of the rest of the money. Sadly the Mercedes had to go back. The lorry was brand new, the first new chassis we'd ever had, and we'd ordered the body to our specifications, with space for six horses and all mod cons, loo, shower and the rest, for ourselves.

Shortly after Helmut's death, Carolyn and I received an offer of sponsorship from Kimberly-Clark through their European chairman, Ron Huggins. He knew I was looking for a sponsor from his brother-in-law, Sam Barr, a well-known breeder of event horses, and he approached me out of the blue. It was a lucrative contract which was for the next two years. The lorry hadn't been delivered by the time Helmut died so it was repainted in the Kimberly-Clark colours, but we retained the ownership of it. Among other things, Kimberly-Clark made Kleenex and Simplicity Freedom sanitary towels, difficult products to promote personally, but we tried. The whole of the back of the lorry was taken up with a huge picture of Carolyn jumping Merlin, with the words, 'Simplicity Freedom'. She hated it!

Later, in November 1991, Kimberly-Clark sponsored the Top of the North Festival meeting at Hexham in aid of the BBC Children in Need Appeal and I was asked to ride in a celebrity flat race over a mile and a half. I duly lined up alongside Lord Oaksey, Jonjo O'Neill and Bob Champion, but my horse, a winning hurdler called Galloway Raider, never showed at any stage. Sometimes Kimberly-Clark had a hospitality tent at events and we had to go to meet their clients, but above all we had to win, ideally starting with the

World Championship at the end of July, 1990.

That was looking increasingly difficult, especially after Greylag was out for the season after pulling a hamstring on the cross-country at Saumur in late April. We presented him for the vet's inspection on the third day, but when he was put in the holding box after the first trot up, we withdrew him before he was to be re-presented. That left Bahlua in pole position for a World Championship ride, even after our first-ever cross-country stop – at the lake – dropped us to nineteenth place at Badminton in early May. My last-chance selection for Stockholm would have been my second Badminton ride, Michaelmas Day, now sound again after several up and down years since damaging a suspensory ligament at Punchestown in 1987. Although he seemed to have been around for ever, Mick was still only twelve when he returned to the big time. He was never a dressage star, but he did a good enough test by his standards to give me hope as he powered away on the anti-clockwise route across the front of the house. For the first time, they had the new water after the Luckington Lane crossings and a filthy pool of sewage it was, as I was soon to discover. He bounced in over the first two hedges and seemed a bit surprised to see the third one but, being Mick, he jumped anyway, stood on an overreach boot as he landed and went down. I got back on and jumped the Vicarage V. Then I thought, 'Sod this,' and pulled up. At Bramham in early June he gave me such a horrible ride that I handed him over to another working pupil, Fredrik Bergendorff, for the rest of his career.

Andrew Nicholson and Andrew Scott were back in the New Zealand team for the World Games, along with Blyth Tait, Vicky Latta and Vaughn Jefferis, three newcomers to Europe who were destined to make a tremendous impact on the sport in the nineties. Blyth had been picked for Gawler, only to have his horse die before the competition started so this was his first chance to ride for his country. Vicky was a practising property lawyer in Auckland who evented as a hobby until she decided to take it up seriously in her late thirties. Her horse, Chief, had been round Gawler with Merran Hain with two falls, but he'd started stopping badly afterwards. That's when Vicky bought him and, through sheer hard work and determination, she got him going brilliantly again. Vaughn comes from Cambridge so I'd known him for a long time. He was about eighteen when I took over Pop's dairy herd in 1982 and he claims that my milking parlour parties were his introduction to the good life. If so, he's certainly built on them since. He'd bought his World Games horse, Enterprise, from Marges Knighton after Seoul so he, too, had a horse with experience at the highest level. The World Championship format allows for a team of four, with the best three scores to count, plus two individual riders. In Stockholm, Blyth, Andrew Nicholson, Andrew Scott and I made the team, with Vicky and Vaughn filling the solo spots.

The Stockholm site was perfect for the inaugural World Equestrian Games because it was so compact. Gawler and Lexington only staged the three-day eventing World Championship, but in Stockholm eventing was one of several equestrian disciplines. This meant that whenever we weren't riding, we could watch the best showjumpers and dressage horses in the world – and indeed the best vaulters and carriage horses, if we'd wished. The Swedes gave us a fine welcome. We stayed in a very comfortable hotel and Carolyn and Lauren joined me for the competition.

The dressage arenas were down by the steeplechase and cross-country courses and the showjumping was in the main stadium near the stables. To get to the dressage, we had to hack through the streets. While I was working Bahlua in the final exercise arena, just before going to do my test, I was cantering him quietly down the long side of the arena when he suddenly pricked his ears and very neatly jumped out over the boards without breaking his rhythm. That was a bit alarming, but it turned out to be a momentary lapse in concentration and he did one of his best tests ever, trying his heart out as always. My new regular dressage trainer, Denmark's Hans Erik Petersen, was thrilled, especially as the marks were better than we could ever have hoped for.

Bahlua was a very fast horse and, as usual, he cruised round the steeplechase well within the time. The urban part of the roads and tracks was very picturesque, on a path round a lake and then back into the park. It seemed as if half the city didn't know there was an event going on, so we had to pick our way through amorous couples, which certainly added interest. The cross-country was a big track and quite twisty, which suited Bahlua because he was very quick and nippy and an outstanding jumper, the perfect combination of bold and careful. It was a very interesting course, quite technical, with lots of variety in the fences. Unlike English courses, it was nearly all man-made and it had to be taken down immediately after the Games because they didn't want permanent jumps in their park.

Bahlua went very well through all the direct routes until we came to the water complex. You jumped in over a big white rail with a drop, took three strides to a bank with a bounce over another white rail back into the water. There were three different options, left, middle or right, but left was the most obvious and we all decided to go that way when we walked the course. I remember telling the others, 'You've got to land over the first part and keep moving forward for the three strides to get on to the bank.' Bahlua landed short after jumping in a little cautiously and, like a fool, I held him for four strides instead of kicking on for three. That meant he arrived on a shortish flat stride, jumped up on the bank and stopped at the rail. I was angry with him because he could have jumped it from there, but I was even angrier with myself for going against my own advice. I jumped the alternative and finished inside the time, but with twenty penalties. Matters didn't improve when one of the New Zealand supporters tapped me on the arm at the finish and said, 'It's time you came home and learned to ride properly.' I felt like telling her in no uncertain terms where she could go, but I restrained myself. Blyth was lucky when Messiah left a leg on the same rail that caught Bahlua and nearly tipped him off, but he got away with it and went into the lead. Andrew and Spinning Rhombus were fourth and I was fifth, so the New Zealand team was in pole position at the end of the speed and endurance day.

The showjumping arena was sand, but sprayed green to look as if it was grass. Bahlua was one of the few horses on which I could almost guarantee a clear round and he duly obliged. Messiah was accurate too so Blyth went clear to confirm his gold medal. Andrew had a fence down but stayed ahead of me to keep fourth place. Without the refusal, I would have taken that elusive World Championship so I was totally annoyed with myself, though delighted that the New Zealand team had won their first-ever team gold medal.

However, the biggest winner, in cash terms at least, was Arabella

Volkers, a friend who still keeps a horse with us today. She works in the City as a merchant banker, but she used to come to Cholderton for riding lessons so she knew what our form was in the run-up to the Games. One day, she went to her bookmakers and asked, 'What odds will you give me on three of the New Zealand team finishing in the top five in the World Games?' They said, '1,000 to 1,' so she put on £500 and won £50,000. She didn't mention her bet or suggest I did the same, sensibly because I would certainly have ridiculed her for even thinking of such a thing. Afterwards, I wish I'd shared her confidence!

The Swedes put on a fairly sober party to mark the end of the three-day event. Then we went to the New Zealand supporters tent, organised as always at the World Championships and the Olympics, by Vicky Glynn, a New Zealander based in Britain. Traditionally it becomes a global watering hole as soon as the corks start popping and on this occasion, we had lots to celebrate. We were joined by the Brazilians and the Poles as well as the Brits and the Irish and anyone else who happened to be around. We had a couple of hours of riotous fun after which everyone left, exhausted by the week's competition, and made their way back to the hotel.

Although Double Take was still too young and inexperienced to compete in Stockholm, he was making quite a name for himself in Britain. Perhaps his greatest – and certainly his quickest – hit in a pretty successful season was in the Area International Trial in Pembrokeshire in August 1990. The first prize was £1,000 which attracted a good field, including the Edgars. It was absolutely bloody miles from Cholderton, much further than I anticipated, and I had to renegotiate my start time after arriving late. We warmed up for ten minutes, jumped a clear round, scorched round the jump off, won the event, picked up the prize money and drove straight off, leaving the other competitors open-mouthed with astonishment.

Back at home, a second mad king awaited me. Alfred the Great had been ridden – and named – by Lizzie, then sold on to another friend, Madeleine Gurdon. As these were the early days of her romance with Andrew Lloyd Webber, Madeleine had other things on her mind so she asked me to take Alfred to the British Championships at Gat-combe. He was a big heavy Irish horse, not a great mover and quite strong, but as honest as the day is long and an excellent jumper. He did well to finish seventh in his first advanced competition, form he confirmed with another seventh at Boekelo in October.

By then, Andrew and Madeleine were engaged and full of plans for the future. Andrew lived at Sydmonton Court near Kingsclere and Madeleine suggested that he should turn the derelict farmyard into a stable complex. Originally it was just to be a few stables, but Andrew never does anything by halves and the plans kept getting bigger and bigger. When he came to Cholderton to see our indoor school with a view to putting one up of his own, he imagined how it could be flooded so that he could stage *The Poseidon Adventure*. His mind was totally theatrical, on a completely different track from ours, but his dream of building an indoor school that would double as a theatre was never realised. Madeleine never got him on a horse and she only needed one or two boxes for her own retired eventers, so she asked us if we'd like to lease the yard and run it independently. At Cholderton, the lack of staff accommodation was always a problem, whereas Sydmonton had a staff flat in the yard, plus a cottage down the road, so there were advantages on that score. Andrew had employed an architect before we got involved, but we had quite a bit of say in the design of the stables. No expense was spared on the building programme so the facilities were excellent. So, after negotiating a deal, we agreed to move in the following spring.

Back in August, I'd received a phone call from Angela Davis, a New Zealander based in England, who'd sold me a horse called Down Under. When I was living in New Zealand, she'd bought a horse of mine which she named Paramount and eventually took to Badminton so our business dealings went back a bit. Now she was offering me the ride on Face the Music, a big chestnut ex-racehorse from New Zealand that she'd taken up to intermediate level. He was a fabulous jumper and she'd done a couple of advanced tracks on him, but he was getting too strong for her. She'd entered for Burghley and she sent him to me on 27 August, which gave me a week to get used to him. I made good use of it, coming third in the advanced at Ickworth on 2 September, before arriving at Burghley for the vet's inspection three days later.

He was quite an uptight horse and his dressage wasn't that good, especially in the early days, so he was midfield at best when the final scores went up. Although our partnership was so new, he gave me a great feel over a fence, jumping cleanly and accurately throughout so that my confidence in him just grew and grew. Our fortunes took an upturn when the organisers measured the cross-country course wrongly so that the optimum time was a minute shorter than it should have been. No one got inside it, but as Face the Music was extremely fast he came closest, which moved him rapidly up the order and into second place. As he was also a superb showjumper, so good he could almost have been a specialist, he went clear on the final day. That meant Mary Thomson had to jump clear to win, but fortunately for me she had a fence down so Face the Music gave me my second Burghley title. It didn't make total amends for my failure in Stockholm, but it was a very nice sweetener, especially as Burghley had been a bit of a jinx for me in my early days.

Angela and her husband, Phil, were returning to New Zealand that autumn so Carolyn and I decided to buy Face the Music, a plan that received a setback when his X-rays revealed a degenerative bone disease in his feet. The vet said it would be unlikely to affect him in the immediate future so we decided to take a chance and at least it put him in our price range. Even so, he was expensive and, as we'd also spent a lot of money on an eventer called Agent Provocateur and a Dutch showjumper called Calvin, we decided we should insure them, something we never normally do. I suppose it was good that they were covered because they all died within a very short period of time, but it seemed such a bad omen that we've never insured a horse since. The showjumper cut himself in a paddock at Sydmonton, just a tiny cut but it severed the tendon just above the knee, and after six months of convalescence he still couldn't bend it, so that was that. Agent Provocateur completed Le Lion d'Angers in 1990 after he came over from New Zealand, but the next season he started falling asleep all over the place. He seemed to be all right when he was competing, but when he was tied to the side of the lorry, he'd sway and jerk awake just before he fell over. One day he was wandering round his stable as if he was drunk so I put him in the field before he hurt himself. The vet diagnosed a brain tumour and he had to be shot. Face the Music's accident at Badminton in

1992 was the most tragic of all.

Another downside of my business is that I often have to take my profit on horses when they're just coming to their prime. That was the case with Peppermint Park and again with Baxter. I loved that horse and I was sad to sell him to Eddy Stibbe in 1990. Equally Eddy loves him and I got as big a kick out of seeing them win a bronze medal in the European Championships in 1993 as if I'd been riding him myself. He was placed at Bramham in 1997 at the age of sixteen, so he's been a wonderful servant for Eddy and, in return, he's had a wonderful home.

By 1990, Pedro was also on the way out, though he still had some way to go before he found the exit. I'd never entered him for Badminton or Burghley because he'd always lacked that last bit of guts and talent to be a top three-day eventer, but he was a consistent winner at any lesser level. After his victory at Boekelo the previous autumn, he was back at Lizzie's for his annual rest when the hounds went through her land. He jumped out of his pen in excitement, but typically failed to clear it and nearly severed his leg at the fetlock, and although he came sound, he was never the same again. Blyth couldn't get on with him, so I took him back, but eventually he started stopping with me as well. At Thirlestane in 1992 he refused at the water, then went to take off at a road crossing with a big ditch in front of it, changed his mind, tried to stop at the last minute and smacked into it head first. I flew over the fence picked myself up, led him back to the boxes and said to Lizzie, 'Take him away.' That was the last time I ever sat on him. Like Any Chance, he went to Steve Gittins for team chasing, which probably suited him infinitely better.

In December 1990, Andrew Lloyd Webber sealed our deal with an invitation to the Australian première of *Phantom of the Opera*, flying us over from Auckland to Melbourne for the occasion. It was a formal black-tie event. The huge party afterwards was attended by lots of celebrities I'd never heard of, but it was a great thrill to be there. On the way out to New Zealand we had a wonderful holiday with Lauren, in the Mutiara Hotel, a huge resort complex on the beach at Penang. The water was beautiful, with coral reefs and coloured fish, perfect for scuba diving, but it was almost too hot to swim in so we mostly stuck to the pool. We only left the hotel once, to buy pottery and other craft items in a neighbouring village, but otherwise we blobbed out for seven days of sheer bliss.

Back in wintry England, I had to assess my prospects of completing a hat-trick at the Barcelona Olympics in 1992. Susan Welman had always hoped to get Greylag to Badminton and 1991 seemed to be his year. He never had good feet and we'd had some problems with corns, so we put new shoes on him a couple of weeks ahead of the event to give them time to settle. He was fine when I rode him in the morning of the vet's inspection, so I didn't even think of trotting him around in advance. If we'd known earlier, we could have got the shoes off and maybe done something but as it was, I trotted him up and he was put in the holding box. He wasn't hopping lame, just slightly off, so I presented him again but he wasn't passed so that was that. He was all right on the grass but on the hard he just felt his feet a bit. It was a bitter blow for all concerned.

Again I was lucky in that I had a last-minute ride on Just An Ace, a young horse who'd been brought on by Robert Lemieux. They'd been to Burghley in 1990, but Robert broke his leg a week before Badminton and passed Ace on to me. He had been getting quite good dressage marks with Robert and I was pleasantly surprised with him, especially after he took all the direct routes across country and got within the time. He was a very careful showjumper so there were no worries on that score and we finished fifth, another good result on a chance ride that seemed to underline my status as Britain's top ambulance chaser! Robert took Ace back after Badminton but in the spring of 1992 he fell out with the owners, Robert and Mary Patrick, and the horse was offered to me. These situations are a bit tricky because you're inevitably accused of nicking someone else's horse, but as Robert and I had been friends for years, I was able to discuss the situation with him. Although he was bitterly disappointed, he knew that if I didn't take the horse, someone else would, so we agreed that I should.

We were due to be up and running at Sydmonton on 1 June, which meant moving during the Windsor three-day event over the last weekend in May. According to Carolyn, the move was hell, but I was otherwise engaged riding Prince Willoughby and Conde d'Seraphim so I got off lightly. Prince Willoughby was another Welman horse, one of the nicest I've ever ridden and very, very talented. He came third in his first three-day event, but he pulled a tendon and although it didn't seem too bad at the time, he never came right. Conde d'Seraphim was also well placed on the third day, but he was a tiny bit footsore after pulling a shoe off on the cross-country and he failed the vet's inspection. He wasn't a good trotter-upper at the best of times and was certainly no worse than he had been on the first day when they'd trotted him up twice, so I gave the head of the Ground Jury, Patrick Connolly Carew, an earful, which didn't go down too well. It was ironic because Willoughby, who had a tendon injury that didn't show, was passed while Conde d'Seraphim, who was a bit footsore, was spun. I'm not sure that they will ever get the formula right for veterinary inspections at three-day events.

Greylag provided some compensation for the Welmans – and, indeed, for me – by winning Burghley in September. He was a very flash mover, but a nervy character who always sweated up on the way to events. If you could get him settled, there weren't many who could do a better dressage and on this occasion, there was only one, David O'Connor on Wilton Fair, who had 45.2 penalties to my 45.4. On the cross-country, Greylag never did himself any favours. He was a very fast horse but he galloped heavily into the ground, and he never relaxed so as to conserve his energy. He wasn't easy on himself or the rider, but he was a good jumper, very straight and bold. The course was difficult that year and I took some of the longer routes, but still finished within the time. When Wilton Fair had a stop at the Trout Hatchery on cross-country day, I was left in the lead, but only by two points from Australia's Greg Watson on his chance ride, Chaka, with the American, Karen Lende, a further 2.2 points behind on Mr Maxwell.

Because Greylag was so tense, he tended to seize up overnight so again I was worried about the vet's inspection. I used one of the new magnetic blankets that relaxes the muscles through electric impulses on his back and that did the trick. When Chaka and Mr Maxwell each knocked a showjump down, I was a fence clear, a great relief because although Greylag was very careful in front, he jumped with a stiff back so he sometimes caught the rails behind. On this occasion, he used up his single life on the ninth fence and clocked up a quarter of a time fault to win by the dangerously slender margin of 1.75. I felt even better for the Welmans than for myself because they'd always been such wonderful supporters over the years, not only of me but of the sport in general. To win one of the big ones was tremendous for them. Mike had lost a leg in the Second World War, but he was always very active until he had a stroke. However, nothing was going to stop him receiving his prize as Greylag's owner, even though he had to struggle into the ring on crutches to get to the ceremony.

For me, it was two Burghleys in a row, after Face the Music's win the year before. He was in the line-up again this time, but they weren't going to measure the course wrongly twice so I knew he'd have to improve his dressage if he was to win another four-star three-day event. He was very tricky on the flat and I spent hours and hours and hours trying to get him to relax and accept the rider, more time than I did on any other horse in the yard. It was frustrating at times because I felt he was making no headway. He'd go all right one day and the next he'd be as bad as ever. He was a fairly hot sort of horse, so he didn't think dressage was particularly for him and it was a constant struggle to show him he was wrong. With his racing background, he had no trouble jumping round Burghley clear within the time and he always went clear showjumping so he finished tenth, a perfectly respectable result that gave me a viable second string for Barcelona.

After three tough days of competition, the winner at Burghley picked up £10,000, quite a contrast to the world record £120,000 prize I'd been jumping for in Calgary the week before. Like Greylag and Face the Music, Double Take was right on track for Barcelona. He was a suspicious sort of horse, perhaps because he'd been broken rather late, but he loved people once he got to know them and he developed into a real character. I was determined to do whatever it took to get him to the Olympics, which meant going to shows turn and turn about with events throughout the season. He made me feel it was all worthwhile by winning or being placed nearly every time he jumped. One of the highlights was the Grand Prix at Hickstead, where he came second, beaten by John Whitaker on Milton, which was about as good as you could get in those days. To make the constant travelling more worthwhile, I had a second horse called Kleenex Boxhill, a good jumper, but not over brave and the girls gave him the rather unflattering nickname Kleenex Snotbox.

I also had a travelling companion in Bruce Goodin, who'd been about five when I worked for his parents during my farmer's apprenticeship days. Back then, he was always nagging me to read him bedtime stories, but in his early twenties he was trying to establish himself on the international showjumping circuit. He decided that the best way to do that was to ship his horse, Reservation, over to Cholderton and base himself with me. We went to Millstreet in Ireland and then to Calgary in early September. Calgary is a fabulous outdoor show, run by Marges and Ron Southern, who are very hospitable people. They have generous sponsors so we were invited and paid for all the way. Double Take was third on each of the first two days which meant I was briefly leading rider of the show. After that, things deteriorated but improved for Bruce, who excelled himself by winning the speed class on the Saturday and coming second in the Grand Prix, the richest competition in the world, on the Sunday.

After Burghley, Bruce and I went to the Paris Masters, a lovely show staged under the Eiffel Tour, and then on a Scandinavian tour to Helsinki, Oslo and Norrköping in Sweden, a very popular circuit with many of the top riders including Irishmen Paul Darragh and Eddie Macken. In Helsinki, Double Take jumped his heart out to win the World Cup Qualifier and came fifth in the Grand Prix, both over huge tracks. The qualifier was very exciting because the top Austrian rider, Hugo Simon, was last to go in the jump off. I'd gone early and quite fast, not flat out but enough to set a target which none of the others had beaten. Hugo intended to put that right so he took Apricot D round at full gallop, only to knock down the very last fence. He'd have won quite comfortably otherwise, but that's showjumping, and I was thrilled to receive a Volvo as part of my prize. John Whitaker has won so many cars that he felt able to give away a Maserati, but no event rider could ever get the chance to be that blasé. The Volvo Estate was a big car and we sold it after a year, but it was amazing to win it. Life on the Scandinavian showjumping circuit is on a different timescale, with the classes starting at 4 p.m. and running on until midnight. We were put up in smart hotels so we'd eat after that, then go clubbing until 2 or 3 a.m. I enjoyed it, but I wouldn't want to do it too often because you tend to drink more on such a nocturnal schedule and after three weeks, I was in need of a serious rest.

The Scandinavian triumph generated quite a lot of interest in Double Take, including a huge offer through an agent. I don't know how firm it was or if the cash was really on the table, but the Germans and the Americans had a lot of money to spend on showjumpers at that time. After my two eventing victories, my dream was to win a medal in the showjumping, so Double Take was definitely not for sale. As I knew I could rely on Bill Hall's unswerving support, I never even checked the offer out. With hindsight, probably I should have done, but we had spent the past three years planning to go to the Olympics, and at this stage it looked as if I had a very real chance of making that dream a reality.

CHAPTER TWELVE
DOUBLE TROUBLE

As the 1992 season got into gear, my main preoccupation was dividing my time between eventing and showjumping so as to give myself the best possible Olympic shot in both disciplines. After his Burghley win, Greylag was my obvious choice for the three-day event because he had the form and the experience. However, the scorching Mediterranean weather in late July would favour a Thoroughbred like Face the Music, so I was keeping my options open. Given Greylag's record of unsoundness, I felt it was safer for him to miss Badminton that spring, but Face the Music was in good form and he needed the experience at that level so I entered him, along with Alfred the Great. Madeleine Lloyd Webber was pregnant with the first of her three children so Alfred, or Clive as we called him, was up for sale. Several people had tried him and one had got as far as vetting him, but he failed so he ended up going to Badminton with me.

Face the Music did his dressage very early on the first day, an advantage for an excitable horse as there are virtually no spectators. He didn't do a winning test, but he was calmer and much more rideable, which raised my hopes for the future. Alfred was always very steady and he did his best, but he didn't have the paces to be a star. Neither of them were at the head of the leader board, but I had no cause for complaint as we planned the cross-country.

That year the course went in a clockwise direction, starting out through Huntsman's Close and the Quarry before heading back to the Lake, the Vicarage Ditch fences and the turn for home. The fence we were all worried about was the arrowhead over the Vicarage Ditch. We'd jumped it in the other direction the year before without difficulty, but this time the ground was very slippery after sudden heavy rain on a hard surface. I'd given the fence a lot of thought and I slightly favoured the longer route, but I still hadn't finally decided as I made my approach. As I was among the first to go, I had no way of knowing how it was jumping, but Face the Music was jumping so confidently that I thought, 'Bugger it, don't be such a wimp,' and turned him into the point of the arrow.

As I did so, I saw some skid marks veering away from the arrowhead, as if a horse had run out, and I thought, 'God, it's slippery,' but by then I was committed. Maybe Face the Music saw them too because in the very last stride, he looked a little bit and moved off his line, not a violent swerve, just a slight adjustment, and we were gone. As he took off, he slipped on the edge of the ditch, crashed into the rail and flipped over the fence. Somehow he ended up trapped underneath the rail on the other side. I was thrown off and as I leapt up to grab him, I remember the horror of seeing the bone sticking out of his leg above the knee. In shock, I turned and yelled at the fence judge, 'Get the vet. He's broken his leg.' He managed to get back on his feet, but he was still trapped behind the rails. He just stood there with his leg swinging, but very quietly, thank God, because it took twenty minutes for the vet to come. It was the most awful time of my life. I was thinking, 'If only I'd gone the long way. If, if, if ... why, why, why ...' especially as it had been a last moment decision to take the direct route. I've had horses die, but never one breaking a leg in a competition and I discovered that it does strange things to you. I just stood there saying sorry to the horse and trying to comfort him until the vet arrived. Then a friend of the fence judge drove me back to the stables before they shot him.

I got a cup of tea and sat outside the stable with Carolyn, feeling numb. In those situations, you don't want to see anyone because they have to say how sorry they are and you have to try to respond. I did hear that two more horses had died – one was Karen Lende's Mr Maxwell, who'd been third to Greylag at Burghley the year before – but the accidents were at different points on the course and there was no suggestion of stopping the competition, though they did take the direct route at the arrowhead out after Face the Music's death. I didn't feel I had to ride Clive, but at no point did I consider withdrawing him. From the day you first learn to ride, people say, 'If you have a fall, you get straight back on and continue,' so the principle of not quitting is deeply engrained. Clive was a very good jumper, but it was a long lonely ride round the roads and tracks mulling over what had happened and wondering how I'd cope with the cross-country.

It had been a last-minute decision to take Clive and he was a stuffy sort of horse, not a Thoroughbred and difficult to get three-day event fit, so I knew the time would be difficult. He liked to take a bit of a hold at the start, trying to pretend he could go fast when he couldn't, but he jumped fabulously through the Lake and onto the Luckington Lane loop three-quarters of the way round the course. Although I didn't push him, he kept galloping at his own speed and he was up to the mark on time as he jumped Centre Walk. At that point he started to feel a bit tired, so I decided against going the direct way over the acute angle at the second Luckington Lane crossing. On the long alternative route, he slowed down on me going in and I thought I'd had it, but I gave him a kick and somehow he heaved himself over the rail and crashed through the hedges. I said to myself, 'Oh God, I'm going to have to pull up,' but I let him canter for a few strides, then clucked at him and gave him a bit of a kick and he took off again. He kept chugging on and eventually I nursed him home, not within the time but not too far off it. He was one of the bravest horses I've ever ridden, obviously very tired but honest and game to the last. I was really chuffed that I'd done it, both for him and for me. Afterwards I had the unpleasant task of talking about the accident to the press, but as there was an alternative at the fence where Face the Music died, I didn't feel I had any cause for complaint against the organisers. I'd been quite abusive to the poor fence judge about waiting so long for the vet, but there had been a genuine mishap of some kind and Hugh Thomas, the director of Badminton, apologised to me afterwards.

Dear old Clive saved that day, and indeed the next one. Showjumping was never his forté and I didn't know how tired he'd be, but he came out perkier than ever, jumped a lovely clear round and finished fifth. He was a really sweet horse and quiet enough for me to ride around with four-year-old Lauren on the front of the saddle. That was the clinching factor for Mike Friedlander, a middle-aged American buyer who wanted a good jumper to do some pre-novice events. As their classification goes on the rider rather than the horse, Alfred was eligible for pre-novice, despite his fifth at Badminton. Mike had just had a pacemaker fitted so he was particularly impressed by the sight of me trotting and cantering over small jumps on a loose rein with Lauren up front. He said he wasn't supposed to get excited, but when we went out hacking to try the horse, he gave Clive a hefty kick and went off at full gallop. I thought, 'Heavens, his heart will never stand it,' but it did and the sale was completed. I saw Mike sometime later and he said he'd had to give up eventing because Alfred had got too keen. It seems a deer jumped out in front of him and he jumped four five-foot post-and-rails before Mike could stop him.

After Face the Music died, Greylag was my number one for Barcelona, with Mayhill in reserve. Mayhill had been placed at Gatcombe the previous year and in his first three star three-day event at Saumur that spring, but the luxury of having a choice ended at the final one-day trial at Althorp. He was a bit of an idle bugger and he flopped off the lorry, stepped sideways and sliced his back leg open on the edge of the ramp. Like an idiot, the groom had taken his boots off before she led him out, but what can you say? After that, it was Greylag or nothing, which wasn't very reassuring. He had odd feet, with the inside of one foot lower than the outside rim, and they were getting progressively worse, despite our best efforts to keep them level with wedged shoes. He competed at Brigstock and Belton one-day events that spring, but the doubts kept coming. I did a lot of fast work because I knew that if he couldn't stand up to training at home, there was no point in taking him to Barcelona. Sydmonton was next door to Ian Balding's racing stable at Kingsclere and he allowed me onto his best grass gallop for my final trial. The turf was hundreds of years old and so beautifully prepared that it was like galloping on air, but Ian was pretty selective about using it for his own horses, so I was deeply grateful for his kindness.

A more official element in the preparation was random drug testing, of both horses and riders. I well remember the afternoon on which the man from the New Zealand Sports Federation turned up at Sydmonton to take a urine sample. He gave me a bottle and I headed for the loo. When I got to the door he was right behind me, so I said, 'Do you mind?'

'Sorry,' he replied, 'but I have to be there when you do it.' When I started to fill the bottle, he was trying to peer over my shoulder which was difficult for him, given my height. I felt obliged to say, 'Hey, is this absolutely necessary?'

'I have to see you actually doing it,' he reiterated, at which point the flow dried up. It took two hours of him watching me drinking water and tea before I was able to produce enough urine for the sample.

Bill Hall died just before Barcelona, a tragedy I had great difficulty coming to terms with, especially as he was only in his early fifties. He'd developed a cancerous tumour on the brain two years earlier, even before he and Judy came to live near Oxford. The doctors said it was inoperable so he had chemotherapy, then went to India to try faith healing. The cancer went into remission and he wrote a book about his experiences, but it came back and he died shortly afterwards. Judy bravely came to Spain with us to watch Double Take, but we were hardly in the mood for festivities. Originally, I'd been terrified of meeting Bill to talk about the Woolrest sponsorship, perhaps because I needed it so much, but he put me at ease immediately and made it clear that he was a man of his word. There was no messing about with Bill: a deal was a deal and it was sealed with a handshake. Over the years, I always knew he was there for me, but I didn't ask too often and he appreciated that. He was one of life's great characters, a bon viveur, convivial and extrovert among friends and we shared a sense of humour. After I married Carolyn, we got on very well as a foursome and Judy still calls us whenever she touches base from her flittings around the world. I realised how much I was affected by Bill's death when one of the New Zealand reporters came up to me and said, 'Do you wish Bill Hall had been here to see his horse?' I don't normally crack under the strain, but I just burst into tears and walked away. The sadness of his death and the stress of the three-day event and the showjumping were too much for me.

The New Zealand team from Stockholm, Blyth, Vicky, Andrew Nicholson and myself, was unchanged for Barcelona and, as world champions, we were obviously among the favourites. Our horses travelled out to Spain by road, accompanied by Wally Niederer, our ever faithful vet. When we arrived, we met up with our equally loyal chef d'équipe, Dennis Pain, who was a high court judge in his spare time. On his first eventing assignment at Gawler, Tinks and Trudy nicknamed him Auntie because he was so good at finding out all the things we needed to know and the name had stuck.

After a lot of discussion as to who should carry the flag at the opening ceremony, the New Zealand Olympic Federation asked me to do it. Back home, they'd held a competition to design a team uniform and the winner had come up with a Spanish-style outfit, with shiny black trousers, frilly white shirt, braces and a sombrero hat. It looked quite smart, but it wasn't the sort of thing you could ever wear again. Carrying the flag was a great honour, but the sad part is that the athletes miss out on most of the ceremony because they're corralled in another arena until its their turn to march into the stadium. In Barcelona, it was particularly galling not to see the opening moment because the guy who shot the arrow to light the Olympic flame was so spectacular. By 1992, there were quite a few familiar faces in the crowd, but of course there are thousands of newcomers so it's not exactly an old pals' reunion. The atmosphere is great because everyone is so relieved to have got there, and there's a celebration once everyone is assembled in the stadium but it's all over too soon.

By now the New Zealand Horse Society had enough money to hire accommodation for us in the mountains near the stables, fortunately as it turned out because the drivers of the courtesy cars were mostly from out of town. As they didn't know where to go any better than we did, we'd usually end up in the wrong place at the wrong time. I had to go in and out more than the other riders because Double Take was stabled at the Polo Club in the city so it was particularly irritating for me. Carolyn and Judy stayed in the centre of Barcelona in an apartment owned by Salvador Fabrigas, a Spanish friend we'd met at La Granja. His father was a Grand Prix racer and a big game hunter, so you were confronted with tables made out of elephant's feet and lampstands made out of antelope's legs the moment you walked through the door. It was all a bit macabre, but they also had beautiful furniture and paintings.

The house that Sante found for us in the mountains was a refuge from the oppressive heat of the city. The horses were in permanent stables set into a hillside on two levels overlooking the woods. Once again, the cross-country was built on a golf course, this time one that was attached to a country club with a swimming pool and tennis courts. We'd work the horses in the early morning cool, then blob out through the heat of the day, which gave us all a chance to catch up with the gossip.

Germany's Wolfgang Feld is one of the most imaginative designers and he built a beautiful cross-country course, not with any particular theme but with a wide variety of fences. I was happy with it because I thought it would suit Greylag, but it was full length and the weather was hotter than in either Los Angeles or Seoul.

The Fédération Equestrian Internationale (FEI) was increasingly aware of the dangers of holding the speed and endurance phase in excessively high temperatures, but the riders were worried that the onus was still on them to make sure their horses weren't distressed. In the bad old days, we would have had no hope of imposing changes on an Olympic competition, but we were gradually finding a voice in a sport that had traditionally been run exclusively by the FEI. Shortly before Barcelona, Robert Lemieux and some of the other leading riders set up the International Event Riders' Association (IERA). I had the honour to be the first chairman.

The organisation was still in its infancy, but the time had come to put it to the test and the ball was in my court. At the chef d'équipe's meeting, the organisers started waffling on as usual, so I stood up and said, 'Look, it's not fair to put the whole responsibility on the riders. In an Olympic Games, no one who is in a position to win is going to canter round to save their horse. It's up to you to make the competition easier on the horses, either by shortening the course or by extending the time.' In the end, they reduced the roads and tracks, but more importantly my protest as the riders' representative made them aware that it was up to them as well as us to look after the sport. They're very quick to jump on us when things go wrong, but they have responsibilities too.

At the start of the Games, we were all invited to the New Zealand official party, a general thank you for the people who'd made all the team arrangements at the Barcelona end. Being typical equestrians, we were the last to arrive and the last to leave. As the drink flowed, we got chatting to the Maori concert party who'd been invited to entertain the guests and they agreed to come out to our place for a barbecue. The British riders were grounded before the competition so they missed out, but everyone else danced and sang to the Maori guitars far into the night.

The three-day event dressage was held in the same place as the cross-country and Greylag obliged with a lovely test, not quite in the lead, but not far off it. He was a fabulous mover and he managed to contain himself to produce one of his best tests ever. His trotwork was spectacular and I think he would have been Podge's equal on the flat if he'd stayed sound for another year or so. Susan Welman came out to see him and we were both delighted with his test. I wasn't thinking, 'Great, now I'll win three in a row,' but as Greylag was an excellent cross-country horse and a reasonable showjumper, I had no reason not to be cautiously optimistic.

Of course, there was always the niggle about his soundness, but I was happy with him and Wally was happy with him as we set off on phase A. The going on the steeplechase was perfect and he was out of the gate at full gallop, pulling my arms out while I tried to steady him without interfering too much. About half-way round, he landed over a fence and suddenly he dropped the bit and lost his action. At the end of the steeplechase when I pulled up, he was definitely not sound. I said to Wally, 'I don't like this.' Wally's advice was to 'trot on for a bit and see if he comes out of it'. It didn't get any worse, but it didn't get any better either, so we had to pull him out at the checkpoint half-way round phase C, a good decision because he'd strained a ligament in his pastern. Although he was close to a full Thoroughbred, he put excessive strain on himself when he galloped by ripping in so strongly and the ligament just went twang. With hindsight, I think I should have backed off him a bit once we arrived in Barcelona, rather than trying so hard to prove that he was sound, but that might not have worked either.

You look forward to the cross-country with a mixture of dread and excitement but when you know you're not going to do it there is a huge sense of disappointment. As I led Greylag away, there was a dreadful feeling of letting everyone down, Susan and Michael, the team and the New Zealand supporters, the whole country really because the Olympics are the one time you become very nationalistic. Although Greylag was uncomfortable rather than in great distress, I was worried that I'd damaged him permanently. When he did come sound, he became a dressage horse because we thought he wouldn't stand up to the strain of any more eventing.

The disappointment of missing out on my gold medal hat-trick was minor by comparison with the overall sense of anti-climax. People who don't know a lot about horses don't realise how much there is to go wrong. They thought that if I'd won twice in a row, there was no reason I wouldn't win again, so some of the supporters were a bit shellshocked when they learned I'd retired. However, Blyth with Messiah and Andrew with Spinning Rhombus had done New Zealand proud with fast clear rounds. Poor Vicky was given a technical refusal when the judges said that Chief had put one foot out of the penalty zone on the approach to the water. It was a dodgy decision because there was some question about whether the zone was properly marked, but the twenty penalties cost her an individual medal. Even so, we were in the team gold-medal position, with a six-fence cushion between us and the Australians in second place.

The next day, Blyth and Vicky went clear, but Spinning Rhombus created total chaos with nine showjumps down. We felt very badly for Andrew because the horse didn't try one inch. He was very tired from the cross-country and the fences were uniformally blue and grey, which meant that there was nothing to catch the eye. Andrew did all he could to help but once Spinning Rhombus started hitting the fences things spiralled out of control and the team dropped to third. At Seoul, Mark Phillips got his team silver medal although he didn't finish, but at Barcelona individuals who didn't finish didn't receive team medals, so I missed out. I didn't mind because I didn't feel I deserved one and, with the showjumping slated to start the next day, I had little time or appetite for celebration.

Double Take was in great shape physically, but he hadn't been jumping as well as he had the previous year. He was a fabulous character, a big cheeky kid, with great big ears and great big eyes. He'd nuzzle up to you in the stable, slip in a quick nip, then turn round with his ears pricked as if to say, 'What me? No way.' He was very small, just under 16hh like Podge, and he tried his heart out, but you had to be careful because he wanted to please so much that he was easily rattled. In 1992, he wasn't getting things dreadfully wrong – he was placed in several classes at Windsor and he won the big Area International Trial at Bramham – but he wasn't at his very best. I found it quite difficult chopping and changing between showjumping and eventing. It's like playing tennis and squash, both racquet and ball games but very different technically. In pure showjumping, you have to be much more accurate because the tests involved are so much more complex, particularly at Olympic level. In order to jump huge combinations and rows of fences with related distances, you need a very careful horse with a lot of scope, which Double Take was, and he has to be in top form, which he wasn't.

The Barcelona courses were imaginative and modern, with random splashes of paint rather than traditional striped poles, but they were big. Harvey Wilson and Maurice Beaston were on the New Zealand team again, with Bruce Goodin as the rookie. On the first day of the competition proper, there was a horrendous storm while I was warming up and they had to call a halt until the rain stopped. When I went in shortly after they resumed, the arena was half flooded, which certainly didn't help. After the two rounds of the team competition, I was the best of the New Zealanders and, as in Seoul, I was the sole qualifier for the individual event a few days later. This time I didn't make the final round, rather to my relief because the course was enormous and Double Take was still a relatively inexperienced eight-year-old. He didn't jump badly, but you can't win every competition and he was never going well enough to win that one.

We'd always planned to sell him after the Olympics and Bill's executors needed to settle his affairs, so Double Take went on the market as soon as we got back to England. I didn't have much time for showjumping that autumn so I got Nick Skelton to ride him in the hope that he'd up his price by winning some big classes. He didn't go well for Nick, so I took him back and we eventually sold him to the Italian Federation in partnership with Arnaldo Arrioldi. Double Take left Sydmonton on 23 July 1993, a very sad day for me because he was always one of my favourites, but Arnaldo is a nice guy with a lovely property and an English groom. I saw them jumping on the Italian team at the Atlanta Olympics, so I know the horse has a good home and that we couldn't have done any better for him.

The deal was negotiated through the agent Louise Tompkins, as we had had some dealings with her earlier. However, some months after the sale, we had a visit from the VAT inspectors who went through all our accounts. It seems that Louise was being investigated with regard to VAT transactions on deals she had done, but thankfully all our affairs were in order because we'd had the huge sort out a couple of years earlier, so it was all cleared up eventually, but the story didn't end there.

Two years later I arrived at Pratoni outside Rome for the 1995 European Championships to be greeted by plain clothes police. They seemed very friendly at first, but soon it became clear that they meant business. They wanted to interview me about the sale of Double Take, at my convenience of course, but if I tried to leave the country without talking to them, they'd arrest me. They strongly recommended that I have a lawyer to represent me. A friend of a friend, who is a lawyer in Rome, said that she didn't feel qualified to represent me because she's not an expert in criminal law. That got me seriously worried. I wondered what kind of criminal case I might be involved with.

I arranged to go to the police station in Rome with a lawyer on my way home at the end of the Championships. What was normally a twenty-minute drive took two hours, so I arrived at 10 o'clock at night, hardly the best preparation for the four-hour interrogation that followed – and I do mean interrogation. The police were conducting an investigation into the affairs of the Italian Equestrian Federation following accusations of corruption. Their line was that we'd got a lot more money for Double Take than we claimed and that we'd secured the sale by paying a backhander to the Federation officials, none of which was substantiated. Double Take was only one of several horses being investigated that had been bought by the Italian Federation through Louise Tompkins. They had records of everything, my bank details, tax records, where the money had gone. However, everything I told them tied in with the evidence they already had, so they had to let me go. The lawyer sat there making notes, then sent me a bill for £7,000 for four hours of not very strenuous work. I eventually settled for £2,500. Louise Tompkins would definitely have been off my Christmas card list from then on, had she not been off it already.

After the disappointments of Barcelona, the highlights of a rather thin autumn season were Down Under's seventh at Boekelo and General Knowledge's sixth at Pau. The dear old General was one of my real character horses, one-eyed after an accident in Katie Monahan's showjumping yard in America, but a genuine jack of all trades. He was bred in Ireland by the Firestones, part of the Johnson & Johnson Corporation, who had a large involvement in racing. As a grandson of Secretariat, his credentials were impeccable and he was only just short of top class on the flat in Ireland and France. When he went jumping, he won big steeplechases in France and America before going showjumping with Katie, but he wasn't really careful enough so she gave him to Marie Courrèges, the daughter of the avant garde sixties designer. Marie evented him in France, but he was too strong for her so she gave him to me and I took him quite quickly from novice to advanced. He was just about ready to do his first three-star three-day event when his stifle started locking up. That put an end to his eventing career so I gave him to Reggie Purbrick as a hunter – the Colonel on the General – and he's still going strong.

In other respects, the months after Barcelona were a time for taking stock of our position on several fronts. Back in 1987, we'd bought a fifty-acre farm in New Zealand as a base for our racehorses, but we'd sold it three years later. A bigger farm was at the top of our shopping list at the end of 1991, but we hadn't been able to find anything we really liked during our annual visit. When news of a suitable property reached us the next May, Carolyn flew out for six days to look it over and signed for it on the spot, so we were now the owners of a 500 acre hill farm in Whitehall. On a clear day, we had spectacular views of Mt Ruapehu 200 miles away. We completed the deal in early January 1993, and stocked it with cattle and 1,000 breeding ewes under the supervision of our manager, Stephen Harper, but with Dad as overseer. There was a small water bore when we arrived, but Dad had to have it drilled deeper to increase the flow. We also had to install and fill thirty water troughs to supplement the streams so that the stock would have enough to drink. In the early days, we had problems with the water drying up and the cattle fouling the troughs, a downer for Dad because he had to clean them out.

Back in Britain, we were living in a large five-bedroomed farmhouse with a swimming pool on the Lloyd Webber estate, but we knew our time was running out. As Andrew and Madeleine were now heavily involved in racing, they were gradually taking over the stables at a time when I needed as many new horses as possible. Over the last two years I'd lost or sold all my best horses and I urgently needed replacements, so 1993 was set to be a period of regeneration, and in more ways than one. From my point of view, by far the best news to come out of Barcelona was that Carolyn was pregnant. One way or another, it was time to move on.

CHAPTER THIRTEEN
FAIRYTALES DO COME TRUE

W E HADN'T PLANNED SUCH A BIG GAP BETWEEN OUR children, but Carolyn had had another miscarriage, at quite an early stage this time. James was placenta praevia, which sometimes means the mother has to lie in bed for weeks without moving. Carolyn refused to do that, but she didn't feel she could ride, as she had when she was carrying Lauren. A caesarean birth is like an appointment at the dentist: 'You will be at Basingstoke Hospital at 9 a.m. on 20 April 1993, and the baby will arrive soon afterwards.' I was allowed into the operating theatre for the birth, so I saw the baby first. We didn't know the sex in advance, but Carolyn always said she was expecting a boy because this pregnancy was so different. I had a few minutes of panic that something might be going wrong when a senior nurse took the child away and started doing things to him, but it was only that the trainee nurse wasn't quite getting it right. Then I just waited until Carolyn came round so we could share the good news.

If the baby was a boy, he was always going to be called James, my middle name and my grandfather's first name. Mind you, Pop was always called Ted rather than James or Jim, but James was named in memory of him. Maria St Just said, 'Darlings, you must call him Wilbury,' after her manor house near Cholderton, but we decided to stick to our original plan. As Lauren was nearly five when James was born, she's always thought of him as her baby and has mothered him right from the start. She changed his nappies and fed him, more than you could hope for, so effectively we had a built in nanny. They don't fight much, perhaps because of the age gap, and they're quite different in character. Lauren can sometimes be almost hyperactive, a whirlwind that's there one minute and gone the next, but she doesn't always think what she's doing. James was more cuddly as a baby and he's turned into a calmer child, but then you have more of an idea how to cope the second time around.

With two children to consider, it wasn't really viable to combine eventing and showjumping at the highest level, so I decided not to replace Double Take after he was sold to the Italians. I was getting fed up with things not working out and I realised that trying to compete on the showjumping circuit was having a bad effect on my event horses. Because I was never at home working them, none of them was going in exactly the way I wanted and they didn't deliver when it really mattered. In eventing, there's no hiding place: you have to do the basic training yourself. The maximum number of horses I can ride in a day is eight or possibly ten for forty minutes each, but I try to restrict myself to six or seven in the interests of sanity. I do nearly all the schooling on the flat and over jumps, but I allow my best students, Brook Staples, Fred Bergendorff and the young British rider, Nick Campbell, for example, to ride the novice horses under my supervision. Although I'm an equal opportunities employer and the girls who've worked for me have been just as talented as the boys, I feel it's sensible to put up boys because there is less change in weight and strength when I get back in the saddle.

In that spring, Peder Frederickson, who is possibly the most talented rider I've ever employed, came to us from Lars Sederholm's yard at Waterstock. He'd represented Sweden at Barcelona on a mare called Hilly Trip and done very well. In the two years he was with us, he competed regularly on my best horses including Mayhill and, on one occasion, Just an Ace, but he was never quite sure how committed he was to the sport. He is as gifted as a graphic designer as he is as a horseman, but, as is often the case with people with loads of natural ability, he's not keen to knuckle down to either discipline. After he left us, Peder set up his own yard, but as yet he's not realised his full potential as an event rider and is now showjumping full time. You certainly need talent to be a champion, but you're never going to make it without drive and an endless capacity for hard work.

With sixteen or seventeen horses permanently in training, what has always been a full time job has turned into a round the clock endurance test throughout the eventing season. The more horses you have, the more organisation there is and the more complicated the entries become. When you're not actually riding, there's paperwork, bills, vets, correspondence, requests for this and that. It is literally endless. Inevitably, I have to compete every weekend and a lot of weekdays from March to October. There used to be a break in July, but that's gone now and sometimes I long to spend a weekend at home and do normal things like mow the lawn or go to the movies with the kids. We've got to the stage where we make ourselves have one day off a week to do something as a family, but even that doesn't always work because it's very hard to divorce yourself from the horses, especially if there's any kind of crisis. You can never shut the office, lock the door and walk away. As for Sunday lunch, forget it. At best, it's a burger snatched at the event.

As James was born four weeks before Badminton, Carolyn was well enough to join me there, though it turned out not to be one of my best years. I had two rides, Just an Ace, who'd come back to me in February after his owners had a disagreement with Robert Lemieux, and Kinvarra, having his final shot at the big time while Sante was busy setting up an airline in South America for Iberia. Just an Ace was a suspicious horse, but a great competitor, difficult on the flat and not the fastest thing on four legs, but a very good and careful jumper. He was by Just a Monarch, but he had a bit of warm blood on his mother's side which probably made him very one-paced so he always had to gallop flat out to make the time. That always puts extra strain on a horse, but he was a proven horse and he'd been going well in the one-day events leading up to Badminton. As Kinvarra was also in form, I was cautiously optimistic, especially after they both did reasonably competitive dressage tests.

It was an anti-clockwise year for the cross-country so I galloped Kinvarra across the front of the house and down towards the first real test, the Mitsubishi M's double of corners at the fourth. I was a little bit wrong to it and the bloody old thing just ducked out at the last

minute – very annoying because he jumped everything else impeccably. At times like that I found his method of making his own
arrangements, perfected over years with Sante, rather trying.

Then it was Ace's turn and he cruised round, making it feel so easy
until we reached the last real test, the quarry, near the end of the
course. You had to trot over the edge of the bank to a vertical rail at
the bottom and either he misjudged it or I didn't set him up enough,
because he clipped the top and somersaulted. Ace got up and trotted
off and I picked myself up and ran after him but he'd rolled right over
me, so I had to be passed by the doctor before I could go on. You can
see me on the television coverage running up and down on the spot
to prove my fitness, then vaulting back into the saddle and away. I
felt all right at the time, but even before I reached the finish I was a
bit shaky and that night I was so stiff I couldn't turn over in bed. Ace
was all right for the showjumping, but poor old Kinvarra tweaked a
tendon and could not be presented for the final day, so we sent him
off to Moisie Barton for a long recuperation and she's been hunting
him ever since.

Apart from James's birth, the spring of 1993 was one of my all time
lows. The first disaster came in March when Conde d'Seraphim
cracked his stifle at Peper Harrow and had to be put down. Then
Down Under, who was going really well through the spring, pierced
his sole at Compiègne. I was two-thirds of the way round the cross-
country and going very well, when I heard the shoe come loose, I
looked down and saw that it was half off. I was hoping it would fly
off altogether, but it didn't. Two fences from home, I pulled up and
discovered that it had twisted round so that two of the nails and the
toe clip were embedded in his foot. I pulled the shoe off and blood
poured out of his foot, so we had to limp sadly back to the stables.

Vlad the Impaler was the third of Lizzie's mad kings to come to
me, but there was no way I was going to ride a horse with a name
like that so I changed it to Cheseldyne. He was talented enough to
come third at Chantilly in 1993, but he wasn't very sound so he too
was dispatched to the hunting field. Then there was Kilcullen Bay, a
decent horse, but very, very difficult on the flat and very strong, even
more so than Michaelmas Day. Antonia Grey, his previous rider,

couldn't hold him so he went to Julian Trevor Roper and then came to me for a time but was eventually sold to the Japanese. Presumably they couldn't hold him either because he's now a contender for the British team with his new rider, John Paul Sheffield.

Worst of all, I had The Visionary, an inappropriate name if ever there was one because I had more falls off him in twelve months than I've ever had off any other horse. He was owned by Mike and Mary Rose Cooney, and previously ridden by Katy Hill, with minimum success and maximum terror. After one hair-raising ride too many, she sent him to me and I took him on at my peril. His peak was coming fourth at the Falsterbo three-day event in Sweden in July 1994, but he was seriously unathletic and not very genuine, as I well remember from Blenheim a couple of months later. He was going so unexpectedly well that I decided not to risk the direct route at one of the last fences. Instead, I presented him with the easy alternative and the swine ran out. I'd gone on riding him for so long because his owners were so nice, but after Blenheim I told them I thought we should sell him. One of Mary Rose's friends burst into tears and said, 'You can't sell dear Henry,' but eventually I managed to persuade them that it was in everyone's best interest.

The Cooneys have a Toyota dealership, so they sponsor our car and they also run Safilo Eyewear, which Carolyn and I promote. Like the Welmans, though, they are primarily owners who have become good friends, so we were desperate to find them a better horse. After 'Bad Vision' went, I bought them a great big lump of a thing called Blue Bay, which turned out to be another disaster. How I could have thought he was of sufficient quality I can't imagine, but I managed to sell him in a part-exchange.

Whenever we go to New Zealand, Carolyn and I scour the country for likely prospects. I like New Zealand horses because they've got a tougher approach and I find that bit of racing as youngsters gets their heads in order and makes them much more balanced. Mind you, it's becoming harder and harder to find anything worthwhile because more people are out there looking; primarily Americans, Dutch, Italians and Koreans. In addition, the price has to be right because it now costs around £4,000 to ship a horse to Britain. In 1995, the pick of the bunch was Word for Word. Word for Word came from Andrea

O'Rian, a friend who'd done a bit of showing and jumping with him. He's well-bred and very attractive so he'd fetched quite a lot of money as a yearling, but he did nothing on the track as a two-year-old which is hardly surprising because he's pretty immature as a seven-year-old. I'd always thought a lot of him, so I persuaded Mike and Mary Rose to buy him. They have also taken a half share in Eye Spy, a horse that had done quite a bit of showjumping with Joanne Bridgeman. He's come on very quickly so, at last, Mike and Mary Rose have a couple of decent horses.

Richard Adams died on the cross-country at the Windsor three-day event in late May 1994, a tragedy that moved me deeply because I knew him well and liked him very much. I'd met him at the Wokingham Equestrian Centre, which was run by his mother, Anne, when he was still at school. He'd come to train with us at Cholderton on and off for a couple of years in the late eighties and early nineties. We had a great bunch of students at the time and we all had a lot of fun together, riding on Salisbury Plain and going out to the pub. Richard was a really nice kid and very keen and talented. When he started the cross-country at Windsor, I was waiting for him at the water jump with David Green. We saw Richard set off and then from a distance we saw his horse fall at the table fence but couldn't see exactly what happened. We waited for him to get up, but nothing happened. Then the ambulance roared up and still nothing happened. Realising it was serious, we went over. It's the kind of fall event riders fear most, the horse landing on you, as indeed Ace had on me at Badminton a few weeks earlier, but Richard was desperately unlucky and he died of internal injuries. I've never been back to Windsor, partly because of my sad memories of Richard's death and partly because the going is either rock hard and poached or bottomless clay that sticks like glue. Both are bad for a horse's confidence and potentially damaging to his soundness, which means he doesn't jump so well, a potential cause for accidents.

Once she'd recovered from her caesarean, Carolyn was keen to get back in the saddle. She had a horse called Choc Wallace, a part-thoroughbred and a beautiful mover and jumper, that she bought from a British showjumper who was in partnership with Paul Darragh. She'd taken him through novice to intermediate before her pregnancy and she felt that now was the time to turn an honest profit on him. The first potential buyer was Julius Meinl, who owns a bank and a chain of convenience stores with branches in every town in Austria. When he arrived at Sydmonton, he thought the horse was a bit small but his wife, Francesca, fell in love with him. I was away at the time, but Carolyn cemented the deal, and an enduring friendship, by taking her out for a four-hour ride over the estates owned by Andrew Lloyd Webber and Ian Balding. Francesca and Carolyn are the same age and they share a sense of humour so we were invited to come to Vienna that autumn to go to the opera. We couldn't go, but we received another invitation to join them for a holiday in Sardinia. We had to miss 1996 because of the Atlanta Olympics, but we went in 1995 and 1997, and have a wonderful time with them, as they are both great fun and very generous hosts. The only problem is that it's very hard to come home to reality after a week out there.

After Richard's tragic death, Anne Adams was very keen for us to buy a part Arab horse of his called Buddy Good. He had a fantastic jump, but he wasn't really the best choice for Carolyn at that time. She'd lost her confidence a bit after having James and she wanted something that would take her round to get her going again. She did take him to a few events but he was very spooky and that made her even more nervous. The partnership came to an end when we went schooling at Lyneham before the 1994 season started. Buddy Good spooked into a ditch palisade, then decided to go almost from a standstill. He didn't make it, sliding sideways down the bank crushing her ankle against the edge of the ditch. She was obviously very sore, but thinking I was doing the right thing, I made her get back on the horse just to walk around. At the end of the day, Carolyn drove herself to the hospital to get the ankle checked and was told it was just badly bruised. A short time later, they rang us to say that they had re-examined the X-rays and that the ankle was broken. She had to go back and have the ankle set in plaster. While Carolyn's leg was in plaster, I took over the ride and eventually he started to go very well, coming second at Falsterbo and fourth at Le Lion d'Angers. He was a lovely little horse, a really good jumper, but too small to carry me beyond two-star level, so I sold him to the Korean rider, Mark Choy, at the end of the season.

At that point, Carolyn thought she might prefer dressage and she bought two Swedish horses with a view to changing disciplines. As I kept catching her jumping them in the school, it didn't seem to be the perfect solution. I think she did two dressage shows and found the pace altogether too slow, so she sold the horses at a handsome profit and they were replaced by an Irish skewbald called Salvador Dali. Carolyn started off by doing a few novice events hors concours, but he did the job beautifully and she was soon riding confidently round intermediate tracks again.

After months of searching for a yard big enough to replace Sydmonton, I had a phone call from Chris Leigh, a man I'd known for years because he did the commentary at events. His family had owned the estate at Stoneleigh and also most of the village of Adlestrop, near Chipping Norton in Gloucestershire. For years, Cynthia Haydon, the doyenne of carriage driving, had run the stables there as a stud for hackneys and thoroughbreds, but she was retiring so it was now up for lease. I'd told Chris I was looking for a new place and eventually he offered me the yard. It was purpose built, with a big triangular block of thirty stables and two staff flats. We had twenty-five acres, mostly fields divided by solid post and rails, and they put in an arena for us.

We finally left the Lloyd Webbers on 31 October 1993, three weeks before we went to New Zealand to introduce James to our families. We did the move ourselves, slogging up and down the A34 in the lorry and humping furniture until I was heartily sick of it. Carolyn and I and the kids crammed into one of the staff flats which was really tiny. It was only while we were away that Chris Leigh found us a lovely newly renovated cottage to rent from Sir Anthony and Lady Bamford. It was pretty small too, so for the next two years most of our furniture remained in the coach house where Cynthia Haydon had kept her carriages.

A lot of the horses went back to their owners at the end of the season, so it was a good time to move. Most of them came back in January, including Just an Ace, my main hope for the World Games in The Hague. While I was away, Annabel Scrimengour worked on his dressage and his progress was impressive, but he never got good enough marks to make it easy for him to win a major three-day event and so far he never has. That year he made a promising start by winning at Belton, so I had reasonable hopes for Badminton. My prospects were further improved when I got a call from the Bevans on the Tuesday before the vet's inspection asking me to ride Horton Point. He was a big chestnut horse, sixteen years old and a real family pet. Over the years, he'd introduced Ros and Lynne Bevan to top-class competition. I'd helped them at events, walking the course and so on, and they'd said if they ever needed another rider, I'd be the one they'd choose. When Lynne broke her collarbone in a nasty fall at Bicton over the weekend, they proved they meant it. In normal circumstances, they would probably have withdrawn him, but this was his last Badminton and they wanted him to make the most of it. I accepted at once, but I gave Just an Ace the better chance of winning because Horton Point, although having jumped flawlessly round Badminton and Burghley for years, had never got anywhere near the time. I thought it was partly the way the girls had ridden him, but he was quite a heavy sort of horse, by no means a Thoroughbred, and I doubted he'd be able to go fast enough however hard he tried.

Originally Lynne had Buckley Province as well as Horton Point in the line up and she wanted them both ridden by 'foreigners', Andrew Nicholson and me. The rules as to who is accepted at Badminton change all the time, but that year, Hugh Thomas, the organiser of the event, would only allow us to compete on chance rides if all the British entries were accepted first, so it was white-knuckle time waiting to see if enough people withdrew for us to get our start numbers. In the end, I squeaked in, but Andrew lost the ride on Buckley Province to the British rider, Graham Law. I was the chosen one because, as Lynne said at the time, 'Horton Point's a funny old horse – if he doesn't like you, he won't go at all – so I wouldn't put up anyone but Toddy.' We finally got the green light at 4.30 on Tuesday evening and I trotted and cantered Horton Point for the first time on Wednesday morning. He was very well trained, like clockwork really, so I called it a day after twenty minutes. I was number one to go on the first morning so I warmed him up for forty minutes and hoped for the best. He was very rideable and he did a lovely test, finishing on 40.6. When all the results were in, he was second to the German rider, Marina Loheit and Sundance Kid, on a score of 37.4. Just an Ace was a victim of what was described in *Horse and Hound* as 'erratic judging'. Berndt Springorum placed him thirty-seventh and Jack Le Goff fourth, a remarkable discrepancy. He was also given a controversial two-point penalty for an error of course when he broke from canter into trot short of the mark on the centre line.

I popped Horton Point over a couple of jumps on the Friday, but I must say I felt a bit nervous setting out first on the cross-country on a horse I'd ridden for less than two hours. There was a problem over what bit I should use because the girls had found him quite strong so they'd used some sort of chain snaffle. Being bigger and stronger myself, I opted for something a little bit milder but I had no way of knowing if I'd made the right choice. I could have changed it after the steeplechase, but when you have your foot flat to the floor the whole way round, the horse doesn't have an opportunity to show you what kind of hold he's going to take cross-country. Ros and Lynne assured me that he was as fit as he'd ever been, but there was just one problem: he always got a bleeding nose when he stopped galloping at the end of the steeplechase and he'd been vetted out at Burghley the year before when he arrived in the ten-minute box with blood on his nostrils.

As it turned out, our partnership nearly ended before that could happen. We had a disagreement as to where he should take off at the first fence on the steeplechase and he galloped straight through the base, breaking the take off rail and almost coming down. That woke us both up and he jumped the rest of the fences fine, finishing with just 0.8 of a penalty after I'd nudged him along every inch of the way. With me on board he was carrying more weight than he ever had before, Lynne had always had to carry quite a bit of lead to make the 75 kg minimum weight, but he was a really gallant old trier and he stuck with it right to the line. At the end of phase B, Ros rushed up with a wet rag and said, 'Before you go back into the park, get off him and wipe his nose with this.' I went all the way round phase C with a wet rag in my hand and just before I came into public view, I cleaned his nose and threw the rag into the bushes, looking round desperately to check that no one had seen me.

I'd walked the course with the girls and their plan was simple: I was to take all the direct routes. I thought, 'Okay, I'll go along with it, but if things don't feel right I'll definitely be taking a few easy alternatives.' I also said to myself, 'Don't set off too strongly because you may be running out of petrol before the end.' I got into a nice rhythm and Horton Point jumped neatly and accurately from the start. On the clockwise circuit, the quarry comes up near the beginning. The aim is to pop in over the stone wall and land neatly on the edge of the bank, but I saw a bit of a forward stride and he took an enormous leap and landed at the bottom of the bank with a hell of a thump. I had my reins at the end of buckle and he was in a bit of sprawl, but we managed to get it together for the arrowhead wall on the way out. After that he gave me a wonderful ride round what turned out to be a more difficult Badminton than most people had foreseen. He was foot-perfect over the bounce into the water, three strides to the step and out over the fence into the second part of the course.

By now, I realised why the girls had trouble getting round without time penalties: when you came to steady him for a fence, nothing much happened. He felt as if he needed a lot of time to set himself up, but if I let him have it, I'd be way down on the clock. I had to force myself to make him keep coming and trust that he knew what he was doing, which he did. He was very neat with his front legs so I said, 'Okay matey, you're going to have to do your bit as well.' He kept galloping and every time we came to a fence, I managed to pick a nice forward stride. As befits a horse doing his sixth Badminton, he was very clever through the coffin and he made nothing of the Footbridge and the Vicarage V so I kept going the short routes and maintained the rhythm. At the centre walk fences the safest method is a steady four strides across the lane, but he pinged the first part and took the second hedge in three strides. I haven't done that on many horses and Ian Stark's great grey tearaway, Murphy Himself, is the only one to do it in two.

With most of the challenging jumps behind me, I was daring to hope for a good result, especially after he cleared the Zigzag and the Mitsubishi Ms as flawlessly as ever. There is a bit of a pull up to the park, but I knew it was now or never so I put my foot down and he responded. He was through the Sunken Road almost before I could blink and then it was just a question of crossing in front of the house to the finish as quickly as possible. As I'd said before, he was hardly Nashwan but, bless him, he gave it everything. Although he wasn't going a lot faster, he wasn't going slower either, and he finished just inside the time. It was the first time Horton Point had ever done that in a three-day event and he'd given me a fabulous ride. The television cameras picked up Ros, with white knuckles and tears in her eyes, as she watched me go round and Lynne said it was agonising following me on the video in the St John's Ambulance tent. Make no mistake, this was their family pet. They'd had him since he was eighteen months old and their parents had had to sell their house and move into a caravan to keep him going.

Marina Loheit was the only person who could beat me and, although it was her first Badminton, she set off as if she meant business. The Sundance Kid was a clever, experienced horse and he took the direct routes fearlessly and fast until he reached the second Luckington Lane crossing. I was getting pretty worried by that point but, inexplicably, he fell at the angled hedge and had to be retired so Horton Point ended the second day in the lead. After a fast clear round, Just an Ace finished on his dressage score of 57.2. With my confidence riding high from my first circuit, Just an Ace made it feel like a Pony Club course and we pulled up from eighteenth to seventh.

My elation took a knock later that night because Horton Point was a bit off, partly from landing so heavily in the bottom of the quarry and partly from the strain of going so fast for so long. Luckily our team vet, Wally Niederer, was around. Together with the Bevan family he looked after him late into the night and early in the morning. We used ice packs and hosing and everything that was legally possible, but he was still a little bit unlevel when we trotted him up in the morning. It was one of the most draining experiences I've ever had because the girls were living on pure emotion, laughter and tears. They had come this far with their old war-horse and no one was going to give up hope, but right up until the last minute we thought he wouldn't get through the vet's inspection. When I trotted him up, it was almost as if the old horse said, 'Right, I've got to make an effort here,' and he trotted up foot-perfect. Then we were all coaxing him, 'Come on you old bugger, jump one more showjumping round and you can retire.' I had Just an Ace to deal with as well, but Horton Point was all consuming. I don't think there was anybody who didn't want him to win, for his own sake and for the Bevans. The prize money alone would help them to build their new house, so there was an awful lot at stake. As the big moment approached, the girls were telling me, 'Just stay relaxed, but don't screw up. Our life depends on this.'

Just an Ace went round with one fence down, so I had a small advantage of knowing the course. Overnight I'd had a fence in hand over Mary Thomson and King William and Karen Dixon and Get Smart, but they'd dropped down the order with 26 and 15 faults respectively. By the time I went in on Horton Point, Blyth and Delta, and Vaughn and Bounce were in second and third places, but the really good news was that I could have two fences down and still win. Horton Point was a very good showjumper, but he was tired and he was sore, so I wasn't counting any chickens. He was clear to the last fence, which was a double, and I remember thinking, 'Okay, you knock them if you want to', but he went clear all the way. It was a magical victory for a real old pro and dear old Ace sealed it for me by coming fifth. His owner, Mary Patrick, had died in a riding accident shortly before so if he'd won it would have been a fitting tribute to her, but it was Horton Point's year. This win was all the more sweet because I had realised one of my eventing ambitions by winning a second Badminton after a fourteen-year gap. However, the real pleasure was the tremendous thrill it gave the Bevan family, a fairytale come true.

Top Hunter at the Lexington World Championships, 1978 – the fence before
our disaster and elimination

THE BURGHLEY WINNERS:

Wilton Fair, 1987 (top); Face the Music, 1990 (bottom)

Welton Greylag, 1991 (top)

Broadcast News, 1997 (bottom)

THE BADMINTON WINNERS:

Southern Comfort, 1980 (left); Horton Point, 1994 (right)

Bertie Blunt won in 1996. In 1995 we lost a stirrup on the cross-country

Michaelmas Day at Burghley in 1986

Bahlua, World Equestrian Games, Stockholm 1990 – where it all ended
at the water

Double Take at the Barcelona Olympics in 1992

Just an Ace at Badminton in 1993 (left)

Kayem at The Open European Championships
Pratoni in 1995 – fourth place (bottom)

Sounds Like Fun winning at Ellerslie, Auckland, in 1986 and ridden by Michael Coleman

I'm Bad – on the way to the start at Tidworth point-to-point in 1987, the year Badminton was cancelled

Word for Word shows
his class at 1997
Gatcombe Open
Championships

CHAPTER FOURTEEN

A 'SECOND HONEYMOON'

I DON'T KNOW WHAT IT IS WITH WORLD CHAMPIONSHIPS, BUT I've never done well in them. My first attempt was Lexington in 1978 with Top Hunter and we were eliminated. My second was with Podge at Gawler in 1986 and we fell in the water. My third was with Balhua at Stockholm in 1990 and we had a stop at the water. Now it was time to try again at The Hague in 1994. Ace's fifth placing at Badminton was a very good performance, so I was determined to put past disappointments behind me as I set off for Holland at the end of July.

The pure dressage and the showjumping were held in the main arena in a big park on the outskirts of the city. The organisation seemed to be under immense stress and everything was a hassle, even straightforward things like getting passes. The officials were also extremely unfriendly, which was surprising because all the other Dutch events I've been to have been fabulous. There seemed to be too many chiefs and not enough Indians and there were little technical hitches along the way. The temporary stabling out by the cross-country was in an aircraft hangar which was very hot and stuffy. The accommodation for the grooms wasn't good and the cross-country was some way away from the main action. The roads and tracks were very long, 10 km on deep sandy going, which was far too much in the extreme heat. The steeplechase was on rock hard going right in the middle of an airstrip which jarred up a lot of horses. The cross-country itself was designed as a true test, with big challenging fences on flat sandy ground.

When we walked the course, the first water gave the greatest cause for concern. You came up a bit of ramp over a small log and dropped down into the pond, then took one or two strides to a difficult arrowhead in the water. Next you went under a bridge and either right up a step with a bounce to a rail or left up a smaller step with a stride to a smaller rail. The consensus was that there would be falls and run outs at the arrowhead and so it turned out to be, but Ace was a very good cross-country horse and I wasn't that worried about it. I remember him flagging when we passed the 7 km post on phase C. It was right by the stables so he obviously felt he'd done enough and I had to kick him from there on, which was a horrible experience because he was normally so willing. However, he recovered well in the ten-minute box and after that he was purring along, jumping beautifully, on time and well within himself, as we approached the water. He went in strongly, jumped the arrowhead and cantered towards the little bank, two-foot, two-foot six inches – the sort of thing you could trot a novice over. I can remember him preparing to take off and the next thing I knew we'd slammed head first straight into the bank. It was the most extraordinary feeling. He wasn't the sort of horse to stop, let alone head-butt a fence, so something must have happened – a hole, a problem with an overreach boot – but to this day, I don't know what it was.

All I could think was, 'Here it is again, my World Championship jinx' and of all of them, it was the most embittering. Top Hunter was ignorance and inexperience, Podge was my fault because he would probably have jumped the fence perfectly well at some other point and Bahlua was naughty, but Ace was completely mystifying bad luck. I could almost feel him start to rise and, as he rose, down we went. Afterwards I asked myself why I hadn't taken the more difficult route. He'd probably have jumped that fine, but who knows?

I landed on the bank so at least I wasn't wet but I was so annoyed that I almost retired. The team was trying to qualify for the Atlanta Olympics and Blyth had had to pull out after Delta fell at one of the earlier fences. I knew our chance would be gone if I didn't finish, so I cantered on and Ace jumped everything else beautifully. It was lucky I did complete because Vaughn won the individual with Bounce and the team ended up in sixth place, just good enough to get us to

Atlanta. As Ace had had a better dressage score than Bounce, jumped clear showjumping and had every chance of a faultless cross-country round, I'm convinced it should – could – have been my World Championship, but it wasn't. My loss was Vaughn's gain. He's probably the most naturally talented rider of all of us, at least over fences. He's got good balance and rhythm, an excellent understanding of horses, a very precise eye for a stride and a lovely classical style. Blyth was the reigning World Champion and Vaughn had psyched himself up to beat him in The Hague. He had really worked at getting himself and his horse fit and it paid off.

In the summer of 1994, I had my first dealings with the colourful Trevor Banks. I'd met him a few years earlier when he'd tried to buy Double Take before the Barcelona Olympics and he came back to me after Horton Point's Badminton victory because he wanted someone to ride his showjumpers. He's a larger-than-life entrepreneur, always involved in complex deals that may or may not work out. He's very charming, very witty, very charismatic, but absolutely everybody warned me, 'Be very careful how you get involved.' He had a knack of attracting major sponsors onto his projects and Reg Bond, the head of a large family-owned tyre distribution business based in Hull, was the man of the moment. He'd persuaded Reg to invest in showjumpers and now he wanted someone to ride them.

Trevor had owned some good horses – Chainbridge, Hideaway and Anglezarke – and employed some good riders – Harvey Smith, Mark Phillips and Malcolm Pyrah amongst them – but he'd come to the end of a long list of riders who had been and gone, having ridden for him. I went along with him because part of the bargain was that Bond International would sponsor my event horses. As it was two years since the Kimberly-Clark contract had finished, that made the deal look very rosy. And so it was, for twelve months or so, but although I'd gone in with my eyes open, things went wrong in the end. Mind you, Trevor had no illusions, as one of his favourite sayings was, 'We're in the honeymoon period now and we need to make the most of it!'

The Bond sponsorship was very generous, not like the Merrill Lynch days, but good for the nineties, and Trevor sweetened it further by saying that he'd buy me a good event horse. Although I didn't know it at the time, his plan was that I'd find one, he'd buy it and sell it on to one of his owners. My search led me to Bertie Blunt, a horse that had been on the market at various times, but for an awful lot of money. In 1993, he'd gone so well round Badminton with his owner, Nick Burton, that he was chosen for the British squad for the European Championships at Achselschwang later that year. After he fell early on, Nick retired on the grounds that there was no point flogging the horse round when he wasn't in the team and he'd incurred sixty penalties. Of course, the British officials thought differently and he got quite a bit of stick along the lines of, 'Why didn't you carry on bravely as one is supposed to do?' – all the usual guff.

In 1994, he did badly at Badminton and became a victim of something that quite often happens to promising British riders. The officials spot a young talent coming through with a very good horse, he gets a couple of results and suddenly the pressure goes on. He's the new white hope, expected to do well every time he goes out, and if he doesn't, he's rubbish. Pretty soon people were saying, 'This is a really good horse and you're messing it up.' Not surprisingly, Nick lost confidence in himself and the horse to the point that he didn't want to know. I told Trevor that Bertie was a bit of a gamble because his form had been pretty average since Badminton 1993. I also consulted Vaughn, who knows Nick quite well. In his opinion, all the horse needed was a good slap round the backside and he'd be fine. Even so, I was still a bit apprehensive as all the other buyers had been scared off Bertie Blunt, and here I was spending a lot of someone else's money on a horse that might never return to form.

It was Trevor who went along to Nick to do the deal. He is a very hard man to resist, a powerful character who always gets what he wants in the end. He won't leave until he does; you tend to give in just to get rid of him. He paid £50,000, less than half the asking price a year earlier, so it was a good bargain, always assuming I could turn the horse around. At the time, I thought Trevor owned him but, when we fell out, I discovered that Bertie belonged to Reg Bond in partnership with Rob and Melita Howell, a couple who ran a construction company in Lincolnshire. They were part of Trevor's coterie at the time and they turned up at events so I always had my little group of supporters, and a very entertaining one at that. Trevor did everything in style and he was always there, a dominating figure, very much at the helm of the ship. At events, it was the same story with lavish hospitality and lots of laughs. We were still in our honeymoon period, having a wonderful time.

Bertie Blunt is a chestnut horse with a white face, at over 17hh bigger than I really like because small horses are much nippier on the cross-country, but a Thoroughbred by Suny Boy. He'd been in training over fences with Nicky Henderson at one time, but he was too big and slow for the racetrack. He is a lovely jumper, a bit excitable at times, and quite fast enough for eventing. He's a pushy sort of character, forever barging and treading on your feet, probably because he was Nick Burton's pet so he was thoroughly spoilt. He isn't nasty, just very impatient and he likes his food, so he'll walk all over you to get it. A reprimand doesn't bother him because he's a tough-thinking horse, not laid back because he has a nervy racehorse streak, but not a real worrier either.

When Bertie arrived at Adlestrop at the end of July, I took him schooling at Hartpury and then straight to Gatcombe in mid August. I was a bit dubious about tackling such a demanding course first time out, but to Nick's credit he admitted, 'All the problems were mine. If you give him a confident ride, he'll be fine.' How right he was. Bertie Blunt was third in the Open Championships and, as far as I remember, I never had a cross-country penalty with him. It was on the flat that things were not so straightforward. It was only when I got him home that I realised he was a headshaker, something Nick had neglected to mention before the sale went through. I was a bit annoyed because it can be a problem in dressage tests in hot weather, but, funnily enough, Bertie never really did it in the arena. He could be appalling warming up but, when it really mattered, he behaved well. It took me a little while to get used to him on the flat, especially in the rein back which he always found difficult. At Gatcombe, he reared up and refused to do it at all, but we were getting the hang of it by the time we got to Burghley a month later.

In the interim, he'd won an open intermediate class at Tythrop Park so I was reasonably confident. Both the flies and the headshaking were terrible in the warm-up area at Burghley, but he calmed down in the arena and did a very competitive test. He's a very smart-looking horse, a good mover and well trained, so he was more than capable of winning the dressage. In fact he didn't on this occasion, but he was well in touch. The cross-country was big, but not unusually so, and I thought I had a good chance of completing the elusive Badminton–Burghley double.

The roads and tracks at the major events are the same year after year so we all know that two-thirds of the way round phase C at Burghley there's a little loop off the main track that takes about two minutes to do. On this occasion, I drove round with my friends just to check that nothing had changed but as nothing ever does we were talking and laughing rather than giving it our undivided attention. On the day, Bertie and I were among the first to set out on the roads and tracks and the steeplechase. No problem. He passed the vet's inspection at the end of phase C and we started on the cross-country, finishing foot-perfect within the time. Again no problem. He didn't take a really strong hold, just galloped along on a nice contact. He'd fight a bit when I tried to steady him in front of a fence and I had to use quite a lot of leg to keep him together because he was so big, but he was such an accurate jumper that he gave me a really good feel.

Afterwards, I joined Trevor and his wife and daughter, plus Reg, Melita and Rob, in the member's tent to await results. We were drinking champagne right near the end of the day when there was a call on the public address system: 'Will Mark Todd please report to the secretary's tent.' When Trevor and I got there, they told us, 'There's been a problem, you've got to talk to Mark Phillips.' They ran us down to the start and Mark came up and said, 'You've been eliminated for missing a checkpoint on phase C.' The man at the checkpoint said he never saw me, but it's a boring job and he may not have been concentrating. Equally I may not have been concentrating because I do tend to trot along thinking of other things, at least I used to – I'm a lot more careful over the precise route of the roads and tracks nowadays. Their argument was that as I'd come in two minutes quicker than the average, I must have missed out the loop, but I often arrive early because it gives you a longer break before phase D.

To this day, I don't know whether I missed it or not, but eventually I had to accept their word for it. What I couldn't accept, especially in the light of the current concern with protecting the horses, was that they didn't stop me before I did the cross-country. The Ground Jury said they had no communication with phase C, but that was their problem, not mine. I felt very strongly that they shouldn't eliminate me for something that gave me no possible advantage when they'd allowed me to complete the cross-country course. If I hadn't been so dumbstruck, I'd have put my case even more forcefully and I wish I had because the injustice still rankles today. If you accept their story, as you have to, I made a mistake, but then so did they. I was furious, all the more so because a good place at Burghley would have made me unbeatable in the Land Rover World Rider rankings which carries a £10,000 first prize. Then there was the prize money at Burghley itself. I think that little incident ended up costing me about £20,000.

The next morning, Bertie was fit and ready to jump, and I felt just awful. As it turned out, I wouldn't have won because William Fox Pitt and Chaka were just ahead of me at the end of the second day and I think he'd still have shaded me into second place if I'd jumped clear on the third day. However, that wasn't much consolation, then or now. I still cringe when I think about it because it was such a basic error for someone as experienced as me to make but, to my face at least, Trevor and his friends reacted very sympathetically. In October, I tried to redeem myself at Boekelo, always one of my favourite events, and it paid off. Bertie and Ace both did quite good tests, but not quite good enough, and went clear on the other phases so they finished third and fifth.

When the British season ended, I turned my attention to the inaugural three-day event at Puhunui. It's not a British set-up in the sense of a castle in a big park, but it's a very attractive venue right on the coast near Auckland International airport and the cross-country has become increasingly sophisticated over the years. In 1994, they invited Karen Dixon to take a chance ride because she and Blyth were neck and neck in the World Rider Rankings. He was a little ahead but she could have overhauled him if she'd done well. As it turned out, she didn't and nor did I on the two chance rides I was offered by people I knew in New Zealand. Everyone had a great time, though, and the organisers have kept their promise to make it bigger and better each year.

Thanks to our international success, New Zealand has an ever-expanding pool of riders and a good infrastructure, with people who know how to set up quality events, as Puhunui proves. With a population of around three million, we can never match the numbers in Britain, but some classes attract 100 competitors. We're regarded as one of the leading eventing nations but, with the exception of Stockholm, we've won individually rather than as a team. The nucleus is Andrew Nicholson, Blyth and myself, with a floating fourth – usually Vaughn, Vicky, Andrew Bennie or Tinks depending which era you're talking about – but we rarely all perform well at the same time. As the three of us are based in Britain, the New Zealanders don't often see us ride. It can be a bit of a hassle to get out there on a strange horse at the end of a long hard season, but these are our country folk and they always get behind us so they deserve our support in return.

Nowadays we get considerable funding from the New Zealand Sports Foundation. It started about five years ago and the money has gradually increased to the point at which our athletes receive reasonable 'pay'. We each receive a cheque quarterly, with the amount calculated on past international performances and medal potential. Blyth, Andrew and I all fall into the elite category.

Although I have absolutely no regrets about my choice of career, I was born at the wrong time to make a lot of money out of eventing. I can't stop the clock and imagine how it would be to be starting in the late nineties, but I choose to think we had more fun than twenty-year-olds do now. On the other hand, it's nice to know that if you dedicate yourself fully to your sport, you can get some reward. Obviously international superstars in sports like football and golf make the kind of money we could never dream of, but thanks to the New Zealand Sports Foundation and the Olympic Committee, we now receive a very fair reward for being at the top. We don't have a lot to boast about in New Zealand, but sport is an obsession and everyone is very proud of the sporting achievements of a tiny population so the financial help is given in a generous spirit. I'm also involved as an ambassador with an organisation called New Zealand Way, which promotes our produce abroad. They represent the New Zealand Wool Board, the New Zealand Wine Board, organisations like that. It's been going for about a year and I'm required to make appearances, wear their branded clothing and generally talk positively about New

Zealand goods. I'm the only rider, but there are other sportsmen – a top yachtsman and a motor racing driver.

Through the winter of 1994–95, my honeymoon with Trevor continued and Bertie thrived, so I hoped I'd be able to make amends for the Burghley fiasco at Badminton. I was also riding Ace and they were both going so well that I'd have been pushed to say which would come out ahead. Ace did his usual honest unspectacular test, but my optimism was dented a bit when it came to Bertie because the warm-up for the dressage was hideous. The flies gathered under the trees near the practice arena and his headshaking was off the scale. Again he settled once he was in the arena and did a decent test, so there was still nothing between them at the start of the cross-country day.

I rode Ace first and he skipped round, making it all seem effortless, as was his custom. It was much the same story with Bertie as he galloped across the front of the house, down towards the Mitsubishi fence and through the Luckington Lane crossings. When we got to the next fence, the pond with the filthy water where Mick had given me a ducking a few years earlier, Bertie jumped in and landed fine. As he took the next stride, I felt my left leg slip and looked down to see the stirrup hanging off my foot. The leather was broken so near the buckle it wasn't even worth stopping to fix it. The Vicarage V, a huge corner over a ditch, was looming and I was thinking, 'What am I going to tell the owners? I cocked up at Burghley on this horse and I just can't do it at two championships in a row. I've got to give it a go.' This all flashed through my mind in about two strides and I knew I had to try to jump it. I'd slowed down so I picked myself up, gathered Bertie up and went for it. He's a very good corner jumper so he'd never run out, but we were still only a third of the way round the course.

Although my instinct was to keep going and see how far we'd get, I knew that if I couldn't do the time there was no point in doing it at all. To achieve that, I had to find a way of galloping between fences without banging on his back. I tried with my weight in one stirrup and that didn't work. Then I kicked out with both stirrups and bumped along, which was agonisingly uncomfortable. The fences kept coming and he kept jumping and eventually I devised a way of keeping my weight in my right stirrup and pulling my left knee up almost over the pommel. A tearaway like Podge or Mick would have been so spooked that he'd have gone faster and faster, but good old Bertie just lobbed along, almost on a loose rein so that I'd interfere with him as little as possible. By comparison with stretches in between, the fences seemed almost easy. As each one came up, I'd sit down, take a contact and put my legs on, but I must give full credit to Bertie because he played his part to perfection. By never trying to deviate, never giving me the slightest anxious moment, he allowed me the greatest possible chance of staying on.

After the Vicarage V, the next major hazard was that horrendous coffin, with very short distances between the rail in, the ditch and the rail out. Even at that stage, I was so exhausted that I didn't know how much longer I could last. The Badminton water is notoriously difficult, with a bounce in and drop to the water, three strides to a step up and a bounce out over a rail. I had plenty of time to plan my approach on the long gallop down to it, but I almost felt like bursting out laughing at the thought of galloping down to one of the most difficult fences in the world with only one stirrup. I calculated that all I could do was put Bertie in the best possible spot to jump the direct route and leave it up to him. He responded magnificently and I thought, 'Phew, I'm half way round, with most of the most difficult fences behind me. Maybe I can hang on to the finish after all.' So on we went, up the staircase and over the keeper's brush to the quarry. I kept checking on my time and amazingly I was quite fast. Even when I'd walked the course, I hadn't liked the direct route at the quarry and I now had a good excuse to go round and play safe. After that, I thought I'd make it and we finished within the time in second place.

I was totally knackered at the finish and later that night my leg ached and I was stiff in my back from holding myself in an unnatural position, but I wasn't crippled. Bertie was also a bit sore in his back, which the vets ascribed to my weight thumping on him. When they'd worked on him with massage and the magnetic blanket, he came right so we weren't too bothered overnight but he wasn't quite sound when we trotted him up the next morning. He was still a little stiff when I rode him out in the park, but he loosened up after a couple of minutes, so I brought him back to Rob, Melita and Trevor and pronounced him, 'Good as gold, no problem.' Then we put him back in the box to get him ready for the vet's inspection and he came out hopping lame. He was still a bit unlevel after we lunged him, but we presented him for the first trot up anyway, but withdrew him before he should have been re-presented.

Ironically, we were more worried about Ace, who'd also had his problems overnight, passed with flying colours, jumped his habitual clear round and finished fourth. He'd tweaked a tendon so he needed a break after Badminton and that was the last time I ever rode him. He was supposed to come back to me at the beginning of 1996 but his owner, Robin Patrick, contacted me and said, 'Look, I haven't spoken to Robert Lemieux yet, but he's had bad luck with his horses, he's got no top horse to ride, and I'd like to keep Ace nearer home so would you mind if I offered the ride to him?' I said that was fair enough, but I was disappointed because Ace was a funny old character, very shy and timid, and I'd become more and more fond of him as I got to know him better. Also I'd worked extremely hard on his dressage to get him to a stage where he was starting to get consistently better marks. Then again, Robert had started him off and I'd taken over from him, so I couldn't turn round and say I didn't want Robert to have him. There was a certain justice in it as well because at that stage I did have a lot of good horses coming on. Furthermore, Ace was an older horse and he wouldn't have been my first choice for Atlanta because he wasn't very fast and he didn't like the heat.

With hindsight, we should have looked into Bertie's situation more thoroughly after the Badminton cross-country – when he got home his condition deteriorated. Eventually Trevor took him up to Newmarket for a thorough examination and the vets discovered that he had pus in his foot, obviously from a bruise. The roads and tracks were particularly rough that year so he'd probably trodden on a stone, possibly aggravating an existing bruise. If we'd realised it was nothing to do with the broken stirrup, we could have treated the foot, put on a pad and maybe completed the event, but somehow it was missed so that was that. It was infuriating having been to two major three-day events without completing, when both times we should have finished in the top three.

After Badminton 1995, I got a call from Owen Moore who'd been riding Kayem for George and Jayne Apter. George owns Studio and

TV Hire, a big props company based in London, and Jayne rode a bit. She'd bought Coco, as we called Kayem, as a young horse from John Poole. She started him off, then sent him to Robert Lemieux, who upgraded him to advanced and rode him in the World Championships at The Hague in 1994. I'd never noticed the horse particularly, but I'd seen him showjumping a couple of times and he really did operate over a fence. Owen Moore had taken over the ride from Robert for the 1995 season, but he'd broken his collarbone, so he asked me to take him to Punchestown. Kayem arrived a few days before the event so I could get to know him, then went to Ireland, did a reasonable dressage and flew round the steeplechase. On the racetrack, one of the nicest steeplechase courses in eventing, good going and big fences encourage the horses to really gallop on. When I pulled up, I thought Kayem didn't feel quite right but I went on for a bit, then realised that he was tying up and it was pointless to continue. After Punchestown, George and Jayne asked if I would like to keep the ride and I was delighted to accept their offer.

Back at home, I prepared him for the European Championships at Pratoni in Italy. For the first time, they were open to riders from all over the world, not just Europeans, so there was an exceptionally strong field. It is a spectacular venue, set among the hills outside Rome, and it was a wonderful event, very friendly with excellent facilities, but relaxed despite being a championship. Buffy Shirley-Beavan, who does our veterinary work, is very good on blood analysis and she'd prescribed extra vitamins and minerals to solve Coco's tying-up problem but he was lame with a bruised foot when he got on the truck to Italy, so there was no certainty he'd compete at all. He's a very cocky sort of horse, very friendly and outward going, a bit grumpy in the stable sometimes, but he loves attention. Because he isn't built for dressage, he finds it quite difficult so I'd had to do a lot of work on that. He is a fabulous jumper, very straight and direct and honest, a credit to Robert Lemieux's early training, just as Ace had been. The cross-country at Pratoni was billed as a three-star, but it was almost as big as a four-star, with challenging fences that caused quite a bit of trouble. Coco cruised round the cross-country course with his customary élan and went clear in the showjumping, which was good enough to just miss out on the medals in fourth place. Lucy

Thompson won the individual gold for Ireland on Welton Romance, the mare she bought from Ginny, with Marie Christine Duroy and Mary King behind her, so I was beaten by three women. Equality is the name of the game in eventing so I'm well used to that, but after a string of defeats snatched from the jaws of victory, I felt that I was overdue for a change of luck.

CHAPTER FIFTEEN

A Hiss and a Roar

B Y 1995, CAROLYN AND I HAD DECIDED THAT WE'D BE
spending quite a few more years in Britain, so it made sense
to invest in a property of our own. We'd bought the 500-acre
farm in Whitehall in New Zealand partly as an investment and partly
as a place to stay when we were out there. With a manager to run it
and my father keeping an eye on it, it was paying its way, but it
seemed ridiculous to have a big farm which we rarely saw while
paying rent on a place in Britain. We had tenants in the house during
1994, but they moved out by Christmas so we spent a couple of weeks
there with the children. Basically it was a camping holiday in a
partially furnished house, lovely scenery but not very comfortable,
and it made us face up to the fact that it was time for a rethink. We'd
already turned down a couple of offers for it, but the prices of cattle
farms were beginning to fall on the back of a meat mountain in
America, the main market for New Zealand beef, so it was a good
time to get out.

We'd been looking for a place to buy in Britain throughout the
previous summer, but we intensified our search when we returned
for the 1995 season. As we were living at Adlestrop three miles down
the road, we'd often drive past Poplar's Farm, but we'd never been
inside. Trevor Banks told us that it was owned by his friends,
showjumper Richard Sumner, and his wife, Patsy. They'd built the
house on the site of a much smaller property in 1989 but, by 1995,
they were in the throes of a divorce so they had to sell. Trevor did us
a good turn by badgering them to sell it to us, rather than putting it

on the market. When we looked round it in April, we realised it was just what we needed, a five-bedroomed house, with twenty stables, several barns and an indoor school, plus 200 acres. We couldn't afford to buy the whole lot but a friend bought 100 acres and leased it to us to keep the place together. We have just under seventy acres of grass and the rest is corn, so at last I'm a farmer again, though most of the work is contracted out.

Initially Carolyn didn't want to come up to the Cotswolds, but we didn't have much choice when we left Sydmonton. Once we got here, we really liked it. It's beautiful, central and quite rural for England unless you go somewhere like Cornwall or Devon. Although Stow-on-the-Wold and Moreton-in-Marsh are very touristy towns, they still have a country feel to them. Occasionally, once or twice a year, Carolyn and I find time to wander around and have lunch in one of them.

The deal on the Whitehall Farm worked out well because we had bought it at an advantageous exchange rate with money from Britain. We made a profit when we sold it, not as much as we would have six months earlier, but a lot more than we would have if we'd waited any longer. By the time we brought the money back to Britain to buy Poplar's Farm, the exchange rate had swung the other way so that, again, it worked in our favour. I can't claim financial acumen, but we were lucky because we were committed to buying Poplar's Farm and we had to sell the Whitehall place to pay for it, no matter what price we got for it. Originally the Sumners were supposed to move out in July 1995, but Patsy had not found anywhere to move to, so the exchange date kept getting later and later. By November, we had a deadline because our lease on the stables at Adlestrop ran out and the trustees were asking for an exorbitant rent to extend it for a few more months. In the end, we told them that the price was unacceptable and rented the stables at Poplar's Farm from the Sumners until the deal went through. It dragged on through the winter, completion dates being set and broken in February and March 1996, and we were beginning to wonder if we'd ever move in. Eventually the Sumners fixed on April Fool's Day, but we insisted on a twenty-four-hour delay, just in case.

Poplar's Farm was well worth waiting for, especially as it was all set up so we could move straight in. The house is Cotswold stone, with big light rooms and an airy feel. The focus is a farmhouse style kitchen, with an Aga, windows looking out over the stables and paddocks and a large table, where we all sit chatting over innumerable cups of coffee. We didn't have to do much to the house, other than decorate it. Carolyn had done a course in interior design in Bath when we were at Sydmonton and Jane Bowyer, one of our most loyal owners, runs a company called Rectory Design, so she was a great help with ideas. We extended the garden quite a bit, planting a lawn and seventy trees, which will change the aspect once they're established. We built an outdoor school and a five-bedroom flat for the staff in the stable area and we were ready to go. Our current team is headed by Sarah Mann, an invaluable help over the past three years because she doubles as a nanny and girl Friday. She hacks the horses out and does a lot of the cantering, but she's also very capable with the children so we can leave them with her with complete confidence, even when we are competing abroad.

For the past few years, Podge had been living happily in semi-retirement on the Whitehall farm, under the loving care of the manager and his wife, but once it was sold there was the question of what should happen to him. If he'd gone to Mum and Dad's, there would have been no one to ride him so he'd just have got fatter and fatter, and anyway they didn't really want the responsibility of looking after an old horse. In the end, the situation was resolved at a dinner with John Mahoney, the chairman of my long-time sponsors, Bell Tea. We were chatting about Podge and he said, 'We'll pay for him to go over to England.' They got a bit of publicity from the press coverage of Podge leaving New Zealand, but it was still an incredibly generous offer. Judy Hall gave him a return ticket when she offered, 'If he doesn't like it at Poplar's Farm, I'll pay for him to come back again.' We've never had to take her up on it, though. The first week he was here, he'd stand in the field looking round with his ears pricked as if to say, 'What's up then? When do the competitions start?' I really believe that the flight and being back in a yard made him think he was going eventing again, and he was in such good form that he probably hoped he was. Although he celebrated his twenty-fifth birthday last October, we still ride him and he loves it here so it's turned out perfectly.

On 1 March 1996, I too had a landmark birthday, my fortieth, which we wanted to celebrate with a skiing holiday with the Purbricks and the Duffs. In the end, nothing got organised so Carolyn said, 'We'll go to Paris, just the two of us, on Eurostar.' Normally she is even more unpunctual than I am, but on this occasion she was very organised and very determined we should arrive at Waterloo station in plenty of time. What she'd planned was that we'd get on the train and the others would wander through the carriage as if by chance to surprise me. What actually happened was that, while in the station bookshop, I heard a booming voice saying, 'I suppose I'll have to buy the old bugger a card at least.' Well, there's no mistaking Lizzie, whether you can see her or not. Initially, I thought, now there's a coincidence, but once I spotted the four of them, Lizzie included, the secret was out.

Coincidentally our hostess on the train recognised me because she'd worked for the American event rider, Karen Reuter, so she kick-started the celebrations by insisting we drink champagne all the way to Paris. By the time we arrived in our suite at the Georges V, we were more than ready to take on whatever the town had to offer, including a nightclub, which a fellow traveller had recommended to Reggie during the journey. After a very jolly dinner on Saturday night, we decided to check the club out, but no one seemed to have heard of it. Eventually we consulted the concierge at the hotel who said, 'My God, it is the limit', so we knew we had to go. It looked quite normal when we arrived just after midnight, with some people dining in one room and in another dimly lit room others gathered round what we took to be a billiard table. Things livened up after a while and I couldn't help but notice the scantily dressed women on the dance floor. From time to time, couples or threesomes would drift towards the billiard room, so we thought we'd go and see what was going on. The answer was just about everything imaginable, either on the table, which turned out to be padded leather rather than green baize, or in a cage in a dark corner. You could either stand and watch, as we did, or join in. The Purbricks had their noses pressed to the bars of cage when Lizzie stopped everyone in their tracks by saying, 'Reggie, the man next to me has got his hand up my dress.' At that point, Reggie read out the club rules which emphasised the need for everyone to be very friendly to their fellow guests, instructions that were certainly being taken literally. The guests looked like normal people, obviously very open sharing normal people, all of them couples, because men weren't allowed in on their own. I assume most of them were regulars, rather than tourists like us, because they certainly weren't there for the laughs.

All in all, it was a fabulous weekend and then it was time to start work in a year that I hoped would peak with Olympic gold in Atlanta. My prospects were not as good as I would have liked because my association with Trevor had ended acrimoniously shortly after we bought Poplar's Farm. Nearly everyone I know has a Trevor story and it always ends in exactly the same way, with disagreement followed by a parting of the ways.

Our quarrel prompted Trevor's decision to sell Bertie Blunt. Given that the horse was a headshaker, the price tag was astronomical in my view. As I wasn't about to do Trevor any favours when people checked Bertie out with me, he couldn't find a buyer, which angered him still further. He took his revenge by bad-mouthing me to the Howells, presumably in the hope they'd take the horse away permanently. The only contact I had with Rob over the next few months was when he sent a dispatch rider to pick up Bertie's passport in the middle of the night. To be eligible for the Olympics, a horse had to be registered in the rider's name on 1 January 1996 so removing my name from Bertie's passport meant I couldn't take him to Atlanta, no matter what happened. However, throughout the whole affair Carolyn and Melita kept in touch, which definitely helped with Bertie and I being reunited.

After the passport incident, I never expected to ride him again but early in 1996 I got a call from Tessa Hood. For the past few years, she and her husband Charlie have asked me to run a pre-season cross-country clinic at their place near Lincoln. Now she wanted to know whether I'd be prepared to include a demonstration on Bertie Blunt in that year's programme. When I agreed, the Howells duly appeared with the horse on the appointed day. To my astonishment, Bertie went completely wild as soon as he heard my voice. It took several attempts to get on him as he reared and cavorted around in extremely high spirits. It was as if he was saying, 'I know this guy, and it means galloping round cross-country courses . . .' He'd been doing dressage and showjumping with Rosemary Morris, a friend of Rob and Melita's who runs a yard near the Hoods', and I represented the thing he loved and missed most. Once I calmed him down, the demonstration went well but I still didn't know if it was a one-off or if Bertie was to come back to me. When the offer finally came, I hesitated to accept but I eventually agreed to ride him in a class sponsored by Rob Howell's company at the Lincolnshire one-day event three weeks later. When Bertie won it, I took him back to Poplar's Farm to prepare him for Badminton.

As he was ineligible for Atlanta, my Olympic choices were limited to Kayem and Ethelred The Unready, a lovely, big, quality horse of Lizzie's, who'd come fourth at Gatcombe in 1995. At that stage, she'd said, 'I have no hope of getting into the British Olympic team, so why don't you take him to Badminton next year and then to the Olympics if need be.' He was a fabulous jumper and I enjoyed riding him in one-day events that autumn, but at Boekelo in October he was so unmanageable that we had a pretty nasty fall at a corner on the cross-country. He'd never misbehaved in a one-day event with me and I believed I could get him out of it in a three-day so I kept faith with him until he went lame behind at the Gatcombe spring event in 1996. As the X-ray was clear, the vets thought the source of the problem must be a bruised sole so they dug deeply into his hoof to locate the cause of the trouble. Weeks went by and still no improvement, but as soon as they gamma-scanned him, they discovered he had a cracked pedal bone. He returned to Lizzie's to rest, but an infection set into his foot. Once the poison spread into the bone, we had no choice but to put him down – a tragic waste of what could have been a very good horse.

Despite this setback, my 1996 three-day event season started with a hiss and a roar, back to back wins at Saumur and Badminton for Kayem and Bertie in successive weeks. Chessman, the winner of the British Intermediate Championship at Gatcombe in 1994, also came to Saumur and turned in the better dressage. When I walked the cross-country, I thought it was demanding enough to ensure that the competition wasn't won on the dressage alone and so it turned out to be. Chessman was normally pretty reliable, but on this occasion he put in a couple of very hairy jumps early on and had a silly stop coming out of the water near the end of the course. Then it was Kayem's turn and he just cruised round, making it all seem effortless. He has a slightly unorthodox jump, but he's very accurate and he loves it. The next day, it was easy: Kayem jumped clear and we won, with Chessman down the field.

Bertie is a striking horse and a good mover so he is well equipped to please the dressage judges, always provided headshaking is kept out of the equation. At Badminton in 1996 he performed fluently and finished just behind the leaders on 41.20, a competitive mark as very few partnerships get under the forty barrier in a major three-day event. It was a clockwise cross-country year, the direction that had worked so well for me when I won on Horton Point in 1994. However, Bertie Blunt and Nick Burton had had a stop in '94 coming out of the quarry by the direct route. After all the disappointments with Bertie, I was desperate that nothing should go wrong so I prepared with extra care in every department, and that included pondering long and hard over whether that stop would come back to haunt him if I took the same direct route in 1996.

On the Saturday, everything worked out as planned. As you can imagine, my concentration never wavered on the roads and tracks and Bertie's experience on the racecourse made it easy for him to complete the steeplechase within the time. Although the quarry came early, I decided to go for the direct route and he jumped it fantastically. Bertie is brilliant across country, not nippy like Podge, but a relentless galloper. Sometimes he gets excited and puts his head in the air in front of a fence, but that's his only flaw. We went on over the Keeper's Rails and down the Staircase, which has a double of narrow arrow-heads at the bottom. He jumped those superbly, keeping a very straight line, and cruised on to the Lake fences. I was up on time at that stage, but I dropped behind when I took it a little too easily between the Vicarage V and the Luckington Lane crossings. Before I'd started, David Green and I had been watching the riders gallop across the front of the house to the finish on closed circuit TV. A camera mounted on rails that ran parallel to the course did the filming. No matter what kind of round they'd had, they all finished with grim faces and lowered heads so Greeny dared me to wave at the camera.

When I heard it start up beside me, I only had one fence to jump and the horse was flying, so I turned and waved and said, 'Hi Mum', though the sound men didn't pick that up. I was so anxious not to make a mistake that I finished with 0.8 of a time fault, but it was still a fabulous round and I ended up on 42.00, a close second to Ian Stark and Stanwick Ghost. Melita and Rob were over the moon, but then again, we'd been in the same position in 1995 and Bertie had gone lame overnight, so we weren't counting our chickens.

Stanwick Ghost wasn't known for his accurate showjumping, whereas normally Bertie was pretty reliable, so I knew that a clear round would put immense pressure on Scotty. Once Bertie had played his part to perfection, I stood outside the arena as Stanwick Ghost started his round. Would there be a groan of disappointment from the partisan British crowd? The answer wasn't long in coming and Bertie was a champion at last. Certainly no horse deserved it more and the win was the sweeter for all of us because we'd so often been on the brink only to have victory snatched away. Rob could hardly believe it, so much so that he played the video almost every night for a year.

And so to Atlanta, where for the first time there were to be two three-day events, one for teams and one for individuals. The change came about because the Olympic Federation decided they couldn't give two medals, one for a team and one for an individual, in one competition. It's ridiculous because that is the nature of the sport, but there are no plans to revert to the old single competition system. The Federation also complain at the cost of running the event, again an absurd reason for change because they've only added to the expense by building two cross-country courses. My biggest objection to the new system is that both competitions are devalued because there aren't enough good horses to fill two events. As each national entry puts the emphasis on the team, the individual competition faces a very real possibility of becoming sub-standard. In Atlanta, the individual gold medal, deservedly, went to Blyth, on the inexperienced Ready Teddy, but I'm sure he'd be the first to admit that he didn't beat the best horses in the world to win.

Kayem had finished Saumur really well, with no signs of tying up, but early in his preparation for the Olympics he'd pulled up a bit sore after a gallop. We'd had him treated and we thought we'd found the spot that was bothering him and sorted it out. We think he'd had an old shoulder injury back in his racing days, or even earlier, and he'd learned to compensate for it by moving in a way that didn't come naturally. This put a strain on his physique, but he stood up to all the training and by the time we left Britain, he was ready to go. He still seemed fine when we arrived, but disaster struck when I gave him his first bit of serious work the next day. Talk about bad timing: in the week before the Olympics, a vital link decided to go twang. At first he wasn't hopping lame, just not quite right, but gradually he got worse and worse. He'd torn the attachment to the muscle that runs up under the shoulder and the whole thing collapsed. There I was, a captain without a horse. And to make things worse, Carolyn hadn't been able to join me as planned because her father had died shortly before the Olympics and she'd had to go to New Zealand for the funeral. All in all it was a pretty devastating month.

One thing about having more or less the same team each time is that the other New Zealanders are almost as experienced as I am and we know each other so well that there's no point in trying to hide anything. Originally, I was going to be in the team but even before we left for Atlanta, we'd decided that it would be safer for Kayem to go for the individual title. Ironically, Ready Teddy was the reserve for it so he only got in when Kayem came out. In the end, the team selected was Blyth Tait on Chesterfield, Andrew Nicholson on Jaegermeister, Vicky Latta on Broadcast News and Vaughn Jefferis on Bounce. Andrew also did the individual on Buckley Province, but it was Sally Clark on Squirrel Hill who came through to take the individual silver medal for New Zealand behind Blyth. The last thing I felt like doing was hanging around when I couldn't take part, and I also wanted to go back to be with Carolyn, but I did stay for a few days to walk the course with the team. Almost any cross-country course would suit Kayem, but Roger Haller had designed this one beautifully, which made me even more acutely aware of what might have been. There had been a lot of advance publicity about the heat, but the distances were shortened and new cooling devices installed – wonderful watermist sprays you could walk through or stand in – so the predicted carnage never came.

After the disappointment of Atlanta, I turned my attention to that elusive Badminton–Burghley double. After his big win, Bertie was so precious that the Howells wanted him near them in Lincolnshire. I told them, 'He's an older horse, just give him ten days in the field, then keep him ticking over for a few weeks before starting his autumn build up.' Rob hunts and they do a bit of showing so they like their horses to be big and round, not eventing lean as Bertie was. When they got him back, Bertie was their golden boy and was treated like the king he is, so they gave him a really good holiday. When he came back into work, he went to Rosemary Morris and I didn't see him until I returned from Atlanta. When he came down to me, he looked fantastic, like you want them to look at the beginning of the year, before you get them really fit, but Burghley was only a month away. Bertie was a big horse with old legs, and he really didn't need any extra weight. I took him to the advanced at Hartpury and although he went very well, I was surprised at how tired he was at the finish. The next day, he was a little bit off so he missed going to the Scottish Championships at Thirlestane. He didn't need the mileage, because he's a very competent horse, but his lack of fitness was a major concern to me, so we had to stoke the work into him. The injury was diagnosed as a minor tweak in his pastern and we thought he was over it when we got to Burghley, but he certainly wasn't as well prepared as I'd have liked. The lack of competition told against him in the dressage when he got rather tense, finishing in ninth place. On cross-country day, he went clear round a very big track and within the time, but at the end of it his pastern swelled up again and he was lame. We worked on it with ice and massage and he was a lot better in the morning, but still not right. When he was ready for the trot up, I said to Rob and Melita, 'I'll ride him for five minutes and if he doesn't come sound, we won't be able to present him.' That's what happened. The vet's scan showed very slight ligament damage below the pastern so he went straight back to the Howells for the winter. The vets had advised that he should be fine to compete again the following spring.

My second Burghley ride was Kingarrie, a sweet little horse owned by Susan Lamb, who'd been a pupil at my first ever clinic at the Wokingham Equestrian Centre in the late eighties. At the end of it, she vowed she'd never speak to me again, but in 1996 she changed her mind and gave me rides on two of her horses, Kingarrie and Kindred Spirit. Kingarrie is normally very honest, as he'd proved when he came fourth behind Blyth and Ready Teddy in the three-star three-day event at Pratoni just before the Olympics. In fact, we would have won had Kingarrie not tripped up and fallen on his knees coming down a bank and been unable to take off for the second element and had a refusal.

As Kingarrie wasn't really established in his dressage at that time, I was pleased enough with his Burghley test, especially as it was his first attempt at a four-star event. On the cross-country, he went very nicely until we came to the sunken road at the back of the course. You jumped a rail, popped down into the road, one stride and out, then two strides to a corner. He's always found it hard to judge the distances in those kind of fences and he decided to bounce the sunken road rather than taking a stride. Even after he'd left a leg coming out and we'd scrambled up the bank, we were still on line for the corner so I kicked him for it and he ran out. With hindsight, I should have pulled him right and gone the long way, but he'd always been pretty good at corners and I thought he could do it from there. After that, he cantered on quite happily until the double of brushes in the main arena. I was a bit half hearted about them and I let him run out at the second one, but we finished. He's always had trouble with his feet and he's not a great mover, but I was not worried about the trot up, especially as the vets had taken a second look at him at the first inspection so they knew that his action was always slightly awkward. To my astonishment, they put him in the holding box on the third day and then they spun him. Although he wasn't in a prize-winning position, I was very disappointed not to finish the competition on either of my rides.

The good news was that I did complete my hat-trick of three-day events in 1996, but only at the very last time of asking, at Pau at the end of October. I was riding Tessa Hood's Just Josh, a handy sort, very idle round the stable, but very strong on the cross-country. He wasn't a great showjumper – he'd dropped to third place behind my other ride, Vambi Charboniere, at our first three-day event at Chantilly in

1995 – however, his main claim to fame is that he won the two-star at Pau in successive years, beating the leading French rider, Jean Taulere, into second place on both occasions. The crowds were out of their seats as all the way round Josh bounced the rails out of their cups and, amazingly, they all bounced back in. In 1996, Jean could hardly believe his bad luck when he lost to Just Josh again. I knew two-star was Josh's limit and Tessa didn't want to ride him any more so he was sold to a woman who was looking for a horse to give her more experience.

CHAPTER SIXTEEN

SO FAR, SO GOOD ...

NOW THAT I'M IN MY EARLY FORTIES, IT BECOMES increasingly important to secure my family's future. Before we had children, I thought I'd like four, and I would certainly have liked a third, but Carolyn is adamant that two is enough and it's really her call. Character-wise, I think Lauren is very like Carolyn, but it's hard to tell how your children will develop as they grow up. Carolyn and Lauren get on very well together, but tend to squabble a bit, as like-minded people often do, and Lauren and James are both pretty stubborn, which they may get from me! So often the children of high achievers are under pressure to live up to their parents, but I have no specific ambitions for Lauren and James other than for them to have a good enough education to enable them to make choices. They're both moderately keen on riding, but nowhere near as keen as Carolyn and I were at the same age, probably because it was a novelty for us town kids whereas they're brought up with it twenty-four hours a day. I hope they get good enough to really enjoy it, and if they do want to take it up more seriously, we should be ideally placed to help them. We certainly don't force anything on them, but James loves animals as much as I did as a child, so he may grow up to be a horseman – or even a farmer.

I look forward to the day when we will be able to go riding as a family, go hunting (if it still exists) or jump round the farm, and play tennis and ski together. I enjoy all water sports, including snorkelling, and Lauren is old enough to try them now, so family holidays are great fun. The academic opportunities are generally better in Britain than they are in New Zealand, so we'll probably stay here at least as long as the children are in school, and I'm in a good position to compensate for any shortage of sports opportunities. Mostly I just hope that we continue to have a good relationship with Lauren and James. You read all these stories about kids going off the rails, running away and getting into drugs, all sorts of horrific things, and that really terrifies me.

In the two years we've been at Poplar's Farm, Carolyn has made tremendous progress in her eventing career in partnership with Regal Scot, a horse we saw on one of our routine talent trawls round New Zealand. He'd been raced on the flat winning once, then schooled over fences but basically he wasn't fast enough. He's a lovely type, not a great mover, but he has a fabulous jump, as we saw when his owner took him over a few hurdles when we went to try him. He's a grandson of Balmarino – a national hero back home after finishing second in the Prix de l'Arc de Triomphe, and he wasn't very expensive so we bought him. When he first arrived at Adlestrop three years ago, I took him showjumping and he won quite a bit of money in a short time. Despite that, I couldn't sell him as a showjumper, and I evented him until he was nearly out of novice. From the word go, he was a complete natural and I kept thinking, 'This is the perfect horse for me to ride in my old age.' He doesn't pull, he's brave and he's very clever, but physically he's never been strong. He was very weak when he first came to us and it took a long time to build him up. He used to get himself quite wound up, especially in the field; he'd gallop round and round without stopping to graze. He always had a sweaty patch on his rump, a sure sign of a long term injury, probably a pulled muscle in his hindquarters from jumping so extravagantly. I thought I must be a bit heavy for him because he sometimes felt unlevel behind on the flat, so I decided the time had come to sell him. When Ian Stark came to look at Regal Scot, he was lame on the trot up and I flung the reins at Carolyn: 'You can have this damned horse, I'm fed up with him.'

It was the start of a great partnership. Regal Scot has never taken a lame step with her and they get on like a house on fire. She loves trying things like massage and homeopathic remedies and she's treated the muscle in his quarters so effectively that it's given no sign of trouble for ages. She's much lighter than I am and Scottie, as we call him, thrives on being a one-woman horse. Dressage is certainly not his forte but she's worked extremely hard with her trainer, Tracy Foster, and he's beginning to get consistently good marks. Carolyn has jumping lessons from Vaughn – never from me because that might lead to arguments – and she nearly always gets a double clear. Scottie is a great horse for her: I know he's going to look after himself and he's going to look after her. From a husband's point of view, that's always the most important thing.

As the sponsorship drought seems to be pretty permanent, we now have several smaller arrangements involving the exchange of goods, rather than money, in return for promotion. Carolyn is very good at fixing up deals, so I leave most of it to her. Badminton Horse Feeds supply almost all our feed and Aubiose our bedding. P&O Ferries allows us travel discounts on their ships and Saab loan us a car. Other sponsors include Robinson's Animal Healthcare Products, Vine Herbal – who make natural healing products for horses – and Safilo UK. Horseware, the equipment suppliers owned by Tom McGuinness, have been extremely loyal over the last ten years, supplying as many rugs, travelling boots and saddle pads as nineteen horses can use. Over the years, Tom has established his Ulster-based company as the largest horse equipment supplier in Europe. Now he is planning a return to eventing himself, initially on Star Man, a promising advanced horse he bought from us. Conversely, I'm expanding my business interests with the Mark Todd collection, a range of rugs, boots and bits and pieces. The Mark Todd close-contact jumping saddle, which I helped design, is already in production in Walsall. The collection is a logical extension of that first project. Most of the items will be manufactured in Hong Kong and they will all be marketed by my partner, Bruno Goyens de Heusch, the Belgian entrepreneur who is already the sales agent for the saddle.

Currently, my major is Husky, now owned by Giuseppe Veronesi, who also has the European distribution rights for all the Ralph Lauren branded products. Giuseppe agreed the Husky deal when he came over to Poplar's Farm to offer me the ride on Vicky Latta's Olympic horse, Broadcast News, in October 1996. Since then our association has gone from strength to strength, boosted by Broadcast News's victory in the European Open Championship at Burghley in September, 1997. I first noticed the horse at Badminton, 1996, when Vicky rode him into seventh place behind Bertie Blunt and me. He is New Zealand bred, by a part Appaloosa stallion with a full blanket of spots over his rump. Although markings don't affect a horses's performance, I wouldn't have agreed to ride Andy, as we call Broadcast News, if he'd inherited the spots because I don't find them attractive. As it happens, he's a gorgeous, almost black horse, nearly full Thoroughbred and very fast and honest.

In the Atlanta Olympics, Broadcast News broke his nose falling at a big rounded bounce early on the cross-country course. As she'd decided to retire, Vicky invited me over to try him when she returned to her base at Gatcombe. Although I'd been impressed with his ability to gallop in his brief Olympic appearance, I was afraid he'd be too small for me but he rode bigger than he looked so I agreed to take him on. He's a timid character, a bit grumpy and very thin skinned and it took me a while to get to know him. After a mixed first season in which he came second at Bramham, and missed Badminton through no fault of his own, I felt that he was finally coming good for the European Championships. When we arrived at Burghley for the event, he was going beautifully on the flat and he was very fit. He doesn't need a lot of work and although he pants and puffs more than most horses, I've discovered that it doesn't mean anything because his stamina is excellent.

As the competition drew near, there were five contenders for the New Zealand team, Blyth Tait on Ready Teddy and Vaughn Jefferis on Bounce, respectively the Olympic and World champions; Sally Clark on Squirrel Hill, the silver medallist from Atlanta; Andrew Nicholson, a brilliant rider and a great team player, on Dawdle, and myself. Somebody was going to have to miss out. I told everyone I was happy to ride as an individual since my horse had had some problems, but I was pretty confident he'd finish the competition. Andrew said much the same thing, but in the end Vaughn was dropped because he made it clear he didn't want to go first in the team. When the question of running order came up, I was convinced I'd be asked to go first, which I didn't really want to do because Andy's dressage is good and you can sometimes get a better mark for a test the later in the competition you go. My preference would be for the number three spot but, as usual, I ended up as anchorman, which can sometimes create extra pressure. Ready Teddy is excitable in the dressage and Blyth said he would explode in front of the vocal second-day crowds if he went last, so I drew the number four slot, with Andrew going first, Sally second and Blyth third.

As the New Zealand team was drawn last, being anchorman meant going last of all, the first time that has happened since my inaugural World Championships at Lexington in 1978. I'm not superstitious, not obsessively so anyway, but as I'd failed to complete on that occasion I hardly felt it was a good omen. Not that I believe in omens ... Okay, I do have my favourite cross-country breeches, but not for reasons of superstition. It's just that I always ride in one pair until they wear out and then I get a new pair. After so many three-day events, my real problem is concentrating enough to get it all together. I used to tape reams of stuff about distances and times onto my wrist before I started on the speed and endurance tests, but now I just note the time allowed for the roads and tracks and leave it at that.

In the dressage, I had to follow the 1997 Badminton winner, David O'Connor, who is always high up the leader board. If your horse goes well, it can work in your favour because the judges are already thinking of high marks, but if he doesn't, it's a lousy draw. Andy is an attractive horse and he very seldom goes badly, but just as we were about to start they announced that David had gone into the lead on a score of 40 and the crowd burst into spontaneous applause. You're always walking a bit of tightrope on a really fit horse and Andy exploded, spinning round and taking off just as the judges were about to ring the bell for us to go into the arena. Although he was more on edge than he'd been before, he settled quite quickly once in the arena and went well until the second flying change – the one from the right leg to the left, which is always his worst direction. I always try to move as little as possible because he's so sensitive, but when I put my leg on for the change, he lashed out at it which lost us a mark or so. Again, he calmed down at once and completed a very nice test on a score of 44.2, in sixth place behind David.

When you're in a good position, you inevitably check the form of those above you and, looking at the leader board, I was reasonably confident that we could move up a bit on cross-country day. The course started with two inviting fences, then bam, you were into it, with the big log drop into the leaf pit at the third. The fourth offered an unattractive choice between a very narrow log with an uphill approach and a bigger but wider log with a dip in the ground in front of it if you went the long way. Those who survived – and several didn't – were faced with one technical question after another. It wasn't just that the course was big, but the rider had to be accurate regarding line and distance and the horse had to be bold and honest. The Trout Hatchery was a difficult fence, with a big drop into the water, followed by a choice between a bank and a bounce over rails into the lake on the left or a slightly larger step, a bounce over a fence under a roof and a stride to a fence into the lake on the right. My instinct was to go for the second option because Andy jumps so big into a bounce that he can't always pick up for the second element. I also approached the Dairy Mound Cobwebs with a lot of respect: you went up two big steps, took two strides to a large, narrow triple-brush, then three more strides on a curve to an even bigger triple-brush. A fence like that requires a lot of impulsion and accuracy, as Lucy Thompson and Welton Romance, the reigning European champions, discovered when they hesitated, had a fall and retired.

As I was last to go, my prospects were fairly clear by the time I lined up for the cross-country. Of those ahead of me overnight, Lucy Thompson, David O'Connor, Finland's Pia Pantsu and Chris Bartle had come to grief, but Bettina Overesch had gone clear across country, within the time, on the grey, Watermill Stream. As I assumed from this that she'd finished on her dressage score, the best I could do was finish on mine, a fraction of a mark behind her. What I didn't know was that she'd had time faults on the steeplechase, meaning I could overtake her – always assuming I went clear within the time myself. From the team perspective, Blyth and Ready Teddy were well up there with a fast clear round, but both Andrew and Sally had had refusals, so New Zealand needed a good round from me if we were to have any sort of chance at the medals.

I wasn't sure whether the undulating terrain would suit Andy, but Bramham is fairly similar to the Burghley ground and he'd gone well there, so I had no particular cause for concern, especially as the going was perfect, with a bit of give in it, and very smooth and well prepared. I managed to find my way round the roads and tracks, not always my strongest suit, and Andy felt superb on the steeplechase, much better than he had at Bramham. Because it was a three-star competition rather than a four-star as Badminton had been, the roads and tracks were eight km instead of ten, the chase was four minutes instead of four-and-a-half and the cross-country was eleven minutes, twenty-three seconds instead of over twelve minutes, three factors that made for an excellent competition with no horse finishing seriously tired.

Andy came in very bright and fresh after the steeplechase and the roads and tracks. His heart rate was an encouraging sixty-six which showed he'd recovered very well, so I knew I was in a position to give it everything on the cross-country. Usually when you're last, the crowds are drifting away as you go round, but this competition held everyone's attention to the end so I wasn't short of an audience. Because the third and fourth fences were so demanding and because Andy is a slow starter, I got on earlier than I normally would and gave him a good canter round. I rode him forward into the first fence, then dropped the reins on him in front of the nice big flowerbed at the second. He gave it a bit of a knock with his front legs and I thought, 'Good, that'll sharpen you up because you're going to need to be jumping the big log at three into the leaf pit.'

Watching the others all day can be an advantage or a disadvantage, but on this occasion it worked in my favour. I changed my mind about two fences, the fourth and the Lion Bridge, when I realised it was possible to take the safer alternatives and still make the time. Andy and I set off well enough, but I was a bit concerned when I was already fifteen seconds down on the clock by the two-minute marker. It may not sound a lot but it's not that easy to make up, especially as I thought I was going pretty fast already. I knew it was important not to panic and I gradually increased the tempo until I was going as fast as possible without being dangerous. As we climbed steadily uphill from fence six, Andy responded brilliantly, answering all the awkward questions at the Trout Hatchery, Capability Cutting, the Dragon fence, the Dairy Mound Cobwebs and the Farmyard. When you turn at the top for the long downhill stretch towards the Lion Bridge, you know how much petrol you've got left in the tank and I was relieved to find Andy had plenty. From then on, he fairly flew, despite giving me a moment's anxiety at the Lion Bridge. As I approached the first part of the obstacle, the seat, he seemed to lose concentration and I thought for a split second he was trying to stop. I jammed my leg on and gave him a sharp nudge with the spur and he did an enormous cat leap over it. He then quickly dropped down the bank into the water, turned and neatly popped over the boat, under the bridge and galloped quickly away on the homeward leg. The last major hazard was a bounce of big angled hedges in the main arena. Although it didn't look inviting, it had jumped very well all day and I'd decided that if I was down on the clock, I'd risk the direct route. Andy was fairly flying by that stage and I'd made up my fifteen seconds, plus the five extra I needed to play safe at the hedges, so that's what I did. In the end, we finished five seconds within the time after one of the fastest rounds I've ever done round a track of that size and difficulty. Andy's not dissimilar to Charisma, nippy and fast, balanced enough to slow down, turn and accelerate on a sixpence, and there can be no higher compliment than that.

As we jogged back to the stables, I could hardly believe it when I heard the announcer say, 'Mark Todd has gone into the lead.' Mind you, my excitement dimmed somewhat when we cooled Andy's feet in iced water in the whirly boots and he came out hopping lame. Once again we had our brilliant veterinary team, Wally Niederer and Mary Bromily, and they decided that it was actually the cold that was causing the problem. Mary's healing hands soon had him back on track, so Carolyn and I were confident enough about the vet's inspection the next day to enjoy a quiet celebration with Giuseppe, Lucia Montanarella his PR person, Lizzie and Reggie at the George in Stamford that evening.

With Bettina Overesch and William Fox Pitt lying second and third, just .2 of a penalty and one penalty behind me, I had absolutely no margin for error in the showjumping. If I'd knocked one rail and all the horses immediately behind me had jumped clear, I'd have dropped to about twelfth so it was white knuckle time as Bettina, the first of the top placed riders to jump, went into the arena. If she knocked a fence, Andy and I would have a cushion, but the gods were on her side. Although Bettina and Watermill Stream gave some of the fences a few dramatic rattles, all the poles stayed in place and she was clear.

Andy is an excellent showjumper, but he hadn't jumped a clear round in a one-day event that autumn. Nevertheless I knew he could do it, I knew I was capable of making him do it and I knew I was going to prove it there and then. As Andy popped flawlessly over the practice jumps, the applause that greeted Bettina's round told me what I didn't want to know. 'There's no way you're going to have a fence down and lose this competition,' I told him as we waited in the collecting ring, but did we both believe it? The track was a fair size, but that in itself wasn't a problem for a horse that jumps extravagantly big. It was the three combinations that represented the real danger: the danger of him jumping in too exuberantly, landing on his forehand and failing to pick up in time to clear the next element. If I'd done my homework properly, he would clear them and we'd win. As we started our round, I drew on my experience as an Olympic show-jumper to banish all self-doubt. As Andy pulled eagerly towards the fences, I steadied him, looked for a stride and urged him on. He responded magnificently and the fences came and went, the two doubles and the nerve-racking treble, until there was just one upright left. He cleared it effortlessly and we were the champions, a supreme moment that was all the more welcome because this time we'd taken on the world's best and won.

William Fox Pitt and Cosmopolitan also jumped clear, taking individual bronze and securing team gold for Britain. New Zealand came a close second, thanks to my win and Blyth's fourth, and ironically, we probably would have been unbeatable had Vaughn been on the team. After the medal ceremony, I did a television interview with four-year-old James perched ecstatically on my shoulders. I'm not sure he knew why he was there, but he certainly enjoyed the moment. Afterwards we had a few drinks with Pedigree Chum, who sponsored the event, and then we drove Andy home.

Exactly a week later, I was stretched out on the floor of my dining room enduring intensive massage over most of my body. The cause of my pain was Hunter's Moon, a big bay six-year-old that I'd always thought a lot of. He was 16h 1in when I bought him in New Zealand early in 1996, but he's grown another four inches since he arrived in Britain. I knew he was a late developer but he'd gone so quickly through novice that I thought he was ready for his first intermediate at Gatcombe the weekend after Burghley. He was so far in the lead after dressage and showjumping that I was expecting to trot up, so he'd proved me right. Mind you, we were all a bit concerned about Princess Anne's new fence, a double of angled hanging logs on undulating ground, but I thought he could handle it. Wrongly, as it turned out. He jumped the first part well, had a big look at the second, chipped in another stride and tried to jump it. Somehow he got his front end over, but fell heavily on the gravelly landing and rolled right on top of me. I lay there winded for a bit, then got up and used a few words I don't usually use in public. I had gravel rash all over me and I was quite sore, though I wasn't going to admit it to anyone. The fence judge didn't want me to go on, but I wasn't concussed and I was determined he shouldn't finish the day on that note, so we jumped the next two fences before I retired. I showjumped two more horses, then allowed myself to be talked out of going across country and went home to lick my wounds.

I could have broken my pelvis, my leg, my arm or even my neck, but somehow I walked away. I notice that I don't bounce back so readily from a real cruncher of a fall nowadays, but that won't stop me, not for years yet, touch wood. I still love eventing and my Burghley win confirmed that I'm still competitive at the highest level, but of course there comes a time when you have to stop. Bruce Davidson is successful on the international circuit as his fiftieth birthday looms, and Bill Roycroft represented Australia in the Olympics when he was sixty, but it's tougher nowadays. I haven't noticed my reactions slowing down yet and I'm quite fit and supple but the time may come when I have to work out to keep in shape, something I'm putting off for as long as possible!

Carolyn and I haven't decided one way or the other about returning to New Zealand, yet. In a lot of ways, I'd like to, but we have to work out how best to earn a living if and when I retire. Teaching is an obvious fall back and I'm happy to do it at any level so long as the pupils try. You can't change anyone radically in a few days, but you can give them a few ideas, a few things to work on, and you usually see some improvement by the time they go home. I prefer teaching on a one-to-one basis on the flat, whereas jumping works well in a group because everyone can learn from everyone else's mistakes. Sometimes people who've barely jumped at all get going over novice fences and feel like they've jumped clear round Badminton, which is as rewarding for the teacher as training advanced riders who are aiming for the top. I have two annual clinics in England, at Lincoln and Wokingham, but I also teach regularly in Italy because the money is much better. The riders are more advanced and I use a translator so that they can understand precisely what I want them to do. In addition, I do the occasional clinic in America and Canada, and although I would never find enough of a challenge in full time teaching, I can imagine expanding on my existing programme in the future.

I also do quite a few lecture demonstrations. I don't enjoy the prospect, but it's fine once you get going. I ride three or four horses, explaining what I'm trying to do as I go. I haven't fallen off yet, but I wouldn't mind if I did because it would make people laugh and I always try to strike a light-hearted note. At the end, the audience are invited to ask questions, but as most of the demos are held in a draughty indoor school in the middle of winter, they're usually so frozen to their seats that they can't wait to leave. I first got into the lecture demo business when I did my Round Britain Rolex Tour after my second Olympic victory in Seoul in 1988. On that occasion, we took in twelve venues in fourteen days, starting in the north of Scotland and working our way south. The tour was arranged by Raymond Brooks Ward, through his marketing company, BEP, and by the end of it I sounded like a broken record. The invitations have kept coming ever since.

I've always had a passion for breeding horses and I can easily see myself spending my retirement running a small stud. I bought my first ropey old brood mares at auction in New Zealand in the late seventies and I've been accumulating knowledge and expertise ever since. Currently we have two New Zealand stallions in Britain, Mayhill, who stands at Clissy and Edward's stud in Devon, and Aberjack, who is already following in Mayhill's footsteps by doubling up as an eventer. From 1992 to 1995, Mayhill covered mares in the spring, then travelled to events in Clissy's lorry so that I could ride him. When the stud season ended, he returned to us to complete the eventing season. He'd probably have been an even better eventer without the moonlighting, but we wanted to establish him as a stallion while he was young. I remember riding him in the three-day event at Saumur, then pulling him off the lorry to serve a mare the moment he got home. On other occasions, he'd cover a mare in the morning, compete in a one-day event, and cover another in the evening. It was an exciting life for him, but tiring at times. We've got one of his yearlings, but his first crop are five years old now and they're looking pretty good, so we should see them in novice events this season.

Aberjack is by Aberlou, the sire of Blyth's two good horses, Messiah and Delta, so he certainly has an eventing pedigree. I chose him because he's a very different stamp of horse from Mayhill and they should complement one another. He'd done nothing other than cover a few mares and hack around the sheep station when we brought him to Britain as a six-year-old in February 1997. He is a beautiful mover with a lovely temperament, so he has everything it takes to go to the top and his first two events in early August were extremely promising. Shortly after that, however, he injured himself so badly on the horse walker that he put himself out for the rest of the season, but I'm looking forward to getting back in the saddle in 1998.

We also have a couple of brood mares at Poplar's Farm, but our main thoroughbred interests are in New Zealand, not least because breeding and training racehorses in Britain is too expensive. We've got three quality brood mares, Sounds Like Fun, who was second in the Oaks just after Carolyn and I got married; her daughter, Cantango, by Danzatore; and Sounds Abound, by Sounds Like Fun's sire, Sound Reason. They're all with Brent Taylor at the Trelawney Stud in Cambridge, where Sounds Like Fun's maternal grandsire, Alcimedes, used to stand. I'm fascinated by bloodlines and my aim is to produce middle distance horses that are capable of winning classic races like the Derby and the Oaks, but of course it doesn't always work out like that.

I first went into flat racing under Jockey Club rules in 1983 when I sold my dairy herd. I had decided to become a full-time event rider, but reckoned I had enough money to spare to fulfil a long-held ambition to buy a nice brood mare. I consulted Patrick Hogan, the leading breeder in New Zealand, and he advised me to choose a well-bred yearling filly, race her and then breed from her. I went to the sales at Trentham racecourse in Wellington and looked at every filly I'd marked, plus a few others. I set myself a limit of NZ$50,000, a lot of money for me at that time. Even now I think I must have been mad, but you have to take a gamble somewhere along the line. I'm not a betting man, never more than a couple of dollars anyway, and I couldn't stand losing money at roulette or pouring it into slot machines, but I'm prepared to take a chance on a racehorse.

Sounds Like Fun was on my list, but I'd always put a question mark beside her, and I ended up buying one of my first choices, Somerford Bay, by Western Bay out of an English mare. I paid NZ$32,000 for her and then I thought, 'Well, I've still got money to spend,' so I looked at my question mark again. She was almost black with a nice face, but very warty. It didn't totally put me off because a lot of yearlings suffer from the same problem. I was watching in the parade ring with a farmer friend called Kit Davison when Sounds Like Fun came under the hammer and I asked him if he'd like to go halves. When he said no, I bought her anyway for NZ$20,000. As there was no way I could afford to race two fillies, I asked another friend, John Bell, if he'd like to lease a half share in one of them. My trainer, Jim Gibbs, has a particularly good track record with fillies and he liked them both so I offered John a free choice. Unfortunately for him, he picked the wrong one but his loss was Mum and Dad's gain because they agreed to lease a half share in the filly he didn't want.

And what a gain it was because Sounds Like Fun turned out to be a real fighter who didn't know how to run a bad race. She matured slowly so she didn't run as a two-year-old, but the next year she won two races before going for the New Zealand Oaks. She didn't have a lot of early speed, but she would settle in just behind the pace and come with a long smooth run at the end. She couldn't stop and then sprint, so she usually had to work towards the outside before making her move. In the Oaks, she ran her usual honest race to come second, beaten fair and square. She won a couple more races, including the Great Northern Oaks at Ellerslie, and ended up as one of the leading three-year-old fillies of the year. Over the next two years she won several more races but never managed to get home first in a Group One race. With an ounce of luck, she'd have won the TV NZ Stakes in Auckland, but she finished third, beaten by a nose and a nose. The winner was Bonecrusher, the Australasian champion at the time, and the second was Horlicks, a mare who went on to win the Japan Cup in world record time. They both had very good runs up the rails, while Sounds Like Fun had to pull out to get a clear shot on the outside. Even after covering that extra bit of ground, she got her nose in front, but the others came back at her on the line. She completed her final campaign in a million dollar race in Sydney, just missing a place after travelling badly, running on a heavy track which didn't suit her. Her career earnings were just under NZ$500,000 so she was certainly a bargain, even before she went to stud. She is a leggy individual and her progeny are just like her so they aren't easy to sell, even though her only two runners are winners. With hindsight, I may not have chosen the most suitable stallions for her because although her offspring have inherited her looks and her fighting spirit, they haven't shown her ability. Not yet anyway.

After Sounds Like Fun's successes, Mum and Dad thought, 'Well, this is really easy,' but they've lost a bit of enthusiasm since they took half shares in our other racing interests, Sounds Abound and Cantango. Sounds Abound may have the same talent as Sounds Like Fun, but she certainly doesn't have the same enthusiasm. We bought her as a yearling and put her in training with Jim Gibbs, but her two-year-old form was dismal. When she started her three-year-old career in the same fashion, we were getting a bit desperate. Under the New Zealand system, horses have to compete in trials, informal race days with twenty races or heats at varying distances, to qualify for a start under Jockey Club rules. When Jim told us that Sounds Abound was showing nothing in her trials up to 1600m, I said, 'Stick her in blinkers, start her over 2000m and send her to the front and if she doesn't do any good that way, we'll get rid of her.' My plan worked! She won her next trial, followed by a couple of races under rules over 2000m. They weren't great races, but some of the horses behind her were going to the Oaks, so we let her take her chance. On the day, she was one of the favourites but she was drawn on the inside which didn't suit her, especially when the handlers spent eight minutes persuading the recalcitrant favourite into her stall. Sounds Abound was a relaxed character so she fell asleep and missed the Jump. When she failed to get up with the leaders at the start, she lost interest and did nothing. Later in the season, she partially redeemed herself by winning the Group Three Centaine Stakes at Awapuni. By that time, we'd begun to realise that she was a real gutsy stayer when ridden from the front, but if she found herself behind a wall of horses, she wouldn't try. She came into work again as four-year-old, but tweaked a tendon before she got onto the track so we sent her straight to stud. Like Sounds Like Fun, Sounds Abound's progeny take after her, but it's too soon to say how they'll turn out. At the moment, racing is a nice little earner, with the emphasis on the little, but like all good horse people, we expect to hit the jackpot soon!

Looking back on my eventing career to date, I can't think of a better way of earning a living. I do what I love, meet a huge range of people and travel the world. What more could you want? Dinner with the Queen? No problem. I've done that twice – and it was hugely embarrassing on both occasions. The dinners were hosted by the New Zealand Commission, so there were quite a lot of people there, but because I'm horsey I was seated next to the Queen. The first time was just after the Los Angeles Olympics, when I was still single. I was introduced to the Queen and Prince Philip and we chatted away over drinks before going in to dinner. As I was putting my napkin on my lap, I noticed that my fly was open. While discreetly zipping it up under cover of the napkin, I could only hope it hadn't been too obvious earlier on. I found the Queen surprisingly easy to talk to, probably because she knows so much about Thoroughbred breeding, and she'd visited the Cambridge Stud just down the road from where I lived.

The second dinner was a black-tie event at the New Zealand High Commissioner's house on 8 February 1996 and, as usual, Carolyn and I were late. Our taxi driver got a bit lost and we were flying around in circles when we came to a road block. 'Hey, what's going on 'ere?' he asked, and I said, 'Don't worry, it's only the Queen. Just drop us off here and we'll run.' As it's not the done thing to arrive after the royal party, the butler shuffled us up the back stairs to enable us to make a discreet entrance. No such luck ... As we strolled in trying to look nonchalant, Prince Philip said, 'Ah, a little late, are we?' At the table, the lady-in-waiting seated on my left was in a complete flap, saying, 'Just wait until Her Majesty talks to you. She'll turn to you when she wants to, but don't speak to her until she does.' The Queen sat down and we resumed where we'd left off 12 years before, chatting easily about racing and other topics.

After the Queen presented me with the prize for winning Badminton in 1980, my next royal assignment was with Prince Edward, when he was at school at Wanganui for a year. He wanted to visit a farm and go for a ride, so the headmaster rang me up and asked if he could come to us. This was in 1983 when I had the dairy farm, so I rounded up a bunch of mates and we spent a very pleasant afternoon in the hills above Kenny Browne's place. We were in a complete dilemma as to what we should wear and we all got dressed up in our jodhpurs only to see Prince Edward turn up in his jeans. My Jack Russell terrier never ever followed me when I went riding, but she did that day, even she knew it was a special occasion! I made sure our route took us past Pop and Mumma's place so they could meet Prince Edward, and afterwards he came back to our old farmhouse for tea. Mum had said, 'You can't let him drink out of those dreadful old mugs of yours,' and she brought over her best china, baked cakes and waited with Dad until we turned up. The prince was very relaxed about it all, a competent rider and easy to get along with, and I think he enjoyed it.

Over the next three years, I'll be gearing myself towards the Olympic Games in Sydney in 2000, with a shot at that elusive World Championship in Pratoni as my immediate aim for 1998. When I went to New Zealand at the end of 1996, I bought a big chestnut horse called Stunning for the Apters, who own Kayem. They came over to watch him run at the Puhunui three-day event before he was shipped to Britain, not a particularly auspicious occasion as he fell at the fourth fence when he was in a winning position: he jumped so boldly into the water that he lost his footing and we were such a wet heap that I didn't bother to go on. It was no fault of his, but so far Stunning seems to be a bit like Just an Ace in that he's unlucky at key moments.

He'd done a lot in a short time in New Zealand, first as a show-jumper with Graham Hart, and then as an eventer with Andrew Scott, and I didn't really appreciate how green he was until I started eventing him in the spring of 1997. It takes horses twelve months to adjust to the seasonal change after the journey from New Zealand, and Stunning didn't have much of a break after Puhanui, so I probably asked too much of him too soon. He wasn't very trustful when he arrived, but he's getting more friendly now and I'm reasonably confident he'll end up okay. He's only eleven so if he comes right in time, he'll be a good prospect for Pratoni and hopefully for Sydney as well.

My other great hope is Word for Word, three years younger and much less experienced than Stunning, but so far he's answered all my questions magnificently. I've ridden him from the beginning so he does everything my way, whereas Stunning has had several other riders and I'm having to retrain him to my way of going. Word for Word is very easy to ride, bold and straight, but not strong across country, or anyway not yet. He's capable of doing an excellent dressage test but his showjumping is a cause for concern, mostly because he's weak and a bit idle. If it improves as he matures, he'll be a very difficult horse to beat.

If I dared to gaze into my crystal ball and see myself receiving a gold medal in Sydney, the horse beside me would be Stunning or Word for Word. Then again, who knows? That's the thrill of eventing. You never have a clue what's going to happen next.

A Competitor's Diary: 1998

1 JANUARY: For the first time in ages we spent Christmas in England – partly because we wanted to spend Christmas in our own home and partly because the children only had about three weeks off school and had to be back by 7 January. I've got four horses back in work now, with the rest all due back some time during the month. At any one time we have around fifteen of our own horses alongside those we train. I've got a nice team to start with – the most proven horse is Broadcast News and my number one aim is to get him to Badminton in the spring. I'm also aiming to ride Stunning and Word for Word at three-star three-day events in the spring. As Robert Lemieux is retiring, I have acquired Just A Mission and I'm looking forward to working with the horse; he was well placed in a two-star in 1997 and every other horse I have had from Robert has been a pleasure to ride. Eye Spy went well in 1997 and our stallion Aberjack is starting out this season alongside Diamond Hall Red and Davy. Carolyn is aiming to ride Regal Scot in an early three-day event this season.

17–24 JANUARY: A ski-ing trip to St Moritz with Bruno and Ebba Goyens de Heusch – and we manage not to break any limbs. We all have a fabulous time based in a hotel right on the mountain, so we can ski straight out the door and back again in the evening. Jurg Zindel arranged it for us and managed to join us a couple of times – he was very hard to keep up with.

28–31 JANUARY: Short trip to Phoenix, Arizona, for a couple of days' teaching arranged by a private contact – it's amazing to go from fresh snow to scorching heat and enormous cacti almost overnight. The crew caught me a rattlesnake suggesting I kill it and take the rattle home as a souvenir, but I soon scotched that idea!

1 FEBRUARY: Aberjack gets colic, caused by a blockage in his gut. When we get him to the Potter's Bar Clinic an operation looks likely, but he picks up when they eventually shift the blockage. He has a catheter in his jugular vein to administer antibiotics but, soon after this is removed, he gets an infection in the wound. His neck and head swell up and he has to be injected with antibiotics in the veins on the inside of his legs. (He is an amazing patient, but I don't think he totally recovered from this over the course of the 1998 season and continuous relapses put paid to his going to a three-day event which was my aim.)

2 FEBRUARY: One of the horses we have in training this season is the gorgeous young New Zealand thoroughbred mare Snap Happy. She is one of the nicest young horses I've ever jumped and moves beautifully. She's got a good attitude and is brave, but this morning as she and another horse were being led in from the field something startled them and they got away from the girls. They galloped up the drive to the house and then took off and tried to jump the hedge into a neighbouring field. Snap Happy must have clipped the wire fence three feet behind the hedge, tripped, then went down and broke her shoulder. Such a tragic accident is sickening – she couldn't even be saved as a brood mare and her death was horrible; we're all gutted. Everybody in the yard loved this horse and it's a very sad loss for us all.

6 FEBRUARY: Dazzling Light, a newcomer to the yard, owned by Varenna Allen (she had been with Jane Holderness-Roddam) arrives along with Just A Mission.

10 FEBRUARY: The first meeting of what is to become PERA – the Professional Event Riders' Association. The idea is to get together

with Andrew Nicholson, Blyth Tait, Eddy Stibbe, William Fox Pitt and Mary King (who can't make the meeting) and a representative from a promotions specialist. We listen to his ideas and begin to develop our own ideas of how the association might work to promote the sport (although eventually we parted company with the promotions people after we discovered that they were in trouble financially). What we want is to get more money invested in eventing and encourage a higher profile for equestrianism outside of the specialist media. I'm very keen to make this work, but not sure how it will pan out – it will be difficult for any of us to find the time to run any sort of outfit alongside our riding commitments, but generally I feel very positive about the possibilities for PERA. Eddy is doing a lot of background work and research and feels the idea is definitely good enough to continue with.

12–20 FEBRUARY: Another ski-ing holiday! We had such a good time in St Moritz we decide to take the kids ski-ing at half-term. Diamond Hall Red's owners Pat and John Smith kindly gave us the use of their chalet in Val d'Isère, and Mick and Mel Duff and their two children came along too. Lauren loves it – she was convinced she would be able to ski before we left home and she picks it up very quickly. James is a bit nervous to start with but by the end of the week he is bombing around as well. Fortunately we meet Lizzie Purbrick's nephew, Toby Boone, and a friend of his who are working out here and they take the kids under their wing for half a day most days. The kids learn a lot more from them than they would from us – and it gives us some time to ourselves.

7 MARCH: We kick off the eventing season at Stilemans. The weather is incredibly wet, every lorry is being towed in and there's a huge queue of vehicles. Hit a winning note with High Street in the novice section. I hope this win is going to set the tone for the rest of the season – but not for the weather!

14 MARCH: We take the novice horses to Charlton Park – Aberjack isn't 100 per cent fit, but jumps a double clear, albeit slowly, cross-country. High Street continues to run well and is third.

15 MARCH: TWESELDOWN We take Diamond Hall Red, Dazzling Light and Just A Mission – it's my first ride on both Just A Mission and Dazzling Light. Just A Mission goes well, Dazzling Light runs out at a corner and Diamond Hall Red comes good going very well. I'm not really trying for a win here, just looking to ease the horses in and see how they're running.

17 MARCH: My old friend David Foster comes to stay for a couple of nights over Cheltenham Festival. We have a fun evening one night together with Lucinda Green and friend Tim Brown – I don't know it, but it will be the last time we see David. (He died in a tragic accident later in the season at a competition in Ireland.) Carolyn and I don't get to the races ourselves.

21–22 MARCH: LINCOLNSHIRE Staying as usual with Tessa and Charlie Hood, who owned a previous ride of mine Just Josh. Carolyn is riding Regal Scot in the Intermediate event when she has a nasty fall, cracking her shoulder and tearing ligaments. I'm out on the course and don't see the accident happen – back at the lorry I'm waiting for Carolyn when Scottie appears back without her. I jump on Scottie and ride back to where she should be, but she's been scooped up by the ambulance giving me a worrying moment or two. It's a real shame, because Regal Scot was going very well for Carolyn and she was really looking forward to the rest of the season – now she will be out for several months and I will have to take over the ride. Eye Spy, Stunning and Word for Word all go OK – so it's a good event barring the drama of the day.

We've been joined at the yard by Tracy Foster who comes two days a week to help school the horses on the flat – we've got so many competing that I'm finding it difficult to fit them all in timewise. It makes a big difference to how the horses are running and makes my life easier having another pair of hands to help us all out. Tracy has been teaching Carolyn for the past year and I like the way she rides and teaches – in the same kind of way I like to do it – so she fits in very well.

23–26 MARCH: To Italy for two days teaching a clinic near Milan –

the European attitude to event riding is very different to the American. The Americans are almost too technical, they over-analyse and make riding more complicated than it really is or should be – the Italians are a bit the opposite. Teaching through an interpreter makes the job more difficult, but all the students are very enthusiastic and fun to teach. I enjoy teaching, but only as long as I don't have to do too much of it!

28–29 MARCH: GATCOMBE Stunning is going much better this year in his two runs so far – an improvement on last year when he didn't go well at all in the middle part of the season. Just A Mission copes badly with the heavy ground and has five rails down in the showjumping. Hunter's Moon gets his first run of the year – I had two quite heavy falls off him at the end of last year, so I'm quite pleased to come home with a double clear. Davy also gets a run.

1 APRIL: Valerie and Michael Parr are over from California to try out Limelight, a very nice little horse we own in tandem with Santiago de la Rocha. I don't have time to do both showjumping and eventing so we had come to the decision that the showjumper should be sold. In the middle of the try-out Limelight overreaches and cuts his heel making him slightly lame. This means four to five weeks of hell getting him through a vetting and he takes for ever to come right. (He has since been going very well and his new owners are delighted with him – and we got another ski-ing invite out of it which is terrific...)

5 APRIL: DYNES HALL I intended to run Broadcast News here, but he has missed some work due to a minor hiccup, so I've left him at home. Word for Word goes well and my first ride on Regal Scot goes really well, he wins the Intermediate section and upgrades to Advanced. The weather has been so wet that the stables are under water – it looks like rain is going to be a constant presence this season.

7 APRIL: Second PERA meeting – the crunch has come with the original promotions people, so we decide to go our own way. Robert

Lemieux and Andrew Hoy join us on the committee.

8–9 APRIL: PORTMAN The weather has been dreadful throughout the spring. This event is very wet and I only run one horse, High Street, who does well to win a Novice section.

12–13 APRIL: Brigstock and Ston Easton events cancelled due to the wet weather meaning that Broadcast News misses out on yet another event. This is both disappointing and worrying as Badminton gets even closer, but on the positive side of things it is pleasant to have a quiet weekend at home. There aren't too many of them during the season. With no event to go to on Easter Monday we decide to take the children to the Cotswold Wildlife Park and enjoy a family outing. Our day is shattered when Brendan Corscadden rings from Ireland to tell us the news that our great friend David Foster has been killed in a tragic riding accident. We are left feeling totally numb. David was one of the most respected and well-liked riders on the circuit and his loss will touch a lot of people worldwide.

15 APRIL: Carolyn and I fly over to David Foster's funeral. I have the very sad honour of being a pallbearer. It is a huge funeral with about 1,000 people from many countries turning up to pay their last respects and to support his lovely wife Sneezy and their three children.

18–19 APRIL: BELTON PARK Aberjack, Broadcast News, Stunning, Davy, Dazzling Light and Regal Scot all get a run. Broadcast News goes exceptionally well considering it is his first run of the season and he finishes second in an Advanced section. Stunning has a stop at the water which is perturbing. I hope the water problem he developed last season isn't coming back to haunt us. He stopped at the water several times last year and so I took him schooling into water and tried to persuade him not to think about it too much.

It's now only three weeks to Badminton and Broadcast News has had only one run – he jumped extravagantly across country and felt great at Belton, but today he is lame with a pulled muscle in his back. I'll have to take it easy over the next few weeks, perhaps use the walker or lead him off another horse to keep the weight off his back.

23–26 APRIL: SAUMUR A run for Word for Word and he scores very well in the dressage and is clear inside the time on the cross-country, though only just … We're down on time at the fourth last, a corner fence, and since he still has a bit of life in him I'm pushing him along a bit when we make an error. I misjudge it and we hit it very hard and I shoot up the horse's neck and all but come off, hanging on by luck rather than anything else. So going into the showjumping, we're in the lead, but showjumping isn't Word for Word's best phase though he's improving all the time. Andrew Nicholson is right behind us on New York – also not a great showjumper – with less than a rail between us. Andrew goes clear and is confident he'll get the win, so we need all the help we can get. Lesley McNaught is here with the Swiss Team and she agrees to help me work Word for Word in before our round and we go in to jump clear and win! A very satisfying result for the year's first three-day event.

When I get home it is to the news that one of the mares has foaled a nice bay colt by Aberjack.

29–30 APRIL: TIDWORTH Diamond Hall Red, Eye Spy and Dazzling Light are all running in the Intermediate and all go pretty well apart from Dazzling Light who naps badly and runs out. Aberjack and Sam Smith run in the Novice section and both are placed. Aberjack is going very well in his events as well as working hard at home covering mares – it's a busy season for him!

1–3 MAY: BICTON Stunning runs very well in the Advanced section and comes third. Because of the early season cancellations, Just A Mission hasn't run for ages which means a lot of my plans for him are up the creek. I wanted to do an early three-day event, but now I will have to put him into a few more one-days first. He has also had a mystery leg infection which didn't help matters so I take him out of the Advanced and put him into the Open

Intermediate instead. There are several riders waiting at the start of the cross-country and there is a one-foot-high log in a dip which I decide to trot Just A Mission at. He immediately refuses and drops his head, depositing me on the floor. It causes great amusement amongst the others. By the end of the day lots of other riders including Andrew Nicholson and Blyth Tait fall off on the cross-country so I don't feel too bad about it. High Street does his first Intermediate and he comes second which is great and better still Diamond Hall Red takes the top spot – all in all it's been a good weekend.

7–10 MAY: BADMINTON The big one. I'm really concerned about Broadcast News having missed so much work and whether he's actually fit enough to compete – we've only had one gallop since the run at Belton and I haven't jumped him at all since. The going is very good which will help – Andy is not a horse that likes heavy ground – he much prefers to be on top of the ground. We are drawn late on the second day and he does his best effort for me so far in the dressage test, putting us in second place. He's the first horse to score over 200 marks from one judge for the new four-star test, so I'm very pleased with him at this point. The cross-country course is big but straightforward and a good galloping sort of track with nothing that particularly worries me. Broadcast News completes the roads, tracks and steeplechase well within himself and at the end of phase C comes in with his respiration rate a little high. This worries me a bit with regard to the cross-country – it's probably a sign of his lack of fitness. I decide that we'll start the cross-country, but that I'll pull up if he feels tired. But he's an amazing little horse and, after we set off, he takes a few minutes to get into it before giving me a very nice ride. The further we go, the better he goes. As we get near the end I'm waiting for him to show signs of tiredness, but he keeps on cruising and we finish comfortably inside the time and in the lead. Great! On Sunday he feels a little bit stiff and the ground jury make us trot up twice, but pass him fit in the end. In his two three-days with me he's gone clear in the showjumping both times but we don't have a rail in hand over Chris Bartle on Word Perfect so we're going to have to go clear to win. Going into the arena last of the field we approach a triple bar to an oxer with a water tray underneath near the middle of the course. I try to shorten his stride to the oxer but he doesn't listen to me and has the front rail off. We've lost it. I'm very disappointed not to have a fourth Badminton trophy under my belt but, considering I didn't think Broadcast News would even start the event, I have to be very satisfied with the result.

14–17 MAY: PUNCHESTOWN Regal Scot and Diamond Hall Red are both running in the two-star (Just A Mission is out of the running due to the minor leg infection) and Regal Scot is drawn first to go of the two. He does a very nice test, if not flash, and is well up after the dressage. Diamond Hall Red, however, gets highly excited and is definitely not on his best behaviour. Both go clear inside the time on the cross-country and are well placed for the showjumping on Sunday. We end up with Regal Scot third and Diamond Hall Red just out of the placings and I feel they're both ready to step up to three-star level. Regal Scot feels fantastic and definitely has a big future.

23–24 MAY: PENTON The ground here has gone from being a bog to rock hard in a matter of ten days or so. I don't really want to run any of the horses on such hard ground, but because of the cancellations earlier in the season we need to get some competition runs in. I go very slowly cross-country and then end up withdrawing the one horse that should run on Sunday.

25 MAY: CLEOBURY MORTIMER With Stunning, Eye Spy and Dazzling Light. Dazzling Light and Stunning go very well and Stunning jumps both the waters well so I'm very pleased with him. Eye Spy gives me a few hairy moments because he jumps extravagantly and then stops – I think he must have jarred himself at one of the big drop fences. It's a worry, because this is his last run before the three-day at Blarney.

29 MAY–1 JUNE: WIESBADEN To Germany with Blyth Tait. I'm riding Just A Mission in the new CIC international one-day event which is incorporated with a big showjumping and dressage show

in the town centre's park. It's a fabulously well-organised show. Just A Mission goes very well and comes fourth, which makes up for a mishap I had just before flying out ... I was delighted to have been asked to be best man at David and Jackie Green's wedding, but because we were a bit late leaving home and then got caught in a traffic jam behind an accident we managed to miss the entire service. Fortunately I didn't have the ring in my pocket! A great time was had by all despite the missing best man – and we had a great time too once we actually arrived. Also on the 29th Limelight finally left for the USA and his new owners the Parrs after his try out in March. Back at home Hendrick Degros has been riding Aberjack and Sam Smith in Novice events and going very well on both.

4–7 JUNE: BLARNEY CASTLE To Ireland with Eye Spy and High Street. High Street has some big questions to answer as this is his first three-day and I'm worried he might be a bit light on experience having only done two Intermediates. And Eye Spy had stops in his last one-day event ... Both however finish in the top half dozen after the dressage test. It's very wet – again – and, as Eye Spy is the stronger horse, he copes the better of the two with the heavy going. Eye Spy goes clear cross-country and High Street goes well too, but with one run out which I partly blame myself for, so overall I'm delighted with him. On Sunday Eye Spy is third going into the showjumping. We go clear to see the two horses in front both have fences down and we end up winning. As High Street also goes clear, I'm very pleased with both horses – not many others managed clear rounds in the showjumping making their performance look even better.

9 JUNE: The Hickstead organisation and the press arrive at Poplar's Farm to launch the big new Hickstead event in July at which each competitor will do a dressage test and showjumping round in the arena and then do a short cross-country before coming back into the arena. Michael Whitaker has flown in from overseas to dress up and ride the new dressage test for the media in our arena on a horse lent by Jane Bredin.

11–14 JUNE: BRAMHAM Non-stop rain all weekend! Stunning is drawn near the end of the field which means the ground will be even more churned up by the time we get our chance. He does his best dressage to date and takes the lead which is very encouraging. But on cross-country day the rain never stops and by the end of the day the ground is badly cut up and very heavy. Stunning has a terrible time on the steeplechase and it's a real effort for him in the conditions. On the cross-country the going is so bad I decide we can't risk travelling fast and so we end up with 15 time faults which drops us to third place. It's disappointing, but Stunning has gone particularly well over a difficult water fence and this pleases me more than anything. On the last day there are very few clears in the showjumping and we have one fence down but it still moves us up into second – all in all I think this is a very good result.

20–21 JUNE: CATTON PARK Cancelled. Rain. Another nice weekend at home!

23 JUNE: Spend the day teaching at my annual clinic in Wokingham.

25–28 JUNE: CHANTILLY Off to France with Just A Mission and Dazzling Light. Both horses do very respectable dressage tests. Dazzling Light is a bit difficult on the flat, but I think she's making good progress now and Just A Mission's very nice test puts him near the lead. It's the showjumping next and Just A Mission and Dazzling Light both have two rails down, which is a bit disappointing, but both go very well on the cross-country. Due to his good dressage test and quick time across country Just A Mission finishes tenth and Dazzling Light ends up in nineteenth place. I'm really pleased that they both went so well across country.

30 JUNE: To New Zealand for three days for a cocktail party! There is a big launch for a new sponsor for the three-day event at Puhinui. I fly out, have two days in New Zealand and then fly back again – originally I was only scheduled to spend twenty-four hours there, but eventually I decided I'd take one day and night to spend at home with my parents. Everyone is very happy with the launch and the

organisers are particularly pleased, so the trip has been very good from that point of view – Puhinui is now getting a bigger international profile which is good for equestrian sport in New Zealand. This is why I feel it is so important I do the trip and give the organisers my support despite the hours wasted in an aeroplane!

7–8 JULY: HICKSTEAD I'm at the new event with Regal Scot – he's the best showjumper we've got and he does a reasonable dressage for his first go at the four-star dressage test. He makes a couple of mistakes in the showjumping and we end up just out of the money. It has been good fun running against the specialist showjumpers though. A hugely enjoyable event with a big crowd who seem to really enjoy it.

11–12 JULY: TWESELDOWN I give Word for Word and Regal Scot a quiet run before they leave for Germany next week for the CIC event at Bonn Rodderberg. Hunter's Moon and Aberjack – doing his first Intermediate event – both go well and get double clears. Word for Word and Regal Scot feel very good on the Intermediate track here.

16–19 JULY: BONN RODDERBERG I'm running Word for Word and Regal Scot in the three-star CIC one-day event and Just A Mission in the two-star CCI three-day so it will be a busy weekend. All three horses do good dressage tests in their respective competitions, particularly Regal Scot who gets a better mark than Word for Word – a very good result considering his relative inexperience. And he was competing against some very good horses indeed including Blyth Tait's Chesterfield and Aspyring (who went on to be first and second at Burghley later in the year). Regal Scot goes clear in the showjumping and Word for Word has a fence down. (Andrew Hoy is in the lead on Swizzle-In.) We go in reverse order for the cross-country. Regal Scot is in second and Word for Word is also highly placed at this stage – he's a very good cross-country horse. If I want to do as well on Regal Scot I'll have to put my foot down and keep up a good gallop all the way round. Regal Scot has never even done an Advanced one-day event, so this really is his first competition at this level. He goes nothing short of brilliantly and I'm delighted that he comes home with the fastest time of the day. Andrew Hoy goes exceedingly well until the second last and then has a stop at a bounce into water that puts paid to his chances, leaving Regal Scot first and Word for Word fifth. In his three-day Just A Mission again goes well across country and after this phase lies in second. Unfortunately we have the last fence down in the showjumping but manage to hold on to second place. Home on Sunday night after a really pleasing weekend.

20 JULY: We leave for a family holiday in Sardinia with the Meinls – picked up in the private jet again which is always an immense treat for Carolyn and me as well as the kids! We have a great time in the sunshine and the sea and Lauren learns to water-ski. Home again the following weekend just in time for the next event.

28–29 JULY: KNAPTOFT Feeling pretty chipper after an incredible season so far – particularly the three-day event results – and we're about half way through. Diamond Hall Red, Eye Spy, Regal Scot and Aberjack will all run here. Aberjack is placed again in the Intermediate event – he really is going exceptionally well especially considering that we still can't get his blood quite right which is worrying. Most of the spring and summer three-days are out of the way now and we are going into the autumn having had a good spring – typically I am wary of things starting to go wrong, but the horses still seem to be in good form. We missed competing at Cornbury due to our holiday and the following weekend due to Anna Hermann's wedding to Simon Hilton in Sweden (we had a great time though). But still, we missed loads of events in the spring due to the wet weather and it didn't seem to affect the horses too badly, so perhaps missing these two weekends won't do too much harm to our chances for the rest of the summer. We do try and let our six full-time staff have a holiday at this time of the year before we get busy again in the autumn.

7–9 AUGUST: HARTPURY A busy weekend. I ride High Street, Aberjack, Eye Spy and Stunning, also Diamond Hall Red, Regal Scot and Word for Word meaning that with our pupils and others based at Poplar's Farm we have thirteen horses competing over this weekend. It's a major operation moving so many people and horses, getting organised and ready. Aberjack goes well and is placed. In the end I decide not to run High Street as he is in the process of being sold subject to vet (everything we own is for sale – our aim is always to build up horses with an eye to selling them on, with competitions being our shop window). Stunning wins the Advanced Intermediate and Regal Scot an Advanced section – a great result for us all. Diamond Hall Red gets his first Advanced run – also his first since Punchestown as he missed Knaptoft with a slight bump on his leg – after a silly stop at a spooky third fence he goes very well.

11 AUGUST: PERA meeting at Poplar's Farm – things are progressing well and we are in advance talks with Husky about their co-sponsorship with PERA of the World Rider Rankings and are just about ready to finalise details of an affinity credit card with MBNA and Mastercard. Both deals would do a lot of good for the promotion of the sport to the general public, which is one of our main aims.

15–16 AUGUST: GATCOMBE The British Championships: the only horse we have in the Championship is Word for Word. He goes well to finish eighth – I've got a ride on Diamond Hall Red in the ordinary Advanced and he goes extremely well to finish fifth. Regal Scot comes in fourth in the Intermediate Championship. I also ride Eye Spy, but he has another off day stopping at the tricky third fence. No wins, but overall everything feels good to me.

18 AUGUST: Teaching at Wokingham clinic – nothing unusual to report. After Knaptoft we decided not to run Hunter's Moon (who we had thought a lot of, but who had been lame on and off all year for no apparent reason) again this season. So we are now trying to tie down exactly what is wrong with him.

22–23 AUGUST: THIRLESTANE We originally have five horses scheduled for the Scottish Championships, but High Street has been sold and Hunter's Moon is not right. I had thought of putting Eye Spy in for his first Advanced event, but I've decided he isn't ready as he wasn't foot perfect in the Intermediate at Gatcombe. So eventually we come up to Scotland with only two horses, Stunning and Aberjack. Stunning goes very well and does a good dressage and a very good cross-country including two water jumps – this is really pleasing as I'm running him with Burghley in mind – and he finishes fourth. Aberjack goes very well to finish second in the Intermediate. He has a big future.

30 AUGUST: HENBURY HALL And the season is building up to the World Equestrian Games in Pratoni del Vivaro in Italy. I've got three horses nominated for Pratoni: Broadcast News, Word for Word and Stunning. Broadcast News is of course my first choice and normally I would take Word for Word and Stunning to Burghley and save Broadcast News for the World Games, but the New Zealand Federation want me to keep a horse in reserve for the Games. I decide to make the reserve Word for Word because Stunning is the more experienced of the two and he can go to Burghley. With luck Broadcast News will run in Italy and therefore it won't hurt Word for Word to have another three-star run in Boekelo. So, the plan is to do the minimum with Broadcast News – he is fifteen years old now and getting on a bit – since he has shown he can do well with the minimum number of runs before a competition like he did at Badminton and should therefore be OK as he is for the Games. And here at Henbury I'll run Diamond Hall Red, Word for Word and Regal Scot...

Word for Word and Diamond Hall Red are running in the Advanced class and Regal Scot in the British Selection team section. Word for Word goes brilliantly to win the Advanced class, but disappointingly Diamond Hall Red has an uncharacteristic two fences down in the showjumping on very soft ground. He's more settled in the dressage and goes well in the cross-country. Regal Scot does a good dressage, but I manage not to look properly at the schedule for his section and the usual order of showjumping and cross-country is reversed so that our lovely clear round in the showjumping is done before the cross-country not after it as it should be and we end up being eliminated – which is very annoying indeed as I know we would have been very competitive in this section.

3 1 AUGUST: HIGHCLERE Today is Broadcast News' first run since Badminton and I must admit he feels a bit rusty! He's a bit too keen in the dressage and as he is still not listening to me has one fence down in the showjumping. Again on the cross-country he feels very keen and because the ground is rock hard and rough I try to keep him steady, but he wants otherwise so we have a somewhat rocky passage. Just A Mission goes well and is placed after jumping a double clear. Eye Spy doesn't go well – I can only assume it's because of the hard ground – and he feels sore in his back.

1 SEPTEMBER: Another sad occasion: Katie Meacham's funeral – two good friends in one year have had their lives cruelly cut short. Tragically, Katie was killed in a freak road accident. It makes you stop and think how precious life is.

3–6 SEPTEMBER: BURGHLEY The first three-day event of the autumn season. As I'd planned, Stunning is our only horse here. He does a good dressage and we're well placed after the two dressage days. When we arrive the going is perfect – they have done a fabulous job in preparing the ground – but from Friday on it starts to rain and doesn't stop. By Saturday morning the course is very wet and because it had been watered earlier on in the week it now soaks up the rain like a sponge and just like at Bramham in the spring the horsebox park is a quagmire and the trade stands are sitting in a sea of mud. I feel sorry for the organisers who worked so hard on the ground. It's a very big track here and like last year's European Championship technical too. This year it's perhaps a little less technical than last, but it is certainly even bigger and right from the start the cross-country is causing everyone trouble. There are a lot of problems for all the riders, and even experienced horses are struggling and making it look very difficult indeed. Stunning is due to run at the end of the day and, by the time our turn comes, the steeplechase course is really cut up and heavy – he's one of the few horses in the second half of the field to make the time for the steeplechase and with hindsight I think he may have pulled a muscle in doing so. We complete phase C in fine spirit and then we come to the ten-minute box and things have gone from bad to worse out on the course. The horses are not handling it at all well. But I'm still hopeful we'll get round OK. I'm doing up the girth to get on before the cross-country and stretching Stunning's front leg when I pull up the girth and the horse flinches a bit which worries me, but I get on and trot round and it feels all right so I get ready to start. At Burghley the difficult fences start early and the third, the leaf pit, is a very big log drop followed immediately by a difficult corner. Stunning is normally quite keen at the start of the cross-country, but this time he's off the bridle from the word go and I have to chivvy him along. He does the difficult Land Rover combination very well and then goes up the long pull uphill and the ground is very soft beneath us and he doesn't feel like he wants to go at all, which is worrying at such an early stage of the course. He continues to jump OK – a bit sticky at the first trout hatchery, but it's a difficult water and he goes through it well enough. Another steep pull uphill and he really doesn't feel like he wants to go on. We jump the corner fence, go up again to the chicken mound and stop at the fence on top, turning to jump the long way out, not particularly well, and carry on feeling very unenthusiastic about the whole thing. We jump one more and then it's Capability Cutting. We jump in over a rail into the Cutting OK and then down a dip and up to a big spread to jump out. Stunning must just have caught his front feet on the far side of the spread because he trips a bit, pushes off with his back legs and as he does so shoots me straight out of the saddle to land flat on my bum. I think, well, we're only halfway round and not going well and since we're well out of contention perhaps the best thing is to take the long walk home. As I said, it could have been a pulled muscle, or perhaps even a virus. We've had a bit of a virus in the yard this summer (we regularly check the three-day horses' blood and some had shown signs of having a virus this year) so it could have been that, I'm not sure. We get him home and when we check him over his blood is OK. David Ponton who does our physio' and acupuncture looks him over and says he thinks Stunning is very sore through his shoulder, so the damage was probably done on the steeplechase. Our first autumn event and we didn't finish which isn't a good start. I don't want to think that this is the beginning of a run of bad luck...

10–13 SEPTEMBER: BLENHEIM I'm riding Regal Scot and Diamond Hall Red who is drawn first of the two to go early on Thursday. Again after working in well, Diamond Hall Red is unsettled in the dressage – I think I'll have to send him off for specialised dressage training to relax him a bit. On the second day, Regal Scot does a very nice test to go into fourth place and I feel very confident about him. It rains again on cross-country day – yet another wet event. Diamond Hall Red gives me a lovely ride on the steeplechase and cross-country. Because he's well down in the placings after the dressage, I don't push him hard, but nevertheless we finish just over time with one time fault. I'm looking forward to the ride on Regal Scot. At the start of phase A Scottie gets quite excited and as soon as we set off he doesn't feel right. The further on we get the worse he feels and by the end of phase A at the start of the steeplechase he's not good at all – Carolyn reckons he's tying up and she's right. We've no option but to withdraw again which is immensely disappointing. I feel sure he would have coped very well round this course, but it's easy to say if, if, if ... Diamond Hall Red finishes the competition and again I'm delighted with his cross-country round – he really does feel capable of jumping at the very highest level, we just need to work on his dressage a bit more. So, two three-day events in a row and two out of three horses have not finished – things are not looking too good.

14 SEPTEMBER: On the Monday after the Blenheim event Malcolm Wharton – a very progressive-thinking organiser – hosts a mini-competition at Hartpury for those horses going to the World Equestrian Games. Most of the American team, the New Zealanders and Australians, one Spaniard and one Japanese rider turn up to compete. The competition is organised by Jim Wolf and Mark Phillips. I run Broadcast News (his last run before the World Games). Regal Scot has shown some signs of virus and after he ties up on phase A at

Blenheim I have to rethink which horse to run where in the run up to the Games. So, I reroute Stunning to Achselschwang along with Just A Mission and move Regal Scot to Boekelo (which will give him more time to recover) where I intend taking Word for Word if he doesn't have to run in Pratoni. I'm very pleased with the way Broadcast News is shaping up for the Games – he goes very well at Hartpury – he's the most trouble-free he's been in the run up to any three-day he's done. Word for Word is also going well and is going to be a very able back up.

We're going to be very busy in the next few weeks what with Achselschwang and the rest – on Tuesday 15th Stunning has cross-country schooling, Just A Mission goes at Upton on Wednesday 16th before going to Achselschwang and I also ride two Novices and one Pre-Novice. It's the first Pre-Novice I've done all year and is on Prometheus owned by Sarah Cumani – he's probably the best-bred horse in eventing being the offspring of Rainbow Quest, who won the Derby and Princess Pati, who won the Irish Oaks. We jump a double clear and then it's Thursday at home followed by the weekend at Gatcombe again.

19–20 SEPTEMBER: GATCOMBE I've been hoping that I'll be able to take Aberjack to a three-day event this autumn but his blood still isn't good and he's not feeling right, so I decide to call it quits for this year and start thinking towards a three-day event for him next year. We'll run Word for Word and Eye Spy here. Eye Spy is sixth in the Advanced Intermediate and I'm very pleased with him given that we're heading for Pau later in the season, and that will be his last run as I will be away from now on.

After this week I'm anticipating a bit of a logistical nightmare with three competitions in a row abroad: Achselschwang, Pratoni and then Boekelo. Andrew Nicholson and Blyth Tait and I all have horses going to all three events and so we've spent some time working out who should take which horses where, when and in whose lorries! Andrew has horses going to Achselschwang so we decide his lorry will take our horses there. Blyth's and my lorries will go to Italy with the New Zealand team horses and Blyth's reserve horse and on from there to Boekelo. Andrew also has one horse going to Boekelo so his lorry will go from England with his horse and both Blyth's and my other Boekelo horses – phew! It's hard work getting the right horse to the right place at the right time.

On the nineteenth our team vet Wally Niederer arrives and trots up Broadcast News and he's lame! So, having been as right as rain throughout the summer, all of a sudden his slightly club right front foot is giving us problems. Wally, the team farrier and my farrier David Smith carefully go over his feet and make a few adjustments and I set off for Achselschwang with Broadcast News getting better but still not 100 per cent sound. I tell Carolyn and Wally that if Broadcast News is not sound by the time the lorry is due to leave, not to put him on it. It's all very fraught...

Luckily he comes sound in time and makes the trip to Italy in my absence. Just to complicate matters even further our lorry went for servicing before the trip only for fatigued metalwork to be diagnosed with a warning that the whole back end could collapse at any moment – the local garage worked round the clock to fix it in time.

24–27 SEPTEMBER: ACHSELSCHWANG Despite the complications in getting here all is going well. Just A Mission is lying about eighth after the dressage with Stunning a pleasing second. Just A Mission goes first and goes well on the steeplechase but going into the cross-country we have a very near miss on fence nine – a brush fence with a bounce to a ditch – and he just doesn't jump far enough over the ditch, catches his front leg, goes down on to his nose and I shoot up round his ears with the reins pitching over his head. Just as I'm about to fly off, he throws his head up shooting me back up into the air and I end up astride his neck but with no reins and not in the saddle. As he gets back to his feet, I wriggle back and try to grab the reins, but he's already taking off and it takes some time to get everything organised again. We lose around half a minute while I get him back under control. He gives me a very good ride the rest of the way though valuable time is lost. We get some time faults but not too many, and I've got a very sore chest where his head hit me on the way up. On top of this, Stunning has a near miss on the steeplechase – looking around at the crowd as usual – going straight through the second fence, but I manage to stay on and he is as good as gold for the rest of the course. He gives me a fabulous ride round the cross-country course, jumping two very difficult water fences very well and I'm delighted with him. We finish well inside the time and go into the lead. On the final day both horses jump clear rounds so Stunning has come good and won this time. The owners, Jayne and George Apter, are delighted, even more so when we win a SEAT GTI car as first prize – a shame it's left-hand drive. This is one of the best three-day events: great competition, organisation and *fun*! Just A Mission finishes up seventh and the competition as a whole is a really pleasing warm-up for Pratoni.

27–30 SEPTEMBER: Andrew Nicholson, Rosemary Barlow (head of the British Supporters' Group) and I fly off to Rome for the World Equestrian Games and meet the horses there. All have travelled well to Rome and we arrive in Pratoni on Monday afternoon. I ride a bit on Monday afternoon, and as we are all a little worried about Broadcast News' fitness after the last scare we go for a really good gallop on Tuesday morning so that the New Zealand selectors can decide which horse I should ride in the Games. Andy felt good on Monday and even after his hard workout on Tuesday morning he pulls up feeling good and still looks good at night. On Wednesday we present both horses at the trot up and both pass. I am confident that Broadcast News is all right and I do my best to persuade the selectors to let me ride him in the competition. I put my neck on the line a little, but he's been first or second in every three-day event we've done together. I get a big shock when the team is announced – I get to ride at number one in the team and not my normal anchor position. Our team is drawn second to go. I'm a bit annoyed at this as normally the best dressage marks come in the afternoon of the second day of tests, so I think my chances of a win might be lessened but nevertheless I'm all the more determined.

1–4 OCTOBER: WORLD EQUESTRIAN GAMES, PRATONI
Two of the three judges were at Badminton and marked us well then and I know the horse is talented on the flat, so perhaps riding so early won't hamper our chances too much. We'll just have to do as

good a test as we did at Badminton and then they won't be able to ignore us. Then we're on and Broadcast News does an even better test than he did at Badminton: there's nowhere I can say he makes even a slight mistake. He flows well and moves beautifully and we get comments from onlookers that it's one of the nicest tests they've seen. We get a mark of 34 and face the prospect of sitting through two days waiting to see if it will be bettered! Bettina Overesch goes late in the second day, does a lovely test and just pips us with 33 and there's only one other mark in the thirties. The rest of the New Zealand team do consistently well in the dressage and we finish the dressage with the team second overall and me second as an individual.

Next day, Saturday, I have cause to be thankful for my early draw – it has rained all night (as it does every night! I don't think any other event could have coped with such a deluge, it must be something to do with good drainage on their volcanic soil), but is dry in the morning. Broadcast News gives me a fabulous ride round a thirteen-minute course – very long, but measured leniently. Around half way there is a double of corners which are huge and with a very short distance between them. I decide we've got time in hand so I'll go the long way figuring we could do this and still be inside the time – since going early it was important we go clear. Phase A of the roads and tracks is shortened due to the conditions and Broadcast News is a bit sticky on the steeplechase taking his time to warm up. On returning from phase C, we find that they've pulled out fence 17, the double of corners, and this will make the time even easier. I really don't have a moment's worry round the cross-country; the further we go, the better he gets and we arrive at the second half jumping well and galloping easily, and finish confidently twenty seconds inside the time. This is great for my individual score, but also a strong start for the New Zealand team. Only Bettina will be able to get ahead of me in the individual competition after the cross-country, so she's the one to watch. Half way through the day it starts raining heavily again and the going changes to cut up and heavy making it difficult for the later horses. Sally Clarke going second for the New Zealand team is having an off-day, her horse just doesn't want to know and they have several stops. Blyth Tait goes clear inside the time and then Andrew Nicholson, who isn't in the NZ team, also goes inside the time. Vaughn Jefferis our anchor-man needs to go clear riding in the worst possible conditions – he gets his clear round, but is just outside the time. Bettina also gets her turn when conditions are at their worst and gets time faults, putting her behind me in the individual event. Worse still, her horse has pulled one of its shoes off and looks a bit lame and the next day it doesn't pass the trot up. So, Broadcast News and I go into the showjumping with a rail in hand over Stuart Tinney of Australia and in good heart. Bettina is out of it and Blyth moves into third. As I have one rail in hand over Stuart and not quite two rails over Blyth, I can still only afford one down. At the warm up Andy feels good and jumps well outside the arena, but the rain worries me. It's already quite soft in the main arena and he jumps best off firm ground and we're due to go last of around seventy horses which is bound to mean the ground will be cut up. Going into the main arena I know Blyth has gone clear so I can only afford to have one fence down – Stuart's had two down so he's out of the running. Vaughn has jumped clear and lies fourth so we've got the team result pretty much sewn up provided I go well. (Andrew has one down and goes to fifth as an individual.) It has been twenty years since I rode in my first World Championships and in between I have never gone clear on the cross-country and so the title has eluded me. I'm feeling pretty confident and Broadcast News really goes at the first jump, the second is an upright and as we come into it he doesn't get high enough and so down it goes. I think, 'Oh God – don't panic'; bumping this fence might have woken the horse up a bit, but at the third, another upright, he does exactly the same again. Bloody hell – I kick and jerk and feel desperate round the rest of the course, but the fences stay up. At the finish we've lost the gold. It is sickening to be so close to the title and still miss out. I should be pleased with World Silver, but having had the gold in my grasp it's natural to be disappointed. New Zealand confidently win the team gold even though Sally had a hard time. Blyth is first, me second, Vaughn fourth, Andrew takes individual fifth place, so all in all it is a superb result for New Zealand. Paula Tornquist has a brilliant ride to take the bronze medal – she's only been riding for eight years and is working full time as a pilot, so to achieve third place at this level of the sport is a terrific achievement.

8–11 OCTOBER: BOEKELO My lorry left Rome early on the Sunday morning driven by Debbie Cunningham, with Word for Word and Blyth's other horse as well as two Aussie horses, heading for Boekelo. It feels strange watching it leave, as if we haven't finished this competition yet, but we have to get the other horses up to Holland. There's been no big celebration because we're all too knackered and I have to fly back to England on Monday morning and then leave Poplar's Farm again with Regal Scot, Andrew Nicholson's and Blyth Tait's horses at 4 a.m. on Tuesday in Andrew's lorry. When we arrive in Boekelo, they've clearly had a lot of rain and it is still raining. Debbie arrives from Rome just before we get there. Regal Scot goes in the first day of the dressage and is in the lead at the end of the day. Word for Word, who's done a lot of travelling, does a good test and just beats Scottie so I am lying first and second. On Friday night it rains *again*; they cancel the roads, tracks and steeplechase making the event effectively a one-day, which is disappointing but the right decision under the circumstances. They also take out some of the fences on the cross-country where the going is particularly bad. A few people withdraw, but my two horses go well given the conditions, particularly Word for Word who goes at the end of the day when the going is at its worst and makes the day's best time. So we end up still in first and second place at the end of the cross-country. There isn't so much as a rail between my two horses, but both can afford a rail down over Blyth who is in third place. In fact Word for Word could have two fences down and still get second place. Regal Scot goes clear in the showjumping and then Word for Word lets his concentration slip – as he often does – and has the last two fences down, so they end up reversing their placings.

All in all it has been a very successful three weeks and the end of what has probably been my most consistently successful season so far, but it still isn't quite good enough to beat Blyth Tait in the World Rider rankings. New Zealand are cleaning up internationally, which is a nice feeling for us all; of the competitions we've been in we won just about everything between us, except of course Badminton.

22–25 OCTOBER: PAU With no horses for Le Lion d'Angers we have a week off between Boekelo and Pau. Eye Spy and Sam Smith make the longer journey down to this ever improving event. Both go well in the dressage and end up well placed. Two clear rounds on endurance day leave me well up the order. Eye Spy in particular feels very good. Sam Smith, in his first three-day and the first time I have ridden him since a novice, copes very well. Unfortunately they both have one fence down in the showjumping and end up seventh (Eye Spy) and twelfth out of a record field of 119 starters. It looks like I will have to brush up my showjumping next year – rails down have cost me too much this year. Phew – I'm glad the season's over.

30 NOVEMBER: At the end of this month it will be back to New Zealand for the three-day event at Puhinui.

As a whole 1998 has been a tremendous year. A season as busy as this year's simply isn't possible without my back-up team. First and foremost there's Carolyn who does most of the organising for all our trips away from the yard and makes sure things run smoothly while I'm away, which is no mean feat. I rely on her a lot for all the details. And then there's the staff who work very hard to keep the horses in the yard going while I'm out and about. Our vets are indispensable – both our team vet Wally Niederer and the yard vet Buffy Shirley-Beavan – as are the physios Mary Bromily and David Ponton and the 'backman' Tex Gamble. It is a team effort all round.

Broadcast News has had two starts at four-star level and two seconds – it's sad that a fence down cost two wins, but that's the nature of the sport; you can't afford to make mistakes. I think we've finally cracked it with Stunning – a second at Bramham and a win at Achselschwang. He's a funny character, but this year he has matured a lot and become more confident and trusting. Next year I hope he'll do better still. Word for Word has had yet another very good season with a first and second in his two big events. I aim to have these three horses in four-star events next spring and would like to take one of them to the Lexington, Kentucky four-star event and the other two to Badminton. Regal Scot still hasn't done a three-star three-day event, so hasn't qualified for Badminton. He has improved in leaps and bounds this year, though, and is potentially one of the best horses we have. He is certainly one of the best jumpers, but because he didn't complete at the three-star CCI he will have to do another three-star event – probably Saumur – next year. Just A Mission was second at Bonn Rodderberg and seventh at Achselschwang – he's another horse with a lot of potential, and he'll do another three-star next year. I think I'll probably take him and Regal Scot to Burghley in the autumn.

Any of these horses could be aimed at the Sydney 2000 Olympic Games, although Broadcast News might just be too old by then. But it is good to have such an event to aim for.

Diamond Hall Red will do another couple of three-star events next year and then his owners may consider selling him. As Eye Spy went well again at Pau he'll step up to three-star in 1999.

The other big step forward of 1998 is the formation of PERA – I'm pleased with the way it has taken off and we will be having another meeting soon to make sure we keep up the momentum. We have donated £10,000 to the Bramham event and will add another £5,000 or £10,000 to Blenheim to boost their prize fund. Somehow I find myself the association's chairman – I think I was volunteered – but I'm enjoying it. PERA is a very good thing: it's high time the riders had a say in the running of the sport and also put something back! But we will need backing from many more of the event riders to make a real go of it. It has been good to get some very positive feedback after some initial doubts and concerns. 1999 should be a good year for the sport as a whole...

MY TWELVE FAVOURITE HORSES

Charisma, my double Olympic champion, is the horse of a lifetime, but a riding career can never depend on a single star, however brilliant. It goes without saying that all my best horses are superb jumpers, brave, honest and clever, or they wouldn't be on the list at all. In other respects, horses are as diverse as people, with individual quirks that make you love them or – in some unlisted cases – loathe them. I like to get horses from New Zealand because they're very settled and well-mannered and they're taught a lot of respect. As they mostly live out, they're not so prone to the grumpy stable vices you can find in horses that have been stabled all their lives. Ideally they're raised on the hills in a very natural environment and this means they acquire good balance from the start. By the time they're yearlings, they're galloping up and down hills, crossing streams and jumping over little logs as a part of their daily routine. By naming my top dozen chronologically, rather than in order of merit – which I would find much more difficult – I hope to show the crucial role each played in my first twenty years at the top.

TOP HUNTER (Toppy) 17h liver chestnut Thoroughbred (TB) gelding, by the New Zealand sire, Head Hunter, who produced good all-round jumpers as well as racehorses.

As a big immature baby, Top Hunter was too slow for the track, but he was a very kind horse with a lovely easy temperament. Lyall Keyte, a neighbour of the Harveys (my employers during my farming cadet days), bought him as a four-year-old and turned him into the best hunter he ever had. His big mistake was lending him to me to ride in the Waikato Area Trials for the Pony Club Championships in 1976 – I liked the horse so much that I persuaded Lyall to let me buy him. In 1978, I took him to the World Championships in Lexington, my first competition outside New Zealand, and although we came to grief on the cross-country, the experience gave me a hunger for international eventing that still persists today. Looking back, it's incredible that a horse should go to a competition like that having done just ten one-day events and one three-day event in his life. He also got to grade A showjumping in New Zealand, which gave me valuable experience, and we competed to medium level dressage.

SOUTHERN COMFORT (Monty) 16h 2in brown gelding, with a lighter muzzle, TB cross, possibly with a bit of trotting blood on his mother's side.

A very handsome intelligent horse, with a big eye and a big heart, he was bred on a sheep station and bought by Garnet and Shirley Woods, farmers in the Hawkes Bay area of New Zealand, as an unbroken three-year-old. As an all-purpose family horse, he'd done quite a bit of hunting and of showjumping up to grade B with several riders before he came to me. He also evented up to intermediate level, doing a couple of three-day events. Again he was a lovely, easy horse to handle, but you could never hit him with a stick. I found that out at my first Badminton when I gave him an encouraging slap and he stopped, put his head down and bucked. I always carry a stick, but I never used it again on him because I've never known another horse that resented it to that degree. Perhaps because he'd been brought up on a sheep station Monty was very nimble and quick thinking, always able to find a fifth leg in an emergency. He needed it at Badminton in 1980 when we sprawled on landing over the Footbridge before going on to win. My first Badminton, my first title: how could I ever forget a horse who gave me that!

CHARISMA (Podge) 15h 3in, dark brown gelding, by Tira Mink, out of Planet, TB, with a touch of Percheron. Handsome rather than pretty, with a lovely eye and exceptional presence, even as a foal.

Apart from his all-round brilliance, Podge is an unusually sound horse, perhaps helped by the fact that he didn't start his international eventing career until he was ten. He is also exceptionally greedy, a cause for concern when it came to getting him three-day event fit. Although he didn't go quite as I'd have liked on the flat, he'd been trained to a fairly high level before I had him and his combination of speed and agility over fences took him to the top as soon as our partnership began. After his gold medal in Los Angeles in 1984, he went from strength to strength – literally – on occasion he almost pulled my arms out. In his final gold-medal winning appearance at the Seoul Olympics, he was so far ahead of the field that his one weakness – his carelessness over showjumps – barely came into the equation. Some handsome horses can look a bit soft, but he was a tough athlete and a real fighter, taking nothing out of himself as he got on with the job he loved. The better he got, the more star quality he developed: no one who meets him ever forgets him.

MICHAELMAS DAY (Mick) 16h 3in, bay gelding, Irish bred by Mad for Money.

Susan Welman bought Mick from the showjumper Cyril Light for Phoebe Alderson to event. She took him through to advanced as a six-year-old, so he did a lot very early in his career. He was friendly enough in the stable, but he didn't find any aspect of eventing particularly easy. He didn't move well and he was very stiff, so he found dressage difficult however hard he tried to please. He was almost too bold for his own good across country. I tried every kind of bit, gags, pelhams, twisted wire bits, whatever, and they all worked for a while, but never for more than a couple of runs. Sometimes he was so strong it was difficult to steer him and every so often he'd make a terrible mistake like miss a fence out altogether, which was terrifying at the speeds he liked to go. Nevertheless he was a real old character, I won a lot on him and I couldn't help liking him for all that I wished he was a little less Irish at times.

BAHLUA (Baxter) 16 h 1in, dark bay TB gelding, New Zealand bred, by Balak, the sire of the Grand National winner, Seagram.

After I bought Baxter from Andrew Nicholson, as a novice with five points he took me to team gold and fifth place individually at the Stockholm World Games in 1990. He was a horse with a big character and a particular favourite. He had a wonderful eye and a very expressive face. He could look grumpy, lay his ears back and pull faces at you when he wasn't in the mood, but it was all play-acting, he genuinely loved being around people. He was always very tricky in his mouth, holding it slightly open so that it was very dry and he's never to this day mouthed the bit – played with it so that it creates saliva – as most horses do. He had a habit of putting his head up in front of a fence and running into it, which he gradually got better about, but he always gave you a tremendous feeling of security, as if he always knew exactly what he was doing. He was an exceptionally smart showjumper, almost good enough to specialise, but he found dressage difficult. His trot was fine, especially his extensions, but there was no hiding the deficiencies in his canter and the judges always spotted them. Like Podge, he is exceptionally sound as he was still proving as a sixteen-year-old in 1997 with his long time owner, Eddy Stibbe.

WELTON GREYLAG (Morph) 16h 2in grey gelding, TB cross by Welton Crackerjack, out of Gorse. Bred by Sam Barr and owned by Susan and Mike Welman.

Welton Greylag was my mount for the Barcelona Olympics, but we had to retire after the steeplechase due to injury. As far as talent was concerned, he had everything he needed to go right to the top, but his temperament let him down on occasion. He was wonderfully kind to look after in the stable and fabulous to ride on the flat: he moved so beautifully that it all seemed effortless. When it came to jumping, he was a bit too over enthusiastic about the job, almost to the point of stupidity at times. He wasn't as self-destructive as Mick, but he got incredibly strong across country and that made him difficult to manoeuvre. Luckily, he was very quick with his front feet, so even if he was wrong, he was able to get them out of the way. We never had a fall or a stop, not that I remember anyway, but he had a way of galloping heavily into the ground that put a tremendous strain on his physique. I was always trying different bits in the hope of getting him to relax and settle, but again they were never effective for long. He won three-day events at Stockholm and Burghley, but his record would have been better still if he hadn't been plagued by injury.

DOUBLE TAKE (Squiff) 16h bright bay gelding, New Zealand bred, by a trotter out of a station hack. Bought as a five-year-old in 1988 by Bill and Judy Hall with a view to competing in the showjumping in the Olympic Games in Barcelona four years later.

Squiff was small but very chunky and strong, a plain horse with a totally charming character. The very nature of his plainness, his great big ears and lovely eyes, made him even more charming. He was quite nervy and sharp to begin with, but he was highly intelligent and he relaxed as soon as he knew what was what. Like Podge, he was a favourite with all the girls. When anyone walked down the yard, his head would shoot out and he'd whinney in welcome. You had to be careful when you were riding him and you certainly couldn't bully him, but he always tried his heart out in the ring. He came second to Milton in the Hickstead Grand Prix and won the Volvo Qualifier in Helsinki with me, but he hasn't done so well since he's been ridden by professional showjumpers. I think the way I rode him suited him and I'd like to have taken him further, but time and cash flow were against it. It's nice to have a horse from the start so you can see his confidence develop. By the end, he followed me round like a dog, a real softie, just like Podge.

MAYHILL (Auk) 17h bright bay horse, TB by Auk, out of Blonde Oak. Bought as an unbroken four-year-old from Dorothy Johnson in Tirau, New Zealand.

A big leggy horse, very handsome and a very good mover, but Mayhill's real strength is his temperament. He was so quiet that the children could go into his stable and we treated him just like the geldings. When he was doing his stud work in Devon, he got a bit more aggressive, but as soon as he came back to us, he knew he was off games and settled back into the old routines. His offspring have inherited his temperament, so we made a good choice in keeping him as a stallion. He was very easy to ride on the flat and over fences, so much so that I used to take him across country in a rubber snaffle. I think he could have done a lot more, but the stud fees were too tempting. I'd like to buy one of his four-or five-year-olds to event fairly soon, just in case I've retired by the time our yearling is ready to compete.

JUST AN ACE (Ace) 16h 2in bay gelding, TB cross, by Just a Monarch, out of an unknown dam, possibly part warm blood.

Bought as unbroken two-year-old by Robin and Mary Patrick and brought on by Robert Lemieux with considerable success. I had a catch ride on him at Badminton in 1990 when Robert broke his leg. Since then we've ridden him in turn, first Robert, then me, then Robert again. He's naturally timid, a bit distrustful in the stable and he hates being touched around his head. Initially, he'd stand in the back of the box, but gradually he came out of his shell. I spent a lot of time trying to get his dressage right because he really was a fabulous jumper, quick thinking and athletic, and I always felt very comfortable on him. His dressage did improve, but it was never good enough to make it easy for him to win a championship, and he never did. When his chance came in the World Championships at The Hague, in 1994, he was robbed by a freak mistake at the water, so he will probably always be the best horse I've ridden who never won a big competition.

BERTIE BLUNT (Bertie), owned by Robert and Melita Howell, 17h 1in chestnut gelding, TB by Sunny Boy, out of Spanish Harpist.

After an abortive racing career as a youngster, Bertie was brought on by Nick Burton and was well established by the time he came to me. He's very thin skinned and ticklish, so he pulls faces and snaps his teeth while he's being groomed, but he'd never bite anyone. For a big horse, he's very nimble on his feet and very good technically over a fence, which makes it pretty easy for him across country, especially as he absolutely loves it. As he's usually well up with the leaders in the dressage, he's difficult to beat, as he proved when he won Badminton in 1996, but he already had big windgalls on his joints when he came to us, which indicates a lot of mileage on the clock. A stone bruise kept him out of the money at Badminton in 1995 and at Burghley in 1996 he injured himself and has not competed since.

KAYEM (Coco) 16h 1in flea-bitten grey gelding, by Absalom, out of White Domino, by Sharpen Up. Bred in Scotland as a sprinter and raced unsuccessfully as a two-year-old.

Like Coco the Clown, he can be quite cheeky, perhaps because he's the apple of Jayne Apter's eye and she spoils him rotten. He came with the reputation of being a bit grumpy – his other nickname is Crocodile because his head snakes round when you tighten the girth – but his personality has improved since he came to us. Initially we were told he attacked other horses so he had to be turned out on his own, but we soon discovered that he enjoys being part of the crowd. He too was started by Robert Lemieux, then sent to Owen Moore, who offered me the ride at Punchestown when he broke his collarbone. Like Just an Ace, he's difficult on the flat, but a scopey, if slightly unorthodox, jumper and spectacularly good across country. We came fourth in the European Championships at Pratoni in 1995 and won at Saumur in 1996, but our Olympic bid failed even before the first vet's inspection due to a persistent shoulder injury. In 1997, he chipped the end off his pelvis on the steeplechase at Badminton. A scan later in the year showed that it hadn't healed properly, so he is to have another six months' rest, but he's only eleven so there's still hope he may be able to compete again at one-day events.

BROADCAST NEWS (Andy) 16h dark brown gelding, TB cross by a part bred Appaloosa. Raised in New Zealand and produced by Vicky Latta, who was placed on him at Bramham, Blenheim and Badminton before she retired after the Atlanta Olympics.

He was fourteen by the time he came to me for the 1997 season, but as he rides rather like Podge, small, very nippy and very fast, I had no hesitation in taking Andy on. 'Bad decision,' I thought after he fell at the third fence first time out, but I changed my mind when he won the European Open Championships at Burghley in

September. He came with his own groom, Penny Burgess, who trained in New Zealand with Podge's faithful groom, Helen Gilbert. Penny is now my travelling groom, which gives me a nice feeling of continuity. Andy is another timid character and a real devil to catch. Penny can usually get close enough to grab him, but I've no chance unless I can get him cornered. I think he's suspicious of men, and he was certainly very doubtful about me when I first had him, but he's a lot better now. He's fine when I'm riding him, but I have to be careful how I use my leg because he's so thin skinned and ticklish.

ILLUSTRATION CREDITS

'With Killarney at the local pony club' by kind permission of Heather Hills Photography, Cambridge, New Zealand

'Mumma and Pop at a family celebration' by kind permission of Heather Hills Photography, Cambridge, New Zealand

'In New Zealand at Mum and Dad's for Christmas 1995' by kind permission of New Zealand Woman's Weekly, Dominion Road, Auckland, NZ

'Taupo, 1983, Charisma and Mark Todd' by kind permission of Barbara Thomson, Whenuapai, NZ

'In the dressage arena during the 1984 Olympic three-day event' by kind permission of Hugo M Czerny, Munich, Germany

'Charisma opening the Commonwealth Games in Auckland' by kind permission of New Zealand Woman's Weekly, Dominion Road, Auckland, NZ

'Top Hunter at the Lexington World Championships' by kind permission of Lynne Bruna

'Wilton Fair' and 'Face the Music' by kind permission of Equestrian Services Thorney

'Welton Greylag' by kind permission of Sara Rance, Bracknell, Berks

'Broadcast News' by kind permission of Kit Houghton

'Southern Comfort' by kind permission of Hugo M Czerny, Munich, Germany

'Bertie Blunt' by kind permission of Paul L E Raper-Zullig

'Michaelmas Day' by kind permission of Equestrian Services Thorney

'Kayem at the Open European Championships' by kind permission of foto di Bruno De Lorenzo

'Sounds like Fun winning at Ellerslie' by kind permission of Turf Photo

'Word for Word shows his class at 1997 Gatcombe Open Championships' by kind permission of John Britten Photography

INDEX

Page numbers in **bold** refer to the favourite horses section, pages 253–262

L.H. Wiener

Ezra en Claire

Een liefde

2011
Uitgeverij Contact
Amsterdam/Antwerpen

Ezra en Claire verscheen oorspronkelijk in de roman *Nestor*.

© 2011 L.H. Wiener
Auteursfoto Tessa Posthuma de Boer
Omslagontwerp Suzan Beijer
Omslagillustratie Getty Images
Typografie binnenwerk Text & Image
Drukker Bariet, Ruinen
ISBN 978 90 254 3752 7
D/2011/0108/962
NUR 301
www.uitgeverijcontact.nl

Misschien was de valk niet de beste vlieger van allemaal – dat was toch de zwaluw die in staat was om wentelend en kantelend een mug van het water te pikken met zo'n fabelachtige finesse dat het oppervlak er nauwelijks van rimpelde – maar wel de ontzagwekkendste: de valk had de beste ogen van allemaal, hij kon bidden in de wind, maar hij kon zich ook als een steen op zijn prooi storten.

Eerst kwamen de valken, maar dan de uilen; met hun kattenogen. Uilen konden onhoorbaar vliegen, ze konden in het donker zien, ze konden hun kop drie kwartslagen ronddraaien zonder te stikken. En ze waren mysterieus. Mensen wisten niet wat ze van uilen moesten denken. Uilskuiken was een woord dat extreme domheid aanduidde, maar tegelijkertijd gold de uil als het symbool van de wijsheid.

Belachelijk was zoiets.

Ezra had zich afgevraagd of hij ooit een valk zou uithalen om groot te brengen. Een valk was meer dan een vogel, hoe moest je het zeggen, een valk hoorde alleen te zijn, soms triomfantelijk keffend, hoog in de lucht, soms strak en stil overkomend op weg naar een plaats voor de nacht; maar altijd alleen, in zijn eigen wereld, waar hij heerste. Een valk uithalen, dat hoorde gewoon niet.

En een uil?

Ja, een uil, dat kon heel goed. Als uilen niet jaagden waren het goeiige lobbesen. Ze hielden van dutjes en rust. Uilen waren eigenlijk poezen met vleugels.

Ezra passeerde de plek waar de spoorbaan door de betonnen tankwal sneed die daar eens door de Duitsers dwars in de duinen was gelegd, parallel aan de kustlijn, een meter dik en bijna tweemaal zo hoog en door de jaren heen met korstmossen bedekt, ooit in een roes van onoverwinnelijkheid gebouwd, maar daarna halsoverkop achtergelaten door soldaten die thuis eerst hun uniform verstopten om vervolgens met hun zwembroek onder de arm weer naar Zandvoort terug te keren.

In de verte naderde een trein, geluidloos aanstormend met bevende contouren. Ezra wilde juist het talud van de spoorbaan afdalen om aan de oversteek naar het golfterrein te beginnen, toen hij op enkele meters voor zich, in het lage struikgewas, een konijn zag zitten, dik en roerloos. Ezra hurkte bij het dier neer en zag dat de ogen gezwollen waren en gesloten. Hij duwde zachtjes tegen het achterlijf, maar het konijn deed geen enkele poging om weg te lopen. Vermoedelijk had het de aanraking niet eens gevoeld. Ezra wist wat het was. Myxomatose: een konijnenpest, door een dokter uitgevonden en zo besmettelijk dat de ziekte helemaal uit Australië was overgewaaid.

In de verte werd nu een gedempt denderen hoorbaar.

Ezra pakte het konijn met beide handen in zijn rugvel beet en tilde het dier op, dat nu zacht piepte en zijn poten traag trappelend bewoog. Als een buidel vol vuil hing het in zijn eigen vel. Ezra legde het konijn dwars over de hete spoorrails, waar het machteloos bleef liggen, in totale uitputting, langzaam uitzakkend.

Even later raasde de trein voorbij en was het konijn veilig.

De vorige keer dat Ezra bij het nest was geweest waren de jonge uilen nog helemaal in wit dons gehuld en bestonden hun vlerken slechts uit blauwe hulzen. Dat was negen dagen geleden. Nu waren ze meer dan drie weken oud en kon Ezra Nestor gaan halen.

Uilen meenemen was verboden, want uilen waren beschermde vogels, maar zo'n beetje alles was verboden en bovendien zou Ezra niet anders doen dan Nestor beschermen. Veertien jaar oud was hij en voor niemand bang. Nestor zou bij hem veiliger zijn dan in de natuur, waar voor jonge vogels van elke soort allerlei bedreigingen loerden. Hij zou hem grootbrengen en sterk maken, hij zou hem muizen leren vangen, hij zou zijn vriend worden en hem dan weer loslaten in de duinen, waar hij Nestor zou heten en de wijste zou zijn onder de uilen, omdat hij in twee werelden had geleefd. Zoals de jongen van mensen die soms waren grootgebracht door dieren – door apen of door wolven – altijd macht hadden, zo zou Nestor opgroeien in de nabijheid van mensen, onder de hoede van Ezra Berger, vogelman te Zandvoort, Holland.

Behoedzaam begaf Ezra zich naar de boom met het uilennest. Hij keek omhoog, maar wat hij toen zag, deed zijn adem stokken. Halverwege de boom hing, dood tussen de takken, een jonge uil. De vlerken waren achter twee dunne twijgen blijven haken. Het witte diertje hing daar alsof het gekruisigd was. De klauwtjes machteloos verstijfd. Ezra schopte tweemaal licht tegen de stam.

Ogenblikkelijk verscheen uit het nest de kop van de volwassen uil. Twee ogen van een soort lichtgevend oranje boorden zich in die van Ezra, zo fel en zo diep, dat Ezra zich even afvroeg of het dier hem zou gaan aanvallen. De oorpluimen stonden recht omhoog, een teken temeer dat het dier opgewonden was. Maar was dit woede of was dit paniek? Ezra wist het niet. Aanvallen paste niet bij uilen, terugtrekken en verbergen was meer hun stijl. Nam de beschermingsdrift bij een uil soms toe naarmate zijn jongen groeiden?

Met stijgende bewondering keek Ezra op naar deze vogel, die weigerde van zijn nest te vluchten en de bedreiging onder hem bestookte met de priemende kracht van zijn blik.

Almaar heter begonnen de ogen van de uil te gloeien en plotseling hoorde Ezra, diep in zijn hoofd, een stem die sprak: *Haal hem weg...* Het was de uil, begreep Ezra.

En toen opnieuw: *Hij heette Nestor...*

Een onhoorbare stem was het, die galmde: *Voor hém ben je gekomen...*

Ezra begon zich in de boom op te trekken, zijn voeten zoekend naar houvast tussen de krakende takken. Toen hij het uitgemergelde lijkje lostilde hoorde hij hoe boven zijn hoofd de uil het nest verliet.

Ezra strekte, als betrof het een ritueel, zijn arm naar voren en opende zijn hand. Zo viel het lijkje precies op de plaats waar hij het moest begraven.

Hij keek naar beneden, naar de witte prop aan de voet van de boom. Lag daar Nestor?

Of slechts het naamloze restant van een der jonge uilen? Het was wel zielig, maar Nestor was het niet, prentte Ezra zich in, omdat Nestor nog leefde, omdat Nestor een van de overgebleven drie was, omdat Nestor ouder moest worden dan Ezra zelf, omdat Ezra dat wilde.

En zo klom hij door naar het nest, om af te maken waarvoor hij gekomen was. Hij haalde diep adem en keek.

En zag twee dode veldmuizen, bestemd voor twee jonge uilen, die blazend als jonge poesjes achteruitdeinsden en driftig met hun snavel klapten.

Nog maar twee... waar was de derde?

Geroofd door een havik of door kraaien?

Ook uit het nest gevallen of geduwd? En daarna door een vos of een wilde kat opgeruimd?

En welke van die twee was het, was nu werkelijk Nestor?

Hem nu nog meenemen betekende dat er nog maar één jong achterbleef en was het niet zo dat vogels slechts een beperkt vermogen hadden om hun jongen te tellen? Zoiets als: één, twee, meer, waardoor de uil die even tevoren nog twee levende jongen had bezeten en één dode, bij zijn terugkeer zou vaststellen dat zijn nest toch geplunderd was en daarop misschien wel alles zou verlaten, met als gevolg dat het overgebleven jong een wisse dood zou sterven?

Zo stond Ezra hoog in de boom en keek naar de twee zich achterwaarts schrap zettende uilen. En hij wist wat hem te doen stond: het al zo geteisterde nest verder met rust laten, het dode jong zorgvuldig begraven, zodat ieder roofspoor in de richting van het nest werd uitgewist en dan weggaan om niet meer terug te komen.

Ezra was van dit besef geheel doordrongen en geheel doordrongen van dit besef maakte hij één hand vrij, pakte wat hem als de kleinste van de twee uilen toescheen uit het nest en stak het van angst blazende dier onder zijn bloes, waar de lange nagels zich in zijn huid haakten.

Zo voorzichtig mogelijk klom Ezra vervolgens naar beneden, groef daar een gat in de grond, legde het dode jong erin en dekte de plek met zand en dennennaalden onzichtbaar af. Daarna drukte hij zich op, waarbij hij de bewegende bobbel in zijn kleding met zijn onderarm ondersteunde.

Op weg naar huis probeerde hij te glimlachen en de naam Nestor nog eens te fluisteren, maar geen van beide lukte.

* * *

Ezra ging het huis aan de achterkant binnen en liep voorzichtig de trap op naar de zolder. Daar trok hij met zijn ene hand zijn bloes omhoog, terwijl hij met de andere Nestor ondersteunde. Ezra hoopte dat Nestor onderweg in de duinen en in de straten van het dorp in slaap was gevallen, want hij had zich al een hele tijd niet meer bewogen, maar Nestor was klaarwakker en hield zijn ogen van angst wijd opengesperd. Dat hij zich zo koest hield was een overlevingsstrategie, intuïtief bekend aan elk dier: houd je als prooi zo stil mogelijk en maak je klein. Ezra tilde de jonge uil met beide handen op tot vlak bij zijn gezicht en keek hem aan. Een hees gesis ontsnapte aan de halfgeopende snavel. Wat een ogen! Als glanzend glas. Zou hij honger hebben? Dat zou toch wel? Jonge roofvogels waren schrokops. En drinken. Hoe zat het daar eigenlijk mee? Moesten uilen ook drinken? In het nest kon dat niet, maar misschien zat er in de muizen voldoende vocht. Mensen bestonden voor negentig procent uit water. En muizen?

Maar hoe kwam hij aan muizen? Saul had er vorig jaar in één middag elf. Als oefening, had hij gezegd. Het was in de winter en hij ving ze met vallen in het kippenhok. Elf. Hij had ze, op volgorde van grootte, naast elkaar in een houten bakje met water gelegd en ze ingevroren. De volgende dag had hij ze in de tuin begraven, in een kistje van ijs. Zouden die vallen nog in de schuur staan?

Ezra zette Nestor zachtjes op de krantenbodem in het oude aquarium van zijn vader, waarin nog maar aan één zijde glas zat en dat hij voor deze gelegenheid uit de schuur had gehaald. Nestor opende zijn snavel nu half maar maakte geen geluid meer. En toen Ezra even later de kamer had verlaten om in de schuur naar muizenvallen te zoeken, zakte zijn kop weldra naar voren en sloten zijn oogleden zich langzaam. Eerst het ene, gedeeltelijk, terwijl zijn kop schuin begon weg te zakken, vervolgens het andere, gelijkmatig zakkend als een verticaal gordijntje. En zo viel hij nogal slordig in slaap, met één halfgeloken oog. Het leek alsof hij daarmee wilde aangeven dat hij de wereld om hem heen nog steeds in de gaten hield, maar in werkelijkheid was hij zo uitgeput door alle ellende die hem overkomen was, dat hij geen macht meer had over de mechanismen van zijn lichaam. Een lichaam dat in dit stadium van zijn bestaan toch al aan alle kanten ongemakkelijke zwaartepunten had en dat hij moest verduren als een bijna niet te torsen last. Aan zijn kop die enorme haak van een snavel die hem volledig topzwaar maakte en aan de onderkant die twee groteske klauwen, waarvan het nut nog totaal onduidelijk was en die hem het voortbewegen tot verlammens toe belemmerden.

Een straal witte smurrie spoot uit zijn onderlichaam over de kopletters van de plaatselijke courant en trof het woord *Zandvoort* vol.

Ezra vond in de schuur geen muizenvallen, wel bijlen en messen en het hakblok van zijn vader. Eigenlijk was het geen schuur, eerder een vervallen loods waarvan het dak en de wanden schots en scheef tegen elkaar hingen en de regen op meerdere plaatsen naar binnen viel. De vele kieren en spleten waren zichtbaar door het witte licht dat ze doorlieten. Toch was de ruimte in halfduister gehuld. Het enige raam was door een kleverig soort aanslag van jaren geel beslagen en afgeschermd door meerdere lagen spinnenwebben en stofragen. De toegang werd gevormd door een vrij opgehangen schuifdeur, die aan de bovenzijde met metalen wieltjes over een rail schraapte. Er stond een oude werkbank, waarop her en der gereedschap lag: hamers, tangen, schroevendraaiers, een metalen afvoerontstopper, conservenblikken met harde kwasten, lege spuitbussen en een verrekijker waarvan een glas ontbrak. Aan lange spijkers hingen diverse verroeste zagen, fietsonderdelen, touwwerk en een halfvergane overall van Louis, die hij bij het slachten aantrok. Ezra hurkte neer en doorzocht een aantal kartonnen dozen met afgedankt huisraad en oud speelgoed.

Het was vooral zijn moeder die werkelijk niets wilde weggooien. 'Je weet nooit of het niet nog eens van pas komt' was een van haar favoriete uitspraken. In een versleten koffer zat oude kledij, alles van zijn moeder, jurken zo oud dat het geen jurken waren maar japonnen, dansjaponnen, met lovertjes en kwastjes. Eerst in plastic omhulsels gewikkeld en daarna een voor een opgevouwen en ter bewaring gegeven aan de tijd. Ezra drukte zich op zijn knieën omhoog en wilde net de schuur uitlopen toen hij Saul in de verlichte toegang van de loods zag staan.

Saul hoorde je nooit en je zag hem nooit; hij was er

altijd ineens of hij was er niet. Meestal niet.

'Wat was je daar aan het doen?'

Ezra dacht na.

'Ik zocht iets.'

'Wat?'

Ezra zweeg.

'Wát dan?'

Maar Ezra volhardde in zijn zwijgen, zijn broer was niet de baas over hem.

'Wat zócht je?'

De vraag was inmiddels uit zijn voegen gebarsten en overgegaan in een dreigement.

Oppassen, Saul kon zomaar een driftbui krijgen.

'Muizen...' antwoordde Ezra toen maar. En om deze bekentenis weer te neutraliseren voegde hij eraan toe: 'Is het nou goed?'

Saul stak daarop zijn hand in zijn zak en haalde er een mol uit tevoorschijn, dood.

'Heb je hier wat aan?' vroeg hij en een brede glimlach trok om zijn mond.

Het in zes stukken snijden van een mol vereist geen speciale ervaring, maar is een tamelijk vervelend en bloederig karwei. Toch stond Ezra erop het zelf te doen. Nestor was immers zíjn uil. Ezra nam het grootste mes, Victorinox genaamd, een lang en scherp vleesmes met een ebbenhouten heft, dat Louis speciaal gebruikte om verdoofde kippen de kop af te snijden aan het eind van het onhandige slachtritueel.

Saul bleef erbij staan en legde de stukjes mol een voor

een terzijde. Plotseling leek zijn aandacht te worden afgeleid. Hij trok zijn hoofd achterover en snoof een aantal keren door zijn neus, zoals een jachthond doet om zich te oriënteren. Hij keek om zich heen en spande het vel van zijn voorhoofd. Toen liep hij weg in de richting van het lege tuinhuis. Ezra zag hoe hij voor de deur bleef staan en aan het zware hangslot morrelde, opnieuw naar boven keek en zijn neus gebruikte, als een dier. Daarna verdween hij om de hoek, waar het geblindeerde raam zich bevond.

'Zie je die tak daar?' had Saul op een dag gevraagd, toen Ezra en hij elkaar toevallig in de tuin tegenkwamen, althans, daar leek het op. Ze stonden onder een der oudste iepen in het laagste en diepste gedeelte, waar Saul een ondergronds hol had.

Ezra had de richting van zijn broers hand gevolgd.

Wat nu weer.

'Die gaat eraf.'

Ezra had niets gezegd, omdat dat gewoon het beste was.

'Wat ik kan zíén,' vervolgde Saul op onheilspellende toon, 'dat is dat die tak binnen een minuut op de grond ligt en dat diezelfde tak binnen vijf minuten helemaal niet meer bestaat!'

Ezra knikte maar, weglopen was nu gevaarlijk.

'Luister. Ik ga eraan hangen en dan zal je zien dat hij doorbuigt, ver doorbuigt, maar niet breekt. Dan moet jij aan mij gaan hangen en dan breekt hij. Oké?'

Saul sprong op en omklemde met beide handen de

tak, die ver doorboog maar niet brak.

'Nu!' commandeerde Saul en Ezra klemde zijn handen rond het middel van zijn broer en trok zijn voeten op.

De tak kraakte, scheurde en brak af.

Saul veerde lenig neer en begon het dunne uiteinde van de tak rond te trekken totdat hij nogmaals brak. Daarna gooide hij beide delen ver uit elkaar de tuin in.

'Zo doe je dat. Gezien?'

Daarna was hij verdwenen.

Eerst dacht Ezra dat Nestor dood was, zo volledig verfomfaaid lag hij op de kranten, maar toen hij neerhurkte en de spijlen van het aquarium aanraakte krabbelde hij overeind en begon hij heftig te blazen en met zijn snavel te klappen. Het duurde even voordat hij Ezra's bedoelingen begreep. Uit angst en de intuïtie om zijn huid zo duur mogelijk te verkopen, rekte hij zich op en deinsde hij onhandig balancerend zijdelings weg tot hij tegen de enige ruit van zijn behuizing klem liep en hij zich nog slechts schuin hangend tegen het glas kon schrap zetten.

Het eerste stukje mol dat hem werd voorgehouden zag hij niet eens. Hij keek er faliekant overheen.

'Nestor, hier...' moedigde Ezra hem aan. 'Kijk dan...'

Maar Nestor staarde slechts in afgrijzen naar dat onbekende monster waardoor hij nu ieder ogenblik kon worden doodgebeten en opgegeten. Hij was uit het nest geroofd en hij ging eraan, dat stond vast. Ezra zag dat hij dat dacht, maar wist niet hoe hij duidelijk kon maken dat hij geen monster was. Geroofd was trouwens het verkeerde woord. Hij had Nestor meegenomen en niet om hem dood te bijten en op te eten, maar om hem groot te brengen en bijzonder te maken, bijzonderder dan alle andere uilen op de hele wereld.

Een uil met ervaring, een uil wijzer dan de uilen van Athene, waarover meneer De Haan had verteld.

*   *   *

Op de begraafplaats Zorgvlied te Amstelveen heeft iedere oude boom een nummer. Op de bast van elk bejaard exemplaar zit een groen ovalen plaatje gespijkerd. Deze registratie heeft op het eerste gezicht iets treurigs, iets Duits, maar blijkt bij nauwkeuriger beschouwing te verwijzen naar een bomenarchief dat zich ergens in de kantoorruimte van deze begraafplaats moet bevinden en bestaat ter conservering van het park, niet ter slechting. Van iedere eeuweling is soort, anciënniteit en conditie bekend en het is zeer wel denkbaar dat een boomchirurg tot de vaste staf van de begraafplaats behoort.

Hoe anders is het gesteld in het dorp dat vroeger Zandvoort was, een dorp waar de dood niet passief aanwezig is, zoals op de begraafplaats Zorgvlied te Amstelveen, maar actief, zoals bij een slopende ziekte, waaraan bijvoorbeeld de Haltestraat, de Kerkstraat en de Grote

Krocht ten onder zijn gegaan, om maar enkele straten te noemen waar in vroegere zomers de hemel onzichtbaar was vanwege de naar elkaar reikende en verstrengelde boomkruinen, maar waar nu in het geheel geen bomen meer staan, omdat ze zijn onttakeld en gerooid en vervangen door parkeermeters, afvalemmers of prentbriefkaartenmolens.

Zandvoort, een dorp waar iedere vierkante meter die uitbaatbaar is, wordt uitgebaat. Zandvoort, het Volendam van Kennemerland. Een serie parkeervakken erbij? Waar nu nog die oude eiken staan? Fotografeer die eiken, maak er een *Ansichtskarte* van, kettingzaag daarna die bomen omver, dek de littekens van hun bestaan af met bakstenen en trottoirbanden en plaats, bij wijze van herdenkingskruis, op ieder graf een parkeermeter. Voorzie de foto van de opdruk *Das alte Zandvoort* en men heeft andermaal handel onder een nieuw geopende hemelboog.

Zo is inmiddels in het dorp dat vroeger Zandvoort was maar nu alleen nog zo genoemd wordt, al het markante verdwenen: gesloopt, kaalgeslagen, neergehaald, gesmoord, verstikt, vergiftigd, verziekt, verpest of verpatst.

De Duinweg te Zandvoort bestaat nog, althans volgens een bordje met de naam Duinweg erop. Een strakke en functionele brandweerkazerne, compleet met slagbomen en automatiese deuren is er nu het enige gebouw, maar op diezelfde plaats stond van 1834 tot 1985 een markant huis, uniek in het dorp vanwege de eigenaardige bouwstijl. Toen de familie Berger dat huis in 1957 betrok, prijkte er een geschilderd opschrift boven de deur. Geen naam was het, eerder een leus: FRYSLÂN BOPPE. En met de voordeur in het midden en ter weerszijden daarvan twee hoge ramen, met de vierkante dakkapel en de hoge kap, waaronder een enorme zolder, was het huis inderdaad gebouwd in de stijl van veel Friese boerderijen. En toch ging deze overeenkomst alleen maar op voor het vooraangezicht van het huis, want aan de achterzijde verrees opnieuw een puntdak, waardoor het huis in feite uit twee delen bestond, die tegen elkaar geschoven waren en in totaal acht kamers bevatten.

Ezra Berger was bijna dertien toen hij in december van het jaar 1957 als zijn privédomein de reusachtige zolder betrok van het voorhuis aan de Duinweg 29.

Saul Berger was toen zestien en bewoonde afwisselend, maar het liefst niet, de twee bovenkamers in het achterhuis, van waaruit hij in zowel westelijke als oostelijke richting de gunstigste uitkijkpositie bezette. De diverse ondergrondse hutten die hij zelf had gegraven of die hij wist, gebruikte hij niet meer actief maar hield hij als noodvoorzieningen achter de hand.

Ooit had men vanaf de Duinweg een vrij en onbelemmerd uitzicht over zee gehad, maar dat was voordat de huizen aan de Thorbeckestraat en aan de Vuurboetstraat bestonden. De benaming Duinweg was in de moderne tijd niet duidelijk meer te plaatsen, al leek de observatie dat het huis op de achterste rand van de oude zeereep stond gerechtvaardigd. Waarom het in Friese stijl was gebouwd en wie verantwoordelijk was voor het opschrift FRYSLÂN BOPPE bleef onduidelijk.

En dan was er nog het tuinhuis...

Het raadselachtige bakstenen huisje, onbewoond en met een hangslot vergrendeld. Het was een huisje zoals kinderen tekenen, een huis in zijn eenvoudigste vorm: vier muren en een dak met een schoorsteen. De muren waren ooit wit geweest, de dakpannen ooit oranje en de schoorsteen ooit schoon. Slechts aan één kant zat een raam. Aan de smalle kant naast de voordeur. Aan de oostzijde waren glazen serredeuren, maar ook deze zaten op slot en zware gordijnen sloten hermeties af wat zich binnenin bevond. Zekere ambtenaren van de afdeling huisvesting schenen meer te weten, maar wilden niet meer loslaten dan dat het huisje niet te huur was.

Ezra's broer Saul had al verscheidene keren overwogen om in het huisje in te breken, deels om uit te vinden wat zich daarbinnen bevond, maar merendeels om er zelf in te trekken, als een hut, bovengronds, een hut van steen, want Saul Berger wilde overal zijn, behalve thuis. Hij had die plannen echter als onprakties verworpen. Wat moest je eigenlijk in dat vieze hok? Nog een jaar of wat en hij was voor altijd vertrokken.

Ezra's vader hield van kippen en hij sprak hun taal. Hij hield minder van mensen, al sprak hij hun taal ook, zij het sporadies. Misschien was dat ooit wel anders geweest, bijvoorbeeld in de tijd dat Ezra en zijn broer er nog niet waren, voor het begin van hun jaartelling, toen Louis Berger nog trompet speelde en Nellie nog met Simon Plas danste. Die tijd moest erg vrolijk zijn geweest. Maar op een dag kwam Simon Plas niet meer dansen.

Toen trouwde Nellie met Louis en zij leefden nog lang.

Nellie aan de voorzijde van het huis, in twee doorlopende kamers, waarvan zij er een gebruikte als atelier en de andere als slaapkamer; een werkgedeelte en een slaapgedeelte. In die twee kamers, feitelijk de zuidwestelijke vleugel van het huis, was zij prakties altijd te vinden, altijd aan het werk, achter de kniptafel, of de naaimachine, met een klant voor de grote passpiegel, of achter de strijkplank, de laatste hand leggend aan een nieuwe japon, een nieuw mantelpak, een nieuw kostuum, of de kleding van haar gezin.

Louis sliep in het middengedeelte van het huis, een diep verschanste kamer aan de lange gang naar achteren, die dwars door beide huisgedeelten liep en vanwaaruit men in geval van nood even gemakkelijk via de achterdeur kon vluchten als via de voordeur.

De oorlog had Louis en Nellie verbonden voor de rest van hun leven, niet als geliefden maar als lotgenoten, niet als minnaars maar als kameraden. Het werd de oorlog die de zin van hun leven uitmaakte, als een pad door duisternis verlicht, als een geschenk uit de hel.

De oorlog was in Amsterdam voltrokken, als een onverbrekelijke verbintenis tussen leven en dood en

wat de dood tezamen brengt zal het leven niet schei-
den.

Het verbaasde Louis Berger niet zeer dat hij kort na de
geboorte van zijn tweede zoon, Ezra, impotent bleek
te zijn, een hoedanigheid die hij nauwelijks als een te-
kort ervoer en zeker niet als een gemis, eerder ging het
om een achterstallige loyaliteitsverklaring: het zij zo en
zie, het was zo. Daar was voor geen zielendokter nog
emplooi.

Nellie dacht hier soms anders over maar zij had haar
eigen loyaliteit die Louis betrof, wellicht meer dan hij
verdiende. Louis, ooit het zwarte schaap van de familie,
alleen bevriend met zijn trompet en zijn Oldsmobile
Roadster. Onverantwoordelijk, verkwistend, met als
voornaamste garderobe een set smokings en ettelijke
paren lakschoenen – *happy times are here to stay* – dagen waren er om in uit te slapen, nachten om in te spelen, in de *Blue Note* of in de dansclub van theater Tu-
schinsky, *La Gaieté*, waar Louis en Nellie elkaar hadden
ontmoet.

'Danst u dame?' waren volgens Nellie de twee eerste
woorden die Louis tot haar sprak. Hij scheen beleefd
en verlegen, maar zijn vraag was louter pro forma, want
Simon Plas was hun wederzijdse vriend en er bestond
in heel Amsterdam geen hartstochtelijker danspaar
dan Simon en Nellie.

'Dame zei ik er niet bij,' hield Louis later vol, tegenover zijn zoons Saul en Ezra, alsof het enig verschil
maakte.

Dronken huiswaarts slenteren langs mistige ochtendgrachten in Amsterdam.

Simon, Nellie en Louis...

Amsterdam?

Dat is geen stad om in te dansen.

Dat is een stad om in te sterven.

Hand in hand en samen, met een laatste kus en een laatste wanhopig gebaar.

En zo vestigde Louis Berger zich in 1948 met zijn gezin te Zandvoort aan de Zee, een dorp dat voor iemand met een afkeer van joden geen slechte keus was. Alleen: het meeste van Louis was in Amsterdam achtergebleven, wat hij van zichzelf nog had meegenomen bestond voornamelijk uit schuld en zelfhaat, een verstikkende last die hem tot in de tweede generatie de mond snoerde en er de oorzaak van was dat Ezra en zijn broer Saul nog tot op hun veertiende, respectievelijk zestiende jaar geloofden dat ze normale mensen waren.

Uiteindelijk was het Nellie die nog eenmaal naar het verleden omzag en haar beide zoons over de Cliostraat vertelde, Cliostraat nummer 29, waar de dood op 11 mei 1940 als gast op de thee was uitgenodigd. Hij had het druk die dag in Amsterdam, de dood, en hij kon niet heksen, kon niet overal tegelijk zijn, maar wel bijna. Jammer dat Louis niet was gekomen, dan was de hele familie compleet geweest. En dat was toch veel gezelliger, zoals bij de familie Witvis, diezelfde morgen nota bene. Altijd al een buitenbeentje, die Louis.

Op eerdere momenten was hij hem toch bijna in de armen gevlogen, slippend in die auto van hem, op het behulpzame grind van een hoge bocht in de Ardennen, twee jaar tevoren. Op weg naar Cannes, naar Antibes en naar Nice. *God*, dat was *close*. Zijn linkervoorwiel hing al boven dat ravijn. En als hij die meid niet bij zich had gehad, rechts voorin, als tegengewicht, dan was het nog net genoeg geweest. Nellie heette die deerne, *aber die Nellie wollen wir auch noch kriegen!*

De dood sprak alle talen, maar hij bediende zich in de vorige eeuw bij voorkeur van het Duits.

Typies dat die zwarte schapen vaak het langst de dans ontsprongen.

Maar ach, komt tijd, komt dans.

Wat is het leven anders dan een poosje machteloos tegenstribbelen?

*   *   *

Het was op een middag geweest, zomaar ineens, toen Ezra koffie voor haar had gezet in het Durobor-door-lekapparaat.

'Wat ben je toch een lieve jongen,' had Nellie gezegd en eraan toegevoegd: 'Soms.'

Ze had Ezra door zijn haar gestreken, die zijn hoofd wegdraaide en zijn gezicht tot een grimas vertrok.

Ezra wilde weglopen, maar Nellie vroeg hem of hij nog iets voor haar wilde doen.

'Ik wil je wat laten zien...'

En ze vroeg Ezra om uit de woonkamer een fotoalbum te halen.

'Dat grote onderop, dat van leer.'

Zelf liep ze naar boven en klopte op de deur van een van Sauls kamers.

De andere ging open en Saul vroeg wat er was. Hij had zijn mouwen opgestroopt en in zijn hand hield hij een elektriese spoel waarvan het koperdraad bijna helemaal was afgewikkeld. Dit koperdraad vervlocht hij in strengen van drie om er strikken van te maken. Aan een van zijn vingers zat wat bloed.

'Wat ben je aan het doen?' vroeg Nellie bezorgd.

Saul antwoordde niet.

'Is er wat?' vroeg hij kortaf.

'Kom even beneden.'

'Ik heb het nu te druk.'

'Saul...'

Ze keek hem aan, twee, drie seconden lang.

Daarna daalde ze de trap weer af, zonder nog te spreken, wetende dat hij haar even later zou volgen.

Ezra had het fotoalbum op de kniptafel gelegd en bladerde het door.

Het was een oud en mufruikend boek, met bladen van een soort viltachtig karton, dik en bruin, met foto's uit de prehistorie, van mannen met glimmend haar en vrouwen met bont en bakken van vierkante auto's met witte banden en boulevards met palmbomen.

'Kom eens zitten,' zei zijn moeder.

En zo begon ze te vertellen.

Waar Louis zich toen bevond is niet bekend, maar dat hij in Haarlem op de Gedempte Oude Gracht bij Slavenburgs bank op de zogeheten 'tikker' stond te kijken en zich afvroeg of dit nu een moment was om te kopen of juist een moment om te verkopen, lag het meest voor de hand.

En Nellie deed, zoals gewoonlijk, het vuile werk.

Eerst op neutrale toon en alsof het een gewoon verhaal betrof, maar langzamerhand onzekerder en zachter. Haar vingers gingen langs de foto's, die af en toe werden voorzien van een naam, of een plaats, een tijd of een handeling. Ze dronk haar koffie uit het glas in de metalen houder, maar Ezra zag dat haar hand licht beefde.

Toen ze was aangekomen bij de maand mei van het jaar 1940, 11 mei om precies te zijn, ging de deur van het atelier open en kwam Saul zwijgend binnen. Hij liep naar het raam en keek naar buiten, draaide zich tijdens het steeds moeizamer verlopende relaas van zijn moeder niet eenmaal om, maar aan zijn houding was te zien dat hij luisterde en dat geen woord hem ontging.

En Nellie vertelde alles, totdat ze stopte.

Ezra wist niet wat hij zeggen moest, zijn moeder huilde nooit.

Even was het akelig stil in de kamer, toen klonk Sauls stem:

'Van wie was dat paard?'

Ezra keek verbaasd op.

'Dat paard op de laatste bladzijde, linksonder,' verduidelijkte Saul.

Ezra bladerde verder door het album en zag op de laatste bladzijde linksonder zijn vader, Louis, in een geruit hemd, met leren rijlaarzen, zittend te paard.

Hij lachte breed, met sterke witte tanden en leek gelukkig.

* * *

'Nestor, je bent niet van mij...' fluisterde Ezra op een middag eerbiedig, maar de uil sliep. Ezra had nogmaals willen uitleggen hoe het zat, dat uilen hoogstens tijdelijk bij mensen verbleven, zoals mensen bij wolven of bij apen, om er beter van te worden, maar steeds als hij daartoe overging viel Nestor in slaap, waardoor Ezra's beweringen uitsluitend nog door hemzelf werden gehoord en het karakter aannamen van voornemens en goede bedoelingen eerder dan van plechtige beloftes en bezweringen.

'Jij wordt de sterkste uil, Nestor, van het hele land. En je mag zelf zeggen wanneer ik je weer moet loslaten.' Ezra had eerst gedacht aan het terrein van de Kennemer Golf en Country Club, waar Nestor ook geboren was, maar dat waren wel schrale jachtvelden, al met al, en met veel te veel publiek. Het circuit was toen bij hem opgekomen, de dennenbossen tussen het circuit en de Zeeweg naar Bloemendaal, daar moest je zijn als uil.

Geen spoorbaan met langs denderende treinen, geen luid lachende sukkels die tussen de bomen naar afgezeilde golfballetjes zochten, maar een bosrijk gebied met muizen in soorten.

'*I know the way*,' fluisterde Ezra en bracht zijn vinger onder het fluweelzachte dons van Nestors kop, die hierdoor wakker schrok en wegdeinsde. Op datzelfde moment werd er op de deur van Ezra's kamer geklopt. Het was Saul. Hij wilde binnenkomen, maar dat ging niet, want de deur zat op slot.

'Ga weg,' zei Ezra, toen hij op de achtergrond het dwaze gegiechel hoorde van Jessie Koper.

'Ik heb een mus bij me, voor je vriend.'

'Hij heeft nu geen honger.'

'Onzin, die beesten hebben altijd honger.'

'Net als ik,' giebelde Jessie.

'Hou jij je kop,' siste Saul.

'Sorry...' proestte Jessie.

Jessie woonde in de Potgieterstraat in Zandvoort, aan de noordkant van de spoorbaan en was soms de vriendin van Saul. Meestal niet. Dan was ze de vriendin van iemand anders.

'Mag Jessie hem even zien?' drong Saul nog aan, op de allervriendelijkste toon die Ezra van hem kende en waar meestal wat achter stak. Maar al zou Jessie belangstelling hebben voor uilen, hetgeen zo goed als uitgesloten was, uilen hadden zeker geen belangstelling voor Jessie, dat was zeker.

Jessie had dikke witte benen en de billen van een big. Dikke witte biggenbillen. Dat had Ezra gezien, door het gaatje in de deur van Sauls kamer, waar een schroef ontbrak bij het slot, waar ooit een ander slot had gezeten.

'Hij heeft geen zin,' zei Ezra op besliste toon.

'Als ik wil trap ik die deur zo in! Weet je dat?' dreigde Saul.

'Doe maar...'

Omgaan met Saul viel te vergelijken met blufpoker, een spel dat Ezra op wonderlijke wijze wist te winnen, al stond zijn grootste troef hem niet bewust voor ogen; het lukte gewoon altijd.

Nu niet doorgaan, voelde hij. Het was gezegd.

Ezra wachtte tot de stilte was teruggekeerd en vroeg zich af wie Nestor eigenlijk wél mochten zien. Zijn moeder, Nellie? Nestor scheen voor haar nog het minste bang te zijn. Dieren hielden van vrouwen. Zijn vader, Louis? Natuurlijk. Ezra kende niemand die dichter bij de dieren stond dan zijn vader. Hij sprak de taal der kippen, als geen ander. En vissen aten uit zijn hand, zoals de goudkarpers uit de vijver, waarvan hij sommige zelfs bij naam noemde. De grootste noemde hij Creon. En dan was er zijn onafscheidelijke makker, de nerveuze dashond Jonker.

Claire?

Ja, Claire, die natuurlijk helemaal, maar dan moest je het wel goed uitleggen. 'Wil je mijn uil zien?' tegen het mooiste meisje van de school, dat daarvoor ook nog helemaal met de tram uit Haarlem moest komen, dat deed ze nooit. Welk meisje begreep zo'n vraag? Ze zou er eens wat achter kunnen zoeken. Nog maar wachten tot Nestor volgroeid was en op zijn mooist. Misschien wel wat kunstigs wilde laten zien. De lege parkietenvolière achter in de tuin zou daarvoor een geschikte oefenruimte zijn. Wat kon hij leren? Een prooi overnemen uit de hand, zoals een valk? Valken waren behendig en snel. Uilen waren traag en lui, het woord uil zei het eigenlijk al.

'Claire...' fluisterde Ezra, terwijl hij strak naar Nestor keek, die zich tot een ronde bal had opgerold en met schokkerige ademhaling leek te slapen.

De mus lag voor de deur, zoals Ezra had verwacht.

Hij raapte hem op en nam hem mee naar het hakblok in de schuur, waar het grote vierendeelmes met het zwarte heft altijd klaarlag. Mussen en spreeuwen waren moeilijker te verdelen dan muizen of een mol, maar waren minder kliederig. Bij het in vieren snijden kraakten er meer botjes en je moest het windbukskogeltje zien te vinden, dat Nestor absoluut niet binnen mocht krijgen, maar het doorsnijden van een muis bood een veel gruwelijker aanblik. Je hield precies twee halve muizen over waar de kledder uit liep, terwijl de stukken mus bolletjes vlees met veertjes werden. De muizenvallen had Ezra niet gevonden, maar hij had er twee bij ijzerhandel Van Zeggelen in de Haltestraat gekocht en in het kippenhok neergezet op plaatsen die Saul hem gewezen had. Altijd ergens langs een rand. Muizen lopen uitsluitend langs wanden en muren en steken nooit over. Hij had er meer gevangen dan Nestor op kon en hoopte dat Nestor spoedig groot genoeg zou zijn om de muizen in hun geheel te verorberen.

De kogeltjes waren diabolovormige stukjes lood, die Ezra in een lucifersdoosje bewaarde. Niet altijd kwam zo'n kogeltje uit de bloederige partjes prooivogel tevoorschijn en Ezra ging er dan maar van uit dat het projectiel de vogel geheel had doorboord, wat meestal al viel af te leiden uit de twee blauwe wondjes aan voor- en achterzijde. Bij in de zijde getroffen vogels had hij het kogeltje nog altijd gevonden. Wáár Saul zijn windbuks verborgen hield wist Ezra niet en dát hij er een bezat was aan zowel Nellie als Louis onbekend.

Mussen en spreeuwen waren de extra lekkere hapjes. Nestors dagelijkse menu bestond uit poulet van slager Gaus, gewikkeld in donsveertjes uit het kippenhok. Het vlees voor de groei en de veertjes voor de spijsvertering.

Op de terugweg naar zolder, met de gevierendeelde mus in zijn hand, bleef Ezra op de overloop staan en boog zich naar de deur van Sauls kamer, van waaruit nu een regelmatig en zwaar hijgen hoorbaar was. Een vreemde stuwing in zijn bloedsomloop kreeg direct greep op zijn hartslag en ademhaling en hoewel zijn ogen niet konden waarnemen wat zich aan de andere kant van de deur voltrok, zwiepten de beelden door zijn hoofd en deden hem duizelen van opwinding. De kracht van deze emoties was als een koorts die in golven werd opgestuwd en hem volledig willoos leek te maken. Het was een even akelig als aangenaam gevoel, dat hem in hevige verwarring bracht en bijna deed vergeten waar hij was. Doorlopen, doorlopen en Nestor voeren, dat moest hij doen! Niet toegeven aan de onweerstaanbare drang zijn oor tegen de deur van Sauls kamer te drukken en zijn eigen lichaam te betasten.

Maar het was te sterk.

Eerst duwde hij zijn oorschelp voorzichtig plat tegen de deur om zich voor te kunnen stellen in welk stadium van verhitting Saul en Jessie zich bevonden. Waren zij nog op weg naar de top dan was hun aandacht voor al het andere op de wereld verdoofd en kon Ezra de kromgeslagen spijker veilig uit het gaatje naast het slot trekken om naar binnen te gluren en met het bloed ruisend in zijn keel te zien hoe mensen het echt deden. Achter gesloten deuren, maar daar dan ook open en bloot.

Was dit wat lang geleden Odysseus ook gevoeld had toen hij zich liet vastbinden aan de mast van zijn boot, om niet op de betoverde rotsen schipbreuk te lijden?

Hadden de sirenen ook dikke witte billen, net als Jessie Koper?

Zou meneer De Haan dat weten?

*   *   *

's Nachts was Nestor wakker.

Ezra kon hem dan horen rondklossen in het aquarium, waar hij zich niet verder waagde dan de lage opstaande rand waartegen vroeger de ruiten gekit hadden gezeten en waar nu de krantenbodem ophield. Maar op een nacht hoorde Ezra hoe Nestor zich over de rand heen werkte en zich over de vloer voortbewoog, moeizaam bonkend en steunend op zijn hele onderpoten, als een alk. In het donker trachtte Ezra de richting te volgen die Nestor was ingeslagen en het leek erop of hij Ezra's bed als eindbestemming had. Met korte pauzes zette hij de overtocht voort en Ezra hoopte dat dit de eerste tekenen van vriendschap waren, een uiting van de behoefte om bij iemand te horen. Bij Ezra, die zo graag zijn vriend wilde zijn.

Een uil en een jongen, dat paste bij elkaar.

Ezra wist dat Nestor hem kon zien alsof het dag was en Ezra blind.

Hij knipte een lichtje aan en zag hoe de uil zijn kop een halve slag ronddraaide in de richting van de lichtbron. Zijn snavel rustte op zijn rug en in zijn van angst starende ogen verkleinden de dikke pupillen zich tot zwarte punten.

'Nestor, kom... kom eens hier...' fluisterde Ezra, terwijl hij zich half uit bed liet glijden en zijn arm over de grond strekte, maar de uil verstrakte zijn lichaam en liet een licht blazen horen. Hij zat nu midden in de kamer. Hoe de dag hem zo onverwacht in het gelaat kon springen was een onbegrijpelijk fenomeen, dat hem volledig ontregelde. Hij draaide zijn kop in een gelijkmatige beweging tweehonderdzeventig graden rond en staarde naar het aquarium, bewoog zich vooralsnog niet. Scheen het doel van zijn onderneming vergeten. Hij formeerde zich weer tot een bol en schurkte zijn veren, waardoor schilfertjes hoornstof in het rond stoven. Daarna zakte hij geheel door zijn poten en staakte hulpeloos ieder initiatief. Ezra kwam nu uit bed en knielde bij hem neer.

'Het is maar voor een paar maanden, Nestor, ik beloof het...'

Ezra dacht aan het naderend einde van het schooljaar en de opdoemende leegte van een zomervakantie. Het dorp overstroomd door luidruchtige Duitse toeristen en Claire weg. Zou hij haar kunnen schrijven?

De uil leek een opleving te vertonen.

Hij kwam half overeind en duwde zijn kop omhoog. Die houding leek eerst iets triomfantelijks uit te beelden, maar plotseling begon zijn snavel op en neer te schokken en gingen zijn bewegingen over in een onregelmatig kokhalzen. Even later lag er op de vloer een natte harige prop, die naar schatting bestond uit de residuen van twee muizen en een mus. Ezra nam het vreemde uitwerpsel tussen duim en wijsvinger op en legde het op de kranten in het aquarium.

'Zie je nu wel, hoe gauw je al groot wordt,' zei hij maar en nam Nestor van de grond op.

'Vind je het saai in het aquarium?' vroeg hij.

Nestors lange nagels klauwden naar houvast in Ezra's vingers. Het zou niet lang meer duren of zo oppakken zonder handschoenen ging niet meer.

'We hebben het er nog wel over...' zei Ezra toen en zette de uil terug in zijn aquarium, maar in het donker lag hij nog een poos lang te luisteren naar het geritsel op de kranten dat evengoed veroorzaakt zou kunnen worden door een hongerige, rusteloze rat.

Wie had hij eigenlijk? Zo vroeg hij zich af. Wie had hij om te vertrouwen?

Saul?

Saul was zijn broer, maar wat zei dat?

Zijn vader? Louis?

Hij geloofde wel dat zijn vader om hem gaf, veel zelfs, maar was hij niet toevállig zijn vader?

En toevallig de verkeerde?

Een angsthaas in plaats van een kerel?

* * *

Van alle menselijke relaties is die tussen vader en zoon wel de ingewikkeldste. Zelfs God de vader wist er niet mee om te gaan, want wat wilde deze vader bereiken? Waarom liet hij op aarde geschieden wat hij in de hemel niet kon uitleggen? Omdat zijn almacht niet bestond? Omdat hijzelf ook maar een zoon was die al eeuwig naar zijn vader zocht, in een groot, duister en leeg heelal?

Verklaarde dat zijn onverklaarbaar zwijgen?

Vaders komen en vaders gaan, alleen de zonen blijven over.

Toen Louis Berger in mei 1945 als enige overlevende van zijn familie aan zijn nabestaan begon, was Saul ongeveer drie jaar oud en Ezra drie maanden. In de oorlog had Ezra's vader niet geleefd, alleen bestaan. Leven kon altijd nog, eerst kwam het óverleven, dat in de dagelijkse praktijk neerkwam op net doen alsof men niet bestond, maar in zijn ultieme vorm eiste dat men zich vanuit het niets verhief in de vaderstand, hetgeen Louis Berger met de onbaatzuchtige hulp van Ezra's moeder nog was gelukt ook, tweemaal maar liefst.

* * *

Geld bestond voor Louis Berger, net als voor ieder ander, als een middel van bestaan, maar dan wel op een zeer eigenzinnige wijze, die in ieder geval niets van doen had met het betalen van rekeningen. Hij had een prikker, een soort puntige spaak op een verzwaarde voet. Daarop spietste hij alle rekeningen die op zijn huis werden afgevuurd, zonder er ooit één te betalen. Niet althans dan nadat hij daartoe middels een dwang-bevel was gesommeerd. Ook dat dwangbevel werd ge-spietst en later eveneens de kwitantie die betrekking had op de uiteindelijke afhandeling en waarop niet zel-den een bedrag stond dat een verdubbeling aangaf van de oorspronkelijke schuld. Waarom dit zo ging? Een-voudig, omdat Louis Berger van mening was dat hij in het casino of op de beurs het geld van de vordering kon verdrievoudigen, in de tijd dat de vordering verdubbelde.

Casino's als speelhuizen der hebzucht waren zandbakken in vergelijking met de beurs, want de beurs was een met bloed, zweet en tranen doordrenkte arena, waarin de zwaarden, de drietanden en de netten waren gesublimeerd tot cijfers. Cijfers als percentages, als prognoses en als saldi. De gladiatoren van toen waren de speculanten van nu, slaven, evenals in de antieke oudheid, die elkaar naar het leven stonden tot vermaak van hun heerser, de Godheid Geld.

Op een dag in een of ander voorjaar deed Louis iets ongebruikelijks wat Ezra behoorlijk in verwarring bracht. Hij toonde Ezra onverwachts een aankoopfactuur van effecten, voor een bedrag van een kleine driehonderdduizend gulden. Ezra wist niet wat zijn vader wilde dat hij zei. Wat moest hij zeggen? Het was een blauw papier. Met een aantal zegels erop geplakt. Louis wees smalend op het bedrag dat de zegels tezamen vertegenwoordigden, zestienhonderd gulden, het commissieloon van de bank.
'Wel veel voor zegels, hè?' bracht Ezra uit.

* * *

'Ezra heeft een uil,' zei Louis Berger op een dag tegen zijn vrouw.

'Ja, al een hele poos,' antwoordde zij.

'Hij wil hem in de keuken zetten,' zei Louis daarop.

'Gezellig,' zei Nellie.

'Dat vinden wij dus goed?' vroeg Louis toen.

'Dat vinden wij zelfs leuk,' antwoordde Nellie.

Louis dacht even na en knikte toen instemmend.

*   *   *

Drie weken nadat de jonge Nestor als dwaalgast tegen wil en dank gedwongen werd zich tot mensenvriend te ontwikkelen, leek hij in uiterlijk toch de uil te gaan worden waartoe de natuur hem had voorbestemd. Zijn gevoel ten opzichte van Ezra had zich geconditioneerd, zoals roofvogels in een dierentuin zich gaan richten op de verzorger die af en toe een handje eendagskuikens in hun kooi komt werpen, terwijl de man zelf een vervangbare handlanger blijft van het repressieve systeem. Eerder is het de verschuivende grendel van hun volière die de aandacht trekt dan de verschijning van de man die het dagelijks rantsoen aan voedsel op de kunstmatig geformeerde rotspartij smijt.

Verbijstering en angst hadden plaatsgemaakt voor felheid en vraatzucht. En als Ezra na thuiskomst uit school met een aantal in kippenveertjes gerolde stukjes poulet zijn kamer betrad, ontwaakte Nestor met een schok uit zijn gedommel en veerde op, met heftig knipperende ogen en stampende klauwen. De vriendelijk aanmoedigende woordjes die Ezra dan sprak leek hij in 't geheel niet te horen. Hij staarde strak naar Ezra's handen en greep het brokje voedsel tussen diens vingers weg zodra hij erbij kon, waarna hij het vervolgens met enkele kokhalzende bewegingen in zijn geheel naar binnen schrokte. Zijn vleugels waren nu bijna volgroeid, bruin van kleur met zwarte dwarsstrepen en zijn borst was bedekt met een dikke laag zacht en goudbruin bespikkeld dons, waarin de vleugels diep wegzakten. Uit zijn kop staken nu twee lange oorpluimen die zijn uiterlijk een strenge aanblik gaven.

Het eerste wat Ezra aan training met Nestor lukte was om hem op zijn pols te laten stappen, nadat hij zijn arm in een langzaam opwaartse beweging onder zijn buik duwde. De uil wiebelde om zijn evenwicht te bewaren, maar het lukte altijd en als Ezra zijn arm enigszins versneld liet zakken dan spreidde Nestor zijn nog gedeeltelijk in hulzen verpakte vleugelpennen uit en bood hij een al bijna vervaarlijke aanblik.

Het volgende stadium was een echte uitdaging.

Ezra zette Nestor op de rug van een stoel neer en hield zijn arm als opstap op ongeveer een halve meter afstand. In zijn andere hand hield hij Nestor een mals brokje in veertjes gewikkeld vlees voor, dat Nestor zou kunnen pakken als hij eerst de sprong naar de arm had gemaakt. Een sprong waarbij hij voor het eerst zijn vleugels zou moeten gebruiken.

Nestors blik hechtte zich aan de prooi en zijn ogen

gloeiden in fel oranje op, zijn kop begon te bewegen, eerst naar beneden, daarna naar links en daarna naar rechts. En opnieuw. Heen en weer, onafgebroken nu, alsof hij de afstand schatte tussen zijn prooi en hemzelf. En toen, plotseling, de aanval. Nou ja, aanval, hij sprong naar voren, waarbij hij onhandig met zijn on- klare wieken waaierde. Maar het lukte.

'Nestor, je kan het!' riep Ezra enthousiast en hield het vlees voor de kromme snavel van zijn pupil, die het onmiddellijk beetgreep en naar binnen werkte.

Daarna gaf Ezra het voedsel nog uitsluitend als Nes- tor er de vliegsprong voor wilde maken, wat eigenlijk niet meer mislukte. Een enkele keer hield Ezra zijn arm toch iets te ver weg, of berekende Nestor de afstand verkeerd en viel hij op de grond, maar dat bleek op zijn ontwikkeling geen enkele nadelige invloed te hebben. Steeds beter begon hij zijn vleugels te gebruiken, totdat uiteindelijk Ezra's kamer te klein was geworden voor de training die Nestor nodig had. En zo geschiedde het in die dagen dat de familie Berger aan tafel zat in hun keuken, terwijl een jonge ransuil met een soort ver- warde gestrengheid op hen neerkeek vanuit zijn tijde- lijke verblijfplaats: een ruïneus aquarium dat boven op de servieskast was geplaatst.

Zijn met van angst tot lichte gespannenheid ver- mengde nieuwsgierigheid veroorzaakte dat hij alles wat zich in de keuken voordeed met volledige aandacht volgde, zodat alle afgewerkte 'viezigheid' uit zijn sys- teem zich in de goede richting ontlaadde boven de kranten op de bodem van het aquarium.

En deze situatie bood meer mogelijkheden.

Niet alleen raakte de uil door het hechtere contact met de familie Berger in versterkte mate gewend aan de aanwezigheid van wezens die zich mensen noemden, maar zijn training kon nu drasties worden verhevigd. De sprong naar Ezra's pols kwam weldra neer op een duikvlucht, die hij keer op keer feilloos uitvoerde, waarna hij zich op Ezra's arm omdraaide, zich krachtig afzette en bijna rechtstandig terugvloog naar de rand van het aquarium. De prooi hield hij daarbij in zijn snavel en kokhalsde hem pas naar binnen nadat hij zich volledig had geherpositioneerd.

Zo was Nestor, na vier weken, een echte uil geworden.

*　*　*

In de Girondijnenstraat te Haarlem bevindt zich al sinds mensenheugenis een dierenwinkel waar men speciale dieren in de verkoop heeft. Voornamelijk vogels, omdat vogels nu eenmaal de mooiste dieren zijn. Honderden zitten er daar al sinds mensenheugenis en tot sint-juttemis onder wit neonlicht in hun kooitjes heen en weer te springen. Rijstvogels, agapornissen, kardinaalvogels, parkieten maar voornamelijk kanaries verbeiden daar hun getralied leven.

Ook knaagdieren zijn hier voorhanden, zoals de cavia, de hamster en de witte muis. Voor deze laatste

soort geldt echter dat waar het een leven in gevangenschap betreft er nauwelijks een gunstiger adres denkbaar is. Een beetje luieren in wat houtwol zal geen witte
muis tot wanhoop drijven en als zij uiteindelijk ver-
kocht worden zullen zij bij een kleine jongen op zijn
kamer met vervroegd pensioen gaan en hun zo nodige
lichaamsbeweging opdoen in een plastic draaimolen-
tje, tenzij die jongen Ezra Berger heet, de vogelman uit
Zandvoort.

Then all hell breaks loose...

Ezra kocht er vier.

Hij kreeg ze mee in een zakje van bruin pakpapier,
dat in de oude Budapester tram ritselde op zijn schoot.
Af en toe vouwde hij het zakje open en gluurde hij door
de spleet naar binnen, waar de levende muizenlijfjes
bibberend over elkaar heen klommen en met hun
krabbelende pootjes tevergeefs een uitgang zochten.
En Ezra vroeg zich af of dit eigenlijk wel een goed idee
was. Nestor moest gaan oefenen in het vangen van een
levende prooi, zeker, maar deze muizen waren zo bang!
In de natuur wist een muis nooit dat een uil op hem
jaagde, totdat hij gegrepen werd en er zich acht kromzwaarden door zijn lichaam boorden. En hij dood was.
Daar kwam geen angst aan te pas. En zo hoorde het
ook te gaan, maar nu? In de bonkende blauwe tram op
weg naar Zandvoort bedacht Ezra dat er kooitjes bestonden, gemaakt van dik koperdraad in de vorm van
een tulband, met een gaatje van boven waardoorheen
de muis naar binnen kon kruipen. De koperdraadjes
in het binnenste van de val eindigden met scherpe pun-

ten in een zich verwijdende cirkel, die terugkeren onmogelijk maakte. Zo ving je een muis levend, een wilde, zoals het hoorde en je kon hem direct geven. Ezra besloot op zoek te gaan naar zo'n kooivalletje en deze vier witte muizen zo snel mogelijk van hun angst te verlossen.

In de keuken liet hij Nestor van het aquarium op zijn hand stappen en nam hem mee naar de overloop boven. Dat was de plek. Hij plaatste de uil op een der hanenbalken en opende de papieren zak, waaruit hij door licht te schudden één muis naar buiten werkte. Met trillende snorharen keek het diertje om zich heen, wist niet wat te doen. Ezra daalde enkele treden in het trapgat, zodat alleen zijn hoofd nog zichtbaar was. De muis keek hem aan en deed een paar passen van hem af, stak zijn snuit schuin omhoog en bewoog zijn lippen. Zou hij het onraad dat zich boven hem bevond kunnen ruiken? Of zat hij zich slechts te oriënteren op zijn omgeving, zocht hij met zijn blik de plinten af op zoek naar een holletje of een ander veilig plekje om in weg te kruipen? Ezra keek naar Nestor onder het dakbeschot. De uil had zijn ogen wijd opengesperd en leek totaal gebiologeerd door de aanblik van de muis, de eerste levende die hij ooit had aanschouwd. Ezra schatte het hoogteverschil op een meter of drie, de afstand op vijf of zes, een tamelijk steile val voor een jonge uil die zijn eerste prooi moet zien te vangen, al kon Nestor goed duiken. Zou hij het wagen?

Zijn kop begon de trage heen-en-weerbewegingen

te maken, waarmee hij de afstand peilde. Zijn bolle oranje ogen fonkelden in zijn kop en zijn oorpluimen stonden in de hoogste staat van paraatheid. De muis trippelde doelloos een eindje over het gladde zeil, bleef toen weer zitten en veegde met zijn voorpootjes langs zijn snuit. Erg zenuwachtig leek hij niet te zijn. Ezra keek een aantal keren van de uil naar de muis en terug en zag dat de muis de aanwezigheid van Nestor in 't geheel niet vermoedde.

Nestor hing nu licht naar voren en de uitslagen van zijn kop naar links en naar rechts waren maximaal. Het was duidelijk dat de aandrang om zich op zijn prooi te storten bijna onweerstaanbaar was. Maar het was zijn eerste keer. En Ezra hield zijn adem in toen Nestor als in een vertraagde beweging zijn nog onvolgroeide vleugels spreidde en zich voorover liet vallen. De vleugelbewegingen kwamen hoofdzakelijk neer op remmende slagen, die een licht ruisen veroorzaakten en met een harde bons sloeg Nestor naast de muis neer op het zeil en gleed onhandig een eindje door.

Mis!

De muis rende weg, stak dwars over en probeerde een goed heenkomen te zoeken voor het monster dat zojuist uit de lucht was komen vallen. En wat zich toen voltrok had Ezra niet verwacht. Nestor sloeg opnieuw zijn vleugels uit, waardoor hij onverwacht snel ronddraaide en zette half lopend, half vliegend de achtervolging in. Die kort duurde, aangezien de muis zich nergens kon verbergen. Nestor stapte boven op hem, eerst met zijn ene klauw, vervolgens met de andere en bleef toen zitten. De muis piepte, eenmaal, een akelig angstig geluid, maar hij stierf niet. Ezra's gezicht vertrok tot een lelijke grimas. 'Kom, Nestor, knijpen...!' beval hij, maar de uil zakte licht door zijn poten en bewoog zijn oogleden traag op en neer.

Dit was niet goed!

Dit was niet zoals het moest!

'Nestor...!' siste Ezra, 'Dood hem...!'

Maar Nestor leek in te dommelen op de nog langzaam bewegende muis.

'Nestor... alsjeblieft...'

De ogen van de muis leken tweemaal zo groot te zijn geworden, als glimmende bloeddruppeltjes kleefden ze aan zijn kop, maar het waren zijn ogen. En nog bewoog hij.

Ezra stond als verlamd op de trap.

Dit was zíjn schuld!

Het was maar een muis, probeerde hij zichzelf voor te houden, muizen bestonden als voedsel, ze hadden wel hun eigen leven, maar ze werden altijd alleen maar gevangen, door uilen, door valken, door wezels, door marters, door hermelijnen. Ze werden ervoor gekweekt in dierentuinen, met handenvol rondgestrooid in de kooien van alle roofvogels die men gevangen hield. Ze waren eerst vergast, waarschijnlijk, maar ze hadden slechts bestaan als voedsel voor andere dieren. Slangen kregen ze levend en daarom werd het voeren van slangen nooit in het openbaar gedaan, nooit voor het publiek, aangezien een toeslaande slang en het in zijn geheel verorberen van zijn prooi een afgrijselijke aanblik boden. Oh, Nestor...!

Ezra wilde weglopen van het tafereel dat zich voor zijn ogen afspeelde, maar hij kon zich niet meer bewegen. De papieren zak op de grond veranderde af en toe ritselend van vorm en Ezra zag dat er enkele gaatjes en scheurtjes in waren gekomen. Het zou niet lang meer duren of de andere muizen hadden zich bevrijd. Doe wat, straks komen ze eruit! Maar Ezra stond als verlamd en aanschouwde willoos wat hij niet wilde zien.

Nestor boog zich naar voren en trok met de punt van zijn snavel aan het oor van de muis, waardoor de kop slap bewoog. Was hij dood? Of hoorde Ezra hem nog piepen? Nee, hij was dood. Acht kromzwaarden. En dan nog het gewicht van de uil.

Maar plotseling, in een laatste wanhopige krachtsinspanning, begonnen de voorpootjes van de muis toch nog te rennen en sloeg zijn staart heen en weer. Er trok een rilling door zijn lijf en nog eenmaal maakte hij een geluid, dat geen piepen meer genoemd kon worden.

Ezra zag dat hij dood was aan de ogen, die nu leeggelopen leken en dof. De uil bleef de muis onhandig aftasten met zijn snavel en de lange haren die daarlangs staken en trok uiteindelijk zijn prooi open onder de staart, waar hij het eerste houvast vond. Er kwam wat bloed, dat werd opgenomen door de witte vacht. Toen meer, dat uitliep op het zeil. Nestors snavel begon drastieser te bewegen en hij scheurde aan een inmiddels gapende wond. Volwassen uilen slikken hun prooi in hun geheel in, met huid en haar, kop eerst. Nooit trekken zij hem stuk, zoals valken en sperwers en haviken en Nestor...

Ezra ademde snuivend door zijn neus en zag hoe Nestor het bovenlijf van de muis los naar binnen schrokte. Daarna tilde hij zijn klauw met het andere deel erin omhoog en begon dat met aandachtige snavelgrepen leeg te eten. En wat Ezra toen zag deed hem verstijven van walging. In een lange streng van glimmende vleesklontjes trok Nestor vijf, zes, zeven, ongeboren jongen uit het gehalveerde muizenlijf, waarbij hij met korte schokjes van zijn kop het totale aantal muizenembryo's in één hap naar binnen werkte...

Toen keken ze elkaar aan, Nestor en Ezra, met Nestors snavelpunt rood van het bloed en Ezra's hart op hol en Ezra begreep dat hij zich in een wereld had binnengedrongen, die niet meer tot die van de mensen behoorde, misschien ooit wel behoord had, maar die vergeten was of weggedrongen, of in onbruik geraakt.

Of niet?

Wat had meneer De Haan verteld?

Ezra wist het niet meer.

Hij was een vogelman, dat wist hij zeker en hij had mussen in vieren gesneden en Nestor partjes bebloede mol gevoerd, dat had hij toch gedaan? Jawel, dat had hij, maar al die dieren waren eerst dóód geweest. Hoe moest je het zeggen. In één keer dood, zoals het hoorde, door een kogel, of een messteek, of een dichtslaande val, maar dit was geknoei, onhandig en onnatuurlijk en nodeloos.

Of toch niet?

Ieder roofdier moest leren doden.

Ezra keek naar Nestor en de uil keek terug, zonder hem te zien, zoals hij naar een boom zou kijken die roerloos uit het trapgat groeide en kokte het slappe en lege achterlijf van zijn prooi op in de muil van zijn snavel, waarin het even bleef steken en de staart als een veter naar buiten hing.

De drie muizen in de papieren zak ritselden onafgebroken, op zoek naar vrijheid en verlossing. Zouden zij iets hebben kunnen bespeuren van het lot dat een hunner was overkomen? Zouden zij bloed kunnen ruiken? Of doodsangst? Ezra wist het niet. Zou je witte muizen kunnen loslaten? Bijvoorbeeld in de tuin, of in het kippenhok?

De uil stapte gewillig op Ezra's pols en even later op de rand van het aquarium in de keuken, waar hij zich schurkte, dik maakte en in slaap viel.

* * *

Claire Meerman was zonder twijfel het mooiste meisje van het hele Lorentz-Lyceum, dat viel door iedereen direct te constateren, maar welke jongen op het gehele Lorentz-Lyceum het meest verliefd was op Claire Meerman viel minder gemakkelijk te zeggen, want verliefdheid was geheim. Vroeger althans. Haar ogen waren zo blauw als het blauw in de vleugel van een Vlaamse gaai en haar haren zo zacht als de borstveren van een uil. Zij kon lopen zonder dat haar voeten de grond raakten en de manier waarop zij zich voortbewoog leek daarom nog het meest op zweven. Haar wimpers waren even lang als de wimpers van een oehoe en ook even zwart. Ze kwam uit het noorden, niet Friesland of Groningen, maar uit het hoge noorden, Noorwegen of Zweden, haar ouders dan, haar moeder, want weinig Noormannen heten Meerman.

∗   ∗   ∗

Het leek erop of Nestor op zijn aquarium in de keuken alleen maar zat te slapen, maar als Ezra binnenkwam om voor zichzelf een boterham te maken of om Nestor iets lekkers te brengen, een dode mus, of nog lekkerder, een dode muis, dan sperde hij zijn ogen wijd open en begonnen ze te gloeien van honger. Om niet te zeggen vraatzucht. Hij richtte zich dan op, waarbij zijn lichaam verstrakte en het leek alsof hij zich klaarmaakte voor de een of andere actie, de een of andere oefening, een sprong, of een aanval, een duik- of een klimvlucht. Dit waren de momenten waarop Ezra hem kwam halen om in de tuin te gaan oefenen.

Gewillig stapte Nestor op Ezra's pols, als die zijn arm met zijn gekromde hand tot vlak bij zijn klauwen omhoogstak of licht dwingend tegen zijn borst drukte en hij bleef daar ceremonieel zitten tot Ezra een geschikte plaats had gevonden om hem neer te zetten en de buik van de uil tegen de tak van een boom of de rand van een hek duwde. Die discipline van opstappen en blijven zitten was eigenlijk vanzelf gekomen, tezamen met de gewenning aan elkaars gezelschap. Het was duidelijk dat Nestor wist wie Ezra was en hem beschouwde als zijn meerdere, als zijn leermeester, als een ouder wellicht, zijn vader, een houding die eens zou overgaan, zoals alle jongere dieren eens hun zelfstandigheid opeisten en solitair werden, en zich afzonderden en wegtrokken, of voor altijd uitvlogen, op zoek naar een eigen territorium, dat zij zelf gingen beheersen en waarvan zij tegelijkertijd een deel werden, door zich te manifesteren als jager en ten onder te gaan als prooi, levend en stervend, meedraaiend in de eeuwige cirkel van de natuur.

Wat deed een uil in de keuken?

Een goede vraag, waarop het antwoord gewoon was dat hij daar zat, de uil Nestor, op een ongebruikt aquarium, een aquarium zonder glas, waarvan Saul kort tevoren onder de verlichtingskap de volledig vergane bedrading had ontdekt die tot op enkele millimeters boven het wateroppervlak was gezakt, zodat het nog slechts een kwestie van toeval was wie er zou worden geëlektrocuteerd, alleen de vissen of ook Ezra's vader, Louis. Hoe Saul op het spoor kwam van dat soort gevaren was een mirakel, groter dan het ontstaan ervan. Louis had zijn oudste zoon bewonderend aangekeken en zijn hand op zijn arm gelegd, maar Saul was weggelopen zonder iets te zeggen.

En nu zaten de vissen in het nieuwe aquarium, de black molly's en de maanvissen en de guppen, maar vissen in een aquarium waren levende doden, als mensen in een huis met alleen maar meubels en kasten en bedden op vloeren van dood hout, waar in de op maat bewerkte balken van de plafonds de dode bomen hun onmachtige kracht toonden in hun verzaagde ziel. Soms had Ezra gedachten waarvan de betekenis hem ontging, maar waarin hij een waarheid bespeurde die later misschien nog eens zou blijken. Of ze zouden vanzelf weer overgaan. Je kon niet altijd de baas zijn over het binnenste van je hoofd. Wel kon je op zoek gaan naar de nesten van vogels en leven in bewondering voor de schoonheid van hun bestaan, om er te zijn als dat nodig was en ze te behoeden voor gevaar en te luisteren naar hun gezang, naar hun gekrijs, of naar hun gemonkel en te voelen dat er een mysterieus leven was, dat in de huizen van mensen niet meer bestond en nog alleen door dieren werd geleefd, alle dieren, maar de vogels in het bijzonder. Hoe konden de mensen dat alles vergeten zijn?

Ten huize van de familie Berger kwamen meer dieren over de vloer dan mensen.

Eerst kwam de hond, natuurlijk, Jonker, de dashond, onafscheidelijk in de buurt van Louis Berger. En dan waren er de kippen, de barnevelders en leghorns en Floris de witte kalkoen, wel vijf kerstmissen oud en de Brahma-haan Piet, die met zijn stramme bevederde poten vorstelijk door de tuin paradeerde. En er waren

parkieten geweest, tientallen, als een kolonie van rede-
loze kwetteraars, waarvan nu nog alleen de lege volière
bestond. En voor de kippenschuur, in een kleine loop-
volière met een schuin dak van golfplaten, de goudfa-
zanten uit China en de parelhoenders en de kwartels.
Maar dat was nu allemaal niets meer vergeleken met
de uil Nestor, die tot de echte natuur behoorde en misschien wel de hele zomer zou blijven, om de mensen
weer te leren kennen, zoals Louis en Nellie en Saul.

En vooral nóg iemand.

'Als je dit in één keer pakt mag je Claire zien,' riep Ezra
Nestor toe, nadat hij hem van zijn pols op een hoge ie-
pentak had geplaatst, zich vervolgens een aantal meters
had verwijderd en zijn hand met daarin een stukje in
donsveertjes gerolde kippenpoulet omhoogstak.

Onmiddellijk vernauwde Nestor zijn gezichtsveld tot
Ezra's hand. Zijn lichaam verkrapte en zijn kop zette
een regelmatige dwarsbeweging in en even leek hij zich
direct te laten vallen om de aanvalsvlucht in te zetten,
maar de afstand was hem kennelijk toch te groot, of
hij werd door iets anders weerhouden, want geleidelijk
nam zijn gespannen felheid af en werd hij weer ronder
en begon hij met schokkerige bewegingen van zijn kop
om zich heen te kijken, als een slaperige poes.

'Nestor, hier!' riep Ezra hem toe en de uil keek nog
wel, maar hij raakte andermaal afgeleid en keek ook
naar het PEN-huisje in de verte, met de twee geglazuur-
de tegels in de muur, een van een haan en een van een
hond, en hij keek naar de schreeuwende meeuwen

hoog in de lucht en ten slotte naar het dak van het af-gesloten bijhuis aan de achterzijde bij de schuur. Waar-om de uil zo plotseling alle aandacht voor zijn training verloor viel niet te constateren, maar Ezra zag dat het misging. Nestor verzette zijn klauwen, draaide zich zo een halve slag om en fixeerde zijn blik vervolgens op zijn nieuwe bestemming. Toen zette hij af. De tak zwiepte ervan. Hij vloog, eerst licht dalend, zo doelbe-wust op het tuinhuisje af dat het wel leek alsof hij zich ertegenop zou storten, maar vlakbij gekomen zwenkte hij schuin weg, steeg scherp hoogte winnend uit boven de bomen en begon met jachtige vleugelslag aan een cirkel boven de tuin. Ezra riep nogmaals zijn naam, maar de uil reageerde niet en zette een nieuwe lan-dingspoging in die echter onzeker werd uitgevoerd en met een harde bons tegen de dakpannen eindigde. Met uitgespreide vleugels en geopende snavel lag Nestor zo enige tijd tegen het schuine dak gedrukt te hijgen, tot-dat hij zich niet langer schrap kon zetten en langzaam, met krassende nagels, naar beneden begon te glijden om zo uiteindelijk vermoeid en versuft in de dakgoot te belanden, waarin hij zich uitschudde en zich op-nieuw op de wereld trachtte te oriënteren.

'Blijf daar staan!' schreeuwde Ezra en hij holde naar de schuur om een ladder te halen.

En Nestor bleef staan, en even later gelukte het Ezra om hem weer op zijn pols te krijgen en hem voorzichtig in de keuken terug te zetten, waar hij voor straf het stukje poulet met veel misbaar in de pedaalemmer weggooide.

Nog een geluk dat Nestor er niet echt vandoor was gegaan. Wie had hem kunnen tegenhouden? En erger, had hij een ontsnapping wel kunnen overleven? Waarschijnlijk niet.

Ezra keek op naar Nestor, die neerkeek op hem.

'Wat deed je nou ineens?'

Maar Nestor had inmiddels zijn aandacht verlegd en was doende de slagpennen van beide vleugels een aantal malen tussen de bladen van zijn snavel door te trekken, waardoor er een fijne regen van hoornstofdeeltjes neerdwarrelde op Ezra's gezicht.

Dit moest worden goedgemaakt, van beide kanten.

Ezra nam zich voor Claires naam niet meer bij zijn trainingsprogramma te betrekken en Nestor moest tonen dat hij vorderingen had gemaakt bij het pakken van een prooi en dat hij zich niet meer door het geheimzinnige tuinhuis zou laten afleiden.

's Avonds kwam Ezra daarom terug, in de keuken, waar het nog warm was en rook naar pannen, jus en vaat. Buiten was het donker. Wat Ezra wilde doen was eigenlijk een experiment. Nachtvliegen. Een vervolg op een eerdere oefening. Of liever, dezelfde oefening maar nu uitgevoerd in totale duisternis. Een oefening alleen aan uilen voorbehouden.

Zo opende Ezra de deur en betrad hij de keuken in het donker. Voetje voor voetje en om zich heen tastend posteerde hij zich in het hart van de duisternis en stak een stukje verenvlees omhoog. Zo bleef hij roerloos staan, als een vriend die een groet brengt, of als een

beul die zijn bijl heft, of als een heilige die omhoog-
wijst. Het maakte geen verschil.

Even leek Ezra te horen hoe Nestor zich op de rand
van het aquarium verplaatste, een licht geritsel, een
vaag geschuifel, maar hij was er niet zeker van. Konden
uilen werkelijk geluidloos vliegen? En konden zij werkelijk zien in het donker? Als katten met vleugels? Nu
moest het blijken, nu moest het vliegend bewijs gele-
verd worden.

En daar!

Plotseling verstrengelden Nestors klauwen zich met
Ezra's hand en was er het lichte suizen van balanceren-
de wieken.

Daar was hij!

Het bestond!

Ezra hield zijn adem in en volgde via de toppen van
zijn vingers hoe Nestor erin slaagde zich weer te ont-
haken en zich middels evenwichtbewarende vliegbe-
wegingen en zonder zijn prooi los te laten, om te wenden en ruisend weer op te stijgen in het niets. Oh!

Een halfwassen ransuil weegt, gewogen op de hand van
een veertienjarige jongen, ongeveer een pond, inclusief
prooi, bijvoorbeeld een in kippendons gewikkeld brokje runderpoulet. Zijn afzet lijkt het gewicht te vermeerderen, maar dit is schijn. De veertienjarige jongen ver-
andert in een zesenvijftigjarige man, en de ransuil
verdwijnt op de eeuwige jachtvelden, in de mist der uilen, maar dat moment van waarheid en wonder, het
moment waarop werkelijkheid en waanzin versmelten

en het leven zijn mysterie onthult, zal nooit meer vergaan.

Een licht ruisen was hoorbaar geweest, alsof een engel
vertrok. In duisternis verschenen en slechts waargeno-
men in het gevoel.

Ezra zuchtte en deed het licht in de keuken weer aan.

En verbrak daarmee de betovering, om Nestor te
zien.

En daar zat, op de rand van het aquarium, met een
stukje vlees in zijn klauw, de uil Nestor, ongeveer zoals
een papegaai die een pinda eet.

Het plotselinge licht verstoorde zijn bezigheden,
waardoor hij opkeek, opkeek vanuit een andere wereld.
En Ezra zag hoe Nestors ogen veranderden en van twee
ronde donkere kralen opgloeiden tot oranje ballen van
vuur die hem troffen als laserstralen, met de hitte van
vloeibaar licht.

En vanuit deze hypnotiserende blik gestuurd zette
de betovering opnieuw in, maar ditmaal een andere en
buiten Ezra's wil.

Het aquarium verdween in het niets en werd een
brede zwarte band, als de onderkant van een kader, dat
zich vervolgens als een verticale lijst rondom hem sloot
als een diep en duister gat, waarin Nestor leek te zweven, maar tot Ezra's verbijstering weldra in volume begon te vermeerderen en uit de duistere achtergrond begon op te doemen.

Een onmogelijkheid.

En toch was het zo, of leek het zo, hetgeen op hetzelfde neerkwam, indien men kon geloven wat men zag en zag wat men geloofde, indien men kon geloven dat er meer was dan men zien kon, meer dan men niet kon geloven.

En doordat Ezra zich overgaf aan wat hij waarnam, willoos maar met heel zijn wezen, begreep hij plotseling wat zich aan hem voltrok: hij was het zélf die gestadig volume verloor en gewicht verloor, die vervluchtigde in wat hij zag en in zijn vervluchtiging naar Nestor werd opgetild en naar hem werd toe gezogen om uiteindelijk in hem te verdwijnen, als een deel van het beeld dat door zijn eigen waarneming was geschapen.

En er was elektriciteit...

Niet voelbaar en knetterend, maar zichtbaar als zwart en hevig licht, als trillingen in de lucht, een storm van trillingen...

Een schokgolf in een laaiend luchtledig.

Ezra wist wat het was, althans herkende wat hem overkwam.

In dromen soms gebeurde dit, van jongs af aan en op onvoorspelbare momenten.

In dromen... waarin hij ophield te bestaan...

Eerst een klemmende druk op zijn hoofd die zijn droom tot een duizeling maakte.

Een nachtmerrie, waarin hij opging in het niets, een diepe duisternis waar werkelijk helemaal niets meer gebeurde, een zichtbaar niets, waarin hij wakker schrok en ontwaakte als in de dood, voor altijd alleen,

voor eeuwig starend in een nachtzwart vacuüm, over-
mand in het besef tijdloos in de ruimte te zijn wegge-
smeten, zonder ooit te kunnen verdwijnen, zoals alle
andere wezens, als zij sterven en weer opgaan in de
elektriciteit die ooit hun bestaan als een vonk heeft verlicht, om de leegte uit te diepen in een eeuwig universum van verbrande energie.

Recht achter de ogen, die scheel keken van de pijn.
Het was Nestor, die steeds groter werd, kijk maar, en
zich verhief, als in een droom,

Ezra tastte naar de tafel voor houvast.

Nam plaats op een stoel, want deze dromen eindigden altijd in hoofdpijn, in het midden van de nacht en
in het midden van zijn schedel.

Hij legde zijn hoofd op zijn armen en kneep zijn
ogen stijf opeen om niets meer te hoeven zien. Maar
in het donker van Ezra's hoofd bleef Nestor zich ver-
heffen. Hij was inmiddels zo groot dat hij zich allang
niet meer in de keuken kon bevinden. Die was opgelost
in het zwarte heelal dat Nestor nodig had om te groei-
en, om zodanig te groeien dat hij Ezra kon pakken als
een prooi.

Het raadselachtige van alles was dat Ezra heel goed
wist niet te dromen en dat het dus niet zo kon zijn,
maar als hij heel goed wist dat het niet zo kon zijn,
waarom durfde hij dan niet meer te kijken? Naar die
reusachtige uil die nu boven hem hing met wieken als
de zeilen van een schip en klauwen als de ijzeren grijpers van een hijskraan... die daar zo geruisloos hing,
in al zijn goddelijkheid, als een majestueuze draak,

licht verend op dezelfde plaats in de zwarte hemel, die hij geheel en al vulde met zichzelf...

Daar was hij!

'Saul...' fluisterde Ezra, terwijl hij zijn ogen tegen zijn onderarm perste.

En daarna nogmaals: 'Saul, alsjeblieft...'

* * *

The schemes of mice and men gang oft agley.

Deze ontboezeming van de Schotse dichter Robert Burns was maar al te waar. Maar uilen, al waren ze nog zo superieur aan muizen en mensen, mochten in dit verband niet onvermeld blijven, want dezelfde uil die de avond tevoren nog met wieken als zeilen en klauwen als ijzeren grijpers in het tijdloze universum van Ezra Bergers elektriese dromen had gedanst, stond de volgende ochtend machteloos vastgesteld in een juspan op het fornuis.

Hij werd 's ochtends om halfzes door Louis gevonden, die hem pas twee uur later aan Ezra liet zien.

'Oh Nestor, wat ben je toch dóm!' verzuchtte Ezra.

Louis stak het gas onder de pan met vet aan.

'Niet doen!' schreeuwde Ezra.

Maar Louis had het gas alweer uitgedraaid en lachte.

Warm water deed de rest.

Maar dom was het wel.

Voor een uil.

*   *   *

Zandvoort was vroeger een mooi en rustiek vissers-
dorp.

Overal was de zee.

Een eiland van natuur was Zandvoort, met ongerep-
te jachtvelden en eindeloze zomers. De familie Berger
was in 1948 in Zandvoort komen wonen op een par-
terreappartement in de Haarlemmerstraat, een van de
twee toegangswegen tot het dorp en tegenwoordig, met
de Kostverlorenstraat, de laatste straat waar nog bomen groeien.

Het was een gevaarlijk adres, niet omdat het dorp
vergeven was van de NSB'ers, want juist die deden hun
uiterste best om te laten merken dat zij met die ver-
foeilijke club niets te maken wilden hebben en ook
nooit iets te maken hadden gehad, wablief, maar het
adres aan de Haarlemmerstraat was gevaarlijk vanwege
het verkeer, dat verraderlijker toesloeg dan heden ten
dage, aangezien het destijds nog niet uit een onafgebroken stroom voertuigen bestond, die elkaar onder-
ling afremden, maar uit individuele bestuurders, met
ieder hun eigen maximumsnelheid, die afhing van een
veelheid van factoren, variërend van de luim van het
moment, het alcoholpercentage in de bloedbaan of de
mate waarin de vroege jeugd als repressief was erva-
ren.

Louis Berger had de stad Amsterdam verlaten als een man met een verscheurde ziel, maar ook als de aartsvader van zijn familienaam, met aangescherpte zintuigen en een feilloos gevoel voor gevaar. Hij had zijn leven in meer dan één opzicht aan Ezra's moeder te danken gehad. In de oorlog doordat zij er wás en hem de kans bood om voor de levende moeder te kiezen die zij zou kunnen worden en niet voor de dode die hij achterliet.

In de stad des onheils was hem ruimschoots de tijd vergund om te oefenen in het uitschakelen van iedere vorm van persoonlijke herkenbaarheid, het onderdrukken van emoties en het veinzen van belangstelling. Zo was hij een kameleontie aanpasser geworden, juist hij, de meest onaangepaste flierefluiter van vooroorlogs Amsterdam, flierefluiter en trompetspeler, bluffer en lakschoenencharmeur, met zijn Oldsmobile Roadster en zijn Cantegalli-kostuums en zijn lapis lazuli manchetknopen en zijn glimmende zwarte haar en zijn vertoornde vader, die dit alles niet langer wilde financieren, maar het toch deed, misschien omdat hij wist dat de oorlog kwam en Nellie, ja Nellie, de schone vissersdochter uit IJmuiden, op zoek naar avontuur, op zoek naar de grote stad, om er te leven en er gelukkig te worden, Nellie, godzijdank geen jodin, die waarlijk alles had om voor te sterven, maar verdomme verliefd was op Louis' boezemvriend en aartsrivaal Simon Plas.

('Kunnen wij die deerne niet samen delen, Simon?')
('Nee vuile smaus, dat kunnen we níét')

Arme Simon, met zijn malle lach en zijn malle plannen en zijn raadselachtige dood in het IJ, in het voorjaar van 1940. Het was eind maart en het water was nog traag van de kou. Hoe ze daar beland waren wist Louis niet meer, daar achter het Centraal Station, vroeg in de morgen. Waren ze dronken geweest? Louis scheen zich te herinneren dat Simon een poos lang zijn arm over zijn schouders had gelegd, maar die herinnering kon zich ook later in zijn hoofd hebben gevormd, hoe dan ook, opeens was Simon de weg overgestoken en naar het eind van een der havenhoofden gelopen. Daar had hij zijn schoenen en zijn jas uitgetrokken en geroepen dat hij het warm had en dat hij een stukje ging zwemmen en hoe jammer het was dat ze nu niet bij de Amstel waren, bij Ouderkerk, waar het water veel aangenamer was en zonder olie. En met een uitbundige kreet was hij erin gesprongen en helemaal naar de overkant gezwommen, met krachtige slag en wit water om zich heen. Hij kon zwemmen als geen ander, die malloot. Aan de noordkant van de stad, pal naast de pont, was hij tegen de basaltblokken opgekropen en had hij het water uit zijn kleding geslagen. Daar in de verte, nauwelijks nog zichtbaar in de grijze lucht, had hij zich omgewend en gezwaaid, met beide armen in de lucht, als een overwinnaar, alvorens opnieuw te water te gaan. En Louis was zelf ook naar het havenhoofd overgestoken om hem te helpen en langs de kademuur omhoog te trekken, als hij terugkwam. Hij had de jas opgeraapt en zich afgevraagd of hij die zo snel mogelijk om Simon heen moest slaan of dat die zich beter eerst van zijn natte bovenkleding kon ontdoen. En toen was het gebeurd. Halverwege de terugtocht hielden de slagen plotseling op en dreef Simons hoofd als een bal op het water. Alle kracht leek weg. Wat was er? Had hij kramp? Raakte hij onderkoeld? Kon dat zo onverwachts gaan? Maar toen verrees hij langzaam en statig tot zijn middel uit het water, bracht met uitgestrekte arm de Hitlergroet en zonk.

Louis schoot eerst nog in de lach.

Nellie was ontroostbaar.

* * *

Weg moest hij, uit Amsterdam, weg uit die dodenstad zonder toekomst.

Nellie stelde Zandvoort voor en zo verhuisde Louis met zijn gezin naar Zandvoort aan Zee, dat toen nog geen dodendorp was en zelfs nog een toekomst leek te hebben.

Louis Berger was slimmer dan hij wilde zijn, zag meer dan hij wilde waarnemen maar had zijn persoonlijke leefwereld bewust beperkt tot de binnenkant van zijn hoofd en wat zich daar afspeelde wist alleen hijzelf. Het verleden werd in zijn totaliteit en voor de duur van de rest van zijn leven opgeborgen in een hermeties ver-

zegelde kluis, vervaardigd van gewapend verdringings-
beton. En niemand uit zijn nieuw verworven wereld
zou ooit nog enig teken vernemen uit die martelkamer,
die vanaf dat moment ook nimmer had bestaan.

Toen in het voorjaar van 1950 Femke van Duivenbo-
den, het dochtertje van de overburen, tijdens haar spel
in de Haarlemmerstraat door een auto werd gegrepen,
waarbij haar pop onder de voorwielen van de auto
raakte en zijzelf onder de achterwielen, stond het voor
Louis vast dat hij ook die plek des onheils zo snel mogelijk diende te verlaten en nog datzelfde jaar verhuisde
de familie Berger naar een oud en bouwvallig huisje
aan de Marnix van Sint Aldegondestraat.

Wat later de Marisstraat zou gaan heten en nog later
de boulevard Paulus Loot bestond toen nog uit oude
duinen en ruggen stuifzand.

Het huisje was voor bewoning eigenlijk niet geschikt
en zou binnen enkele jaren moeten worden gesloopt,
maar het stond geheel vrij en dicht bij het strand en
was voorlopig groot genoeg. Nellie liet zowel beneden
als boven de tussendeuren wegbreken en vervangen
door gemetselde bogen en ontwierp een van antieke
baksteentjes opgetrokken monumentale open haard,
die 's winters als een tempel van vuur en warmte alle
tocht en kou in een gloed van gezelligheid verzwolg.
Als brandstof diende de onuitputtelijke voorraad
wrakhout van het strand, in de eerste jaren door Louis
gezaagd en gehakt, maar op zijn zesde al grotendeels
door Saul als zijn taak opgeëist.

Vanuit de bovenkamer keek men recht op zee en niemand kon ze zien, Saul en Ezra Berger, als ze dan het raam openden en samen met een grote boog zo in de duinen plasten. Saul won, altijd, maar soms woei de westenwind zo hard uit zee dat de plas tegen het huis en in de kamer werd teruggeblazen. En soms wisten Nellie en Louis niet waarom de jongens boven het zo moesten uitschateren van plezier.

Nellie richtte boven een klein atelier in en zette daar haar naaimachine voor het raam. Zo begon haar loopbaan als kleermaakster, eerst bestaand uit verstelwerk, reparaties, het innemen of uitleggen van kleding, maar geleidelijk begon zij ook zelf modellen te ontwerpen en kwamen er klanten met modebladen om kleding op maat te bestellen, klanten die terugkwamen en voor wie Nellie patronen op naam bewaarde, die weer tot nieuwe ontwerpen konden worden omgewerkt.

Zo vestigde zij langzamerhand een naam.

En zo verstreken zeven warme winters en zeven warme zomers.

Eenmaal per jaar trad Nellie op in een uitvoering van de Zandvoortse Operette Vereniging, waarin ze meestal de hoofdrol speelde, want ze kon heel mooi zingen. Zij en mevrouw Petrovitch, de echtgenote van Dragan Petrovitch. Zij waren de zangsterren van de vereniging. Dragan Petrovitch was voorzitter van de plaatselijke winkeliersvereniging en uitbater van het bekendste etablissement in het dorp, de Bar-Bodega Petrovitch, die pas 's avonds om acht uur openging en waar louche zaken werden gedaan, met vrouwen en drank, althans volgens Saul, die dat soort dingen wist.

Toch stond de familie Berger na een aantal jaren in het dorp als buitenissig bekend, want alles ging daar anders. De vader deed het huishouden, haalde de boodschappen en kookte het eten. De moeder verdiende het geld. Zij was zelfstandig en werkte thuis. Onfatsoenlijk was het niet, want het waren uitsluitend vrouwen die daar aanbelden. En soms kon je haar horen zingen, vooral als boven het raam openstond, dan leek ze zowaar wel een Italiaanse operazangeres. Tot in de Brederodestraat klonk haar stem.

* * *

In de tweede maand van Nestors training, kort voor de zomervakantie, had hij in de jacht een graad van behendigheid bereikt die voor geen enkele wilde uil zou onderdoen, meende Ezra Berger, vogelman te Zandvoort. Op de overloop bleef hij geen tien seconden meer op de hanenbalken zitten om met zijdelings bewegende kop en vlammende ogen de afstand te schatten tot de prooi die Ezra beneden op het zeil voor hem neerzette. De witte muis had zich nog niet op zijn omgeving georiënteerd of Nestor was al feilloos op hem neergedaald, waarbij hij zijn vleugels alleen als remflappen bewoog. Acht kromzwaarden doorboorden de muis vervolgens en doodden het dier snel en schoon, geklieder kwam er niet meer aan te pas en of de muis een mannetje was of een vrouwtje en in welk stadium van ontwikkeling hij verkeerde kwam niet meer aan het licht, want Nestor verorberde zijn prooi in zijn geheel. Het diertje diende als voedsel, stilstaan bij zijn angst was zinloos. Die angst en de pijn zo kort mogelijk laten duren, daar ging het om.

Ezra had zich afgevraagd of muizen in de vrije natuur misschien nog een andere functie konden hebben dan als voedsel dienen voor andere dieren, maar hij moest op die vraag het antwoord schuldig blijven en toen hij het aan Saul vroeg kreeg hij ten antwoord dat ieder dier bestond als voedsel voor andere dieren en dat alleen de mens doodde voor zijn plezier. Een typiese Saul-reactie, die meer vragen opriep dan beantwoordde en waar je dus niets aan had.

Buiten was het vangen van een muis moeilijker.

Niet alleen bevond Nestor zich dan altijd op grotere afstand tot zijn prooi, maar de muis kon zich in de tuin ook beter tussen het gras en de andere begroeiing schuilhouden. Maar ook in de tuin hadden de muizen geen enkele kans en was Nestors superioriteit indrukwekkend. Ezra had de muis meestal in een plastic bekertje dat hij eerst omhoogstak om Nestor te laten zien dat het zover was en dan tegen de grond hield tot de muis met trillende snuit en schokkerige bewegingen tevoorschijn kwam, om enkele voorzichtige stapjes in de tuin te wagen.

Dan floot Ezra met een toon die verliep van laag naar hoog en begon Nestors kop heen en weer te scharnieren en liet hij zich even later naar voren vallen om met zwenkende en zwalkende vleugelbewegingen te naderen en vlak voor de landing zijn klauwen naar voren te strekken en zich, licht afremmend, op de muis te zetten.

Al na de eerste paar weken had Ezra Nestor geen vogels meer gegeven.

Hij was een vogelman en een vogelman trekt geen mes om een vink te halveren of een spreeuw te vierendelen en dan als voedsel te offeren aan een andere vogel. Nu vingen uilen in de vrije natuur af en toe ook vogels, dat was waar, maar muizen vormden hun normale prooi en muizen waren er in overvloed. Witte in de winkel en grijze in het kippenhok. Bovendien was Ezra voor het schieten van de vogels afhankelijk van Saul en zijn luchtbuks en ook dat stond hem tegen. Om de muizen uit het kippenhok levend te vangen had Ezra een poos lang een rond kooivalletje met van boven een gat geprobeerd, maar dat lukte maar zelden. Klapvallen waren veel doeltreffender, al waren dode prooien weer minder geschikt om mee te oefenen.

Witte muizen waren favoriet. Ze waren onder alle omstandigheden goed te zien en bewogen zich traag als zij werden klaargezet. Fokken was geen doen, want Nestor at er één per dag en hoeveel muizen moest je dan wel niet hebben om dat tempo bij te houden?

Tweemaal had Saul hem een levende grijze muis gebracht, die hij in zijn broekzak had zitten, maar Ezra hield Saul liever op afstand, want diens belangstelling kwam alleen maar voort uit bemoeizucht, of verveling. En het was eerder machtsvertoon dan hulp. Beide keren had Saul erop gestaan om de muis zelf in de tuin te laten neerploffen en beide keren was het diertje in de struiken ontkomen en was het nog lastig geweest om Nestor weer op te nemen en mee naar binnen te krijgen.

Opvallend was hoe het tuinhuisje een mysterieuze aantrekkingskracht op Nestor uitoefende, die uit niets te verklaren viel, al had Saul wel eens opgemerkt dat uilen verzot waren op heksen en dat het hem niet zou verbazen als in het tuinhuisje ooit een heks had gewoond.

'De lucht van die hut bevalt me niet,' had hij daarbij gezegd. Maar op Ezra's vraag wat hij dan rook had hij geen antwoord gegeven.

Hoe ruikt een heks?

Wanneer Ezra Nestor op een tak in een der bomen had neergezet en met de prooi wegliep naar een geschikte plek in de tuin, vloog de uil meestal eerst over naar het tuinhuis, waar zijn nagels op de dakgoot schraapten en tikten, als hij zich met tastende stappen omdraaide op de zinken rand.

Dat Nestor buiten ook zomaar kon wegvliegen als hij dat wilde, had Ezra in het begin op het onzalige idee gebracht om Nestors harige klauw met een manchet van stof te omwinden en daaraan met een kleine veiligheidsspeld een lange dunne ketting vast te maken, van maar liefst vijftien meter lang, gekocht bij ijzerhandel Van Zeggelen in de Haltestraat, een soort ketting die bedoeld was om rubber afvoerstoppers aan kranen te bevestigen en veel te zwaar om op deze manier te gebruiken. Bovendien raakte de ketting al bij een van de eerste keren in de war en ging het daarna faliekant mis. Ezra was nog hard achter Nestor aangehold, maar had niet kunnen voorkomen dat de nietsvermoedende uil met een schok naar de grond werd neergerukt en daar hulpeloos bleef liggen, met gespreide vleugels, niet meer in staat omhoog te komen. Door deze stommiteit kon Nestor de poot waaraan de ketting had vastgezeten een poos lang niet gebruiken en hield hij die opgetrokken in de warme bescherming van zijn borstveren. En Ezra besloot het risico van wegvliegen dan maar te nemen en de training uitsluitend op het vasthouden van aandacht en de belofte van voedsel te baseren, een aanpak die Nestor trouwens probleemloos overnam. Niet eenmaal probeerde hij uit de tuin naar de omringende huizen weg te vliegen. En tot Ezra's verbazing bleek hij zelfs in staat om een muis met één klauw van de grond te lichten, de prooi onder het terugvliegen naar de dakgoot in zijn snavel te steken en met slechts halve steun van zijn gewonde poot weer te landen, waarbij nog alleen de staart van de muis uit zijn bek hing, als een roze veter.

De muizen.
Eigenlijk het enige zielige aan dit alles was dat de

witte muizen, diertjes die zich ergens in een kunstmatige omgeving voortplantten met geen ander doel dan te worden gebruikt als voedsel of als experimenteel organisme, slechts één enkel moment in hun leven in de natuur kwamen, een natuur waartoe zij eigenlijk behoorden, maar die zij nooit eerder hadden aanschouwd en nadien ook nimmer meer zouden aanschouwen, aangezien juist dat ene moment, het enige in hun leven waarbij zij niet in gevangenschap verkeerden, hun dood inluidde.

Ezra wilde hier niet te lang bij stilstaan, omdat er anders een vervelend gevoel bij hem werd losgemaakt, een gevoel waarvoor hij bang was, een verwarrende mengeling van machtswellust en mededogen. Eens had hij in een filmjournaal gezien hoe witte muizen als bijvoeder werden gegeven aan de reigers en roerdompen in het Naardermeer, dat tijdens een strenge winter was dichtgevroren. Met dozen tegelijk werden deze diertjes daar in het harde berijpte gras gegooid, waar ze door de uitgehongerde reigers achter elkaar werden opgepikt en levend doorgeslikt. Dat ging zo hebberig dat sommige reigers in hun vraatzucht een dikke prop in hun nek kregen van de opgeschrokte muizen. En het raadselachtige gevolg van dit walgelijke tafereel was dat Ezra een afkeer in zich voelde opkomen die des te raadselachtiger was aangezien dit gevoel zich keerde tegen de muizen en niet tegen de reigers, tegen de weerloze slachtoffers en niet tegen de vraatzuchtige daders. Juist de weerloosheid van al die muizen wekte een vreemd soort erbarmen op dat zich

tegen zichzelf teweer begon te stellen en zich omvorm-
de tot een emotie die rationeel geen bestaansrecht behoorde te hebben, maar die zich desondanks manifes-
teerde.

Wat was dit voor gevoel?

Een gevoel dat Ezra in lichtere vorm ook onderging
als hij een muis bij zijn staart vatte en hem door de
lucht liet zweven naar de plaats van zijn dood. Een
vreemde mengeling van medelijden en minachting,
van schuldgevoel en leedvermaak, van fascinatie en afkeer, het onverenigbare besef zowel beul te zijn als behoeder.

En de kippen.

Was Ezra's vader Louis onderhevig aan hetzelfde
tweeslachtige gevoel?

Dat was een vraag die Ezra zich wel eens had gesteld,
een vraag die als zovele vragen omtrent zijn vader nooit
beantwoord was.

Louis Berger hield van kippen.

Hij hield van kippen meer dan van mensen.

En hij fokte fraaie rassen: de oer-Hollandse barne-
velder, maar ook minder bekende soorten, zoals de Ply-
mouth Rock en de zwartglanzende Harz-hoender. Hij
had een aantal ruime rennen achter het huis, en een
geheel overdekte behuizing en hij liet de kippen ook
regelmatig loslopen in de tuin. Hij zorgde altijd voor
verse groente, bloemkoolstronken en ander groenteaf-
val, omdat het goed was voor de dieren en de dooiers
er zo mooi oranje van kleurden.

Maar hij slachtte ze ook.

En dat ging eigenlijk heel raar.

Soms wekenlang niet en soms meerdere per week.

En altijd bij zonsopgang, als iedereen nog sliep.

'Hij geeft ze eerst een klap met een plank,' wist Saul, die alles wist. 'En dan legt hij ze op het blok en snijdt hun kop eraf.'

'Veel te omslachtig,' voegde hij eraan toe.

'Hoe zou jij het dan doen?' vroeg Ezra, nieuwsgieriger dan hij eigenlijk wilde zijn.

'Ik? Gewoon, tussen m'n knieën dat kreng en dan: krak!'

Hij beeldde uit wat hij bedoelde door zijn vuisten op elkaar te leggen en ze met een korte, rukkende beweging uiteen te trekken.

Ezra knikte maar en dacht aan zijn vader, die toch absoluut van dieren hield, van Jonker het meest, maar ook zeker van zijn kippen. Zou hij werkelijk denken dat zijn methode van slachten de beste was, of was het een ritueel met nog een andere betekenis? Kreeg hij bij het slachten misschien ook dat bepaalde gevoel, een opwelling waarover niet te praten viel, omdat je het niet kon uitleggen, omdat het privé was. Hoe moest je het zeggen? Of was het andersom en wist zijn vader tijdens het slachtritueel een bepaald gevoel juist te onderdrukken en zelfs weg te nemen? Of kwam dat, gevoelsmatig, op hetzelfde neer?

Triomf of Angst, beide kon men uitschreeuwen.

Beul of Behoeder, het was dezelfde hand.

Dood of Leven, het was één bestaan.

Louis was Ezra's vader, dat was een zekerheid, maar wie was hij écht?

En Saul was zijn broer, maar wat was dat, een broer?

Ezra wist het niet.

En Nellie?

Ja Nellie, zij was zijn moeder, wat viel daar nu verder nog van te zeggen?

Toen Ezra zeven was zat zij eens zeer hard te werken in haar atelier aan de Marnixstraat. Zij had in die tijd niet voldoende klanten voor maatwerk en had een grote opdracht aangenomen bij het confectiebedrijf C&A, dat bekendstond om zijn wurgtarieven. Zij moest voor hun herfstaanbieding in wel honderd damesmantels mouwkappen stikken, wigvormige opvulsels voor de schouders, want in die tijd vonden vrouwen rechte schouders interessanter dan ronde. Nellie deed alleen de mouwkappen, dan werden de mantels weer opgehaald en op een ander atelier verder afgemaakt. In de logistiek van C&A gold de gouden clausule: *niet alles op tijd klaar, dan helemaal geen geld*. Een wel heel onbeschofte versie van het latere in de Amerikaanse schadevergoedingsadvocatuur opgeld doende *no cure, no pay*.

Maar Nellie kon snel werken en zag het contract als een uitdaging.

Het was zomer en het raam stond open.

Alleen Nellie en Ezra waren thuis, zoals zo vaak.

Louis was naar de beurs in Amsterdam en Saul zat vermoedelijk ergens in een ondergrondse hut.

In het raamkozijn zat Akka, de kauw, de vreemdste kauw van de hele wereld, want in een van zijn vleugels zat een spierwitte veer. Louis en Nellie hadden de jonge vogel een jaar tevoren voor Ezra gekocht, op de Botermarkt in Haarlem. Akka vloog vrij rond in en om het huis en deed wat hij wilde, maar het leukste van alles vond hij het om, zittend op Ezra's schouder of pols, voor een spiegel gehouden te worden, waarbij hij dan door zijn poten zakte en onophoudelijk en op verstaanbare toon zijn eigen naam begon te schreeuwen. Hij was voor niemand bang en hield van keten. Zo kwam het wel voor dat hij plotseling van buiten kwam aanvliegen en Nellie liet schrikken door pardoes op haar naaimachine neer te ploffen, een machine van het merk Bernina, met een brede, platte landingsbovenkant. Succes verzekerd.

Als Ezra uit school thuiskwam vloog de kauw hem al van verre tegemoet, om op zijn dwars uitgestoken arm te landen en op zijn schouder te springen en hem onder het lopen zacht knorrend te knuffelen, met een wriemelende snavel in zijn haar.

Hoe was het toen gebeurd?

Daar viel slechts naar te gissen. Ezra wilde Nellie helpen door een stapel mouwkappen voor haar klaar te leggen en maakte er een spelletje van. Hij stapelde ze een voor een op elkaar, totdat er een wiebelende toren ontstond die hij door nauwkeurig manoeuvreren voor instorten moest zien te behoeden. Zo naderde hij de kniptafel. Hij moet daarbij tegen Nellie's elleboog hebben aangestoten en stevig ook, want plotseling was de wijsvinger van haar linkerhand onder het metalen voetje van de naaimachine geraakt, die bonkend tot stilstand kwam. Ze had gegild, tweemaal, van schrik en pijn, twee kreten die overgingen in een aanhoudend kermen. Ezra wist niet wat er gebeurd was en keek om en zag zijn moeder in verbijstering staren naar haar hand en de naald van de machine die dwars door haar nagel stak. Het zilveren voetje was losgeschoten en lag naast haar hand. Er was geen bloed.

'Oh, Ezra..., wat moet ik doen,' kermde ze.

Maar Ezra wist het niet. Hij was zeven.

Gelukkig wist Nellie het zelf.

Met haar rechterhand begon ze voorzichtig het wiel rond te draaien dat aan de zijkant van de machine zat en waardoorheen de drijfriem liep die de spoelen op-wond. En zo draaide ze de naald langzaam omhoog en ontkruisigde zichzelf en stak haar trillende wijsvinger in haar mond. En huilde niet, maar nam Ezra op schoot en begon hem te troosten, terwijl Ezra zich klein maak-te en wilde dat ze hem uit het raam gooide of van de trap af smeet.

Nellie, logies denken was niet haar sterkste kant.

*   *   *

Waar was het misgegaan?

Met het uithalen van Nestor?

Was Nestor van Ezra's verlies de oorzaak of het gevolg?

Of zou alles anders zijn gelopen als Louis Berger het recept dat zijn vader op 10 mei 1940 voor hem had uitgeschreven en waarmee hij zelfstandig de bestanddelen zou kunnen mengen om zich alsnog bij zijn ouders en zijn broer te voegen, uit eigen beweging aan Ezra en Saul had getoond, als bewijs van zijn loyaal en onvoorwaardelijk vaderschap, in plaats van het zijn leven lang heimelijk in zijn portefeuille te dragen, als een oningeloste schuldbekentenis? Zou Saul dan eindelijk eens thuisgekomen zijn als broer en niet als ontheemde mythiese halfgod uit de verhalen van Homerus en meneer De Haan? En Ezra zelf, zou hij zich dan minder schuldig hebben gevoeld over het hem opgedrongen verraad? Over zijn wanhopig falen als zoon en als broer? Zou hij dan zichzelf geworden zijn, zoals Claire zichzelf was...?

Ezra en Saul, zij waren Louis' laatste kans geweest, de rechtvaardiging van zijn beslissing om zich van zijn eigen vader af te wenden en alleen verder te gaan, zelf vader te worden en zijn gezin te leiden in geluk en te behoeden voor gevaar.

Waarom had hij alles niet zelf verteld?

Waarom was hij halverwege gestopt?

Was hij opnieuw ondergedoken?

Ditmaal dieper dan vroeger.

Eerst in Ezra's moeder.

Later in zichzelf.

En voorgoed.

Waarom?
Louis?
Lou?

*   *   *

Uiteindelijk was het initiatief van Claire uitgegaan, Ezra was daartoe niet in staat. Hoe verliefder hij op haar raakte hoe verlammender haar aanwezigheid op hem werkte. Er waren dagen dat hij nauwelijks naar haar durfde te kijken. Wat een onzin eigenlijk, waarom pakte hij niet gewoon zijn pen en een vel proefwerkpapier en schreef de zin 'Ik vind je zo mooi' neer? Dat wás toch zo? Ja, dat was zo. Claire was oogverblindend. Zelfs jongens uit de eindexamenklas, die in een groep bijeenstonden en lachten en praatten, staakten soms hun overleg en keken om als Claire langsliep. Keken elkaar daarna aan en lachten wat.

Waarom sprak men het minst met diegene om wie men het meest gaf?

Waarom namen de gedachten dan de woorden weg, werden daden door fantasieën vervangen? Oh, werd Claire ooit maar eens bedreigd, zodat Ezra ten minste kon bewijzen wat zij voor hem betekende.

Als Ezra aan het eind van een schooldag terugliep naar het station van Haarlem kwam het steeds vaker voor dat Claire met haar fiets naast hem kwam rijden, stapvoets, moeilijk sturend, omdat ze zo langzaam gingen.

'Hallo Ezra...'

'Claire...'

Ze wist altijd wel een onderwerp te bedenken waarover ze konden praten, dingen die die dag op school waren voorgevallen, zoals onverwachte schriftelijke overhoringen, die ze dan als 'een smerige streek' afdeed, maar waarvoor ze altijd een hoog cijfer haalde, of de verwijfde maniertjes van meneer De Haan, die ze dan vervolgens 'toch wel een schat' noemde.

Ezra liep dan gemaakt glimlachend mee, voortdurend knikkend en zijn hersens pijnigend om zelf ook eens iets te zeggen, zodat zij om hem kon lachen, wat niet meeviel en bijna nooit lukte.

Eén keer een beetje, ongeveer.

Het was toen een poosje stil geweest en beiden gingen zwijgend voort.

Of Claire die stilte ook als pijnlijk ervoer wist Ezra niet, maar zelf kreeg hij het er behoorlijk benauwd van. Iemand móést wel iets zeggen, maar wat?

En toen, als vanzelf, hoorde Ezra de woorden die alleen hij gesproken kon hebben. En de enige woorden die hij had: 'Ik heb een uil...'

Tot Ezra's verbazing schoot Claire toen in de lach, waarop hij hevig begon te blozen. Erger kon niet. Lachen om iets wat niet grappig bedoeld was...

'Ik ook,' zei Claire toen, nog steeds vrolijk en het was duidelijk dat ze Ezra niet had uitgelachen.

'Ja, echt waar, ik heb óók een uil. Hij staat op mijn

kamer, op een plank, naast een kluut en een piranha en een koffervis en een, eh... sperwer. Ik heb ze gekregen van een oom, die vroeger opgezette dieren spaarde.'

Ezra knikte en keerde weer terug uit het luchtledige waarin hij zojuist was opgelost. Waarom was hij zo geschrokken, dit kón toch gewoon.

'Wat voor soort uil is het?'

'Weet ik het. Hij is behoorlijk groot, dat wel. Ik gebruik die dieren als modellen, om na te tekenen.'

Meneer Verhoeven had eens een tekening van een koeienkop in de hoogte gestoken en aan de klas laten zien en daarbij gezegd: 'Wie dit kan maken is heel begaafd.' De klas had moeten lachen om Claires tekening, omdat de opdracht was geweest: teken een portret van iemand om wie je heel veel geeft. Meneer Verhoeven had het lachen verkeerd begrepen, omdat hij docent was aan het Lorentz-Lyceum, en had vervolgens uitgeroepen: 'Wat zijn jullie toch stom' en hij voegde er na een korte adempauze aan toe: 'Met z'n allen! Kijk dan, hoe dit is gedáán! In één lijntje, achter mekaar door en in één keer goed. Zoiets kan Picasso alleen maar probéren.'

Ezra had getracht Saul na te tekenen, maar dat was mislukt, want hij kon zich nog maar moeilijk herinneren hoe Saul eruitzag.

En toen had zich een toevalligheid voorgedaan, zo toevallig, dat men bijna zou geloven dat het geen toeval meer kon zijn:

Ezra vroeg: 'Wil je hem eens zien...?' vroeg Claire.

Nu bloosden beiden tot aan hun navel en kon Claire niet meer fietsen. Ze stapte af en hing van het lachen over haar stuur.

Ezra voelde een flits, diep in zijn buik, als een messteek van geluk.

*　*　*

'Waarom ga je nu niet mee?' vroeg Claire even later, terwijl ze met haar fiets aan de hand naast Ezra meeliep.

'Nu?'

'Ja, nu meteen. Hoe laat moet je thuis zijn?'

'Eh...'

Claire wachtte het antwoord niet af, maar stelde geestdriftig voor om bij haar thuis thee te gaan drinken en haar uil te bekijken.

Ezra werd nu zeer nerveus en kon geen woord meer uitbrengen.

Wanneer gíng je eigenlijk met iemand, vroeg hij zich in stilte af, terwijl ze samen verderliepen en Claire hem vertelde dat er bij haar 's middags nooit iemand thuis was, omdat allebei haar ouders werkten. Alleen haar oudere broer kon er zijn, maar die zei nooit wat.

Ezra knikte.

'Hij doet niets anders dan lezen en vioolspelen.'

Ezra zweeg over zijn altsaxofoon, thuis in de zwarte

koffer, die hij in bruikleen had van de Zandvoortse fan-
fare en die men al tweemaal had teruggevraagd, omdat
hij nooit meer kwam, omdat hij nooit meer blies op
dat stinkende mondstuk in de vorm van een eenden-
snavel.

'Kan hij goed spelen?'

'Oh... dat zal wel, ja, hij zit op het conservatorium,
dus...'

'Het conservatorium? Zo zo...'

Ooit was Ezra zo trots geweest op het zilverkleurige
instrument in de met groen satijn gecapitonneerde kist,
met al die vernuftige kleppen, stangetjes, beugeltjes, lip-
jes en veertjes. Nu nog leren het te bespelen, te beheersen en de baas te worden. Er melodieën uit tevoorschijn
toveren, als een volleerde muzikant, als Charlie Parker
of Piet Noordijk. Ooit. Maar veel verder dan voorspel-
bare marsmuziek was hij nooit gekomen en eens tijdens
een uitvoering op de Hannie Schaftschool had hij van
louter zenuwen helemaal geen noot uit het instrument
kunnen krijgen.

Wat een idioot woord eigenlijk, conservatorium, het
deed eerder denken aan een zaal met opgezette dieren
dan aan een muziekschool.

Hij keek Claire aan en wist niet hoe hij moest zeggen
wat hij dacht.

Ze keek terug en glimlachte.

En hij dacht: wat ben je toch mooi!

Als je naar Claire keek dan zág je haar niet alleen, je
vóélde haar ook.

Je hele lichaam ging ervan tintelen.

Het huis van de familie Meerman stond aan een stil park even buiten het centrum van Haarlem. Ook van binnen was het huis stil, doodstil zelfs, want de oudere broer was niet thuis. Zijn viool was er wel, die lag tussen mappen muziekpapier op een enorme zwartglimmende vleugel die in een hoek van de woonkamer prijkte. In de glooiende holte van het instrument stond een uitklapbare metalen lessenaar.

Ezra keek om zich heen en zag hoge ramen met gaasgordijnen die een lichtgrijs licht doorlieten, witgeschilderde kastdeuren van bewerkt hout en een zoldering met cirkels, ribbels en bloemmotieven in goudgeverfd stucwerk. Er lag een vloer van oud parket in twee kleuren bruin, waarmee ingenieuze randen waren uitgebeeld en precies in het midden van de kamer een soort platte zon, opgebouwd uit taartpunten met gekantelde vlakken. Claire was naar de keuken gelopen om thee te zetten. Ezra kon horen hoe zij bezig was met een fluitketel en bekers, maar het geluid leek van veel verder te komen, uit een andere wereld. Ezra had het gevoel dat hij droomde. Een halfuur eerder was hij nog op weg geweest naar huis, naar Zandvoort, naar Nestor, om te oefenen, zodat ze samen binnenkort Claire konden uitnodigen, voor een demonstratie in de tuin. En wie weet zouden ze later, met zijn drietjes, naar de duinen bij het circuit kunnen gaan om Nestor daar zijn vrijheid te hergeven. Het moment van triomf, waar alles om te doen was geweest, Nestor weer vrij en Claire en Ezra bij elkaar...

En nu stond hij hier, bij haar thuis, door haar gevraagd, om naar haar uil te gaan kijken. Een dode.

Was dit nu goed of juist helemaal verkeerd?

'Pas op, heet...'

Claire duwde hem een beker thee in de hand.

'Zullen we maar naar boven gaan,' stelde ze voor, 'hier beneden valt toch niets te beleven.'

'Ja, goed idee...' stamelde hij.

Het was eigenlijk een vreemd zinnetje, althans, als je er wat achter zocht.

Móést hij er wat achter zoeken?

Ezra dacht aan Saul en aan Jessie, maar hij probeerde de beelden van Jessies witte lijf met alle kracht uit zijn hoofd te bannen. Zo wilde hij aan Claire helemaal niet denken!

Ze liep voor hem de trap op.

Haar kamer bevond zich aan de achterzijde van het huis. Er was een groot balkon dat uitkeek over een brede en diepe tuin, die als vanzelf leek over te gaan in het park erachter.

'Hier woon ik,' zei Claire en zette haar thee neer op een breed werkblad. Daarna opende ze de deuren naar het balkon tot een spleet en koppelde ze in die stand aan elkaar met een koperen haakje.

Langs de ene muur stond een divan naast een schemerlamp en een laag glazen tafeltje. Aan de overzijde zag Ezra een prachtige kledingkast van glimmend donkerbruin hout. Op het werkblad stonden glazen potten waaruit penselen staken, er lagen diverse tekendozen en schetsboeken en vastgeprikt in het midden een tekening in wording. Er hing een eigenaardige lucht. Geen petroleum of terpentijn, maar wel zoiets.

Een bed zag Ezra nergens, maar bedden waren voor gewone mensen, niet voor goden en godinnen.

'Kijk daar,' zei Claire toen en wees achter Ezra naar een open kast met planken, waarin een groot aantal opgezette dieren stond. Tientallen.

'Zijn dat je modellen?'

'Ik oefen erop. Ze zitten mooi stil. Maar ik oefen op alles.'

Ezra liep op de kast toe.

Het opvallendste vogeltje vond hij een blauwborst, die was gefixeerd met open snavel, alsof hij zong, al had het wel iets zieligs zo. Tamelijk bijzonder vond hij ook een koekoek, met zijn onevenredig lange staart. Zeldzaam was een raaf, met zijn enorme haksnavel, maar de grootste vogel was een roerdomp, die nergens tussen paste en boven op de kast was geplaatst, met zijn puntige snavel schuin omhoog, haast tegen het plafond. Van een fazantenhaan stak de staart naar buiten weg en onder de gespreide vleugels van een jagende sperwer stonden een spreeuw en een lijster veilig beschut. Een van de vogels was inderdaad een uil. Ezra tilde hem met twee handen naar buiten.

'Dit is een velduil,' zei hij deskundig en bekeek de vogel van alle kanten.

'Oh,' antwoordde Claire, terwijl ze in een map met tekeningen bladerde.

'Die komen nog hoofdzakelijk voor op de Waddeneilanden...'

'Gôh...'

Ezra zag dat de uil verkeerde ogen had, veel te donker, een tint lichtbruin, terwijl de ogen van een velduil een duidelijke gele kleur hebben. Ook de ogen van de sperwer moesten eigenlijk geler, maar Ezra zei dit niet. Hij zette de uil voorzichtig terug.

'De meeste uilen jagen 's nachts. Velduilen niet, dat zijn eigenlijk niet eens echte nachtvogels. Ze vliegen laag en worden daarom vaak overreden.'

'Wat zielig...'

Claire leek nauwelijks te luisteren, al deed ze wel geïnteresseerd.

Naast vogels stonden er in de kast ook andere dieren, die Ezra niet allemaal van naam kende. Hij zag een wezel en een hermelijn en diverse martersoorten.

'Dit is een boommarter,' zei Ezra en hij streek met zijn vinger over de zijdezachte rug.

'Dit ook,' antwoordde Claire en ze trok een penseel uit een pot half omhoog.

Ze lachte eerst, maar werd daarna rood in haar gezicht.

Ezra lachte uit beleefdheid een beetje mee.

'De meeste mensen denken dat uilen overdag niet kunnen zien, maar dat is niet waar,' ging hij zenuwachtig verder. 'Het zijn wel nachtdieren, maar ze kunnen overdag ook alles zien. Net als katten. Alleen op een warme zomerdag raken ze verblind. Door de warmte...'

Ezra had Claire ook nog willen uitleggen dat de ogen van een uil niet alleen licht kunnen waarnemen, maar ook warmte en dat een prooi, zoals bijvoorbeeld een fouragerende muis, zich 's nachts lichtend aftekent te gen de koude achtergrond.

Maar plotseling trok Claire een vel papier tevoorschijn uit een stapel op het werkblad.

Ze toonde Ezra een tekening, een houtskooltekening, een portret, van Ezra.

'Goed gelukt, vind je niet? Die hondenogen... En uit mijn blote hoofd!'

Ze lachte kort en luid.

'Hier, je mag hem hebben, als aandenken. Hij is al gevernist.'

Ze rolde de tekening op, deed er een elastiekje om en stak hem Ezra toe

'Wat aardig van je...'

Ezra vroeg zich af of Claire en hij nu met elkaar 'gíngen'.

Daar leek het vervolgens wel op, want Claire draaide haar hoofd schuin weg en zei op een opzettelijk nagemaakt toontje: 'En nu, Ezra Berger, mag je me kussen.'

Ze maakte er een toneelstukje van, waardoor het gemakkelijker ging.

Wat was ze toch apart.

'Een kus... oh ja...,' zei Ezra haperend en hij liep op haar toe om haar op haar wang te kussen, in de overtuiging dat hij nooit zou leren hoe je met mensen om moest gaan en op het allerlaatste moment draaide ze haar hoofd dan ook weer terug en raakten hun lippen elkaar, of beter gezegd, kuste ze hem op zijn mond.

Ze sloot daarbij haar ogen, terwijl Ezra de zijne juist opensperde.

Nu moest hij zeggen hoe mooi hij haar vond, prentte hij zich in en dat hij al bijna twee jaar van haar droomde en dat hij haar nóg een keer wilde kussen, wat hij ook best zou durven, als op datzelfde moment geen vioolklanken uit het benedenhuis te horen waren geweest.

Het scheen Claire niet te deren.

'Er is een bijzondere expositie in Het Goede Uur,' zei zij toen.

* * *

Claire ging Ezra voor naar binnen.

Het was haar idee geweest om naar deze expositie te gaan, want Hylke Buwalda was heel bijzonder. Hij was pas vijfentwintig, maar had al een aantal belangrijke prijzen gewonnen. Een gedreven kunstenaar, die dag en nacht werkte en de mooiste miniaturen kon maken. Als gravure, pentekening of in olieverf.

De zware houten deur piepte op de stenen dorpel en er rinkelde een belletje. Ze waren op voorstel van Claire rechtstreeks uit school gekomen en zetten hun tassen bij de kapstok. Ezra keek verwonderd om zich heen, hij was nog nooit eerder in een café geweest en als ze allemaal zo gezellig waren ingericht als *In 't Goede Uur* dan zou dit niet de laatste keer zijn. Oh nee.

Hij had zojuist een nieuwe wereld betreden, dat voelde hij. Overal aan de donkerbruine muren hingen antieke attributen en kunstvoorwerpen. Op diverse niveaus bevonden zich aparte zitjes met knoestige houten tafels. Het was een artistiek café, dat was duidelijk te zien.

Er kwam een oude man tevoorschijn.

Hij had een wit hemd aan met korte mouwen en liep op pantoffels. Zijn wijde broek hing in bretels om zijn dikke buik. Achter een der bretels stak een geblokte theedoek. Zijn droge grijze haren staken alle kanten op en hij deed Ezra denken aan Albert Einstein, de grote geleerde van wie in het lokaal van meneer Iddekinge een ingelijste foto hing.

'Hallo Claire, meissie...' zei hij en hij omvatte haar gezicht met twee handen en kuste haar met een smak. Ezra zag dat zijn ogen waterig stonden en glommen.

'Dit is Ezra,' zei Claire. 'Ezra dit is Jacques, hij is een tikje vreemd, maar daar wen je gauw genoeg aan. We willen even boven kijken. Goed?'

De man stak Ezra zijn hand toe.

'Ezra, de schriftgeleerde! Wat een prachtnaam. Ben je een jongen van joodse komaf?'

'Eh...'

Claire trok Ezra aan zijn arm mee naar de trap.

'Ezra, geen antwoord geven, hoor. Wie vráágt nu zoiets.'

De man hief zijn armen ten hemel.

'Schaam je je er soms voor? Ik ben het zelf, al mijn hele leven!'

'Ik geloof het wel... een beetje.'

'Schaam je je een beetje?'

'Ik bedoel, ik bén het... een beetje.'

Jacques boog zich voorover, keek Ezra strak aan en sprak plechtig: 'Dat kan niet, jongen, je bent het, of je bent het niet.'

De woorden van Jacques troffen Ezra als een vermaning.

Hij kuchte nerveus en knikte zo beleefd mogelijk.

Claire trok hem mee naar het trapgat.

Toen ze boven waren hoorden ze Jacques in het trapgat roepen dat Ezra een profeties boek had geschreven dat ten onrechte voor apocrief werd gehouden.

'Hij heeft ook de bijbel in het Hebreeuws vertaald. Onthoud dat!'

Even later gevolgd door de op lagere toon uitgesproken overpeinzing dat hij dat beter niet had kunnen doen.

'Wat is apocrief?' wilde Ezra weten, maar Claire haalde haar schouders op.

'Weet ik het. Hij gebruikt altijd van die moeilijke woorden. Dat krijg je als je te veel leest. Hij kan hele stukken uit boeken uit zijn hoofd opzeggen. Vooral als hij gedronken heeft.'

De expositieruimte was stil en mooi.

Aan de ene zijde keek men uit op de Korte Houtstraat en aan de drie overige muren hingen de schilderijen en prenten van Hylke Buwalda. Ezra had nog nooit eerder een schilderijenexpositie bezocht en was erg onder de indruk. Temeer omdat Hylke Buwalda een voorkeur voor dieren scheen te hebben en je precies kon zien wat alles voorstelde. Het was allemaal zo nauwkeurig gedaan. Maar wat Ezra opviel was dat de kunstenaar iets anders bedoelde dan hij uitbeeldde; nee, niet iets anders, meer. Er viel meer te zien dan waar je naar keek.

Zo zag Ezra een klein houten paneeltje, niet groter dan het deksel van een sigarenkistje, waarop in precies de goede kleuren een baars stond afgebeeld. Het water waarin de vis hing was niet meer dan een lichtblauwe gloed en waterplanten werden gesymboliseerd door een enkel klein groen stengeltje aan de uiterste rand. Ook het wateroppervlak was te zien, ongeveer op tweederde van het paneel. Daarboven was de hemel, in blauw van een iets donkerder tint. Met een flard bijna opgeloste wolk. De vis was op zichzelf al voldoende om er een mooi schilderijtje van te maken, vond Ezra, maar de kunstenaar had nog iets meer gedaan, waardoor alles helemaal anders werd. Schuin achter de baars hing een dobber in het water. Kaarsrecht, met gekleurde ringen en het drijfkurkje in felrood. Aan een nylondraadje hing een minuscuul zilveren haakje, waarvan zelfs het aasloze weerhaakje nog was afgebeeld. Boven het wateroppervlak uit stak het steeltje van de dobber, wit met een oranje puntje. Een hengel was nergens zichtbaar.

'Vind je dat mooi?' wilde Claire nu weten.

'Ja, heel mooi... maar ook... eh...'

Ze kwam naast hem staan en pakte zijn hand.

Ezra had aan schilderijen nog nooit eerder zo gedacht, dat zij meer konden betekenen dan zij uitbeelden.

'Die vis is er geweest,' zei hij.

'Wat?'

'Die baars...'

'Is dat een baars?'

'Ja... die gaat eraan.'

Claire fronste haar wenkbrauwen.

'Hoe zie je dat dan?'

'Aan die dobber en die haak. Je hoeft er alleen maar een made aan te hangen en die baars is er geweest.'

Claire schraapte haar keel.

'Ik wou dat hij die dobber niet geschilderd had,' ging Ezra verder. 'Zo maakt het schilderij je ongerust, juist omdat die vis zo mooi is.'

'Misschien moet je er niet zo diep op ingaan...'

Ze liet zijn hand los en liep naar een hoek van de expositieruimte, naar de muur waarachter zich het Nieuwe Kerksplein bevond.

'Hoe vind je dit?'

Ze wees op een pentekening in ongeveer hetzelfde formaat als het portret dat zij van Ezra had gemaakt. Ingelijst achter glas zat Claire daar zelf. Zij was naakt. Op haar blote schouder zat een raaf. Zijn lange nagels lagen niet zachtjes op haar vlees, zag Ezra toen, maar drongen er diep in. Bij iedere nagel was een kuiltje te zien. Er zou bloed moeten zijn, constateerde Ezra, maar in plaats daarvan zat Claire te glimlachen. Dat kon dus niet. Ze hield haar handen ineengevouwen voor haar buik, zodat je gelukkig niet alles kon zien.

Ezra begon nu heftig te blozen.

'Wat heb je...?' vroeg Claire.

'Ben jij dat?' vroeg Ezra, om maar wat tijd te rekken.

Claire legde een hand op haar voorhoofd en streek haar haren weg.

'Af en toe ben ik zijn model,' antwoordde ze, op een toon waarin Ezra duidelijk kon horen dat ze haar woorden zo gewoon mogelijk wilde laten klinken.

'Het lijkt anders helemaal niet,' zei hij vlak.

Claire haalde haar schouders op en vervolgde op dezelfde toon: 'In ruil daarvoor geeft hij mij weleens les, wat heel bijzonder is, want hij wil eigenlijk geen leerlingen.'

Ezra voelde hoe een onmachtige driftbui zich van hem meester maakte.

'Ik ben de enige...' zei Claire.

Ezra probeerde lang en diep adem te halen om haar niets te laten merken.

'En alleen als hij er zin in heeft,' vervolgde ze.

'Hoe oud is hij?'

'Vijfentwintig, geloof ik.'

Met haar hand nog steeds op haar hoofd liep Claire naar een hoek van de zaal.

'En deze...?' vroeg ze toen, met nu een vreemde trek om haar mond.

'Hoe vind je deze?'

Ezra keek naar de plek die Claire hem wees en verstijfde.

En besloot op datzelfde moment dat Claire Nestor nooit te zien zou krijgen.

Nooit meer.

Nooit!

* * *

Maar 's avonds in bed kwam reeds de twijfel.

Waren de tekeningen die Hylke Buwalda van Claire had gemaakt niet alleen maar bedoeld om haar schoonheid tot uiting te brengen? Ezra probeerde dit te denken en niet al het andere. Hylke Buwalda was kunstschilder en misschien was dit dan wel gewoon. Net zo gewoon als naar de dokter gaan. Een dokter was een man, maar als hij dokter was dan was hij alleen dokter.

Kleedt u zich maar even uit.

Kunst, wat was dat eigenlijk?

Had meneer Verhoeven op school dat niet al eens verteld?

Kijken naar symbolen, meer zien dan er was. Maar dat was nu precies wat Ezra die middag zelf had ontdekt, toen hij keek naar de baars, met de dobber, zonder hengel, naar de haak, zonder aas, naar het schilderijtje dat een wereld was op zich en dat mooier was geworden doordat Ezra het begrepen had, zoals ook de schoonheid van de vis verhoogd werd door de dood die hem bedreigde. Die ontdekking had Ezra met trots vervuld, want hierdoor had hij beseft over een vermogen te beschikken, waarvan hij eerder niet wist dat hij het bezat, een manier van kijken, maar meer nog, een manier van zien. Maar nu was het ineens veel ingewikkelder en zelfs beangstigend, want dit nieuwe besef van het bestaan van onzichtbare waarheden en symboliese gedaanten, leidde nu tot het stellen van vragen waarop de verwarrende antwoorden nieuwe vragen bleken te zijn.

Zo was er Claires schoonheid.

Was haar schoonheid dan niet privé?

Uitsluitend en alleen van haar?

Hij had het haar niet durven vragen uit angst uitgelachen te worden. En wat zou zij anders hebben kunnen doen dan hem uitlachen. Zij kon hem moeilijk gelijk geven en toch op die wijze voor Hylke Buwalda poseren.

Op die wijze...

Maar precies op die wijze had hij vaak van haar gedroomd, alleen in zijn bed, wanneer in de duisternis van zijn gevoel Claires schone lichaam zo blank en zacht was en hijzelf zo hard als een man, een ridder te paard, om Claire te redden uit de klauwen van monsters en mannen zonder gezichten... in een bloedig gevecht van leven en dood, om haar te bevrijden, als een prins zijn prinses, in een gevecht dat hij won en verloor... en won...

Claire had gemerkt hoe geschokt hij was, maar wie gaat daar nu zo liggen, zo... open en bloot...

Zou Jacques het weten?

Zou Ezra eens alleen teruggaan naar Het Goede Uur om het hem te vragen?

Ezra voelde dat hij Claire kwijt zou zijn als hij de laatste tekening in de hoek van de expositieruimte als vunzig zou afwijzen.

Die vunzige tekening van Claire moest een formule bevatten die verborgen zat in de uitbeelding zelf, anders was alles verloren.

Wat was een kunstenaar?

Iemand die de dood kon uitbeelden zonder hem te laten zien? Zonder geraamte, zonder schedel en zonder zeis? Maar dat konden de fotoalbums van Ezra's ouders evengoed. En beter. Die waren niet te torsen van de dood.

Dat was de vraag: wat had de kunstenaar Hylke Buwalda met die laatste tekening bedoeld?

Die houding van Claire... uh... de schoonheid van de vrouw... naakt... dus op haar allerschoonst... als een meisje... uh... die daar ligt in een houding... in een houding, die twee dingen... uitbeeldt... een meisje en een moeder... als symbool... uh... een schakel tussen de dood en het leven... eerst het leven... dat er nog niet is... het meisje is het leven en de moeder is het nieuwe leven... of... uh... zij is beide... dus... want... uit die houding wordt men geboren... ter wereld gebracht... maar eerst... in diezelfde houding... is er de liefde... uh... een man... die niet stond afgebeeld... maar op het paneeltje met de baars ontbrak de visser... dat schilderijtje was gemakkelijk... was Claire... uh... de vrouw in haar twee uiterste gedaanten... als minnares... als in een roes... achteroverliggend op haar rug... met opgetrokken benen en... uh... wat was het woord... vunzig... nee, uh... aanlokkelijk... ja... afstotelijk... ja... verlokkend... ja... schaamteloos... ja... onbeschaamd... ja... ja... onverbloemd... ja, als een bloem... een zwarte bloem... dat was het... een zwarte bloem waaruit de hele wereld ontluikt.

En na lang wikken en wegen besloot Ezra dat het heel aparte tekeningen waren die de Haarlemse kunstenaar Hylke Buwalda van zijn vriendin en toekomstige vrouw Claire Meerman had gemaakt, omdat het niet om Claire zelf ging, maar om een uitbeelding van de oervrouw in de wereld, de oervrouw in het algemeen, zoiets.

En de volgende dag op school duwde hij Claire een briefje in de hand met niet daarop de woorden: *Ik hou van je*, maar vier andere woorden, die hetzelfde betekenden en de enige woorden die hij had: *Wil je Nestor zien?*

* * *

Het was op een zaterdagmiddag, kort voor de zomervakantie van het jaar 1959. Nestor was al een poosje in absolute topvorm geweest en Ezra wist zeker dat de demonstratie zou lukken. Toch was hij nerveus. Er hing zoveel vanaf. Zijn plan. Zou Claire Nestor echt zo mooi en bijzonder vinden als Ezra hoopte? En zou ze hem op haar arm durven nemen, of op haar schouder? Of misschien zelfs wel een prooi omhoog durven steken en die door Nestor laten pakken? Het beeld van de klapwiekende uil met Claire als begeleidster wond Ezra op, gaf hem het gevoel dat Nestor en Claire en hij bij elkaar hoorden. Of preciezer nog: dat Nestor van hen beiden was. De uil Nestor, die zij dan samen de vrijheid zouden geven in de duinen bij het circuit. Claire en Ezra.

Nestor, Ezra en Claire.

Er klopte misschien wel helemaal niets van, maar op de een of andere manier leken die drie namen bij elkaar te horen. Als klank, als geheel, ja, hoe eigenlijk? Je kon het niet bewijzen, een heleboel dingen waren op een aparte manier zoals ze waren; aanwezig. Of juist afwezig. En... ja, Saul bijvoorbeeld, die was altijd afwezig, hij kon niet anders, maar hij was toch Ezra's broer, als het erop aankwam, die mussen neerlegde voor de deur van Ezra's kamer en schroefgaten in de deur van zijn eigen kamer openliet...

Ezra wist zeker dat Saul dichterbij was dan hij kon laten merken.

Wist of hoopte, wat was het verschil?

En gold hetzelfde ook niet voor Louis, zijn vader?

Zijn onmachtige vader en zijn machtige broer?

Zij waren er gewoon, altijd.

Claire arriveerde met de trein.

Een hele trein te vroeg stond Ezra bij het station te wachten.

Een hele trein was een uur en een uur was weinig als je op iemand wachten moest, althans als het iemand was om wie je gaf.

In gedachten verzonken begon hij de trappen langzaam op en af te lopen, terugdenkend aan die keer toen hij drie hele treinen te vroeg was geweest. Hij was toen zeven en Nellie had hem beloofd een horloge voor hem mee te brengen uit Amsterdam, als cadeau omdat Ezra Nellies hand onder de naaimachine had gestoten, waardoor de nagel van haar wijsvinger tweemaal volledig was doorboord. Nellie zou pas met de trein van halfzes terugkomen maar Ezra had het in het doodstille huis niet meer kunnen uithouden, waar alleen het tikken van de oude klok hoorbaar was geweest en het tjilpen van de mussen in de goot.

Drie eigenaardige uren waren dat geweest, op het station, niet omdat Ezra de tijd die daar zo overmatig heerste had weten te doden door in een vast en langzaam tempo de treden van de twee stationstrappen op en af te gaan, één trede per seconde, zestig per minuut, en zo onophoudelijk aftellend, maar aangezien hij een groeiende zenuwachtigheid onderging bij de vrees dat Nellie haar belofte zou kunnen zijn vergeten en zij zich tegenover Ezra dan zou moeten schamen. Trap op trap af. En nergens in Zandvoort nog horloges te koop.

De eerste trein, een handjevol passagiers die hun

kaartjes moesten laten zien bij het hek, waardoor er even een opstopping ontstond.

('Sorry, Ezra, maar ik had het zo druk.')

('Geeft niks, doet je vinger nog pijn?')

Trap op trap af.

De tweede trein, meer passagiers, een grotere opstopping.

('Ach, lieverd, helemaal vergeten.')

('Geeft niks, doet je vinger nog pijn?')

Trap af trap op.

En dan, eindelijk, de trein des onheils.

Onder de passagiers bevond zich ene Nellie, de moeder van Ezra Berger, de vogelman van Zandvoort. Je kon haar van verre herkennen, met haar hoed schuin op haar hoofd en een rag van zwart gaas voor haar gezicht. (Of was dat op een vroegere foto? Nakijken!) Zij lachte naar Ezra en hief haar hand naar hem op, waaruit een langwerpig doosje stak.

En even later stond er in de tijd van Ezra's leven één moment voor altijd stil en werd hij de trotse bezitter van het allermooiste uurwerk van de hele wereld, een horloge met dikke groene wijzers die licht gaven in het donker.

De secondenwijzers van de twee stationsklokken te Zandvoort aan Zee, de ene op het perron beneden en de andere in de hal boven, wandelden nog steeds in hetzelfde tempo op de wijzerplaat rond als Ezra op de trappen, stap voor stap, hielden bij het passeren van de laatst geleden minuut één seconde pas op de plaats om

de grote wijzer de tijd te geven naar de volgende minuut te verspringen. Ezra berekende dat de secondenwijzer dan dus per seconde 1/60ste van een seconde te
snel moest lopen om precies op tijd te komen.

Dezelfde nervositeit beving hem als zeven jaar tevoren.

Trap op trap af.

Als Claire hun afspraak nu eens vergeten was?

Trap af.

Als ze nu eens niet in de trein zat?

Trap op.

Als ze nu niet in de trein zat?

Trap af.

Niet in de trein zat?

Trap op.

Niet in de trein?

Trap af.

Niet?

Nestor was ook al zo onrustig geweest.

Ezra had voor de zekerheid een laatste korte oefening
met hem in de tuin gedaan, een soort generale repetitie,
vanaf de dakgoot van het verlaten tuinhuisje. En het
was wel goed gegaan, daar niet van, maar toen hij de
uil na de beloning in triomf op zijn vuist omhoog-
gestoken had en zijn arm in een overwinnaarsgebaar
langzaam op en neer had bewogen, zodat Nestor zijn
vleugels voor evenwicht moest uitslaan en hij op zijn
allermooist was, waardoor Ezra de gebruikelijke vreug-
dekreet niet in kon houden, was Nestor ineens wegge-

vlogen en had hij maar liefst tweemaal boven de tuin gecirkeld alvorens buiten adem neer te strijken op de rand van de oude parkietenvolière. Tweemaal. Dat had hij nog nooit eerder gedaan. Eenmaal helemaal rond was het meest geweest en dat was al heel lang geleden.

En toen Ezra zijn hand onder Nestors buik duwde om hem te kunnen optillen weigerde de uil koppig en deinsde hij blazend terug.

'Wat heb je nou?'

Geen antwoord.

'Kom... kom nou...'

Eindelijk.

'Wil je buiten zitten? Het is lekker weer en er staat geen felle zon.'

Ezra opende de deur van de volière en plaatste Nestor op een gladde, volkomen kaalgekloven tak, waar de uil zich breed uitschurkte en zijn vervaarlijke snavel langs zijn lange slagpennen begon te trekken, ongeveer zoals een poes zich wast.

Daar was zij!

Oh God!

Temidden van een deinende zee aan passagiers.

Ik moet haar kussen, flitste het door Ezra's hoofd, alsof dat de gewoonste zaak van de wereld was. Op haar wang, niet op haar mond, dacht hij erachteraan. En dan onder het lopen haar hand vastpakken. Ja, dat was het beste. En als het kan moet ik haar om iets laten lachen. Ja.

'Hi, Ezra!'

'Hi, Claire!'

Ezra's verliefdheid deed hem duizelen.

De secondenwijzer op de stationsklok pauzeerde, haperde, stokte...

Zo stonden ze daar, terwijl de badgasten rondom hen naar het strand wegstroomden.

('Zeg nu iets!')

'Ik heb wat voor je meegebracht,' zei Claire en ze gaf Ezra een opgerold vel papier, bijeengehouden door een zwartfluwelen lint. Ezra trok het lint los en ontrolde het papier. Het was een pentekening, in Oost-Indiese inkt, een portret, van Ezra, het tweede, maar ditmaal was niet slechts zijn gezicht afgebeeld, maar ook zijn hele bovenlichaan, dat veel krachtiger leek dan in werkelijkheid.

De tekening eindigde halverwege.

Ezra's benen ontbraken, maar zijn gelaat had een stralende uitdrukking. Zijn ogen waren overdreven groot gemaakt en leken te fonkelen.

Aan de onderzijde van de tekening waren twee schaduwplekken zichtbaar waar Ezra's liezen begonnen en precies in het midden krulden enkele zwarte haartjes over de rand.

'Hoe vind je hem?' vroeg Claire en ze giechelde.

Maar ze gaf zelf het antwoord.

'Mooi, hè..'

Ik heb niets voor haar, dacht Ezra.

En hij kreeg het gevoel alsof hij langzaam in het niets oploste.

Onderweg naar de Duinweg was het Claire die het gesprek gaande hield.

Ezra had haar niet omhelsd, pakte onder het lopen niet haar hand, slaagde er niet in om haar te laten lachen en kon eigenlijk helemaal geen woord uitbrengen. Een duidelijker bewijs dat hij smoorverliefd op haar was viel niet te leveren.

Een bewijs uit het ongerijmde.

Gedachten had hij te over.

Ze raasden door zijn brein.

Eén gedachte overheerste daarbij alle andere: Nestor, red mij!

* * *

'Dit is hem dan...' stamelde hij.

'Wat een mooi beest, Ezra!'

Claire haakte haar vingers in het gaas van de volière en staarde in werkelijke bewondering naar de uil, die zich uit zijn dikke slaaphouding half oprichtte en zijn kop langzaam in haar richting draaide. Het ging goed, dacht Ezra. Nestor verhief zich traag en opende slechts één oog om Claire te bekijken.

'Ik vind hem echt heel prachtig,' zei Claire, 'wat een ogen, zeg!'

En inderdaad, Ezra zag nu dat Nestor ook zijn tweede ooglid had opgetrokken en Claire strak bleef aankijken. Geleidelijk verhief Nestor zich verder. Zijn lichaam versmalde en zijn oorpluimen kwamen omhoog. Ezra wist wat dit beduidde: onraad. Claire kende deze reflex niet en meende dat de uil zich voor haar extra opdofte.

'Hij heeft snorharen. En wimpers!'

Ezra keek van Nestor naar Claire en van Claire naar Nestor en concludeerde dat er iets helemaal verkeerd ging. Wat had Nestor nu toch?

Plotseling gingen de serredeuren open en verscheen zijn moeder.

Ook dat nog!

'Wie ben jij, kind?' vroeg ze op vriendelijke toon.

Kind!

Claire liep op haar toe en stelde zich voor.

Nellie was volkomen ontoonbaar, vond Ezra. Zo armoedig, in dat lange werkhemd, een soort overall, waarvan ze er verscheidene had en die ze in een halfuur in elkaar flanste.

'Claire, wat een mooie naam...' hoorde Ezra haar zeggen, terwijl hij naar zijn voeten bleef kijken.

Nestor schuifelde over de tak naar achteren.

* * *

Nestor was op zijn mooist, die dag, net als Claire.

Ezra ging de volière in en de uil stapte gewillig op zijn pols.

Zij waren alleen in de tuin, die eveneens op zijn

mooist was, al was het jammer dat alle vogels bij de verschijning van Nestor uitgeweken waren naar veiliger oorden.

Nellie was na haar vriendelijke begroeting van Claire weer naar haar atelier teruggegaan. Waarom was zij daar eigenlijk ineens geweest? Zij had Ezra toch wel vaker met Nestor zien oefenen?

Zou Nestor overigens weten hoe belangrijk dit moment voor Ezra was? Waarschijnlijk niet. Hoe kon hij het weten? Vogels konden soms de toekomst voorspellen, maar dat was al lang geleden. De vraag daarbij was of die vogels – het ging meestal om arenden of valken – zelf wel wisten hoe de toekomst die zij voorspelden eruit zou gaan zien. Wat meer konden zij tonen dan louter de schoonheid van hun verschijning? En wat meer konden zij bewerkstelligen dan zich op een zeker moment op een zekere plaats te manifesteren? Maar wie bepaalde hun koers? Waren het niet altijd de goden die hen door het luchtruim zonden, als symbolen van hun wil?

'Zeg maar wat ik moet doen,' zei Claire vrolijk.

Ze liep met Ezra en Nestor mee naar het midden van de tuin.

'We kunnen hem hoogstens drie keer laten vliegen,' legde Ezra uit. 'Hij doet het alleen voor een beloning en na een keer of drie krijgt hij er genoeg van. Uilen zijn luie vogels, eigenlijk. Het liefst slapen ze de hele dag. Dus ja, drie keer.'

'Maar moet ik helpen?' wilde Claire nu weten en ze stak haar vinger naar Nestor uit, alsof ze hem wilde aanraken, waarop de uil zijn kop wegdraaide.

Daaraan had Ezra niet gedacht.

'Durf je hem op je arm te nemen?'

'Bijt hij?'

'Nee, nooit.'

Ezra keek om zich heen en maakte een plan om het optreden van Nestor samen met Claire te doen. Beter kon niet, dacht hij opgetogen. Nu waren ze echt met z'n drieën en op de beste manier.

Plotseling zag Ezra Saul verschijnen, boven in zijn kamer, voor het raam. Een zwijgende gestalte, die zich achter het donkere glas posteerde en daar beweging-loos bleef staan. Niet vlak voor het raam, maar iets te-rug in de kamer, zodat alleen zijn hoofd en zijn boven-lichaam zichtbaar waren.

Saul was naakt.

Was Jessie daar ook, boven?

Juist nu?

Maakte het uit?

'Moet je dát zien,' zei Claire, en ze wees op Nestors kop, terwijl haar wijsvinger in de lucht een kruis te-kende. 'Als je goed kijkt zie je een witte X tussen zijn ogen en zijn snavel, zie je dat? Het is net een oude wijze man.'

Eerst Nellie, nu Saul, dacht Ezra, wat gebeurde er al-lemaal?

Alleen Louis ontbrak nog.

Moest hij stoppen of doorgaan?

Claire stond met haar rug naar het huis en Ezra leid-de haar in de richting van het lege en verlaten tuinhuis.

'Ik denk dat als je hier gaat staan, dat het dan wel lukken zal. Meestal start hij vanaf deze plek. Hier, steek je arm maar uit. Kom, Nestor, stap op, kom...'

En Nestor plaatste, tastend, een klauw op Claires arm, die daarbij een kreetje slaakte van angstig plezier.

Ezra haalde zijn eigen arm langzaam neer en Nestor trok zijn andere klauw op Claires arm bij.

'Wat wéégt hij weinig!'

Ezra liep terug in de richting van de volière en haalde een plastic zakje met vlees uit zijn zak.

'Oh gatver!' schreeuwde Claire opeens. 'Precies op mijn schoen!'

Ezra zag wat er gebeurd was en bedacht dat als Nestor andersom had gestaan Claire nu onder de witte smurrie gezeten zou hebben.

Wat ging alles stroef!

'Hij is zenuwachtig... Wil je liever stoppen?'

'Nee Ezra, het geeft niet,' gaf Claire moedig te kennen. 'Ik draai me nog meer naar je toe. Zo goed?'

Dit zou echt niemand doen, dacht Ezra.

Niemand.

Nooit.

En toen zag Nestor Ezra's hand met het wiebelende stukje prooi erin omhooggaan en onmiddellijk boog hij zich voorover en begon afstand en diepte te schatten door zijn kop ritmies heen en weer te bewegen.

Eindelijk was het dan zover!

'Nu, Nestor nu!' riep Ezra.

En Nestor vertrok.

Niet uit de drabbige, stinkende goot van het tuinhuisje, maar vanaf de sierlijke, slanke arm van Claire Meerman.

En daar kwam hij!

Oh God...!

Eerst laag naar de grond zwevend, daarna met enkele korte vleugelslagen snelheid winnend en vervolgens met gestrekte wieken in een schuine, steile boog omhoog, rats!

Claire applaudisseerde.

'Bravo Nestor!' riep ze en ze maakte een sprongetje van plezier.

De uil pakte het stukje poulet voorzichtig uit Ezra's hand en kokte het naar binnen. Daarna schudde hij zich uit, zoals na een vlucht zijn gewoonte was, en keek Ezra doordringend aan, in afwachting van nieuwe instructies.

Zou Claire het werkelijk zo opwindend vinden als ze voorgaf? Het leek er wel op. En toen ze vroeg of zij nu de prooi mocht ophouden wist Ezra het zeker. Hij liep met Nestor op zijn arm naar haar toe om haar het vlees te brengen. Onder het lopen flitste zijn blik nogmaals omhoog naar de kamer van Saul, maar die stond niet meer voor het raam.

Claire pakte het lokaas tussen duim en wijsvinger beet.

'Heb je gezien hoe ik het deed?'

Claire hield haar arm dwars omhoog en bewoog het reepje vlees heen en weer.

'Iets hoger.'

'Zo?'

'Zo ja.'

Ezra liep met de uil terug naar de volière.

'Nestor, nu komt het erop aan, hè,' sprak hij op zachte en ernstige toon. 'Claire is mijn vriendin. Wij horen bij elkaar. Doe het nu heel speciaal goed... oké?'

De uil draaide zijn kop van links naar rechts honderdtachtig graden om, daarna van rechts naar links. Was er iets?

'Dit is het moment van de waarheid, Nestor.'

Een vreemd gevoel ging door Ezra heen, een voorgevoel van onheil. Wat kon dit zijn? Vreesde hij dat Saul naar buiten zou komen en zich met hem en Claire zou gaan bemoeien? Nee, daar had het niets mee te maken. Maar wat was het dan?

Te laat om nu nog te stoppen.

Zeggen Claire ik doe het toch maar niet. Zeggen ik denk dat Nestor het zo niet begrijpt. Zeggen lieve Claire ik durf het niet. Zeggen Claire jij kunt het wel, zeggen het ligt niet aan jou. Zeggen nee Claire.

Claire...

Ezra stond nog met zijn rug naar haar toe.

Hij slikte en wist dat het mis zou gaan, maar wát er mis zou gaan en hoe érg, kon hij niet weten.

Toen draaide hij zich om.

Daar stond zij.

Ze had haar lippen van spanning getuit.

Haar ene voet was wit, haar andere zwart.

Ezra hief zijn arm op en voelde Nestors klauwen verstrakken.

'Voorzichtig...' maande hij nog, toen de uil zich voorover liet vallen en kort boven de grond naar Claire toe scheerde.

Het meisje zag hem komen en bleef rustig stilstaan, zoals ook geboden was, maar op het laatste moment, toen de roofvogel haar scherp stijgend naderde en zijn klauwen vooruitstak voor de landing, zonk onverwacht alle moed haar in de schoenen en slaakte zij een kreet van angst.

Ze keek wild om zich heen en wilde wegrennen, maar wist niet waarheen.

De uil probeerde een botsing nog te vermijden door met woeste vleugelslag een bijna haakse wending in te zetten, maar juist in die richting deinsde ook Claire weg.

En Nestor vloog haar vol in het gezicht.

*   *   *

Claires gezicht zag eruit alsof ze met volle vaart in het prikkeldraad gelopen was. Ze was op haar knieën gezakt en hield haar beide handen beschermend voor haar gelaat, maar Ezra had de rode krassen van Nestors nagels al gezien.

Nestor zat op de dakgoot van het tuinhuis en was nog nooit zo smal geweest. Zelfs zijn poten hield hij nu gestrekt. Zijn oorpluimen stonden recht omhoog en zijn ogen priemden op Claire neer. Het leek op woede, maar het was ontreddering.

'Oh Ezra... Ezra...' kermde Claire, 'mijn oog...'

Het was haar linkeroog, dat dikke rode druppels huilde.

Ezra knielde naast haar op de grond neer en sloeg zijn arm om haar heen.

Dit gebaar was tweeërlei.

Het was voor het eerst.

En het was voor het laatst.

Op één moment.

In de tijd.

* * *

Nestors nagels krasten tegen de kartonnen bodem van de doos, het was een ongemakkelijk verblijf, want hij kon er net niet in staan. Ezra liep over de kale noord-boulevard tot voorbij het grote hek dat toegang gaf tot het buitenterrein van het circuit. Hij wist dat de afrastering verder in de richting Bloemendaal overal grote openingen vertoonde, gaten waardoorheen de jongens kropen als er autoraces waren, op weg naar de grootste uitdaging die er op zo'n dag bestond: het zonder toegangskaart bereiken van de hoofdtribune. Maar nu bevonden zich nergens politiemannen te paard op de heuvels in de duinen. Er was niemand. Alleen Ezra liep daar, met de uil Nestor, die hij moest terugbrengen, omdat de tijd gekomen was.

De avondlucht was zoel.

De zee geurde zilt in een zachte westenwind.

En de zinkende zon gloeide langzaam bloedrood op.

In de verte kleurden de dennenbossen zich in blauwe nevels. Hoe verder weg hoe dieper blauw, maar zo ver hoefde Ezra niet te gaan. Als Nestor daar zijn nieuwe leven wilde leiden dan moest hij er zelf maar naartoe vliegen. En dat zou verstandig zijn, want in die verste bossen kwam haast nooit een mens, niet meer. Ook daar moest eens een oorlog zijn geweest, dat was nog steeds te zien. Bunkers stonden daar niet, maar er liep een breed grauw pad van ingewalst gruis, dat ooit kon worden versperd door twee enorme betonnen helften, die op hun ronde achterzijden konden draaien en met hun rechte voorzijden hermeties worden neergelaten. Ooit, toen zij nog deel uitmaakten van de dwars door de duinen gelegde 'Duitse muur', een betonnen verdedigingswal voor het geval de bevrijdingslegers bij Zandvoort zouden landen. Maar nu stonden deze massieve blokken beton als machteloze mastodonten weggekanteld en versteend. Van kettingen of takels geen spoor.

Af en toe bleef Ezra even staan om een van de kleppen op te tillen die de doos aan de bovenzijde afsloten en die hij onder het lopen met zijn duimen dichthield. Dan keek hij naar binnen en wilde iets zeggen tegen de uil, om hem te kalmeren en vast voor te bereiden op het moment.

'Nestor...' fluisterde Ezra dan, maar meestal volgde er niets. Dan keek hij alleen maar.

Wat viel er nog te zeggen?

Dat het allemaal niet meer gaf?

Dat Nestor er niets aan kon doen?

Dat Ezra hem nooit had moeten uithalen?

Moest hij dát zeggen?

Moest je altijd zeggen wat je voelde, tegen iemand om wie je gaf?

Ezra schoof eerst de doos door het gat en kroop er daarna behendig achteraan, zijn hand voortdurend op de kleppen. Hij daalde de zeereep aan de achterzijde af en keek om zich heen. Nog steeds niemand te zien. Goed. Zoals verwacht. Nu voortmaken. Het werd al minder licht, zeker tussen de heuvels en straks in het bos.

'We zijn er bijna. Ik weet een goede plek.'

De duinen bloeiden en waren op hun mooist. De dennenbossen overheersten als veilige domeinen, maar tegen de flanken van de heuvels groeiden dichtvertakte vlierbomen. En op de vlakkere gedeelten stonden hier en daar groepjes zilverberken.

De uil zou zich overal kunnen verbergen.

En Ezra besloot dat het einddoel bereikt was.

Mislukt weliswaar, maar toch bereikt.

Doorzetten nu.

Naar de plaats van het afscheid.

Met ieder zijn eigen leven in het verschiet.

Toen Ezra de beide kleppen van de doos opendeed en zijn hand onder de uil schoof was een licht blazen hoorbaar en het klappen van Nestors snavel. Reflexen, die meer een automatisme waren dan op Ezra gerichte agressie.

Uilen tilt men niet op, althans geen volwassen uil, die verzoekt men plaats te nemen op een arm. Ezra zette de doos op de grond, knielde erbij neer en hield zijn arm uitnodigend bij de opening.

'We zijn er, jongen...' zei hij op opgewekte toon.

Nestor stapte tastend uit de doos op Ezra's linkerpols en schudde zich uit en knipperde met zijn ogen. Zijn kop maakte schokkerige bewegingen en draaide bijna geheel in het rond.

Ezra trapte de doos plat en schoof hem met zijn voet uit het zicht onder de takken van een duinroos, waar hij na verloop van tijd vanzelf wel zou vergaan.

Een gepaste afscheidsgroet was niet nodig en zou ook niet lukken want Ezra's keel zat dicht. Hij liep nog een eind in de richting van het dichtstbijzijnde dennenbos en schatte de gunstigste afstand.

Nog ongeveer twintig meter verwijderd van de eerste bomen bleef hij staan.

Het was zover.

Ezra sloot zijn ogen en gooide de uil omhoog.

En Nestor zette zijn vlucht in, dalend naar de grond, zoals thuis, maar ditmaal was er geen opdracht en was er geen prooi. De uil won hoogte en zette een draaiing in. Ezra zwaaide met zijn armen.

'Nee!' riep hij uit. 'Het bos, Nestor, het bos!'

Maar met een grote boog keerde Nestor terug, landde op Ezra's schouder en sloeg hem daarbij met zijn vleugels om de oren.

'Oh Nestor... snáp het nu toch...'

Ezra stak zijn arm achter zijn hoofd en liet de uil zijn vertrouwde positie weer innemen, waarna hij tot de rand van het bos liep en naar een geschikte boom zocht om de vogel in neer te zetten.

Iedere boom was eigenlijk geschikt, maar Ezra besloot om Nestor niet aan de uiterste rand te plaatsen. Iets verscholen, dat was het beste.

En dan?

En dan zo snel mogelijk weg.

Wat anders?

Door Nestors buik zachtjes tegen de tak te duwen en zijn arm langzaam te laten zakken, dwong Ezra de uil om over te stappen. Een bekende handeling op zich, maar nu ging het moeilijk, moeilijker dan thuis in de tuin.

De uil blies.

Hij was uit zijn doen, begreep niet wat de bedoeling was.

'Het stikt hier van de muizen...' zei Ezra maar.

Nestor maakte aanstalten om weer op Ezra's schouder te springen.

'Nee! Niet doen!'

En Ezra holde weg in een onscherpe wereld vol tranen.

Niet omkijken... gonsde het door zijn hoofd, maar soms moet men wel omkijken, of men wil of niet.

Achterlaten is het moeilijkste dat er is.

Omzien kan gedwongen zijn.

Hopend op vertroosting.

Uitstel van verlating.

Zo gaat het soms.

Een leven lang.

Maar omzien kan ook noodlottig zijn.

Andere voorbeelden dringen zich op.

Vergeefse ontsnappingen aan de dood.

Zo dan bleef Ezra toch staan, van plan om nog éénmaal om te kijken.

Nestor was onzichtbaar, zoals het moest, gelukkig.

Er was alleen het groene bos.

Zou Nestor hém nog kunnen zien?

En op het moment waarop Ezra besefte dat juist door te blijven staan de uil zou kunnen denken dat hij verwikkeld was in een nieuwe oefening, maakte Nestor zich los uit de achtergrond van het bos en kwam hij gezagsgetrouw op Ezra toevliegen, over een afstand die hij nog nooit eerder had hoeven overbruggen.

Halverwege de overtocht werd zijn vleugelslag onregelmatiger en vielen de eerste tekenen van vermoeidheid waar te nemen. Af en toe kantelde hij weg en had hij moeite om zijn evenwicht te hervinden. Zou hij het wel halen?

Ezra begon met steeds snellere pas terug te lopen.

Plotseling verschenen dansend in de lucht twee heftig kekkende kokmeeuwen, die duikvluchten en schijnaanvallen begonnen in te zetten. Nestor probeerde zo goed mogelijk koers te houden, maar toen even later uit het niets ook nog een kraai verscheen die zich met een rauwe kreet bijna op hem stortte, deinsde de jonge uil schuin weg en sloeg daarbij tegen de grond, waar hij in angstige verwarring en met korte bewegingen van zijn kop het vijandige gedrag van zijn belagers afwachtte.

Maar Ezra naderde op tijd en Nestors vijanden hielden krijsend afstand.

'Oh... kan je dan helemaal níks goed doen,' beet hij de hijgende vogel toe, die geheel in de war niet meer wist waar de uitgestoken arm van Ezra voor diende.

'Kom op nu! Het is al bijna donker!'

Hij dacht aan Claire. Hij was haar kwijt, dat wist hij zeker. Nu stond hem nog maar één ding te doen. Misschien zou Claires oog dan genezen.

De uil was bang.

Ezra voelde onder de terugkeer naar het bos hoe het dier zich tegen hem aandrukte in de kom van zijn schouder. En voelde hij ook niet Nestors hart dat daar zo bonkte? Of was dat van hemzelf?

Hij betrad het dennenbos opnieuw en besloot Nestor een eind dieper op een tak te zetten, waardoor de uil hem moeilijker zou kunnen volgen. Maar Nestor wilde niet meer overstappen.

En Ezra moest hem dwingen met zijn vrije hand.

De uil blies en stond wijdbeens en opende zenuwachtig zijn vleugels en klapte met zijn snavel.

'Rotuil!' schreeuwde Ezra toen. 'Laat me los!'

De reiger leek Ezra niet te hebben opgemerkt.

Stokstijf stond hij daar en strak bleef hij voor zich uit staren, alsof hij in diepe meditatie verzonken was.

Ezra was dwars door het donkere dennenbos gerend om het Nestor onmogelijk te maken hem te volgen en was er aan de oostzijde weer uitgekomen, die daar schuin afliep naar een soort vallei. Hij had zich van de helling laten afglijden en zich toen stilgehouden om op adem te komen en zich te oriënteren op de richting naar huis.

Zo ver als hier was hij nog nooit gegaan. De schemering was nu ingetreden en hij zou fors moeten doorlopen om nog voor donker terug te zijn. De snelste weg was via het gruispad, althans het eerste stuk en dan de duinen door, tot bij het binnenterrein van het circuit en daarna langs de varkensfokkerij en de modderkommen terug naar de spoorbaan. Hoe lang zou dat nog lopen zijn?

Ezra keek om zich heen. De bodem in het laagste gedeelte van de vallei bestond uit een gecraqueleerd patroon van uitgedroogde plakken mos. Had hier ooit water gestaan? Grondwater misschien?

De reiger stond aan de rand van de droge diepte.

Ver weg van het eerste water.

Hoe kon dit?

Zou hij zich deze plaats van vroeger herinneren?

Maar zelfs als hier vroeger water had gestaan dan zou er nog geen vis gezeten hebben. Wat was hier gaande?

Ezra kwam overeind en liep langzaam op de vogel toe. De reiger negeerde hem geheel, wat ook al eigenaardig was. Dorre twijgjes en kurkdroge grond kraakten en knisperden onder Ezra's voeten, maar de vogel reageerde niet. Pas toen Ezra vlakbij was en bij hem neerhurkte, draaide hij zijn spitse kop half in Ezra's richting. De lange dunne kuifveren bewogen in een zuchtje wind.

Zou hij verdwaald zijn?

Ezra stak zijn hand langzaam uit en legde zijn vingertoppen op de rug van de grote grijze vogel. De reiger knorde en wilde wegstappen, maar bij de poging daartoe viel hij bijna om. Ezra tilde hem nu met beide handen op en voelde hoe uitgemergeld hij was.

Zou hij nog wel kunnen vliegen?

Overveen was niet ver weg. De Brouwerskolk, de Zanderijvaart, het Houtmanpad, vis genoeg. En Zandvoort was nog dichterbij. De Vijverhut, het kanaal in de Waterleidingduinen. De reiger bevond zich eigenlijk vlak bij zijn redding.

En Ezra wierp hem in de lucht...

De reiger slaakte een hese kreet en zeilde terug naar de grond. Landen kon je het niet noemen, neerkantelen was een beter woord. En na de tweede keer wist Ezra dat hij deze reiger moest redden. Als het dier zelf te zwak was om voedsel te vangen, dan moest hij eerst aansterken, in de lege volière thuis in de tuin.

En zo nam Ezra de reiger onder zijn arm en begon hij aan de lange tocht naar huis. Over het gruispad, door de duinen van het binnenterrein, langs de varkensfokkerij en de modderkommen, over de spoorbaan en de nauwe straatjes van het oude dorp, om maar zo min mogelijk mensen tegen te komen.

Het tillen van de reiger was op zich niet zwaar, wel werd het lastig door alle uitsteeksels die voortdurend naar alle kanten bewogen. Vooral de kop met de lange scherpe snavel vormde een probleem. Ezra probeerde de snavel vast te houden, deels om de vogel stabieler te kunnen vervoeren, deels om een onverwachte beet of houw te voorkomen, maar juist het vastpakken van zijn snavel kon de reiger niet verdragen. Zo veerden de kop en de lange hals ongemakkelijk op en neer en raakte Ezra uitgeput van het overpakken en verschikken.

Volhouden.

Volhouden, daar ging het om.

'Ja, hij is ziek, ja, hij moet naar de dokter,' stelde Ezra de enkele dorpelingen die hij in het halfduister tegenkwam gerust.

Eerst naar huis nu en dan snel naar Keesman en Ter Weer.

Meneer Ter Weer woonde boven de winkel.

Wat had je?

Wijting?

Spiering?

Makreel?

Verkochten meneer Keesman en meneer Ter Weer ook zoetwatervis?

En zo kwam Ezra eindelijk thuis.

Met de slappe reiger in zijn armen.

De hals van de vogel hing als een slang naar beneden en zijn snavel sleepte haast over de grond, maar hij leefde nog. Ezra kon zijn hart in zijn hand voelen bonzen.

Hij legde hem zachtjes neer in de donkere volière.

Om hem heen in de tuin leken de bomen een kring te vormen van zwijgende zwarte druïden.

De poten van de reiger staken als gekruiste stokken onder hem uit.

'Misschien gaat het morgen beter,' zei Ezra geruststellend. 'Ik zal om aal vragen, die glijdt makkelijk naar binnen. Hou nu vol, ik ben zo terug.'

En hoewel Ezra zelf uitgeput was, drukte hij zich met zijn handen op zijn knieën op, om nog een keer terug te gaan naar het dorp, naar de Haltestraat, naar de viswinkel van Keesman en Ter Weer, want dat was de plicht van een vogelman. Wat zou het niet geweldig zijn als hij de ten dode opgeschreven reiger nog kon redden. Wie kon weten of het wegbrengen van Nestor op een geheimzinnige manier te maken had met het vinden en redden van deze reiger? Ja, zo was het. Er moest zoiets zijn. Er was een verband. Dat kon gewoon niet anders.

Maar op datzelfde moment begon de reiger met schokkende bewegingen van zijn kop te krijsen. Ezra schrok van de rauwe kreten, die hem als zweepslagen troffen, want hij kon ze verstaan. Geen angsten waren het die de zieltogende reiger hem in het gezicht kreet, maar verwijten.

Ik stond daar om te sterven...
Het was de plaats...
Waar bemoeide je je mee...?
Stukmaker, die je bent!

Ezra's hoofd zakte naar voren. De nagels van zijn duimen persten zich zo diep in de toppen van zijn wijs-
vingers dat hij geen andere pijn meer kon voelen.

Toen hield het krijsen op en was er een hand op zijn
schouder.

Hij keek om.

Het was Saul.

*   *   *

Zo werd het winter.

Claires oog genas, maar ze kon er niets meer mee
zien.

Zij schreef Ezra een brief, waarin stond dat ze hem niet
haatte.

En Ezra?

Die schreef een brief terug, waarin stond dat Nestor
dood was.

Hij hoopte dat het zou helpen, maar dat was niet zo.

Op school konden ze elkaar gemakkelijker ontlopen
dan zij beiden hadden gedacht.

Als hij maar lang genoeg wachtte...

Wie wist de toekomst?